RETRIBUTION

C.J. PETIT

Printed in the United States of America

First Printing, 2018

ISBN: 9781091031951

TABLE OF CONTENTS

This is book is dedicated to Z.T. Armstrong, a good man, and a proud Texan. He's a kindred spirit and a man I've never met yet feel honored to call my friend. When we do finally meet, we'll spin yarns and await our wives and best friends.

PROLOGUE

September 11, 1874
West Texas

Joey couldn't believe it as he held the gunbelt in his hands and just looked at the revolver as his older brothers stood around him.

"That Remington's got me through a lot of scrapes, Joey."

Joey nodded but kept his eyes on his first pistol as he said, "Thanks, Buck. I'll take good care of it, too. When can I try it?"

His second oldest brother, Drew, replied, "Well, let's go out back and you can fire a few rounds and I'll show you how to load it."

Joey's eyes snapped back to his brothers and said, "I already know how to load it, Drew. I can clean it, too. I just ain't never shot one before."

"Well, let's all go out back and see what you can do with it," shouted Fred.

Joey didn't reply but pulled the belt around his waist and then met with a bit of a problem when he ran out of notches before he could get it tight.

Buck laughed and pulled the gunbelt from Joey's waist, pulled his knife from his gunbelt's sheath, and drilled a new hole in the leather strap before handing it back to Joey.

Joey was red-faced when he accepted the gunbelt back from his oldest brother but quickly forgot about his embarrassment about being so skinny and strapped it around his narrow waist until it was snug. He grinned back at his six older brothers, quickly turned, trotted out the back door, crossed the small back porch, and stepped out onto the empty terrain of west Texas.

He hadn't gone twenty feet when Buck exclaimed, "Joey! There, to your right about fifty yards!"

Joey turned his eyes in that direction and spotted a coyote ripping at something, probably an armadillo. He glanced at Buck who was still pointing at the coyote, who didn't seem to even care about the armed humans.

Joey unlashed the Remington's hammer loop, pulled his new pistol from the holster, thumbed the hammer back, and aimed it at the distant coyote. He knew that there was little chance of hitting the animal with the old, .31 caliber pistol, so after just a small delay, squeezed the trigger.

The smaller caliber pistol didn't have the same sound as the larger .44 caliber pistols his brothers all carried, but after the sharp crack and the cloud of gunsmoke boiled from its muzzle, the .31 caliber bullet spun across the one hundred and forty-six feet and slammed into the right hip of the coyote, knocking him onto his side.

The coyote yipped loudly with the hit and was using its forelegs to try and drag itself away as Drew shouted, "Holy damn, Joey! You got him on your first shot!"

His six brothers began to crowd around him pounding on his back and shouting their congratulations as Joey stared at the wounded coyote, not even feeling the pistol in his hand.

Earl then said, "Well, let's go, Joey. You gotta finish him off."

Joey was still stunned that he'd hit the coyote and almost didn't notice his feet moving as his six brothers urged him across the dry ground. He stared at the wounded animal as it struggled to make a fruitless attempt to escape the predators that were approaching him.

The coyote was too young to understand the dangers that humans represented and would never be able to pass on the lesson as it finally just lay on the ground, panting, watching the pack of two-legged animals approach.

The six men and one boy neared the coyote, stopping just ten feet short.

Buck said, "Finish him, Joey. Put one right through his head."

Joey heard his oldest brother's order, but most of his attention was focused on those pained brown eyes looking at him. His pistol was still smoking in his hand and he wished that one of his brothers would do it but knew that they wouldn't.

Buck looked down at his kid brother and snarled, "It's time to be a man, Joey. Kill it."

Joey slowly raised the pistol, pulled back its hammer, and aimed it at those searching brown eyes. He tried to control the pistol's dancing front sights, but the more he tried, the more they moved.

Drew screamed, "Shoot the damned thing!"

Joey closed his eyes and yanked the trigger. He felt the pistol buck and heard the report, but he heard nothing from the coyote. He'd missed at ten feet!

He expected to hear his brothers' laughter at the miss as he opened his eyes, but instead, there was only silence as he stared at the dead coyote. His bullet had blasted a hole right between those sad eyes, and he felt nauseated.

After ten seconds, Earl exclaimed, "Lordy, Joey! That was right between the eyes! And with that old Remington, too!"

A second round of congratulatory back thumps followed as Joey slipped the pistol back into its holster and fixed the hammer loop into place, still staring at the coyote's lifeless carcass.

Buck said, "Well, Joey, you're a man now. Go ahead and bury that critter and then come into the house. We have another birthday surprise for you."

Joey nodded as the six brothers all turned and walked back to the house.

After they were out of sight, Joey slowly walked to the poor excuse for a barn and found the equally sorry example of a spade that hung from the back wall.

How did he make both of those shots? The Remington was almost fifteen years old and probably had a thousand rounds run through that rifled barrel. He'd never even fired a gun before and really didn't even try to hit that coyote. He'd aimed too high and should have missed. Then the killing shot was with his eyes closed and a wavering gun sight. Both of those bullets should have flown harmlessly into the Texas dirt but had hit the stupid coyote. *What was wrong with him?* He should have been proud of his apparent shooting prowess but had almost vomited in front of his brothers.

As he walked with the shovel back to where the coyote's carcass lay beside the ripped armadillo, he wondered why he felt so bad. His six older brothers never felt bad when they killed anything. He felt as if he'd let them down by his girlish concerns about killing a damned coyote.

Joey began digging a hole as he tried to remember if he'd ever seen any of his brothers feel sad about anything they did. They were all heroes to him for as long as he could remember. They were all tough, hard men who didn't take guff from anyone. They did as they pleased, and no one challenged them.

Buck, Drew, Earl, Fred, Glen, and Hank Hogan were all much older than he was. Today was his thirteenth birthday, and the youngest, Hank, was already twenty-five. They all looked like brothers, too. The tallest, Drew, was only two inches taller than Earl and Glen who stood five feet and eight inches tall. They all had black hair and brown eyes and wore similar heavy moustaches. Each of them now carried a Colt Model 1873 chambered for the same .44 metallic cartridge that their Winchester '73s used. They even wore matching brown leather vests and dark brown Stetsons.

As he dug, he felt more out of place than usual with his sandy brown hair and hazel green eyes. He hadn't earned his brown leather vest yet, either. Now he'd behaved like a sissy in front of his brothers, even if they didn't notice it. Buck had given him his old Remington as a birthday gift, and he'd sullied it by acting like a coward. He should have shot that coyote with a smile on his face and then laughed with his brothers when he'd made that first impossible shot.

Joey tossed the spade to the ground and slid the coyote's carcass into the hole before kicking the remains of his last meal in with him. He pulled off his ragged flat hat, wiped the sweat from his brow with his left sleeve, and, before he replaced the hat, he glanced back at the house before he looked at the dead coyote in its shallow grave.

He simply said, "Sorry," then put his hat back on, picked up the shovel, and began to fill the hole.

Once it was done, he headed back to the barn, replaced the shovel, and then left and walked to the trough to wash off the dirt.

After he had water flowing from the pump, he ducked his head underneath the rushing water, felt the cooling splash on the back of his head and neck, stood, rubbed the water on his face, and started the water again to rinse.

When he felt reasonably clean, he pulled his hat back on, and headed for the house to see what other surprise his brothers had for him on his birthday. He knew it wasn't a cake because none of them cooked very well. He did almost all the cooking and cleaning. He was almost like the woman of the house, and after that display over the coyote, he thought he'd earned it by being so girly. He surely wasn't as tough as his brothers.

Joey entered the kitchen and found all six of his brothers sitting around the large table drinking old coffee.

"Well, here's the birthday boy!" exclaimed Earl and followed with a snicker.

Buck said, "Nope. He's not a boy anymore. He's thirteen and he's got a pistol now. He just showed he's a man, so there'll be no more boy talk."

Joey tried to smile at the compliment, but the truth kept his lips in place.

He lifted the coffeepot from the cookstove and was relieved that it was empty before asking, “So, what’s the other birthday surprise?”

Buck replied, “Have a seat, Joey.”

Joey sauntered the eight feet, pulled out the only empty chair left, and sat down.

“Now that you’re a man, Joey, we’re gonna let you come on our next job,” Buck said.

Joey was thrilled to hear that he’d finally be allowed to accompany the brothers on one of their exploits. He knew what they did, more or less, and having to stay at the house while they were out making money had branded him as just a kid. But now, things were going to be different. Maybe they’d even give him a brown leather vest.

“Where are we going?” he asked excitedly.

Buck replied, “We’re heading north to Warwick. It’s more than a half day’s ride, but it’ll be worth it.”

Joey hadn’t been further away than Hinkley, so a long ride was going to be a real adventure.

“When are we leaving?”

“Tomorrow morning before sunup. We’ll pack this afternoon, but right now, I’ll tell you what we’re gonna do.”

Joey nodded as Buck explained the upcoming job. He wasn’t surprised that it involved robbing the bank in the town, but it didn't bother him. Banks and bankers were thieves. They took everybody's money and then sometimes, they wouldn't even give it back to them. It was just as bad as those stores and other businesses. They could sell things for less money, but they milked folks for all they could get. His brothers made them all pay for their greed by taking their money and now, he was going to help them.

After Buck had detailed how they'd enter the bank and keep the sheriff busy while they took the money, he finally reached Joey's role in the job.

Buck had drawn a basic map of the town, the nearby Fresh Water Creek, and the topology surrounding the town.

He pointed at the series of hills north of Warwick and said, "Now Joey, here's what you'll be doing. You'll be on this hill right here, with your pistol. What we're gonna do is, after the job, we'll ride real fast north out of town. Now if there's law after us, you'll see them. We'll ride past you and it'll look like we're heading for the Red River and the Nations, but what we're really gonna do is circle around the hill behind you and ambush 'em on the other side."

Joey nodded as if he understood the plan, but asked, "What do I do with the pistol?"

Drew laughed and replied, "What do you think you do with your pistol? You shoot at the bastards!"

"From way up on that hill? They'd be too far away, wouldn't they?"

Buck answered, "Yeah, but your shooting will slow 'em down and make 'em think we're on the hill with you. That'll give us time to make it around the hill and surprise 'em on the other side."

Joey still didn't comprehend his role in the bank heist, but said, "Oh. I understand now."

He was relieved that he wouldn't have to shoot anyone because, after the coyote incident, he wasn't sure if he could.

The planning done, at least as far as Joey's role, Drew said, "Why don't you fix us some lunch now while we go over what we need to do, Joey?"

"Okay, Drew," Joey answered as he stood and headed for the cookstove.

He happily prepared to cook his brothers' lunch knowing that tomorrow, he'd be going on his first job with his big brothers. His heroes.

CHAPTER 1

September 12, 1874

County Sheriff John Warren was sitting in his office in the back of the county jail and had just passed an amusing anecdote to Deputy Dan Sheehy, who had laughed appropriately.

"It's your own fault, boss. You shoulda had boys," Dan remarked followed by a chuckle.

"Don't blame me, Dan. It's all Minnie's fault. I did all I could to make boys," the sheriff protested with a grin.

Dan was still laughing when they both heard the jail's front door open and slam closed followed by the sound of hurried steps.

"Boss, we got a problem!" exclaimed Deputy Lou Sanborn as he raced down the short hallway.

The sheriff was already rising from his seat as his second deputy rounded the doorway.

"What kind of problem?"

"I was riding in from the Double H and just as I was coming in from the east, I saw six riders heading in from the west. I might be wrong, but I think it's the Hogan brothers."

"Damn it!" the sheriff swore under his breath as he stepped quickly out from behind his desk and snatched his hat from the wall peg.

"Alright, let's get ourselves armed. Dan, you grab the shotgun. Lou, you and I will use Winchesters. Let's go!"

The three lawmen scrambled from the sheriff's private office heading for the large front office and the gunrack on the back wall and almost made it before all hell broke loose.

Out in the streets of Warwick, the six Hogan brothers had seen Deputy Sanborn run into the jail and had to alter their plans, but not by much. As Earl and Drew headed for the bank, Buck, Earl, Glen, and Hank pulled their Winchesters and, remaining in their saddles, formed a line facing the jail, which scattered the citizens in the street and on the boardwalks.

Buck was on the eastern end of the line and watched Earl and Drew hastily dismount, lash their horses to the bank's hitchrail, and enter with their Colts drawn. Once he was sure they were inside, he shouted, "Now!"

The four brothers then began to fire into the jail in a steady, but not hectic pattern to ensure they wouldn't run out of ammunition until they were ready to make their escape.

"Jesus!" screamed Deputy Sanborn before he dropped to the floor when the first group of .44s drilled through the jail's thin wooden walls.

Sheriff Warren and Deputy Sheehy both shouted similar expletives and fell face-first to the unfinished wooden floor as bullets continued to blast through the front of the jail.

"Let's crawl out through the back!" shouted the sheriff over the din.

Neither deputy acknowledged the order but followed the sheriff's lead as he began to snake his way down the hallway while lead slammed into the floor and walls around them.

Even as he crawled, Sheriff Warren was thinking about how they'd be able to stop the Hogan brothers. If they could make it out the back, they could split up and go around the sides of the feed and grain and the hardware stores which bookended the jail. They never had a chance to get their hands on the shotgun or Winchesters, so they would be outgunned, but he knew they had to take the chance to stop those bastards.

The four mounted brothers had begun to stagger their Winchester fire which enabled two to reload while the other two kept firing. Buck would glance over at the bank every few seconds, waiting for Drew and Earl to emerge.

Inside the bank, Drew and Earl followed Buck's plan, and while Earl kept his cocked pistol trained on the two customers and four employees, Drew ran behind the cashier's cage to fill a canvas bag he had tucked under his belt.

Drew began ripping the currency from the cashiers' drawers and noticed that the safe door was closed. It would limit their take, but time was critical now, so after the drawers were empty, Drew backed out from behind the cashiers' windows.

Once clear, he shouted, "Let's get outta here!"

As he and Earl quickly backed toward the doorway, they each fired a round whose purpose was to put everyone on the floor. Drew upped the ante and aimed at the cashier on the left because he wanted to. The young man took Earl's .44 high in the left side of his chest, smashing through ribs and his lung before drilling into the wall behind the cashier's cage. Earl's shot punched through the cashier's cage on the right before ricocheting off the safe.

Buck heard the two gunshots from the bank, turned, and saw his brothers hurry out, trailing gunsmoke as they did.

Drew had his stuffed canvas bag with him and tossed it into his saddlebag before he and Earl mounted and waved to Buck.

Buck shouted, "Let's go!"

The other three brothers all took one more shot at the jail before they wheeled their horses to the east and galloped out of town, catching up to Earl and Drew in just seconds. Then the six brothers all turned north toward the hills and the Red River and Indian Nations just a few miles away.

The three lawmen had clambered to their feet and were exiting the jail when the firing suddenly stopped. They ran out the back door and before they split, Sheriff Warren held them in place as he heard the fading hoofbeats.

"They're running. Let's go straight out the alley!" he said loudly before turning to his left and trotting away.

The deputies followed, both drawing their pistols before they turned into the alley between the jail and the feed and grain store. Sheriff Warren already had his pistol cocked as he began to slow before entering the street sixty feet in front of them in case one or two remained behind to provide covering fire.

When Sheriff Warren reached the main street of Warwick, he found it shrouded in a fog of gunsmoke, but empty of Hogan brothers.

"They're gone! I'm going to the bank and check on injuries. Dan, you and Lou get our horses," he said loudly before he began to jog to the bank across the street and two buildings to his right.

Deputy Sheehy didn't acknowledge the order, but he and Deputy Sanborn raced to the nearby livery to get their three horses as their boss headed for the bank. Townsfolk were already coming back onto the street.

Sheriff Warren slowed before he hopped onto the boardwalk with his pistol drawn and cocked, not really expecting to find any of the robbers. It only took a few seconds to scan the interior of the small bank and only saw frightened customers and employees.

He released his Colt's hammer, holstered his pistol, and shouted, "Is anyone hurt?"

One of the two cashiers, Jimmy Wright, stood from behind the cage and said, "They shot Ed Schmidt. He's dead."

After hearing the sheriff's voice, the bank president, Tom Henderson, stepped out of his office and said, "What happened? Who was it?"

Sheriff Warren replied, "It was the Hogan brothers. We're going after them right now. Can you take care of Ed's body?"

"We'll take him to Bryson's Mortuary."

Sheriff Warren just nodded, then quickly turned and jogged out of the bank to get to the jail and retrieve their Winchesters, so they could hunt those bastards. A posse of angry citizens was already forming as he reached the jail.

The six Hogan brothers had slowed their horses to a medium trot after leaving Warwick. They had already ridden a long way that morning and still had another ten miles to go to reach the Nations. Buck kept checking their backtrail as they rode, not knowing how many lawmen, if any, had survived their fusillade of .44s.

"So far, so good," he announced loudly after they'd ridden two miles out of town and nobody had emerged, then asked Drew, "How much did we get?"

Drew shouted back, "About six hundred, I think, but I ain't sure. Their safe was locked."

"Not a bad haul," Buck yelled back, although he'd been hoping for almost four times that amount.

———

On the top of the hill five miles north of town, Joey could see his brothers approaching easily. He'd heard the massive amount of gunfire and had been impressed with the firepower. He had even seen the gunsmoke cloud above the town in the afternoon sun but wished he'd been down there to watch the robbery. He wanted to be able to see that greedy banker's face when his brothers took away the money he'd robbed from the townsfolk.

He had his Remington in his hands, preparing to do his part. He'd cleaned it and loaded it last night and was ready to do his job as he continued to watch his brothers ride away from the town. His old gelding was hitched to a mesquite bush at the bottom of the hill and grazing on some of the sparse grass. He glanced down at the horse and snickered. Just another few short miles away was the Red River and all along the river were trees and lots of grass, but not here.

As he watched his brothers, he finally asked himself how they were going to return to their house near Hinkley. It would have to be a wide turn to avoid the law but then, he tossed his concerns aside. Buck had done the preparation and he'd probably already planned for the escape.

Joey saw the posse emerge from Warwick before his brothers did and wished he could warn them, but figured they'd spot the posse soon enough. So, he just prepared to do his part in luring the posse into the trap that Buck had designed.

It was Earl who first spotted the posse led by Sheriff Warren when it made its turn to the north to follow their trail. The posse was almost three miles back, but they were on fresh horses, and there were a lot more men than he'd expected. It was a huge dust cloud and he wasn't even sure how many riders were after them.

"Here they come, Buck!" he shouted.

Buck turned to see the posse in the distance and was stunned by the size of the posse as he yelled, "Keep up this pace until we get to Joey's hill, then we'll make our break. That kid's gonna be our insurance."

He was glad he'd set Joey on the hill now as the kid would probably buy them the extra time that might be the difference between getting hanged or making it to safety.

For the next few seconds, each of the brothers was turned in his saddle to watch the posse as it closed the gap, and one by one, they turned back to the front as they saw the first hill and could see Joey on its summit.

"Joey's up there, Buck," shouted Hank unnecessarily.

Buck didn't reply but kicked his horse into a canter, which was quickly matched by his brothers.

Sheriff Warren, his two deputies, and six Warwick citizens who had asked to join him noticed the increase in speed, which had matched their own, but the sheriff maintained the canter rather than tire the animals any more than they already were. He guessed that the Hogans were going to head for the Nations, but at their current speed, their horses might be too tired to make it past the Red River, but it would be close.

Joey watched as his brothers rode rapidly toward his hill and as instructed, he stayed low rather than standing and waving, which is what he wanted to do. But they all waved to him as they passed to the west of his hill and he decided it would be okay now, so he stood and waved before dropping back down to the ground and looking for the posse.

"Did you see that?" Deputy Sanborn shouted.

"Yeah. I saw him," Sheriff Warren yelled back.

This was a new wrinkle. There were only six Hogan brothers, so they must have recruited someone else to join them. Now the game had changed. The sheriff had no idea how many guns were on that hill and he had to come up with a solution quickly because it was just another three minutes away.

After Joey had disappeared, Buck just gave a 'come on' wave to his brothers as they passed behind Joey's hill and turned northeast toward the Red River and the protection of the Indian Nations on the opposite bank. They just needed Joey to do his job and hold up the posse for a few precious minutes.

Joey was watching the posse approach and didn't turn to see where his brothers were headed. He assumed that they were riding around the other hill to the east and he wouldn't have been able to see them anyway.

———

Sheriff Warren shouted, "We're going to split up before we reach that hill. I don't know how many guns are up there, but I figure the Hogan brothers are heading for the Nations. I'll swing west with Charlie and Jimmy and we'll take on whoever's on the hill. Dan, you and Lou take the other four men and circle around the east of the hill, and continue the chase. Stay out of range of the hill. We'll follow you after we clean it up."

"Okay, boss!" Dan shouted as the posse split into two groups, three veering to the left and six to the right.

———

Joey watched the posse break up and wondered how it would affect Buck's plan to catch them by surprise after riding around the hill. He never even considered how precarious his own position was as he readied his Remington. He knew the lawmen would never get close enough to be in range of his pistol, but that wasn't the point of his being there. He was supposed to get their attention to distract them from his brothers' attack, and it was time for him to do his job.

Joey then stood tall on the summit of his hill, and yelled, "Come and get me!"

Sheriff Warren was startled when he heard Joey's shouted dare. It sounded like a kid's voice, but it didn't matter. He'd watched the other six riders disappear around the eastern end of the hill to chase after the Hogan brothers, so his job was just to clear the hill quickly and then go to help his deputies and the rest of the posse. The partial posse was on an equal firepower footing with the Hogan brothers but doubted if any of the men aside from his deputies could match the Hogans in proficiency.

Joey knew the three members of the posse had seen him, so he pointed his pistol in their direction, cocked the hammer, and squeezed the trigger. But instead of the loud blast of the gunpowder going off, his ears reported the not-so-loud click of the firing pin falling on empty metal.

Joey panicked, cocked the hammer again, aimed, and pulled the trigger with the same sickening results. He repeated it four more times, but the useless Remington wouldn't fire! *What was wrong with the damned thing?*

There was nothing wrong with the Winchesters that Sheriff Warren and his two citizen posse members owned and soon opened fire at Joey at about a hundred and twenty yards.

The ground around Joey's feet began to explode as he continued to cock and fire the useless handgun, somehow expecting it to fire. But as the Winchester fire continued, he finally turned and raced down the hill for his horse, still not even thinking about where his brothers might be or where he would go.

The sheriff had seen him run and quickly set his gelding to a fast trot, followed by the others as they rode around the base of the hill to get a shot at the retreating non-shooting shooter.

Joey's legs were windmilling down the hill as he stumbled and ran, his useless pistol still in his hand. He was just fifty feet from his horse when his right foot hit a rock and he fell face forward into the downslope. He tumbled the rest of the way in a cloud of dust, his pistol flying into the air before he came to a stop just fifteen feet from his horse.

Joey was groggy after the fall and tried to sit as the dust filled his eyes. He wanted to scream at his own failure to do the one simple job that his brothers had entrusted to him. *He never even got a single shot off!*

He was still sitting when he heard pounding hooves approaching and didn't care if they shot him. He deserved his fate. He'd failed his brothers and his heroes, but he knew that they'd be arriving soon, so the lawmen would pay for chasing the Hogans.

Sheriff Warren spotted Joey on the ground and shouted, "Charlie, stay here and tie the kid up. I'll be back in a little while."

Charlie Bascom yelled back, "Can I rough him up some?"

An irritated sheriff screamed back, "No! Just tie him up! If he tells me you did anything else, I'll put you in jail with him!"

Sheriff Warren and Jimmy Hill kept their horses moving and shot off to the northeast to catch up with the rest of the posse while Charlie Bascom dismounted and pulled his rope from his saddle.

He approached Joey and snarled, "If it was up to me, I'd be stretching your neck with this rope. But they'll do it soon enough, I reckon."

Joey looked up at him and snapped, "I don't care. You'll never get my brothers."

As Charlie began wrapping the heavy rope around Joey he said, "Brothers? The sheriff said there were only six Hogan brothers."

"Well, he's an idiot like all of them badge owners, 'cause I'm one too, and proud of it!"

———

The six Hogan brothers hadn't heard any gunfire from Joey, and they weren't happy about his failure but figured it didn't matter as they were just four miles from the Red River and were almost home free. Then things changed when Glen noticed the six-man posse appear from around the hill.

"They're still comin'!" he shouted.

Five other Hogan heads swiveled on their shoulders and Drew shouted, "Son of a bitch! That damned kid didn't even slow 'em down!"

Buck yelled, "We can't worry about that now. We've got to get across the river!"

But their horses were close to exhaustion after the long morning ride and their escape run from Warwick. The animals hadn't even had a decent break in four hours. Nonetheless, their riders put their spurs to their flanks to urge them on toward the Red River and safety.

Deputy Sheehy knew they were gaining on the Hogan brothers and that their horses were probably almost finished, but he also knew they were just a couple of miles from the Red River. The river itself was an obstacle that could slow them down enough, so the posse might be able to pick them off as they crossed, but he didn't want to have to use that last-ditch advantage. At this time of year, the river was at a low level and they might be able to cross it quickly.

Deputy Dan Sheehy shouted, “Let’s move!”, then kicked his horse to a canter and pulled his Winchester.

His fellow deputy did the same, and so did the other four men.

Half a mile behind them, Sheriff Warren and Jimmy Hill saw them accelerate and matched their speed.

Buck had just glanced back, seen the posse closing, and looked ahead at the river. It was going to be close when Drew’s horse began to lag. He was already at the back of the pack because his horse was slowing earlier, so no one noticed when the gap between him and his brothers suddenly increased.

“Hey!” Drew shouted when his horse began wheezing as it frothed at the mouth and stopped.

Buck and Earl both turned, and saw Drew already two hundred yards back, but the posse was only another four hundred yards behind Drew, and he could see two more posse members closing as well.

Buck made an instant decision and it was to have Drew fight a delaying action so he and the other brothers could make it to safety across the Red River.

“Shoot ‘em, Drew!” Buck screamed to his brother, which served as a signal to his other brothers to keep riding.

Drew was furious for being abandoned out here but wasn’t about to give up. Unlike the others except for Earl, he knew that they’d murdered that cashier in the bank and would hang in Warwick. He wasn't about to face the noose, so he quickly dismounted, grabbed his Winchester from his almost-dead horse's scabbard, and dropped to the ground to hold off the posse.

Deputies Sheehy and Sanborn knew they were riding into a Winchester's line of fire and quickly pulled to a stop just two hundred yards from the man on the ground.

"You boys stay here," he shouted to the four civilians, "Me and Lou will take care of this one."

"They're getting away!" shouted one of the non-lawmen.

"No, they're not. The sheriff is right behind you," Deputy Sheehy yelled back.

Sheriff Warren was a hundred yards back now and saw the brothers still pulling away. They were eight hundred yards ahead and less than a mile from the river. They were going to make it, regardless of what he did, so he kept riding to talk to his deputies.

When he was close, he said loudly, "There's nothing we can do about the others now. They're almost at the river. We'll spread out and start an enfilade of fire on the one on the ground. If he gives up, cease-fire and let me take over."

"What about our money?" asked Jim Hill.

The sheriff ignored him and said, "Dan, you swing to the left. Lou, you take the right. Stay about a hundred and fifty yards out and lob some shots into him. I'll do the same from the front. Let's go."

Sheriff Warren pulled his Winchester, cocked the hammer, and started his gelding forward at a walk while his deputies split wide and began to circle around Drew.

Drew knew he was a dead man but would rather die by a bullet than a noose, so he just waited for them to get within range.

The sheriff was well aware of Drew's situation. Whenever he'd faced a man who was going to hang, he'd make a fight of it, regardless of the odds. He'd gotten into one gunfight where the outlaw was throwing rocks at him while he faced a loaded Winchester. He'd hanged three days later.

Drew watched the sheriff get closer, raised the angle on his Winchester's barrel, and fired.

Sheriff Warren saw the smoke and flame and then heard the .44 whiz past his left ear too close for comfort, so he pulled his horse to a stop and opened fire himself. He heard the fire from his deputies just seconds later and the ground around the prostrate Hogan brother began popping with dirt volcanoes.

Drew fired a second shot at the sheriff and then felt the burn and shock of a bullet as it hit his right thumb, almost taking it off. He screamed in pain but knew there was nothing else he could do now. He just hoped his brothers had made it safely across the river as he cursed that damned little bastard Joey.

———

Buck and his remaining four brothers all crossed the Red River without a problem as the gunfire ceased from the south, and it was only when they were safely in the Nations that Buck realized that Drew's saddlebags contained their haul from the bank robbery. It was too late to go back and retrieve it and all they could do now was to figure out a way to return to Hinkley before the law got there so they could collect their things and move on.

———

Sheriff Warren dismounted first and as the others stepped down, walked to the fallen Hogan then noticed the mangled, bloody right thumb, picked up the Winchester, and tossed it a few feet away before he pulled his Colt from his holster and lobbed it near the repeater.

Drew didn't say a word, but just glared at the sheriff.

As Deputy Sheehy approached, the sheriff stood and said, "He's not going to be shooting anything anymore. Let's get him on his horse and bring him back to see the doc. I'll see if he's got something in his saddlebags that we can use to wrap that bloody hand."

Deputy Sheehy nodded and the sheriff walked to Drew's still wheezing horse, flipped open his left saddlebag, and was more than pleasantly surprised to find the bag containing the bank's money. He pulled it out, along with a spare shirt, and walked back to the now-standing and bleeding Drew Hogan.

The sheriff tossed the shirt to Deputy Sheehy and said, "Use this. The good news is that this one had the bank's money."

Dan Sheehy grinned and said, "I'll bet that'll make his brothers unhappy."

"You boys get him on his horse, and I'll go back and get the kid."

"*He was a kid?*" asked Deputy Sheehy in disbelief.

"Yup. I'm guessing around twelve or so. When he shouted, 'come and get me', I thought it was a girl at first."

"Are we gonna hang a kid?" asked Deputy Sanborn.

"It's not up to me. That's Judge Madsen's call, or maybe Mister Underwood's."

While Drew was having his bleeding mess of a thumb bound, the sheriff mounted and rode quickly back to the hill where Charlie had tied Joey, pulled his horse to a halt, and dismounted.

He stepped over to the bound boy, unwrapped Charlie Bascom's rope, and handed it to him.

Charlie glared at the kid, handed the sheriff Joey's pistol, hung his rope, mounted, and waited for the sheriff, hoping he at least swatted the kid a few times.

Joey had been watching the gunfight and knew that it had been Drew that had been shot. He may not have been able to tell the difference between his brothers at a hundred yards or more, but Drew's gelding had a light tan tail that made him stand out.

After the rope was removed, Joey stood, brushed off the dust, and glared at the sheriff as he asked with a sneer, "You killed Drew, didn't you?"

"No, son. He's shot, and he'll probably hang, but we didn't kill him," the sheriff said as he examined the old Remington that Charlie had handed him.

"Is this the pistol you were using?" he asked.

“The damned thing didn’t even fire. Not once! Stupid gun,” Joey snapped in frustration.

The sheriff cocked it and pulled the trigger getting the same empty click. He saw the filled chambers and asked, “Who loaded this thing?”

“I did. It’s loaded, but it didn’t work.”

“You forgot to add new percussion caps, son. You can’t use them more than once, you know.”

If Joey was frustrated before, he felt like an idiot now. *Why didn’t his brothers tell him about the percussion caps?* He’d seen Buck load the pistol but didn’t remember him putting on the caps.

The sheriff slid the pistol into his waist and said, “Okay, son, get on your horse and we’ll head back to town.”

Joey didn’t move but asked, “Where are my other brothers?”

His question startled the sheriff and he asked, “Brothers? They’re your brothers? I thought there were only six Hogan brothers.”

“No, I was the last one. Did you kill all of them?”

“Nope. We only caught you and the other one. He had all the bank’s money, though. Your other brothers all made it to the Indian Nations. and I can’t follow them there.”

Joey smiled, said, “Good,” and walked to his horse.

The sheriff mounted his own gelding and didn’t even bother taking the kid’s horse’s reins as he started southwest.

For a few seconds, Joey thought about turning his horse around and racing to the river himself, but he was so ashamed of himself, he knew he couldn't face his brothers after letting them down. He was glad they were all safe but felt bad about Drew getting shot. It was his fault that they shot him and might hang him, too. He wasn't afraid about getting hanged himself either. If Drew was going to hang, he'd ask to go first.

As they rode along, the sheriff asked, "What were you doing up on that hill, anyway? Did you really think you could stop a posse with this popgun?"

Joey was inclined not to answer, but then thought he might as well confess, so the sheriff would know he was part of the heist.

"I was supposed to fire at you, so my brothers could have time to ride behind the hill and surprise you from the side. It would have worked, too, if I hadn't screwed up loading my pistol."

John Warren shook his head slowly and said, "They weren't going to ride around that hill. They were headed for the Red River straight away. I think they just put you on that hill to distract us, so they could gain some ground."

Joey whipped his head to look at the sheriff and snapped, "You're lyin'! My brothers wouldn't do that! Your posse was just too big, and they had to get to the river."

The sheriff shrugged and said, "Believe what you want, son. But I sent two deputies and four civilians after your six brothers. From what I heard about them, they're mighty handy with those Winchesters and Colts, so why didn't they just shoot it out with the posse? They would have had an advantage while I was here dealing with you."

Joey opened his mouth to defend his brothers again but quickly closed it as he tried to come up with a logical reason for their hasty retreat to the river. He knew they weren't cowards like he was. They were all tough and brave. They were his heroes.

———

They reached Warwick as the sun was low in the sky, and after leaving Joey in his bullet-riddled jail, Sheriff Warren went to visit Doctor Gillespie's office to see about the other Hogan. He dropped off the bag of loot with the bank before continuing to the doctor's office.

He entered the outer office and found his two deputies waiting for him.

"How is he?"

Dan Sheehy replied, "The doc had to take off his thumb, but says we can bring him to the jail when he's done."

The sheriff said, "I've got the kid in the first cell, so I'm going to head back there."

"Okay, boss."

The sheriff left the doctor's office and instead of going directly back to the jail, turned and walked down the main street another block, then turned left down a side street and after passing two houses, turned down the walk of the third.

He hopped onto the porch, opened the door, and walked inside, hanging his Stetson on a hook before crossing the parlor.

His wife, Minnie, was in the kitchen and heard him enter, but his first greeting was from his three daughters, who were helping her with the cooking.

"Papa!" shouted his oldest, fifteen-year-old Mary.

Twelve-year-old Bessie and ten-year-old Cassie added their greetings as their father entered the kitchen, smiled at them, and kissed his wife on the cheek, who then opened the oven door and slid in the biscuits she and her girls had just made.

She wiped her hands on her apron as she asked, "Tell us what happened, oh mighty sheriff. We heard all the gunfire in town and then they said that you and a posse chased after the robbers."

He poured himself a cup of coffee as he replied, "That's pretty much it. The Hogan brothers rode into town and they were spotted by Lou Sanborn, but before we could get to the Winchesters, they opened fire on the jail and robbed the bank. They killed Ed Schmidt, too. We chased after them and shot one, but the others escaped to the Nations. We got the bank's money back, though. The wounded one is over at Doc Gillespie's now."

"Did anyone get hurt?" she asked.

"No, ma'am, but there was one odd thing about this. We were chasing after the Hogans and we reached a hill north of town and there was another Hogan we didn't know about waiting for us with his pistol. He was supposed to slow us down, but he didn't load his pistol properly, so we caught him. He's in the jail now and I need to head back over there and have a talk with him."

"What's so odd about that?" Minnie asked.

"He's maybe twelve or thirteen years old and thinks he's a tough guy, like his brothers."

Then after a short pause, he looked at his wife and said, "You know, I may be reading him all wrong, but I think he doesn't understand what bastards his brothers really are. And there's something else odd about him."

"And that is?"

"He doesn't look anything like them at all. The Hogan brothers look as if they were created with a cookie cutter. Black hair, brown eyes, about the same height, and facial features. This kid has hazel green eyes and light brown hair. His face looks different, too. If he's their brother, then I'm his mother."

Minnie laughed and said, "I know that's not true because you can't have boys."

The sheriff grinned and said, "I blame you for that, Minnie. Anyway, I'm going to head back to the jail. Can you send something over when you're finished cooking?"

"You aren't going to eat here?"

"Later, but I need to feed my prisoners. I should have two by the time those biscuits are done. I want to talk to this kid before his brother shows up. It might be interesting to see what happens when the big Hogan does show up, too."

"Well, good luck with that," she replied as she returned to cooking.

Her husband put the coffee cup in the sink and sequentially kissed his daughters, ending with Cassie before leaving the kitchen and after grabbing his hat, departed from his home.

In the jail, Joey lay stretched out on his cot, still trying to figure out why his brothers had just ridden straight for the river. They wouldn't leave him to face the posse by himself. There must be another reason. Then he almost smacked himself in the head for not seeing it in the first place. The sheriff was lying to him. Of course, he was. He was trying to trick him into giving up his brothers, so he could catch them and hang them all.

Satisfied with his conclusion, Joey put his hands behind his neck and smiled. He was just too smart to be tricked by some lawman. Then there was that threat about hanging Drew too. He knew that they didn't hang people for robbing banks. Yup, Joey was sure that the sheriff was just a liar.

By the time the sheriff walked into his jail, Joey was feeling pretty good about himself.

Sheriff Warren closed the door behind him as he entered his office and ignored Joey as he took the seat behind the front desk and opened a drawer. He pulled out a stack of wanted posters looking for the Hogan brothers and after flipping through the pages, found Drew's and smiled. There was a three-hundred-dollar reward on his head and that meant he'd get a hundred dollars added to his account after splitting it with his deputies. The money was important because his three girls were closing in on marrying age, and if they were boys, it wouldn't matter. But Minnie was already talking about hope chests and trousseaus, whatever they were.

After sliding the remaining posters back into his desk drawer, he finally swiveled the chair around to talk to his young prisoner.

"What's your name, son?" he asked.

Joey started to answer 'Joey', but decided that he was a man now, and replied, "Joe. Joe Hogan."

"Well, Joe, you've got to know that you're in a bit of trouble. You can hang for what you and your brothers just did, you know."

Joey snorted and said, "That ain't gonna happen. They don't hang men for robbin' banks. Even I know that."

"You've got me there, Joe. But if you know that, you know we do hang them for murder."

Joey sat up quickly and his eyes popped wide as he asked, "*Murder?*"

"Yes, sir. In addition to the ones that your brothers have committed elsewhere, it seems like one of your brothers got a bit of an itchy trigger finger in the bank and put a .44 through one of the cashiers, a young man named Ed Schmidt. Ed was a popular young man in town, and I don't believe a jury is going to take too kindly to his murder. Now you just told me you're a Hogan, so that makes you complicit in the murder. Do you understand what that means?"

Joey glared at the sheriff and laid back down, stared at the ceiling, and replied, "I don't care if you hang me or not. You ain't gonna get me to turn on my brothers."

"As long as we're bringing that subject up, I want to know something. When I looked at your brother, I just can't see the resemblance. How come you look so different from your brothers? Did you have a different mother?"

His mother wasn't a subject Joey wanted to discuss. He only had a vague recollection of her because she'd died when he was four, and even thinking about her made him sad. The last thing he wanted now was to appear to be a sissy, so he didn't reply and just closed his eyes.

Sheriff Warren shrugged and pulled out some blank sheets of paper to write his report of the robbery, chase, shootout, and capture. It wasn't going to be a short report, and he wasn't sure how he was going to portray young Joe Hogan yet either. Despite his assertion that the boy could hang, he knew that it was highly unlikely. His age, separation from the actual robbery and murder, and lack of participation in the escape all pointed to his being sent to the Texas State Reformatory near Gainesville.

He was almost halfway through the report when Deputies Sheehy and Sanborn entered escorting Drew Hogan.

Joey turned at the noise, saw his brother, and then bounced off the cot and shouted, "Drew!"

Drew was in a bit of a daze, but was so furious about what had happened, he just glared at Joey as the two deputies led him to the second cell and after setting him on the cot, they left the cell and slammed the iron-barred door closed.

Joey ran to the bars separating the two cells and shouted, "Drew! It's me, Joey!"

The three lawmen congregated around the front desk as Sheriff Warren set down his pen and watched the interaction between the two Hogans. The sheriff was the only one of the lawmen that wasn't surprised by the hostility Drew was showing the kid.

Joey thought he understood why Drew was so angry at him and finally said, "I'm sorry, Drew. The stupid gun didn't work at all. It was my fault, too. I didn't put the percussion caps on. It's all my fault that you got shot, Drew. I'm sorry."

Drew just snapped, "Shut up, you little bastard!"

Joey may have thought Drew as angry, but he'd never called him anything like that before. He just stood in stunned silence looking at his brother.

Deputy Sheehy then asked, "Do you need me for anything, boss?"

The sheriff continued to look at Joey and replied, "No. You and Lou can head home. You can write your reports in the morning."

"Thanks, boss. Are you gonna stay here all night?"

"Nope. I'll leave after I finish my report."

"Okay, boss," Dan said as he and Lou Sanborn left the office.

Sheriff Warren was wondering if Drew's comment about the boy being a bastard was meant more as a statement of fact than an insult and decided he'd stay long enough to find out.

He stood and walked around the outside of the first cell and looked at Drew as he sat on his cot and continued to glare at Joey, who had remained with his hands around the iron bars separating the two cells.

Sheriff Warren said, "You know, Hogan, you shouldn't call your brother that name just because he looks different. He might think he's not even related."

Drew looked away from Joey and kept the same malevolent stare as he looked at the sheriff before a slight, wicked smile spread across his lips.

"You think that little bastard is a Hogan? He ain't no brother of mine. He ain't nothin'. Most of us didn't even want to keep him around, but first Pa and then Buck figured he'd be useful 'cause he didn't look like us. But when the chips were down, the little bastard wasn't worth spit."

Joey couldn't understand what Drew was saying at first and then he realized that by disavowing him as a brother, he was trying to save him from the noose. It was what brave men and heroes did. He went from being stunned and sickened by what Drew had said to being proud of his older brother.

John Warren, on the other hand, believed every word, and asked, "Didn't your father marry his mother?"

Drew snickered, glanced at Joey, and said, "Marry her? You gotta be stupid. There were seven of us in that place and after Ma died, my pa got kinda lonely for female company. So, me, Buck, and my pa went over to this farm near Lickville and grabbed these two sisters. Their husbands had gone off to fight in the war and left 'em alone.

"One of 'em had this kid, and like I said, my pa thought he'd be useful. We kinda put the sisters to work around the house, but mostly to keep us happy. The older sister died after just a year and his ma died a year later, and we wanted to get rid of the kid, but Pa and then Buck said we had to keep him around and act like he was our brother."

Joey still wanted to believe that Drew was making this all up, but he had even vaguer memories of another woman that his mother had called Liddy or Libby or something. *Why couldn't he remember?* He couldn't even remember his mother's name.

Before the sheriff could ask another question, Joey quietly asked, "What was my mother's name?"

Drew turned to look at Joey, laughed, and said, "We called her Aggie, but I don't remember her last name at all, 'cause we didn't care. Don't you remember your whore mama's last name, little boy? We all had her, you know, sometimes we'd all just line up by age. Her sister was Lydia and she killed herself, but your precious mama couldn't 'cause if she did, we told her we'd dump her little kid down the well if she didn't behave. But she got herself pregnant and died havin' the baby anyway."

Joey suddenly realized that Drew wasn't making this up to save him from the noose or for any other reason. He was telling the truth. It was more than just an admission that he wasn't Joey's brother. Drew was saying how he and his brothers had kidnapped his mother and her sister and used them like prostitutes until his aunt killed herself and his own mother died having one of their babies. He was beyond sick when he realized that he was nothing.

Sheriff Warren turned to look at Joey, saw the vacant look on his face, looked back at Drew, and said, "Shut up, Hogan, or I'll cheat the hangman and shoot you right now."

Drew just snickered and laid down on his cot, ignoring the throbbing pain in his right hand. He felt good about hurting that little bastard. He should have been dropped down the well years ago.

Joey finally turned, walked slowly to his cot, and sat down, his eyes still staring blankly ahead. Aggie. That's all he knew about his mother other than she and her sister Lydia had been kidnapped from her farm outside of Lickville. And now he knew he wasn't even a Hogan anymore but now he was glad that he wasn't one.

The sheriff sat back down at the desk, dipped the pen into the bottle of ink, and continued to write his report. He couldn't imagine the shock that the boy was going through right now. He went from being a wannabe outlaw to being just a crushed, lonely kid and wondered if he could do anything about it.

He had finished the third page of his report when the door opened, and his three girls all entered carrying trays. They were all smiling at him, and he smiled back, even though he wasn't really in a smiling mood.

"Hello, Papa," said Mary happily as she carried her tray across the office and set it down on the desk.

"Hello, Papa," Bessie echoed as she set hers down.

"Good evening, Sheriff Warren," Cassie intoned seriously as she set the tray with coffee and cups on the desk and she looked at him and giggled.

After each of his daughters set down their trays, they looked into the cells to see the boy that their father had arrested in the bank holdup and shootout. None had ever seen anyone under fifteen in jail before, except when their father had locked up Ned O'Neill for trying to kiss Mary three months ago.

Joey heard their voices, but nothing mattered as he languished in the incredible revelation that Drew had exploded inside of him.

"Do you want us to stay and take the empty trays back, Papa?" asked Mary.

"No, dear. Thank you for bringing the food. I'll bring them back when they're clean."

"Okay," Mary replied before she and then Bessie kissed their father on his cheek and quickly traipsed out of the jail.

Cassie stayed behind, which wasn't unusual behavior for her, so neither sister waited for their youngest sister.

"Is that him?" she asked as she pointed at Joey.

"Yes, that's him. I think you should return with your sisters, Cassie. He's not very happy right now."

"Is it because he's in jail or something else?"

"Something else. I'll explain later. Okay?"

Cassie nodded, but then walked slowly around the desk close to the cell and stared at Joey.

He finally noticed that she was there and snapped, "This ain't no circus or zoo. Leave me alone."

Cassie said, "Just because you're sad doesn't mean you have to be rude; you know."

"You're the one who's rude, little girl. Go away."

"I'm not so little. I'll be eleven in another two months."

Joey angrily said, "You look like you're eight with those pigtails and freckles. Go away!"

Cassie's eyebrows furrowed as she replied, "I like my pigtails. If you think your mean words are going to make me cry, then you're wrong. What's your name?"

"It's none of your business."

"My name is Cassie. Cassie Elizabeth Warren. So, what's your name?"

Joey sighed and said, "Joe. I don't know my last name."

“How can you not know your last name?”

Before he could answer, Drew laughed from the back cell and shouted, “’Cause he don’t know what it is!”

Cassie shouted back, “I wasn’t asking you. You shut up!”

Joey was shocked that a ten-year-old girl would tell an adult to shut up, especially a tough man like his brother…or ex-brother.

Drew must have felt the same way and shot up from his cot snarling, “Ain’t no little girl gonna tell me to shut up!”

Sheriff Warren finally said, “Then I’ll tell you to shut up, Hogan,” then added in a much softer tone, “Cassie, why don’t you head home? Tell your mother I’ll be there in another half an hour or so. Okay?”

Cassie turned to her father and replied, “Yes, sir.”

She turned, walked past the desk, and then before she left the jail, she turned back and said, “Goodnight, Joe.”

Joey didn’t reply but watched the girl leave the jail, thinking she was the strangest person he’d ever met. Granted, he’d never met many people before, and almost no girls, but she sure was different, even from her older sisters.

John Warren wasn’t the least surprised by Cassie’s talk with Joe or her chastisement of Drew Hogan. He loved his youngest daughter as he loved his other two but pitied the poor man that would marry her in a few years.

He rose and brought a tray of food to each cell, slid them under the bottom of the cell door, poured a cup of coffee, and passed them through the bars. He was somewhat surprised that both of his prisoners accepted the food and coffee without saying a word but was grateful for the lack of resistance.

———

In the Nations, Earl, Fred, Glen, and Hank Hogan sat around a campfire while Buck paced around the perimeter.

"We sure as hell can't go back to the house. The law will be waiting for us by the time we get there."

Earl held his hands before the warming fire and said, "We told you Joey would be trouble. He screwed it all up."

Buck snapped, "It wasn't his fault and you know it. If you want to blame somebody, blame me. I didn't figure they'd get a big posse together that fast. I don't know why the kid didn't fire, but it didn't matter. Get over the kid and let's talk about what we're going to do starting tomorrow."

"I say we swing east a bit and find ourselves a town where they don't know us," suggested Hank.

"What about food?" asked Fred.

Buck replied, "All right. Here's what we'll do. Tomorrow, we ride east, cross the river again, and find ourselves a ranch or a farm. We rest up, collect what we can, and then take our time to figure out where we'll go."

Earl then asked, "What about Drew? We ain't gonna let him hang, are we?"

Buck shrugged and answered, "We don't have any choice. They'll be watching for us and if they can send a posse with nine men in just a few minutes, there's no way we can ride in there and save him."

Earl then added in a low voice, “I hope they hang that kid, too. Little useless bastard.”

Buck didn’t reply but noticed the other three nodding. Even he was regretting his decision to let Joey stay with them for all these years, and even more for including him on the job.

———

While his prisoners ate, Sheriff Warren finished writing his report and collected their empty trays. He pointed out the chamber pots in the corner before he stacked the trays, blew out the lamps, and left the jail.

As he walked back to the house and his own meal, he thought about Joe and tried to formulate some way to help the boy. He wasn’t sure if it was because he never had a son or whether he just liked the kid, but the reason didn’t matter. He’d talk to the prosecutor tomorrow when he dropped off his report. Maybe the kid wouldn’t have to go to reform school after all.

———

After the sheriff had gone, Drew launched into a long sequence of stories about Joey’s mother and how he and the other brothers had used her. It seemed that the longer he talked, the more vivid and lurid the stories became, and Joey tried to block his voice from his mind but failed.

It wasn’t until almost eleven o’clock before Drew finally was silenced as the pain from his thumb-less right hand demanded his attention. He drifted off to sleep twenty minutes later, but Joey stayed awake still trying to remember anything he could about his mother that hadn't come from Drew's poisoned mouth.

Before the sun had risen the next morning, the Hogan brothers crossed back into Texas and headed east. They'd ride for another couple of hours in that direction before they made a turn to the south and found a farm or a ranch. They needed food and a place to call home until they could come up with a better arrangement.

Sheriff Warren was the first one into the office and had the heat stove going when Deputy Sanborn arrived followed shortly by Deputy Sheehy. He let them handle the prisoners' needs, including sending Deputy Sanborn to the café for their breakfast as his daughters were in school.

He picked up his report, left the jail, and headed for the county offices to talk to Mister Lucius Underwood, the county prosecutor. He was going to ask that they not press charges against the boy as his only real crimes were yelling at the posse and falling down the hill, but he knew he'd have to make a convincing argument for two reasons. Lucius Underwood was a stickler for the law, even the gray areas.

Technically Joey Hogan, or whatever his name was, had participated in a bank holdup that had resulted in a murder and could hang. Most men would see that as unfair, but not Mister Underwood. The second reason was that Ed Schmidt, the dead cashier, was his brother-in-law, and the sheriff was sure that the prosecutor's wife had demanded the utmost punishment for all those involved in the murder of her sister's husband.

So, as he entered the offices of Mister Underwood, he had no idea what to expect but didn't have long to wait.

After giving his report to the prosecutor, he sat and waited as the attorney read the five-page account. The sheriff was watching his facial expression for an indicator of what he would say when he finished and already had a good idea when Mister Underwood laid the statement onto the desktop.

"Well, John, I think this is a pretty solid case. Those two are both going to be charged with bank robbery and murder. The trial will be this afternoon at three o'clock."

"Why so fast, Lucius? Usually, it's at least two days."

"Because we all saw them do it and the townsfolk are in an uproar and demanding justice."

"If they're demanding justice, why are we charging the boy with those crimes? He didn't do a damned thing other than stand on a hill and yell at us."

"He's a Hogan and I'm not going to let him turn into another of those thugs. You let five of them get away and he's not going to run back to their welcoming arms, so they can come back here and terrorize this town."

"He's not going to do any such thing. I'll be more than happy to pull the lever on the gallows for Drew Hogan, but just let the kid go. Give the boy a chance to grow up before you decide to end his life."

Lucius Underwood's eyes narrowed as he replied, "You did your job and brought him in, John. Let me do my job now."

Sheriff Warren knew he'd lost the argument, if there really had ever been one, and nodded, stood, and left the office. He walked out into the sun, pulled on his Stetson, and headed for the Western Union office. He may not be able to stop the boy from getting hanged, but he might at least be able to let him climb the gallows steps knowing his real name.

After sending his telegram to the town marshal in Lickville, he returned to his offices to let his deputies and the prisoners know about the afternoon's trial.

The door was barely open when he heard the surly voice of Drew Hogan already lambasting the kid about what a stupid coward he was and that was what had marked him as not being a Hogan more than his lighter hair and hazel green eyes.

He hadn't hung his hat before shouting, "Shut up, Hogan!", then asking, "Dan, why are you and Lou letting that blowhard make so much noise?"

Deputy Sheehy answered, "He just started up again. We shut him up a little while ago."

As he hung his hat, the sheriff said, "Well, we don't have to put up with him much longer. Mister Underwood scheduled their trial for this afternoon at three o'clock."

"Already?"

"He wants to show the folks how good he is, I guess," he replied as he walked to the heat stove and poured himself a cup of coffee.

Deputy Sanborn asked, "What about the kid?"

"He wants them both to hang. I argued with him, but he's dead set on it. I imagine his wife laid down the law."

Dan Sheehy leaned back in his chair and said, “I forgot about that. Ed Schmidt’s widow is his wife’s sister.”

“Yup. So now, all we can hope is that Mister Jones will get the jury to see the other side of the story.”

Lou Sanborn snickered and said, “If they can get Winnie Jones out of his rocking chair.”

The sheriff didn’t comment as he walked past the cells and into his office.

Joey had spent most of the morning ignoring Drew’s almost constant diatribes about him and his mother, none of which were new after the first half hour last night. His opinion of the Hogan brothers had been radically altered once he believed that Drew hadn’t been lying.

They fell from the pantheon of heroes to the depths of depraved villains in just minutes. His only wish now was that he wouldn’t hang so he could seek vengeance against the men who had murdered his mother because that was how he saw it. But after the useless Remington incident, he knew he had a lot to learn, and even then, he wasn’t sure he had the fortitude and the will to do it, even if he wasn’t hanged. Those begging eyes of the coyote still haunted him. *If he couldn’t put down a damned coyote, how could he face five tough killers?*

Drew started up again, only in a much lower voice, but Joey ignored him as he sat on his bunk. He’d held out hope that he wouldn’t hang, but the sheriff had made it sound as if there was little chance of his escaping the noose, and felt like a bigger fool than he had when he’d stood on the hill pulling the trigger of a pistol that wouldn’t fire. He was going to hang for just being there.

Less than two hours later, Mister Winthrop Jones, their defense attorney, entered the office.

"Morning, Winnie," Deputy Sanborn said when he saw him enter, "Come to see your clients?"

"In a moment but first, I need to see your boss," the lawyer said as he shuffled across the office.

Mister Winthrop Aloysius Jones was as unlikely an attorney as could be expected to be found in a small town in West Texas. He'd been a captain in the 27th Texas Calvary during the war and while he served, rather than waste all the time between battles and skirmishes, as many had done, he read the lawbooks that the adjutant had brought with him. After the surrender, he'd passed the bar and returned to his home town of Warwick, which had been mostly ignored by both sides.

He really wasn't that old at fifty-two, but in his last major engagement of the war, a Union cannonball had killed his horse and the resulting fall had shattered his right tibia rendering him a cripple. His premature white hair added to the effect of aging and those that didn't know him thought he might be seventy years old or more.

Drew watched him shuffle past and huffed in derision, not that the defense attorney mattered to him at all. He knew he was going to hang, and all he could do now was to make Joey miserable.

Joey hadn't even paid attention as he lay on his cot imagining ways to get even with the five Hogan brothers, knowing that's all he would ever be able to do...imagine.

"Morning, Mister Jones," Sheriff Warren said as he stood behind his desk.

“Morning, Sheriff. Mind if I sit?”

“Not at all,” John Warren said as he took his own seat.

“I read your report over at Lucius’ office and had a chat with my colleague. I was surprised that he’s going for a conviction for robbery and murder of the boy. After reading your report, it sounded as if the boy did nothing at all except try and slow you down with a non-functioning pistol.”

“I can understand why he’s mad, but that shouldn’t cloud his judgement. I was going to ask that the boy not be charged with anything, but he went to the other extreme.”

“Let me ask you, John. When you’re on the stand, and I ask you specifically about the boy, will you testify to that?”

“Of course, but there’s something else you should know. He’s not even a Hogan brother. He thought he was until that loud-mouthed one we have in the cell next to him told him otherwise.”

“He isn’t? It’s not in your report.”

“I know, I already wrote it and figured it wasn’t important until after I talked to Mister Underwood, and besides, I don’t have any proof other than the garbage that Hogan bastard had been spewing, and he surely won’t testify to save the boy.”

“Well, that might make a difference anyway. I’m going to go and talk to my clients. Can you and your deputies vacate the office?”

“How much time do you need?”

“Oh, about an hour, I believe.”

"We'll go and get some lunch then and be back here just before noon."

"Thank you, Sheriff."

The two men rose and the sheriff waited for the defense lawyer to exit his office before following him down the short hallway, collecting his hat and his two deputies, and exiting his office. He trusted Mister Jones not to open Drew Hogan's cell for his own protection, but once outside, he stopped his deputies.

"Dan, stay here and make sure Hogan doesn't try anything. Lou, I want you to climb the church tower and keep an eye out for the rest of the Hogans. They might try and get back here to spring Drew loose, but I don't think so. If they didn't come back last night, they're not coming. After I get some lunch, I'll relieve you, Dan, then you get something to eat and you can relieve Lou."

"Okay, boss," Lou replied before jogging toward the church on the western end of town. The bell tower was the tallest structure in town, but even that was just thirty feet high.

Even as Lou Sanborn was climbing the steps to the church tower, Drew Hogan's five brothers were already almost twenty miles east of Warwick and still riding southeast.

As Lou settled in his position, Earl Hogan was the first to spot the McPherson farmhouse in the distance.

At two-thirty, Sheriff Warren and his two deputies escorted a shackled Drew Hogan and an unfettered Joey to the county courthouse for trial. The sheriff's decision not to bind Joey was ostensibly because there was only one set of shackles, but the real reason was that the sheriff didn't want to portray the boy as a criminal. He wasn't sure it would make any difference, though.

Once they were all settled in the courtroom with the two defendants seated beside Mister Jones and the sheriff seated at the prosecutor's table with Mister Underwood, it was just a matter of waiting for the entrance of Judge Lawrence 'don't you dare call me Larry' Madsen.

Judge Madsen took his job very seriously and had been the county judge for six years now. He was a firm believer in the decorum of his courtroom, which was somewhat unusual in West Texas where most judges were almost as rowdy as the defendants.

At exactly three o'clock, they all stood as the judge floated into the courtroom, took his seat, and gaveled the trial to order.

After the clerk read the charges against the standing defendants, Mister Underwood gave his opening statement to the jury. Sheriff Warren looked at the twelve men and spotted all six of the men who had ridden on the posse with him and another that was a bank clerk. The other five didn't seem to be in a forgiving mood, either. He hoped their anger was all directed at Drew Hogan but doubted it.

Mister Underwood quoted the law that those assisting in a crime were just as guilty as the perpetrator, then explained how the boy had been planted to aid the escape of his brothers.

It was only then that the sheriff realized that the prosecutor didn't know Joe's true parentage and wondered if Mister Jones would spring it now or later.

As the prosecuting attorney was ending his argument, a messenger entered the courtroom, looked around, found the sheriff, walked to the aisle, and held up a yellow sheet to show the judge, who then nodded.

The messenger handed it to Sheriff Warren, quickly backed away, and left the courtroom, knowing he wasn't going to get a tip anyway.

John Warren read the message, smiled, and slid it into his pocket just as the prosecutor ended his opening statement, turned away from the jury, and took his seat beside him.

When the defense attorney gave his opening statement, he stayed with a more humanistic approach, saying that if the law was interpreted as far as the prosecutor seems to believe, then the waitress who had served the Hogans their lunch could be charged as well. He didn't mention the lack of familial bond between his two clients, nor did he mention that the brothers hadn't eaten lunch in Warwick.

The prosecutor couldn't call any of the jury members as witnesses but called each of his deputies first which surprised him somewhat but shouldn't have. After their discussion this morning, Mister Underwood wasn't about to let the sheriff sink his case that he'd build against the kid.

As he interrogated Lou and Dan, it was obvious that he was trying to paint Joey as just another gang member. Ironically, he was concentrating so much on trying to prove his point about the boy's involvement he made almost no effort at all in his case against Drew Hogan. Maybe he understood from the jury selection that it wasn't necessary, and he was probably right.

In his cross-examination of his deputies, Mister Jones tried to parry the prosecutor's thrusts against Joey as well, and in his defense of Drew, he was only able to get the witnesses to admit that they hadn't seen who had gone into the bank and killed Ed Schmidt.

That turned out to be a moot point when the prosecutor called the second cashier who identified Drew as the man who had actually pulled the trigger, not that it mattered much. Mister Jones' argument was that all the Hogan brothers looked the same and he could have been mistaken. It was also the first inkling of his attempt to separate Joey from the Hogan brothers.

The prosecutor rested his case, raising the eyebrows of Judge Madsen when he hadn't called Sheriff Warren to testify.

That was rectified when Mister Jones called the sheriff to the stand as his first and only witness, surprising the prosecutor, who hadn't even bothered to look at Mister Jones' short witness list.

After he'd been sworn in, Mister Jones asked, "Sheriff Warren, you and your posse chased the Hogan brothers just minutes after they ran, is that correct?"

"Yes, sir."

"They were almost halfway to the Nations when you turned north, so what were your chances of catching them before they made it safely across the Red River?"

"Oh, I'd say less than fifty percent. Their horses were tired and ours were fresh but making up that much distance in such a short time would have been difficult."

"What effect did the boy's challenge from the hill have on the chase?"

"Almost none at all, other than my decision to split the posse into two parts. I took two men to clear the hill and sent my deputies and four others around the east to run down the Hogans."

"And that's when they caught Drew Hogan?"

"Yes, sir. We caught the young man at the bottom of the hill. He'd fallen down, and I left Charlie Bascom to tie him up while Jimmy Hill and I caught up with the rest of the posse. Drew Hogan's horse had stopped, and he was on the ground with his Winchester. The others were already at the river, so my deputies and I spread out and engaged him with our repeaters. After his right thumb was shot off, he surrendered, and we brought him in."

"And what about the lad?"

"He never got a shot off because he didn't even know how to load a percussion pistol. He never gave us a hard time after I untied him, either."

Then Mister Jones turned, took two shuffling steps toward the jury, and without turning asked, "Sheriff, did you learn anything about the boy's background since he's been in your jail?"

"Yes, sir. I learned quite a bit. Drew Hogan seemed to be very angry with him because he'd failed to slow down the posse as he was supposed to do. He then launched into a loud and vicious diatribe in which he told Joe that he wasn't a Hogan at all."

That statement caused an audible gasp from the jury and the small audience.

The defense attorney quickly turned and asked, "He's not a Hogan? Surely, you must be mistaken, Sheriff. Perhaps the older brother was just trying to protect his younger sibling from punishment."

"No, sir. I'm sure he wasn't. I now have documentation to prove it as well."

A pleasantly surprised defense attorney asked, "How are you so sure?"

"Drew Hogan told him that his mother and her sister lived on a farm near Lickville and the brothers had kidnapped them during the War of Secession when their husbands were gone. The boy was around two years old at the time. Mister Hogan said that they abused the women and that his mother's sister killed herself before his mother died in childbirth a year later. This morning, I sent a telegram to the marshal in Lickville and asked if he knew of any women that had been taken from a farm outside of town during that time period and I just received a confirming telegram. What Drew Hogan said was true and Joe isn't his brother at all."

Mister Jones smiled and said, "Thank you for your diligence, Sheriff. No more questions."

The prosecutor wasn't pleased with the lawman but stood to cross-examine him anyway.

Joey was flummoxed by the news and as Mister Jones slowly took his seat, he wanted to know more about what the sheriff had found, but all he did was stare at Sheriff Warren as the prosecutor began his questioning.

"Does the boy's parentage really matter according to the law, Sheriff? We don't excuse outlaws who aren't related, do we?"

"No, sir. But in this case, we're dealing with a boy who had been told nothing but lies his entire life. I don't think hanging him for being ignorant will help anyone."

"But he had a pistol in his hand and was attempting to shoot at you and the rest of your posse; wasn't he?"

"Yes, sir, but I think even he knew he couldn't reach us with that pistol at that range. It was a .31 caliber and only had twenty grains of powder in each cylinder. If I'd known that, I would have ignored him altogether. In fact, I'm pretty sure that the Hogan brothers left him on that hill as bait just to slow us down while they made their escape. He was under the impression that they'd be coming around the side of the hill to catch us by surprise, but their tracks never even strayed from a straight line to the Nations. They were leaving him behind because they didn't care about him at all. He wasn't one of them."

Mister Underwood knew better than to press the issue any longer, so he just said, "No further questions," and walked back to his desk.

The sheriff joined him at the prosecution's table seconds later, but the prosecutor never turned to look at him. The sheriff knew the lawyer would shoot him if he had the chance and he suspected that his wife and sister-in-law would get in line behind him, but it didn't bother him one bit.

Then it was just a matter of closing arguments which were surprisingly similar to their opening arguments before the jury stood and walked to the jury room to discuss the case.

They were out longer than anyone expected, not returning for another thirty minutes. When the judge asked for their verdicts, the foreman announced guilty on all charges for Drew Hogan which was no surprise, but the sheriff and Joey both held their breaths waiting for the foreman to declare his fate.

"We, the jury, find the defendant, Joe Hogan, to be innocent of the charge of murder, but guilty of the charge of accessory to robbery."

Joey exhaled, knowing he wasn't going to hang but didn't know what would happen now.

The judge nodded as the foreman returned to his seat and sentenced Drew Hogan to hang the following morning at eight o'clock before looking at the boy.

"Young man, you will be sent to the Texas State Reformatory until you are eighteen. I suggest you make the best of that time and never step inside a courtroom again."

He banged his gavel, intoned, "Court adjourned," then as everyone stood, stepped down from his bench, and with his judicial robes swirling behind him exited the courtroom.

As Deputies Sanborn and Sheehy each took one of Drew's arms to escort him back to jail, he turned to Joey and snarled, "You got me hanged, boy, and you can figure you're safe now, but my brothers are gonna come after you."

Joey was still unsettled by his not being a Hogan and by the reprieve from the noose and didn't even notice what Drew had said as he stood to follow the deputies. It was only when they'd walked halfway to the back of the courtroom that he comprehended Drew's very real threat.

He didn't hear the sheriff slide in behind him as they continued to head out of the courtroom with Drew's clanking shackles marking each step.

John Warren had thought about going to talk to the judge and see if he'd change his sentence and just release the boy to his custody. But he knew that the judge rarely changed his decisions or his sentencing and besides, he'd have to convince Minnie to let him stay with them and they really didn't have the money anyway. But he would have to warn the boy about what he'd find at the reformatory. They may call it a reform school, but it was filled with a lot of older, tougher kids who had been shaving for three or four years. It was then that he decided he'd be the one to escort the boy to Gainesville.

When they reached the jail, Deputy Sheehy removed Drew's shackles before pushing him into his cell and slamming the door.

When they closed the door behind Joey, he walked to the bunk and sat down, still shaken by the events of the past two days. It was difficult for him to get his mind focused on anything.

It was only when Deputy Sanborn asked, "You need us for anything else, boss?" that the sheriff realized how late it was. The sun was already setting, and he needed to get the prisoners fed. It would be the last meal for Drew Hogan.

"Um, no. I'll take care of it, Lou. I'll need you both in early tomorrow, so we can set up the gallows."

"Okay, boss," Lou replied.

The two deputies left the office as Sheriff Warren leaned back in the chair and blew out a long breath.

The town couldn't afford to hire a hangman, but Sheriff Warren had gone to Austin three years earlier to learn the art of stretching a man's neck. He'd had to do the job three times since then and it still gave him the creeps. He was silently terrified that one would drop and then just wiggle at the end of the rope like a worm on a fishhook. He may have believed that Drew Hogan deserved his fate, but the idea of a failed execution still weighed on him.

Three minutes after his deputies had gone, Sheriff Warren followed them out the door and headed to his house to get some dinner and food for his prisoners. Usually, he'd just go down to Rupert's Restaurant and get some food for anyone he had incarcerated in his jail, but sometimes it was more convenient to just take something back from the house. He also wanted to talk to his wife about the trial.

After hanging his hat on the homemade hat rack in the front room, Sheriff Warren headed for the kitchen. He hadn't announced his arrival as he usually did, but the closing door and footsteps served that purpose as he entered the kitchen and was greeted by eight smiling female eyes.

"Hello, Papa. What happened?" asked Mary.

"We had the trial this afternoon and Hogan will hang tomorrow morning. The boy will go to the reformatory in Gainesville."

Minnie said, "I guess that's better than hanging him."

"I suppose," he said as he ran his fingers through his dark brown hair.

"You don't seem happy about it," Minnie said.

"I'm not. The boy isn't even one of the brothers. I feel really bad about him. He's not like those Hogans and now we're sending him to a place that will probably teach him to be that way."

"You were right? He's not their brother?"

"No, let me tell you what I found out."

"Have a seat and we'll eat while you tell us."

He nodded and sat in his normal place as his wife and daughters quickly filled the table with food and drink.

As they ate, he told them what Drew had said the night before but hadn't told Minnie about it yet until he received confirmation of the story.

When he finished, Cassie asked, "What did he say when you told him his real name?"

John Warren paused with a fork full of pork roast on his fork as he replied, "I forgot to tell him that. I've got the telegram in my pocket, and after we got him and Hogan back into their cells, I just thought about what we'd have to do in the morning."

"Are we going to bring supper over to the jail?" asked Bessie.

He replied, "Yes, ma'am. As soon as we're finished," then he looked at Minnie and said, "I'm going to escort him to Gainesville rather than send one of the deputies. I want to talk to him."

Minnie nodded and smiled at her husband, understanding why he would want to do it. There were three daughters at the table but no sons.

For the rest of the meal, the conversation stayed away from what he had to do tomorrow because each of them understood how much he hated doing it, even knowing it was necessary.

Forty minutes later, the sheriff and his three daughters entered the jail with their trays of food, attracting the attention of his two prisoners.

After they'd set the trays on the desk, unlike the night before, all three girls stayed near the desk while their father took one of the trays and slid it under the cell door for Drew Hogan. He took the tray and the cup of coffee and sat on the cot without saying a word.

Joey was watching the sheriff and ignoring the three staring girls, wondering why they were still there. That strange one with the pigtails and freckles was in front, too.

He was surprised when the sheriff didn't bring his tray but simply unlocked the door and swung it wide.

"Come on out, Joe. You can eat at the desk. I need to give you something and explain what will happen to you now."

Joe didn't reply but nodded and followed the sheriff out into the office and sat at the desk in the big chair. The two younger girls removed the covers from the food and took the plates from the tray and set them before him while Mary poured his coffee.

Then the two older sisters pulled up chairs and sat down while the pigtailed girl just stood and stared at him with her arms folded as he began to eat.

"Joe, tomorrow, after we hang Drew behind the jail, I'll take you to the reformatory near Gainesville. Do you know what a reform school is?"

He swallowed some creamed potatoes, shook his head, and replied, "No, sir."

John noted the respectful form of address before he explained, "The purpose of the school was to give troublemaking boys a chance to make their lives better. The idea was to have boys enter the school, learn normal school things and a trade, so when they turned eighteen, they wouldn't become outlaws."

Joe looked up at the sheriff and asked, "But it don't work that way?"

"Not as often as it should. They let some of the bigger boys have their way with the younger ones by being bullies and don't do much to stop it. I don't know why, but that's the way it is."

"I'm not that small."

"How old are you, Joe?"

"I turned thirteen the day before yesterday," he replied before taking a bite of his biscuit.

The sheriff shook his head and said, "Well, happy birthday. But I'll agree with you, you're big for a new thirteen-year-old, but not that big. There are sixteen and seventeen-year-olds in there that could give me a hard time and probably will if they come this way when they turn eighteen."

Joey just nodded as he ate some of the tasty roast pork. There was nothing he could say anyway. It was where he was going, and he'd have to learn how to survive.

When Joey didn't reply, the sheriff said, "I forgot to give you this. It's from the town marshal in Lickville."

He pulled the yellow sheet from his pocket and set it on the empty tray, expecting Joey to pick it up, but he continued to eat which surprised Sheriff Warren as he'd expected the boy to be anxious to know what his name was.

Joey was very anxious to know what was on the sheet but was ashamed to admit that he couldn't read at all, not a lick.

Of course, it was Cassie who realized why he hadn't bothered with the telegram. She snatched the telegram from the tray and asked, "Can't you read at all?"

Joey turned pink and wanted to deny his shortcoming, but instead mumbled, "It don't matter if I can read or not."

"Of course, it matters. You're not stupid, are you?" Cassie asked sharply.

Joey stared at the skinny girl with her pigtails and freckles and snapped, "No, I ain't stupid! I just never been to school at all."

"Then when you get to the reform school, learn to read and write. Maybe I'll even write letters to you."

The sheriff was holding back a grin as his two older daughters stood aghast at Cassie's sharp tongue.

"I don't want any letters from you and even if I learned to read and write, I sure ain't gonna write any letters back."

"You're just too afraid to let anyone know you're smart. Aren't you?"

Joey was even more flummoxed as she chastised him. He simply had no answer.

After he didn't reply, Cassie opened the telegram and read aloud:

SHERIFF JOHN WARREN WARWICK TEXAS

TWO SISTERS AGNES ARMSTRONG
AND LYDIA WHITE DISAPPEARED in 63
ARMSTRONG HAD BOY NAMED JOE
BOTH HUSBANDS KILLED IN WAR
NO LAW HERE BACK THEN
IF BOY FOUND ARMSTRONG FARM IS STILL THERE
BAD CONDITION

MARSHAL AL THOMAS LICKVILLE TEXAS

"Your name is Joe Armstrong," Cassie announced as she held out the telegram to him.

Joey took the telegram and looked at the letters, not understanding them at all. But he had a name now. He was Joe Armstrong but didn't know if he had a middle name or even if his birthdate was right.

He folded the telegram, slipped it into his shirt pocket, and asked, "Sheriff, is there some way for me to know more? I don't even know if I have a middle name or who my father was."

Sheriff Warren nodded and said, "Sure. I'll tell you what, Joe. When I take you to Gainesville, we'll swing by Lickville and see what we can find out. Okay?"

Joe finally managed a smile and replied, "Thank you, sir."

"You're welcome. Now finish eating, so I can go home with my girls."

He nodded and quickly went about finishing his dinner.

Drew had almost laughed at the whole conversation, but when it's your last meal and you didn't even get a choice in what was on your plate, laughter didn't come easily.

When Joe finished eating, he put the plates back onto the tray and handed it to the feisty, freckle-faced girl almost as a peace offering and said, "Thank you."

Cassie accepted the tray and replied, "You're welcome."

Then she turned and grinned at her sisters as if she'd won a prize at the church raffle and waited while her father stood, blew out the lamps, and led her and her sisters out of the jail, leaving a surprised Joe, now Armstrong, sitting at the desk.

Drew was stunned to see that Joey was still outside the cell and after he was sure that the sheriff wasn't about to return, he loudly whispered, "Hey, Joey! Get me outta here! Get me the keys. They're right there!"

Joe turned, looked at Drew, stood, and walked toward the keys as Drew grinned, but continued past the ring hanging on its peg, entered his cell, and pulled the door behind him with a decisive clang.

"You, stupid little bastard!" Drew shouted.

Joe just lay on his bunk with his hands behind his neck and smiled as Drew continued to curse him.

Outside, just beyond the light from nearby windows, Sheriff John Warren was smiling from the moment he'd watched Joe return to his cell. He pulled his hammer loop back in place, turned to his daughters, and said, "Let's go home, ladies."

———

Pauline McPherson was almost catatonic as she fixed the food for the five men who had invaded her home hours ago. She knew that they would kill her before they left, and it was just a question of when they decided to do it. Her husband, Steven, had been caught outside as he tended their meager crop. He never carried a gun anyway. Her two boys had been trapped in the small barn while they were harnessing the mule, and all she'd heard was the gunfire that told her that they were dead.

What had happened to her after they were dead made her wonder if her husband and sons hadn't been treated more mercifully.

———

Just after sunrise, Sheriff Warren and Deputy Sanborn were out behind the jail setting up for the hanging. They would use the same rope they'd used for the last hanging over a year earlier when they'd stretched the neck of Ron Tillson who had accused another poker player of cheating before shooting him at the Warwick Saloon and Billiard Hall.

Once everything was ready, they descended the gallows, walked between the feed and grain store and the jail, and returned to the office.

The two prisoners had just finished eating breakfast and Joey was sitting on his cot as Drew stood with his left hand gripping one of the iron bars, glaring at him.

"They're gonna get you, Joey. It might not be tomorrow or the next day, but one of these days when you ain't lookin', they're gonna fill you full of lead."

Joey turned, looked at Drew, and said, "You're wrong, Drew. They ain't gonna get me. When I get out of that reform school, I'm gonna hunt them all down one by one for what they did to my mother."

Drew cackled and spit at Joey and snarled, "That's all you'll ever be able to do to my brothers, you sissy. I saw how you closed your eyes when you had to shoot that coyote. You ain't nothin' but a coward."

Joey's eyes narrowed as he calmly replied, "Not anymore."

Drew was going to add another threat but lost the incentive when the sheriff and his other deputy walked into the room and the sheriff said, "Let's get him ready to go."

Sheriff Warren expected that Drew wouldn't go quietly, and he was proven correct when the bully began to scream at the three lawmen as the sheriff unlocked the cell door and rushed them when the door was swung open.

He began to swing and kick at the sheriff and deputies as they tried to put him under control, and as the deputies tried to grab his wildly swinging arms, Sheriff Warren stomped on Drew's left foot, making him yank the foot from the ground as he screeched in pain. Once he was one-legged, the deputies had no problems getting him cuffed and then shackled.

Joey just watched the man who had acted so hard and tough just seconds earlier suddenly start sobbing before going limp, making the lawmen have to drag him from his cell. His shackled boots were sliding along the wooden floor as the sheriff walked out of the office and his two deputies each grasped one arm of the whining, begging Drew Hogan out of the jail.

As the door closed and the sounds dropped, Joey sat, still confounded by the overwhelming realization of just how much of his life had been a lie, from his name, and his admiration of his brothers to the truth about his mother. It was as if he'd lived his life in a prairie dog hole and never knew what the sun was.

He pulled out the telegram he couldn't read and recalled what he had just told Drew. He had said it as a response to Drew's threat about his brothers hunting him down, but suddenly it was much more. At that moment as he stared at the indecipherable words on the sheet of yellow paper, he decided that he had to do it, no matter how long it took. He had to make the brothers pay for what they had done to his mother, but he had lied when he said he wasn't a coward anymore. He was scared to death at the thought of facing them.

Joey was still staring at the telegram when the door opened again and was surprised it was unlocked, but even more surprised to see that strange, pigtailed girl enter and close the door behind her.

She didn't say anything but walked to the desk, turned the chair around, and then plopped onto its hard, wooden seat.

“Why aren’t you in school?” he asked.

“It’s Saturday. There’s a calendar right on the wall,” she answered as she pointed.

Joey didn’t bring up that he couldn’t read a calendar either and asked, “Why aren’t your sisters with you?”

“They’re with their friends, so I came here.”

“Why?”

“I wanted to talk to you.”

“About what?”

“I wanted to make sure that you didn’t do anything stupid when you got to reform school. You should go there and learn to read and write and not let those bigger boys make you mean like them.”

Joey said, “I’ve already decided that when I get out, I’m going to go after the Hogans for what they did to my mother. Is that stupid?”

“No. I can understand that, and if I were you, I’d do the same thing, but what I meant was that you shouldn’t change into a criminal like most of those boys. You can go after those men when you get out without being a criminal.”

Joey sighed and said, “What difference does it make to you? You’re just a silly girl with pigtails and freckles.”

“I’m a girl with pigtails and freckles, but I’m not silly. Pretty soon, my freckles will be gone and then I won’t have pigtails anymore. I’m going to have a ponytail and then a lot of boys will want to be my boyfriend.”

Joey snickered and said, “So, you’re going to have a ponytail and a boyfriend. I’m never going to see you after I leave, so it doesn’t matter to me at all.”

Cassie hopped back to her feet and approached the bars and looked at him with her piercing brown eyes.

“It had better matter to you, Joe Armstrong because you are going to come back and be my boyfriend.”

Joey’s mouth dropped open as he stared at her and he began to laugh.

“I ain’t never comin’ back here. I’m gonna be goin’ all over Texas if I have to, tryin’ to find those Hogans. I ain’t gonna have time for girlfriends.”

Cassie didn’t laugh but said, “I’m just telling you that I’m not going anywhere until you return, and when you learn to read and write, you’d better send me a letter. Goodbye, Joe.”

Cassie then turned, her yellow flowered print dress swirling into the air before she, her pigtails, and her freckles crossed the floor, opened the door, and left the jail.

Joey just stood in total disbelief. That girl was crazy!

———

The hanging went as well as could be expected. Judge Madsen had to be there, but there was a decent crowd to witness the execution, too. Drew’s behavior, if anything, got worse as they dragged him up the gallows' steps.

After the black hood was placed over his twisting, contorting head and snugged down, both deputies had to stay there and support him while Sheriff Warren went back to his release lever and without any formalities, pulled it. The trapdoor opened and after one snap and a few spontaneous jerks, Drew Hogan died.

They lowered his body to the ground, the crowd dispersed, the mortician collected the body and the three lawmen restored the gallows to its unused state before they returned to the jail.

Once he saw them enter, Joey didn't have to ask if Drew was dead even though he hadn't heard anything. He was surprised to see a strained look on Sheriff Warren's face. It was as if he was going to be sick.

"What's next, boss?" asked Deputy Sheehy.

"I'll plan on taking Joe to the reformatory tomorrow, so I'll be gone for a few days. Dan, you'll be in charge. If anything serious comes up, like those Hogan brothers trying to avenge Drew's hanging, send a telegram to the reformatory and I'll get back here as soon as I can."

"Do you think they'll show up?" Dan asked.

"Nope. I was worried about them showing up during the hanging, so I had Charlie watching from the bell tower. Once he saw the hearse roll away, he came back down. You should be okay."

The sheriff then walked to the cells, took the key ring from the wall, and unlocked Joe's door.

"Joe, you're still technically under arrest, but I'm going to trust you to not do anything stupid. You're safer with us than if you tried to run away."

Joey stood and said, “I wasn’t going to run away, Sheriff. I’m kinda lookin’ forward to goin’ to reform school. I know that sounds stupid, but I ain’t never been to school of any kind before. I need to learn as much as I can.”

The sheriff looked at Joe, nodded, and said, “That’s a good attitude to have, Joe.”

Joe walked out of the cell and then once he reached the main office took a seat on a chair near the front desk as Deputy Sanborn sat in the chair behind the desk.

“Are we going to stop at Lickville tomorrow, Sheriff?” Joey asked.

“That’s the plan, but it’ll probably be the day after tomorrow. It’s not in my county, but we can swing south and then head east to Gainesville. It’ll only add a few hours to the trip and it’s going to take us three days anyway.”

“Three days? How far away is the reform school?”

“Oh, about a hundred miles, I reckon, but we can pick up the train in Henrietta, so we’ll only have to ride about sixty miles before we get there.”

“This is as far as I’ve ever been from the house that I grew up in near Hinkley. I ain’t ever been on a train, either.”

“Is that where the Hogan brothers lived?” asked the sheriff.

“Yes, sir. I don’t know how they got it, but it’s about a two-hour ride northwest of Hinkley. I didn’t get to go into town very often, but they did.”

"Well, I'll notify the sheriff down there about the place, but I don't figure they'll be heading back there now. They'll probably find some other ranch or farm and take it."

"Take it? Like just...take it?" Joey asked with wide eyes.

"Yes, sir. Probably just like they took your mother and her sister from their farm and probably the place where you were living. There were six brothers and their father for a while. That was a lot of firepower and manpower during the war when most men were gone. It still is, too. There are five of them with Winchesters and Colts and they can overpower most households without a shot being fired."

Joey sighed and said softly, "I always thought they were like heroes. Right up 'til Drew began to scream at me. Even then, I figured he was just tryin' to save me from hangin'. It was only when he started talkin' about my mother that I figured it out. I feel really stupid."

"Just ignorant, Joe. We're all ignorant of something. When you get to that reform school, you learn as much as you can. Don't let those older bastards try and turn you into another Hogan. I think you're better than that."

Joe smiled and said, "That's what your girl said. The crazy one with the pigtails and freckles."

The sheriff smiled and said, "That's Cassie. She says what's on her mind and she's smart as a whip too, but she's far from crazy. I pity the poor boy she decides to marry, though."

Joe almost told the sheriff that she had already told him she had said she wanted him for a boyfriend but thought she was just being crazy again anyway, so it didn't matter. But those eyes of hers scared him a bit. *How can anyone say something like that?* Besides, she was only ten years old, and nobody knew what would happen even in the next week, much less years in the future. Look at what had happened to him in just the two days since he'd turned thirteen. His whole world had been turned upside down and inside out.

But now he was determined to set it right and when he was eighteen, he'd do what he promised Drew he would do. He'd find those five Hogans and let them know he was an Armstrong.

CHAPTER 2

Even though it was a Sunday, Sheriff Warren wanted to get underway. He'd surprised Joe by inviting him to his home for breakfast before they left, and Joe had found himself more than just a little uncomfortable. It wasn't because of his lack of manners or that they made him feel unwelcome, it was just that the strange, pigtailed girl kept glancing at him, almost as if she was evaluating him.

Her sisters, on the other hand, were decidedly pleasant, and he thought both of them were prettier, too. Especially Bessie, who was almost his age. Now there was a girl worth returning to have as a girlfriend. She even smiled at him a few times.

Mrs. Warren had packed food for their trip, and the sheriff surprised Joe again when they entered the livery and he was given Drew's horse to ride. The gelding had recovered from his abusive ride two days ago and his saddle's stirrups had already been adjusted to his height.

What was even a bigger surprise was when he saw the Winchester sticking out of the scabbard. He guessed that it wasn't loaded and figured that two apparently well-armed riders would be less likely to be waylaid by highway bandits.

After getting into the saddles, they walked their horses back to the sheriff's house, so he could say goodbye to his all-female family. Joey tried to look away when the sheriff dismounted and kissed each daughter before embracing his wife and giving her a real kiss, but still glanced back a few times. He'd never seen anything like this before, and even their breakfast had been a revelation to him. Everyone seemed so happy and none of it involved beating or shooting someone.

Finally, around ten o'clock, he and Sheriff Warren, after giving one last wave to his ladies, rode east out of Warwick and picked up the pace to a medium trot.

Once out of town, they continued along the road in silence for the first ten minutes or so before Joey asked, "Sheriff, are there bullets in this Winchester?"

He didn't turn but replied, "Of course, there are bullets in the Winchester, but they're called cartridges, Joe. Saying something like that to the wrong man will mark you as someone who doesn't understand guns. It's always wiser not to say anything unless you're sure of what you're saying."

"What's the difference?"

"A cartridge has the primer, powder, and the lead bullet all together in a brass casing. Guns like the Winchester and that Colt that's in your right saddlebag use .44 caliber cartridges. That popgun Remington that you were given used a .31 caliber ball that had to have the powder dropped into the cylinder before ramming in the lead ball and attaching a percussion cap to the nipple in back for it to fire. They took a long time to reload, but even at that, having a .31 caliber pistol is a lot less dangerous than a .44 or a .45."

"I have a lot to learn, don't I?"

"Yup. I brought the Winchester and Colt along, so you could practice along the way. Okay?"

"I'll get to shoot them?"

"Unless you'd rather not. I'll make you another deal, Joe. If you keep your nose clean in that reformatory and come out of there a good man, then you come back to Warwick and I'll give you that Winchester and the Colt. They belonged to Drew Hogan, so they rightfully should go to you, anyway."

"What about this horse and saddle?"

"By the time you get out, he'll be a bit too old. We get horses fairly often, so if I know you're coming back, I'll save a good one for you. I'll keep the saddle in good shape, too."

Joey asked, "Why are you helping me, Sheriff?"

"I have two reasons. The first is that I don't want to see your life wasted, and the second is that all I have is daughters and I've never been able to spend any time with a boy to show him what he needs to do to grow up right. Now I'm only going to be with you for three days, but I'll tell you as much as I can, so you'll have a better chance in that prison they call a reform school."

Joey nodded and said, "Thank you, Sheriff."

John Warren smiled at him and said, "You're welcome, Mister Armstrong."

Joe smiled at the name and at the thought of getting to fire the Winchester and the Colt.

———

The lessons began when they took their first break three hours later. As the horses drank from a bitter stream and ate some dry grass, Sheriff Warren had him take the Winchester from its scabbard and explained the repeater's operation. He interspersed his technical explanation with the rules of using guns that Joey had never heard before. They all made sense, but he recalled many instances where the Hogan brothers ignored even the basics, like pointing a loaded pistol at someone just for fun or shooting first before they knew what the target was.

The firing itself was another revelation when he found that the sheriff's instructions clarified the whole targeting and shooting sequence. He hadn't understood anything about ballistics or how to control his body, so the sights stabilized.

It was during the target practice that Joey told him about the coyote.

"I felt terrible for shooting him the first time 'cause I thought I'd miss. Then I had to close my eyes when I had to shoot him again."

The sheriff was sliding .44s into the Winchester's loading gate as he replied, "That's because you're a good person inside, Joe. Shooting someone or even a critter should be a hard thing unless it's to put food on the table. I'll bet the Hogans didn't feel bad about shooting folks or animals."

"Have you ever shot anyone?"

"A few outlaws. It's not so hard when they're shooting at you, but once it's over and you have to go and pick up their bodies, it makes you sick."

"Is that why you looked bad after hangin' Drew?"

"Yes, sir. I hate that job, but I know it has to be done. I can't make one of my deputies do it, either. It wouldn't be right."

Joey nodded but didn't believe he really understood.

They mounted their horses again after the extended target practice break and continued toward Lickville.

Joey's other, more important lessons could be conducted on horseback. Almost everything that Sheriff Warren was telling him was either totally unknown to him or completely different from what the Hogans had told him. One of them was that when the Hogans, or any other thief, stole from a bank or a business, he was taking from the community.

He explained how storekeepers and butchers all had to pay for what they had available to sell and that they really didn't make as much money as people thought. Even the bankers were crucial to a town's welfare. If his brothers had gotten away with even that six hundred dollars, the bank might close, and regular people would lose their money.

By the time they stopped to set up camp, Joe's head was reeling with one revelation after another.

They dismounted near a less bitter creek and unsaddled their horses. The sheriff didn't bother making a fire, but he and Joe shared some of the food that Mrs. Warren had sent along.

For the rest of the night they talked, and Joey's world continued to expand.

The next morning, before they set out, Joey was given some target practice using the Colt and had some problems controlling the powerful handgun. His sheriff mentor told him that it wouldn't be a problem when he was bigger.

They were on the road again before nine o'clock and just before noon, Lickville came into sight. Warwick may not have been a metropolis, but it was much larger than Lickville.

"That's what Warwick looked like when I arrived there in '66," Sheriff Warren said loudly.

Joey nodded, wondering if his mother had ever taken him into town.

They entered the town, and as there were only fourteen buildings, were able to find the county offices quickly, dismounted, and tied off their horses. It may not have been much of a town, but it was the only one in the entire county.

They entered the clapboard building that was in dire need of a good whitewash and soon found the records office.

The clerk stood from his desk when they entered and asked, "Can I help you?"

"This is Joe Armstrong, and I need to get a copy of his birth certificate if you have one."

He looked at Joe and asked, "Agnes Armstrong's boy?"

Joe replied, "Yes, sir. I just found out two days ago who I was."

"Well, son, I'm going to disappoint you. They didn't make any birth certificates back then because of the war, but I can tell you some things about your parents if that'll help."

Joey nodded and said, "It'll help."

"Well, your father and mother owned a farm about four miles east of town, just south of the road. It's still there, but I don't know what condition it's in. Nobody lives there, of course. Your father and your uncle went off to war, so her sister moved in with her. Both of their husbands died. Your father's name was Zeke. Your mother's name was Agnes and her sister's name was Lydia White. They were both very pretty ladies and had to run the farm after the men left. It was hard on them and we didn't even know they were gone until their taxes weren't paid."

He looked at John and asked, "Can I guess that you're the sheriff that sent the telegram asking about them?"

"I am. Do you know Joe's birthdate?"

"Not exactly. But I know he was born in late spring of '61 because Zeke came in bragging about having a boy. I had to remember that after the marshal stopped in."

Joe looked at the sheriff, wondering if would make any difference.

Sheriff Warren then asked the clerk, "Could you do me a favor and make up a birth certificate for Joe? I'm taking him to reform school because those same bastards that took his mother and her sister from the farm robbed a bank and used him as a pawn. If we can even get him out of there a few months early, I'd appreciate it."

The clerk glanced at Joe then nodded and said, "Give me a minute."

He pulled out a form and picked up a pen, dipped it into a bottle of ink, and began to write.

He asked Joey, "What do you want for a middle name?"

"Do I need one?"

"Not really, so I'll just make you Joe Armstrong with a birthdate of March 11, 1861. Is that okay, Sheriff?"

"That's fine."

After filling in the rest of the form, he left it on the counter and asked, "Could you tell me what happened?"

"Sure. But we've got to get moving."

Sheriff Warren told the story as quickly as he could, then he pocketed the new birth certificate and thanked the clerk before he and Joe left the office.

John treated for lunch at a small café that only had three tables. The food wasn't bad, but it wasn't great, either.

Just an hour and ten minutes after entering the town, they mounted their horses and headed east out of Lickville.

As they left the small town behind, Joe asked, "That birth certificate means I'll be getting out in March instead of September, doesn't it?"

"Yes, sir. That's why I asked for it."

"Can we stop at the farm on the way?"

"I thought you might ask, so keep your eyes peeled to the right. I don't recall seeing anything on the way in."

"I didn't either."

Thirty minutes later, John spotted something that might be remnants of a building, pointed, and said loudly, "I think that might be it."

Joe had been expecting a standing building but when his eyes followed the sheriff's finger, he could see what appeared to be a cleared area with some debris scattered about. They turned off the road and headed for the remains and as they drew closer, it was apparent that it probably was the farm where he'd been born. It was a lot smaller than he'd expected, too.

They walked their horses close to the scattered boards and other debris and then the sheriff pulled his gelding to a stop and dismounted. Joey soon followed.

After letting their reins drop, the man and boy stepped among what was left of the farmhouse.

"What happened to it?" Joey asked as he surveyed the ruins.

"I don't know. It could have been a tornado or just scavengers looking for lumber. The barn was over there, and there's even less wood on the ground."

Joey began kicking the weathered boards as he scuffled through the mess. He'd hoped to find something that belonged to his mother, not even thinking about his father. It had been his mother who had suffered after he'd gone.

John just walked slowly behind Joey and after he'd kicked one board and moved past, something flashed in the Texas sun from where he'd overturned the piece of old lumber. He leaned down and picked a hair comb out of the dirt and brushed it off as Joey continued to walk away. Two of the tines were broken, but the whalebone comb wasn't in bad condition.

"Joe, you might want to look at this," he said, holding up the comb.

Joey turned around and began walking back as he asked, "What is it?"

"It's a hair comb. It's what women use to keep their hair up. It might have belonged to your mother."

Joey took the comb from the sheriff and turned it in his hand as he examined it.

"How do I know if it's hers?"

"I don't think you ever will, but remember the clerk said that this was your parents' farm and your mother's sister only moved here to help work the land. So, I think the odds are that it belonged to her."

Joey nodded but didn't reply as he studied the broken decorative hair accessory.

After almost a minute, he looked up at the sheriff and said, "I can't take this with me to the reformatory. Can you keep it for me until I get out?"

"I'd be happy to do that for you, Joe."

Joe handed the comb to the sheriff, who slipped it into his vest pocket and they both turned and headed back to their horses, mounted, and headed back to the roadway and continued eastward toward Henrietta.

As they rode and talked, the sheriff continued his lessons, and they passed within eight miles of the McPherson farm which still housed the remaining Hogan brothers.

Just before sunset, the sheriff found a rudimentary campsite and they pulled off the narrow road and dismounted.

Ten minutes later, the horses were unsaddled, and even though they ate a cold supper, there was a small campfire burning. It was surprisingly chilly, or at least it felt that way.

“When will we get to Henrietta?” Joey asked.

“Tomorrow afternoon, I think.”

“Then how long before we get to the reformatory?”

“The train will take three hours, and we’ll probably leave on Wednesday morning, so it’ll be that afternoon.”

Joey stared at the small flames and said, “I’m kinda scared.”

“You’d be stupid not to be scared, Joe. It’s all unknown to you, and I’d be afraid myself.”

“What will I have to do in there?”

“I don’t know, to be honest. You’ll have to go to classes and probably do chores because I do know that the reformatory is supposed to be close to being able to run on its own. You know, grow its own food and such. It probably doesn’t come close to doing that, but it sounds good to the voters.

“What you need to do, Joe, is to keep quiet and learn the ropes of the place. Try and find a friend or two that’s like you, a boy who is trying to put things right.”

Joey nodded and asked, “Did you have any brothers?”

The sheriff snickered and replied, “No, sir. I’m doomed to forever live in the company of females. I had five sisters growing up, then I thought at least I’d have a few sons after I got married, and we only had girls. I blame my wife, of course, but she points to my five sisters and wins the argument."

Joey then looked at the sheriff and asked, "What's wrong with the pig-tailed girl? The one with the freckles. Is she crazy or somethin'?"

"What makes you ask that?"

"Things she told me. She kinda scares me, too."

John laughed and said, "Cassie can scare anyone, but to answer your question, no, she's not crazy. In fact, she's probably the most level-headed person I know."

"Then why does she say those crazy things?"

"Cassie is easily the smartest person I've ever met, and probably the most frustrated because of it. She was reading before she was five and by the time she started school, she probably could have been placed with the fifth or sixth years. But Miss Timmons, the teacher, wouldn't let her advance faster than a grade a year.

"I asked her about it and she said that it didn't matter with girls because they were all just going to get married and have children. I was going to argue with her, but as much as I hated to admit it, she was right. When I explained it to Cassie, she understood, of course, but it was still immensely frustrating to her. She's incredibly bored at school, but at least she was allowed to read the textbooks of the upper classes, but she finished with those and there's no library in Warwick, so she's stuck again."

Joey didn't want to bring up the subject but wanted to know, so he asked, "Why would she tell me that I was gonna come back and be her boyfriend? I can't even read or write."

The sheriff turned to look at Joey with raised eyebrows as he asked, “She told you that?”

“Yes, sir. And that’s why I thought she was crazy.”

“I wish I could tell you why she’d say that, but I can’t. I could ask her when I get back, but I think it’ll come out anyway. She talks to me more than she talks to her mother, anyway.”

“Why? Is she a tomboy, too?”

“No, she’s far from that. She’s very much a ten-year-old girl except for her mind and her manner. She talks to me because she believes I understand her better. Her mother is already setting up Mary, our oldest, with her hope chest for when she gets married and will soon begin to do the same for Bessie. Cassie doesn’t want to do that. She wants something different but doesn’t know what yet.”

“She said I had to write letters to her when I could read and write, but I told her I wouldn’t.”

“You may as well because she’ll probably start writing letters to you anyway.”

“Can’t you tell her to leave me alone?”

“Nope. That’s the last thing I’d do. She’d see it as a challenge, and she loves challenges.”

Joey sighed and then changed the topic to the Hogan brothers.

“Where do you think my bro…I mean, the Hogans are now?”

"Either they're still in the Nations, or they're back in Texas looking for someplace to hide out until things cool off."

"So, they could be just a couple of miles away?"

"I suppose so, but I wouldn't want to run into them right now. Would you?"

Joey exhaled loudly and replied, "No. I suppose not."

"You've got to know when to fight and when to walk away, Joe. Never give the other guy an advantage if you don't have to. Let them call you names and even laugh at you. That doesn't matter because what they think isn't important. When you have to fight, do it on your terms, not theirs."

"How did you get so smart about things?"

"The same way you will, Joe. You learn when you lose and make mistakes. You've already started out with a lot of bad information from the Hogans, but now you've also learned what not to do. You've been learning a lot without knowing it. Think about how we ran them down and even now, they're on the run because they don't know if some other sheriff or marshal knows about them. They didn't learn from their mistakes, but you can."

Joey nodded and said, "Okay."

John Warren looked at the boy and hoped he really did understand because he'd need every bit of savvy to get through the next four and a half years in the reformatory.

———

Over the miles and hours of their long ride to Henrietta, Joey continued to ask questions and receive the best answers that Sheriff Warren could give him to prepare him not only for the reformatory but for his life beyond.

The sheriff had spent quite a bit of time in between their conversations to try and understand why Cassie had said she'd want to make a boyfriend out of Joe. She surely didn't know him very well and, despite her intelligence, she was still only ten and made ten-year-old mistakes.

Then there was Joe himself. He obviously had no intention of even giving Cassie the opportunity after he finished his time at the reform school. Besides, just as Joey himself had determined, no one could predict the future, although, with Cassie, he wasn't so sure.

———

They reached Henrietta just after two o'clock in the afternoon and stopped at a nice café for a late lunch before checking the train schedule and finding that the eastbound train departed at 7:10 in the morning.

They dropped their horses at the closest livery to the train station and walked to the Stern House to get a room. Joey commented on the name as they entered the establishment.

After dropping their saddlebags in their room, they returned to the boardwalk and just took a seat on one of the three benches in front of the hotel where they could watch any trains that might roll past. There weren't many as Henrietta was near the end of the line.

"Do they give us prison clothes?" Joey asked.

"No, I don't think so. From what I hear, they have a big storeroom of clothes that are outgrown by their original owners. As the boys grow, they exchange their things for the next size up. So, when you get there, they should give you another pair of britches and a shirt or two."

"I have to tell 'em that I can't read or write, don't I?"

"Yup. Don't be embarrassed, though. When I was in the army, I'll bet that not even half of those boys could read or write."

"Really?"

"Did the Hogans read or write?"

"I think so, but they didn't have any books around. How long will it take to learn?"

"It depends on how hard you try, Joe. You're a smart kid. If you put your mind to it, I'll bet you'll be reading in no time."

Joey glanced over at the sheriff and asked, "Why do you think I'm smart? I ain't acted very smart."

"You've asked a lot of very good questions since I first met you, Joe. You acted out of ignorance, not stupidity. Even if Cassie doesn't get her way, I'd be happy to have you come back and stay with me."

Joe flushed and said, "Thank you, Sheriff. You know, Bessie is pretty."

John smiled and replied, "Yes, she is. She's just as pretty as her older sister Mary, but I'll bet that Cassie is going to be the prettiest of them all."

Joe's eyes widened as he exclaimed, "*Her? Pretty?*"

The sheriff kept watching the station across the street as he said, "You never looked past her freckles or pigtails, Joe.

Learn to get past the first impression. I watched her sisters grow past their freckles and I'm convinced that Cassie will turn out to be a very impressive young lady."

Joe tried to picture Cassie without the freckles or pigtails and couldn't, so he just said, "I guess."

A westbound train appeared on the eastern horizon and the sheriff said, "There's our train, Joe."

"But it's only Tuesday afternoon."

"It's got to be turned around and serviced when it gets to the end of the line at Fort Belknap. The crew needs to get some sleep, too."

Joey nodded and kept watching the train. He'd never even seen one before and was fascinated with the speed of the thing as it neared Henrietta. When he had first seen it, it seemed to be moving slowly, but the closer it got, the faster it appeared to be moving.

About half a mile from the station, the train began slowing and as the big locomotive passed, the wheels began to turn backward screeching against the steel rails as sparks and steam flew everywhere as Joey sat transfixed at the sight.

He continued to watch in silence as the passengers disembarked and the train took on water, but no coal. There weren't any passengers going to Fort Belknap, so just fifteen minutes after stopping, the engine began yanking the trailing cars out of the station.

Joey couldn't wait to have his first train ride, even if it was taking him to the reformatory.

———

After a hurried breakfast the next morning, Joey and Sheriff Warren boarded their train. The sheriff just showed his badge and filled out a form rather than buying tickets.

Once on board, John let Joey have the window seat, so he could watch the landscape pass. He'd made the trip to Gainesville six times before when he was transporting prisoners to the Texas State Prison which was just four miles down the road from the reformatory.

The train ride was uneventful and after the first few minutes, Joey lost his enthusiasm, so they continued talking about how he should handle himself at the reformatory. The topic was becoming more important with each rotation of the steel wheels that were carrying him to Gainesville.

Surprisingly, it was Sheriff John Warren who was growing sadder as the train neared their destination. He knew that he wouldn't be able to visit Joe because of the distance unless he had to deliver another prisoner to the state prison. In just the few days he'd known the boy, he'd begun to see him as his missing son.

"Maybe I'll be bringing a prisoner to the state prison and stop by sometime, Joe."

"I'd like that, Sheriff."

"When you get out, Joe, you're going to be an adult, so when you come to Warwick, call me John."

Joe grinned as he nodded, not knowing how to address him now.

———

Forty-five minutes later, they stepped onto the Gainesville platform and walked across the street to a livery where John rented two horses. He had a small notebook he kept in his pocket for expenses for reimbursement by the county, so he pulled it out and wrote down the cost for the rental and they rode to a restaurant and stepped down.

After they'd taken their seat and placed their order, Joey said, "I guess this will be the last good food I get for a while."

"You never know. They might serve steak every day in the reformatory."

Joey laughed, and so did the sheriff as they sipped their coffee.

After they finished their lunch and John entered the cost in his notebook, they exited the restaurant, mounted, and rode out of Gainesville.

"I've never been to the reformatory before, but I've seen it on the way to the prison. It's as scary looking as the prison is, though."

Joey just nodded as he was focused ahead trying to get a glimpse of his new home for the next four and a half years.

Four and a half years sounded like forever to Joey as their horses plodded along. He didn't even shave yet and wondered how that worked. *Did they give them razors or let their beards grow? Would they trust them with sharp weapons like razors?* The questions he'd never asked began boiling into his mind, but before he could ask any of them, the reformatory popped up on the horizon.

"Is that it?" Joey asked.

"That's it. It looks different from the last time I saw it, too. The fences aren't there anymore."

Joey's heart began to pick up its pace as the reformatory began to grow before his eyes.

As he remained staring at the looming edifice, he asked, "Will you write me letters too, Sheriff?"

"You bet. I'll let you know what the Hogans are doing, so you can keep track."

"I guess that I'd better learn to read fast."

Sheriff Warren didn't reply as they approached the long access road to the reformatory, and he could already see boys of all sizes working in one of the fields.

"Do I have to do that?" Joey asked.

"I don't know, Joe. I'm sure they'll let you know what your chores will be."

Joey nodded as they continued west down the long drive.

They arrived at the gates and Joey was surprised that they weren't even closed as they rode through and soon reached a large building that had TEXAS REFORMATORY SCHOOL painted in fading letters above its only entrance and dismounted.

After tying off their reins, the sheriff and his prisoner entered the doors and approached a uniformed guard at a small, ugly desk.

"Bringing in a new kid, Sheriff?" he asked as he looked at them.

“Yup. This is Joe Armstrong. Here’s the court order and his birth certificate,” the sheriff said as he set the documents on the desk.

The guard pulled out a green ledger, opened it and took out his pen, dipped it in the bottle of ink on his desk, and began to make entries in the ledger.

“Okay, kid, you’re all registered. Just go through that door on the left. Tell the guard you’re eleven-fourteen.”

Joey looked at the sheriff, tried to force a smile, and began to leave when John grabbed him by the shoulder and turned him around.

He then shook Joey’s hand and said, “Good luck, Joe. You’re going to be a good man.”

Joey thought he’d cry, so he just nodded and turned and walked across the room, opened the door, and passed into his new life.

After he closed the door, John turned to the guard and said, “That kid has had a hard time of it. He and his mother were kidnapped when he was two by a family of seven thugs. They abused her until she finally died giving birth to one of their spawn. He was only four then, and they raised him as if he was a brother.

“He believed them until they tried to rob our bank and they left him to serve as their rear guard. It was only because we caught one of them that he learned the truth about his true family, and he realized what they were. He’s a good kid and he’ll be returning to my town when he’s done. I’d appreciate it if he was looked out for at least for the first month or so.”

The guard nodded and said, “It’s really not as bad around here as most folks think. We got a new warden two years ago and he’s made a lot of changes.”

“That’s good. Well, I’ve got to get back to my town before my deputies let it go to hell.”

The guard laughed as Sheriff Warren turned around and left the office.

After mounting his rented horse, he took the other horse’s reins and left the reformatory at a trot, hoping that the guard had been telling him the truth about the new warden.

Inside, Joey walked into a room where another guard was sitting behind a slightly better desk reading a dime novel.

He looked up and said, “Who are you?”

“Joe Armstrong. The other guard said to tell you I was eleven-fourteen.”

The guard set his thin booklet down and turned and walked to a large closet, opened the door and pulled out some clothes, and set them on his desk near his novel.

He then closed the door to the closet, picked up the clothes, and said, “Okay, come with me.”

Joey followed the guard out a different door and was led into a large office occupied by a balding man with a huge beard wearing a dark wool suit.

“Warden Smith, this is Joe Armstrong, number eleven-fourteen.”

“Thank you, Mister Farnsworth.”

The guard set the clothes on the warden’s desk and left the room.

“Have a seat, Joe,” the warden said.

Joey was surprised at his affable manner but sat down.

“First, if you don’t mind, I’d like to know why you’re here.”

“Well, sir, you see, I was raised by a bunch of men I thought were my brothers…”

The warden leaned back in his chair and folded his fingers as Joey told the story. The warden had heard a lot of disparate tales of broken homes and abandoned, wayward youths since he’d been appointed to the position after the last warden had been found to be privately hiring the boys out to whoever had the funds. It had been quite the scandal and the governor had appointed Aaron Smith to clean up the reformatory’s reputation before the Texas Women’s League tore the place down.

But Joey’s tale was remarkable for several reasons, and one of them begged a question.

So, when Joey finished, Warden Smith asked, “Do you know why they allowed a four-year-old boy to stay with them?”

“No, sir. But I know that only the oldest brother, Buck, really wanted me there. At least that’s what Drew told me in jail.”

The warden shook his head and said, “Well, you’re here now. You may have noticed the absence of walls or fences. I took down the fences when I took over two years ago. That’s because the nearest town is four miles away and if any of the boys want to run away, they'll be caught soon enough. But the other reason is that I wanted this to be a place where the boys could become good men. Now there are still quite a few bullies about, so don't think this place is like a normal school. We can't watch them all the time, but if you have a problem, tell a guard.

"If you wish to attend classes, like a normal school, they're held each morning between eight o'clock and noon. After lunch, you will be either doing chores or learning a trade. We try to be as self-sufficient as possible to reduce the burden on the taxpayer, so we do have many different choices. Do you know what you'd like to do?"

"What can I do here?"

"Well, you can work out on our fields, cook, bake, butcher, or work in the livery with our horses. You can learn to work iron in our smithy or masonry and carpentry."

Joey thought about the different jobs and said, "Could I work as a blacksmith?"

"That's a very good choice, especially as our smith is down to a single apprentice right now. Do you have any questions?"

He had hundreds of questions but replied, "No, sir."

"Very good. Just go back and see Mister Farnsworth again and he'll assign you to a bed and a box. Then he'll set up your schedule."

Joey nodded and then stood and said, "Thank you, sir," before picking up his clothes and leaving the warden's office to find Mister Farnsworth with his fears greatly diminished.

———

Sheriff Warren returned to Gainesville, dropped off the two horses, and barely had time to catch the westbound train to Henrietta.

As the last of the town passed by the window, he looked out to the south and tried to catch a glimpse of the reformatory, hoping that Joe would be okay. He pulled the woman's hair comb out of his pocket and examined it closely. It was just an inexpensive accessory to keep a woman's hair where she wanted, but he knew it meant much more to Joe. It was all he'd ever have from his mother and wondered if he could find out more about his parents after he returned. Maybe he had more family who could tell him more. He realized that he didn't even know Joe's mother's maiden name, but when he had a chance, he'd take another ride to Lickville.

At the McPherson farm, Earl and Fred had been given the task of burying Mrs. McPherson near her husband and children because Glen and Hank had dug the first, much bigger hole.

They might not be able to enjoy her anymore, but at least the place was quiet.

When Sheriff Warren stepped out onto the platform at Henrietta, before he went to get the horses, he stopped over at the Western Union office to check on any messages from his deputies.

There weren't any, so he relaxed and checked into the hotel rather than get his horses. He'd start out fresh in the morning.

Joey had his schedule in his hand as he sat on his bunk, for all the good it did him. Mister Farnsworth had read it to him and shown him where he had to go in the morning and then gave him a tour of the expansive reformatory. There were two floors in the large dormitory, and either by design or by odd coincidence, most of the hardened, unteachable boys were on the upper floor. Joe guessed it was to make it harder for them to escape.

He'd seen a lot of the other boys going about their chores, and most didn't even act as if they'd seen him, but two of the boys who needed to shave, gave him threatening glances as they passed. Joey hoped they weren't going to occupy a bed close to his.

But as the other boys returned from their chores or apprenticeships, he was relieved to find that his new neighbors were both about his age and seemed reasonably friendly.

Soon, Lippy O'Reilly and Pete Spencer were filling his ears with the information he'd need to make his next four and a half years at the reformatory better.

When Joey finally went to sleep that night, he was determined that he'd be ready to do what he needed to do when he left in fifty-four months, which sounded a lot better than four and a half years.

CHAPTER 3

December 11, 1874

Joe was stacking the clean plates on the shelf behind the food line when Pete Spencer entered the kitchen and caught his eye.

"What's up, Pete?" he asked as he put another plate on top.

"You got a box over in the post office."

"I got a box? Really?"

"Yup. We were kinda surprised, so we're all waitin' to see if it's somethin' good, too."

Joe laughed and said, "If it is, I'd be surprised."

He set the last of the clean plates on the tall stack and followed Pete out of the kitchen. Today was a chore day and he was assigned to kitchen duties, which weren't bad. Latrine duties were the worst.

"Did you see who sent it?" Joe asked as they exited the kitchen and turned right down the wide hallway.

"Nope. I was just told you got somethin' and to let you know."

"The only one who would send me anything is Sheriff Warren."

"Maybe one of his girls sent you somethin' that smells like roses," Pete said with a snicker.

Joe didn't reply because he was a bit curious if Cassie had followed through with her threat, or promise, depending on who was listening, and sent him a letter. He couldn't write very well, but his reading was okay for someone who'd only been learning for a few months. Mister Fletcher, their teacher, had told him he was doing really well and should be at the third-year level by March.

He was also determined to learn to speak properly. Sheriff Warren had explained to him that when we spoke, those who listened categorized us automatically and it was better if they didn't think they could fool us.

He and Pete turned into the small office and Joe approached the desk. It wasn't really a post office, because so few boys sent or received mail. It was just an empty storage closet that served that purpose along with administrative notes.

"Do you have a box for me, Al?"

Al Hill was already pulling down the box when Joe asked and slid it across the tiny desk.

Joe picked it up, looked at the writing, and saw that it had come from Warwick, which was just about the only place where it could have originated.

"Thanks, Al," Joe said before he and Pete left the office and headed for their dormitory.

"It smells good," Pete said as he sniffed the outside of the box.

Joe had already made that astute observation when he'd picked it up and was surprised that no one had opened it 'accidentally' before he'd claimed it. With the miniscule amount of mail that passed in or out of the reformatory, when a rare package showed up, it attracted a lot of interest.

They made it to their bunks, and Joe sat down as Pete sat on his bed two feet away eagerly awaiting the opening.

He had to untie the strings binding the outside of the box before he finally pulled open the flaps and found a tin, which was the source of the delicious aroma that portended an equally delicious treasure inside.

Wanting some measure of privacy for the rest of the box's contents, Joe opened the tin, took out two of the molasses cookies, and handed them to Pete.

"Thanks, Joe," Pete said as he snatched the treats and immediately bit into one.

Joe closed the tin without taking one himself as the other contents of the box intrigued him more. He hadn't heard from anyone since he'd been dropped off and hoped that there might be some news.

Under the tin, he found two envelopes and a small wrapped gift. He took the two envelopes and looked at the handwriting. Both were printed rather than script, which he appreciated. He still had a hard time reading the flowing letters.

One was from the sheriff, and he guessed that the second one was from Cassie.

He opened the sheriff's first and had to read it slowly, mouthing each syllable by syllable to make sure he got the word right. It took him a while to understand most of the words.

Dear Joe,

We're sending this early to be sure it gets there before Christmas.

I heard that the Hogans took over a ranch and murdered an entire family about 25 miles east of here. They sent a dozen Rangers to hunt them down, but they scattered, and the Rangers didn't get any of them.

I went to Lickville and found out more about your mother. Her maiden name was Elliott and she used to live near Buffalo Creek. I haven't found any relatives yet.

I asked Cassie about what she told you and she didn't explain much. I wasn't surprised.

How is it going? We think about you often and hope you are doing well.

Write when you can.

John

After reading it once more by words and sentences, Joe folded the short letter and slid it back into its envelope. He noticed that the sheriff had signed it with just his Christian name. He was disturbed to read that the Hogans had murdered an entire family, knowing he had once regarded them as heroes and men to be admired. They were nothing but thieves and murderers.

He then opened the second letter and wasn't surprised when he noted the author's name on the bottom.

Dear Joe,

I know that you can read this now. You are a lot smarter than you think you are, or I wouldn't want you for a boyfriend.

I still have my pigtails and freckles, but it's only been a few months since you saw me last. I had my eleventh birthday on November 7th. I wish I could have sent you some of my mother's pie that she baked for me, but the best I could do was to send you these cookies that I baked myself. I'll bet you are surprised that I can bake cookies.

My father told me that you thought I was crazy. I can understand that. Sometimes I wonder myself. One of these times, I'll explain why I told you what I did.

Have a good Christmas and write me a letter when you can.

Cassie

Joe had to read the letter three times to get a better idea of what she was writing. Some of the words were too big, and he had to work them out. He didn't want anyone else reading the letter. Even though she wrote that she still wanted him as a boyfriend, somehow, it didn't sound as crazy in a letter as it did when she had just said it while he was behind bars.

Pete had already finished both of his cookies and was hoping for more when Joe took out the wrapped box. He debated about not opening it until Christmas but was worried that leaving it that way would only encourage one of the malcontents to steal it when he wasn't looking. As it was, he'd have to empty the tin of cookies today to keep them away.

Joe set aside the letters and the rest of the box and took the small, wrapped gift and pulled the ribbon from the outside, and ripped the paper.

He opened the box and found a silver pocket watch inside resting on a red cloth. He slid the watch out of its box and popped the cover open. It wasn't running, so he'd need to match it to the only clock in the reformatory, the big clock in the dining hall.

On the inside of the cover was an inscription, but it was in script, so he had to take each word apart letter by letter before he was able to understand it.

To Our Joe
Merry Christmas
From the Warren Family

Joe closed the watch and slid it into his pocket. It was even more precious to him than his mother's comb.

Just a few minutes later, the other boys all began to return to the dormitory before returning to the dining hall for supper. Lippy saw the tin and it wasn't long before Joe handed out most of the cookies to greedy hands but saved two for himself.

He bit one and was impressed with Cassie's baking skills. There were enough crumbs and broken cookie pieces on the bottom of the tin for later, too.

———

That night, when the boys were allowed free time, Joe went to the reformatory library to write his reply to the sheriff.

As he took his pencil in hand, he paused as he wondered how he should address it.

Finally, he decided to be himself and carefully began to write in block letters.

DEAR SHERIFF

I GOT YOUR LETTER. THANK ALL FOR THE WATCH. I LIKE IT A LOT.

I AM LEARNING TO READ AND WRITE AND TO BE A BLACKSMITH. I HAVE TWO FRIENDS. I HAVE NOT HAD ANY FIGHTS.

I WILL WRITE BETTER NEXT TIME.

JOE

It took him almost ten minutes to write the short letter, and even that was frustrating. He then addressed an envelope and slid the letter inside.

He was going to seal it but then sighed, took out another sheet, and began to write again. He used Cassie's letter for some of the spelling.

DEAR CASSIE,

THANK YOU FOR THE COOKIES. I ONLY ATE TWO. OTHER BOYS ATE THE REST.

I AM SORRY THIS IS SHORT. I WILL WRITE BETTER NEXT TIME.

HAPPY BIRTHDAY. I DON'T THINK YOU ARE CRAZY.

JOE

He was going to just put the second letter into the same envelope, but decided it should be separate and wrote a second envelope and slid the one-page letter that was really just a second note into the second.

As he sealed both envelopes, he was surprised to find he was more embarrassed about Cassie receiving his childish letter than the one he'd sent her father. Maybe it was just because she was more than two years younger than he was and could write much better. He then reread her letter and wondered if she was using smaller words knowing he would have a hard time reading big words.

Joe walked to the post office, dropped both letters into the box and went to the dining hall, and set his new watch. Once it was ticking, he closed the cover and headed back to his bunk, determined to learn even faster.

As he lay on his bunk examining the watch, Joe reread the script. He'd just been in Warwick for a few days and had only been to the Warren home once, yet he regarded them as his real family already. Maybe it was the letters that made him feel that way.

Since he'd been in the reformatory, he had noticed that the boys were comprised of three types. About a quarter of them really should have been in prison rather than the reformatory, half of them should be here, and the last quarter should never have been sent to this place. He wasn't sure which of the three was his.

The other startling observation he'd made was that the majority had no families at all, and most of the others had families that didn't want them back. There were a lot of bitter boys in the Texas State Reformatory, but he was determined never to be one of them.

He had a watch and a family that wanted him to return.

March 17, 1875

Joe left the furnaces of the smithy and stepped out into the cold air, the chill smacking his sweaty forehead and arms. He had grown accustomed to the sudden temperature change whenever he left his job at the smithy and enjoyed the sensation.

He'd been dangerously awkward when he'd first begun his apprenticeship at the blacksmith shop and had almost cut off one of his fingers when Mister Vinton caught his hand before he swung the mallet. But just like his time in the classroom, he'd learned quickly, and the blacksmith already regarded Joe as his best apprentice of the five he had working with him. The blacksmith shop sounded appealing to many of the boys, but after just a few days, they would invariably switch to less-demanding skills.

Joe enjoyed the work and the skills he was learning and didn't mind the muscle he was adding, even at his young age. The next youngest apprentice was already fifteen.

After returning to the main building, he swung by the post office as he had every day now. He'd received and sent two letters to Cassie, who served as the Warren family correspondent. In each of her last two letters, she'd reported no earth-shattering news. The Hogan brothers seemed to have split up into different groups, making it more difficult to track them all, but none had returned to Warwick. Nor had her father found any of his Elliott relatives.

In each of her letters, she'd expanded her vocabulary, amazingly mimicking his own rapid improvement in his own use of the language. It was as if she was watching him learn over his shoulder. She might not be crazy, but she certainly was spooky.

Al Hill saw him enter and said, "I've got a letter for you, Joe."

Joe was grinning as he accepted the envelope and quickly examined the address. It was from Cassie.

"Thanks, Al," Joe said as he turned and quickly left the post office and headed back to the dormitory.

He reached his bunk, sat down, and anxiously opened the envelope. For the first time, it was written in script, so obviously Cassie thought he was ready for the change and, of course, she was right again.

He was smiling as he began reading.

Dear Joe,

Happy birthday to the only person I know who has three different birthdays and doesn't know if any of them are right.

The big news is that the two of the Hogans showed up in Horace with two other men to rob the bank. There was a gunfight and the marshal was killed. They shot and caught one of them, but not a Hogan. He said that there were three gangs that had Hogan brothers now and offered to tell them where one of them was, but they hanged him instead.

I asked my father if he would show me how to shoot a gun and he said not until I was at least thirteen. I think I'll keep asking until he gives in. It's my way.

Bessie asked if it was okay if she wrote to you, too. I told her it was a free country, so I won't even mind if you write back to her. It's not like you agreed to be my boyfriend anyway. Bessie is nice.

How is it in reform school? Sometimes, I think I go to reform school here. The only thing that's different is Miss Timmons doesn't wear a guard's uniform. That's because it wouldn't look right with the pointy hat she wears at night when she rides her broom.

I still have my freckles, but I've started wearing my hair in a ponytail to try and look older. I'll admit it doesn't work, though. I'm beginning to believe that I'll have my freckles when I'm sixty.

My father gave me your mother's hair comb to keep safe. I cleaned it as best I could.

You only have forty-eight months left, so stay safe.

Cassie

Joe reread the letter three more times, as he usually did. It was getting harder already to picture Cassie. He'd only seen her for a couple of hours. What was odd was that he could recall Bessie better. Maybe because he'd found himself staring at her a few times.

He returned the letter to its envelope and walked to the library to write his reply. He didn't really write it in cursive yet, but sort of a bastardized printed script that was probably more difficult to read than either.

Once there, he took out her letter and spread it out, to make sure he didn't misspell any of the words she had used. He had the giant dictionary nearby, too.

Dear Cassie,

I just got your letter about the Hogan gangs. Part of me wants to be out there trying to help stop them and part of me hopes they're all caught before I get out.

When I first learned about what they did to my mother, I was so mad that I wanted to chase after them right away, but now, I think it would be better if they were caught. It's not like I'm afraid of them, at least not a lot. I want to do things now. I'm learning how to be a blacksmith, and I'm good at it. I don't want to be one when I get out, but it showed me that I can be what I want to be.

When your father was taking me here, he told me that you didn't like that you couldn't do what you want because you're a girl. I think that's stupid.

Joe sat back and looked at the last line of the letter and thought it didn't sound right, so he crossed it out and continued.

~~I think that's stupid.~~ I meant that they should let you do what you want, too. I know your father thinks you should. He said you were the smartest person he ever met. I think so, too. Of course, most of the boys in here are pretty stupid or they wouldn't be here. Me included.

Your teacher may be a witch, but I think we are going to have changes here soon. Some of the boys heard that they are sending a new warden and replacing some of the guards because people aren't happy that we are being treated nice.

I don't think your freckles will stay on much longer. Your father said you will be really pretty.

I have to go now. Forty-eight months doesn't seem too long.

Thank you for remembering the first of my birthdays and taking care of my mother's hair comb.

Joe

Joe reread his letter and hoped he hadn't sounded too much like a boyfriend. He folded the sheet, slid it into its envelope, wrote the address, and then dropped it into the box.

———

Four days later, he received a letter from Bessie and took it to his bunk, not knowing what to expect. He noticed that the letter had a hint of lilac scent, which wasn't a good idea in the reformatory. He'd avoided the older toughs that were all on the second floor, but that didn't mean that he was immune. Those rumors about the coming change were becoming more detailed and none were good.

He opened Bessie's letter and he immediately noticed that her delicate, precise script was different from Cassie's less feminine hand.

Dear Joe,

I hope you are doing well. Cassie let us read your letters and I'm proud of how you're learning so quickly.

I wish I could have spent more time talking to you while you were here. I wish that the judge didn't send you to that reform school. You could have just stayed in Warwick and gone to school here. We would be in the same year, too. That would be really nice.

This summer, I'll be going to my first social, and I wish you could take me rather than having to go with Mary. Cassie is too young, of course. She won't be able to go for another two years.

Cassie told you about the Hogans and I think that they're horrible men. They seem to think all of west Texas belongs to them. There just aren't enough lawmen. Even the Rangers seem to have trouble finding them. Cassie thinks it's because they run into the Indian Nations after they do something bad.

Write to me when you can. I won't let Cassie read it, so you can write whatever you want.

With Affection,

Bessie

Joe didn't know what to make of Bessie's letter. He was partly thrilled that the pretty Bessie had wanted him to take her to the social, but at the same time wondered why Bessie would keep Cassie from reading his reply. He also noticed that Bessie seemed to make a point out of Cassie being too young to go to the social.

He decided he'd write his reply tomorrow night after thinking about what to say in the letter.

The upcoming changes were officially announced the next morning when Warden Smith called all two hundred and sixty-four boys into the dining hall. There weren't enough chairs for them all at the same time, so the older boys were standing, ringing the room. There were no guards.

The suddenly tired-looking warden looked out at his charges and said, “Boys, I’m sure many of you have heard that you will be getting a new warden soon. That rumor is true and on the first of April, Mister Phelps will be taking over the operation of the school. It seems that there was some dissatisfaction among the voters that you weren’t being punished enough. From my understanding, there will be many changes in the way that the school will be run.

“All I ask of you is to keep a steady head on your shoulders and wait for the day when you walk out those gates as a man. The youngest of you, Billy Higgins, has seven years and two months to go, but the time will pass, gentlemen.

“Most of the guards will be reassigned over the next two months as well. Despite the many changes that you will see, I have been assured that the morning classes will continue, and Mister Fletcher will remain as your teacher. There is one other thing I can assure you, and that is that each of you will remain fondly in my memory.”

He then gave a short wave, and then some of the boys began to clap for Warden Smith, and soon most of them were standing and applauding for an obviously affected warden as he smiled and left the room.

Joe noticed that the tough boys ringing the room weren’t clapping, but they were smiling, and he recognized the first change before the old warden even left the room. The bullies would have their way, or at least they believed they would.

During their morning classes, Joe used the time to write what he expected might be the last letters he would be able to send. One of the rumors was that mail would be stopped. He didn’t know if that was possible or even legal, but he didn’t want to take the chance.

Joe wondered just how bad it was going to be as he wrote his first letter. He decided to write a reply to Bessie first because he'd already composed it in his head last night.

Dear Bessie,

I was happy to receive your letter, and I hope you enjoy the social. I can't dance any better than I write anyway, so it is better that I'm not there.

I wouldn't be in your year in school because you can read and write better than I can. Your handwriting is very pretty, too.

The Hogans are going to be a curse on west Texas for years, I think. I'm glad that I'm not one of them.

I'm sorry this is so short, but I'm writing it in class and don't have much time.

He paused before closing the letter, wondering if he should use the same words that she had written in her letter, but decided to play it safe and simply wrote:

Joe

He knew he should have written more, or made it sound friendlier, but he was worried about Bessie for some reason that didn't make any sense to him. He knew he should have been worried about Cassie, not Bessie.

After writing her name on one of the two envelopes, he slid the brief missive inside and set it on his part of the table before taking his second sheet.

Dear Sheriff,

I haven't written to you since I was writing to Cassie, but I wanted to let you know that I will always be grateful for the help you gave me when I didn't even deserve it.

I wish I could have stayed and learned more. You taught me more in those few days than I'd learned in all of my life before that, and probably more than I ever will.

I promise that I will never let anything turn me back to that bad life.

Thank you.

Joe

He knew it was shorter than it should be, but he felt it told the sheriff enough for him to understand.

After addressing and closing the second envelope, he set down to write what would probably be the last letter he would write for years. He didn't know why he didn't pass the information about the new warden to the sheriff, but he just felt that he should tell Cassie instead.

He tried to write this better than anything he'd written before, so he took his time with each word.

Dear Cassie,

We've just been told by Warden Smith that he will be leaving soon, and a new warden named Phelps will be taking over on the first of April. I think the new warden and guards will be strict and not let us write anymore.

So, this will probably be the last letter you receive from me, and I may not get any more of your letters. I will miss them. Each day I would walk to the post office hoping to find one. I know that sounds silly because you are only eleven, but you really aren't, you know. Inside, I think you're a lot older than me.

I wrote a letter to Bessie and she said she wasn't going to let you read it, but if you could read it, it wouldn't make you feel bad.

I also wrote one to your father to thank him for all that he did for me. I want to thank you too, Cassie. I know I told you I thought you were crazy at first, but I know that you're not crazy. You are special. A good special.

I promised your father and I will promise you that I won't let whatever happens these next four years change me back to being the stupid, angry boy that I was before. I will keep learning every morning until maybe I can read and write as well as you.

When I leave here in four years, I will come back to Warwick and if you still want me to be your boyfriend, I won't mind, even if you still have freckles.

With Affection,

Joe

Joe then reread the most important letter three times, checking the spelling and grammar. He wanted it to be right. He thought about taking out the last paragraph about being her boyfriend because if she was as pretty as her father said she was going to be, there would probably be other boys lining up for the honor.

But despite that, and even coming to the sudden realization that she would only be fifteen when he returned, he carefully folded Cassie's letter and inserted it into the addressed envelope.

After classes for the morning were done, Joe dropped off the letters at the mailbox. He was initially surprised that his were the only letters in the box and realized that very few of the boys had families or at least families that wanted to hear from them. Maybe the few others that wrote letters believed they had more time.

Joe's suspicion that the changes would start sooner than the new warden's arrival proved correct, when as soon as the lights were out that night, four of the big thugs from upstairs invaded the younger dorm. They didn't do anything but walk between the bunks letting the smaller kids know that their days of protection would be coming to an end.

March 26, 1875

The postman delivered three letters to the Warren home that morning, and Minnie Warren was the only one at home at the time. She looked at the three envelopes with raised eyebrows. She hadn't known that Bessie had written to Joe and thought that he might be interested in her middle daughter. She'd seen him furtively glancing at her during their one meal but thought nothing of it at the time. She wondered if it had taken Joe six months to work up the nerve to write to Bessie, and she smiled at the thought.

But it was the letter to John that created the greater curiosity, so she slid the other two into her dress pocket and donned her shawl and hat, tied the hat's ribbon to keep it in place, and left the house.

She entered the jail a few minutes later, spied Dan Sheehy behind the desk, and asked, “Is he in?”

“Yes, ma’am,” Dan replied as he half-stood.

Minnie waved him down as she bustled past him and soon reached her husband’s open office door.

John had heard her voice and was already standing as she entered, removing her hat as she did.

“What brings you here this morning, ma’am?” he asked as he smiled.

As he was returning to his seat, Minnie sat down and offered him his letter.

“This came with two others from Joe today.”

“Two? He sent two letters to Cassie?” he asked as he accepted the envelope.

“No. One was to Bessie,” she replied, watching his reaction.

But all she got was a bland, “Oh,” as John opened Joe’s letter.

Minnie watched him read the single page as a smile spread across his lips and he slid the letter across the desk for her to read.

Minnie began to smile as she read Joe’s words, but then asked, “Why would he write this, John?”

Sheriff Warren suddenly realized why Minnie had asked her question. *Why had he written it?* It sounded almost like a deathbed confession.

“I don’t know. I wonder if he explained it in either of the other two letters. I guess we’ll have to wait until the girls come back from school.”

She nodded and put her hat back on before saying, “It’s going to be a long five hours.”

“I’m sure it’s not that bad, Minnie.”

His wife rose and said, “I hope not,” before turning and swishing out of his office and left the jail.

The sheriff picked up Joe’s letter again and reread it. As proud as he felt from what Joe had written, he was growing more concerned about the implication of what he didn’t write. He suddenly agreed with his wife. It was going to be a long five hours.

———

Since the initial foray into the lower dorm, two groups of older bullies formed what could only be described as gangs. They were carefully watched by the current guards, but the boys didn’t do anything overt, so there was nothing they or the warden could do to stop them from socializing.

The population of the reformatory quickly coalesced into three types: the bullies, the indifferent, and the victims. While some of the younger and smaller boys were bullies, the majority of them had already been victims of the milder bullying that took place under Warden Smith’s watch. Only a couple of the older boys fit into the victim category, but the biggest group was made up of the boys who preferred to remain in the background as much as possible.

Surprisingly, most of the boys of the victim class began to recognize Joe as their protector. He hadn’t done anything to earn that position, but there was something about the way he carried himself that attracted the weakest boys to him.

Joe's dedicated work at the smithy had added bulk to what should have been a thin frame. He was only five feet and seven inches and probably weighed less than a hundred and forty pounds, but there was no fat on his young body, and his arms and chest were much more developed than a normal fourteen-year-old, even if he probably wasn't really fourteen yet.

But it was more than just his strength that led the other non-bullies to seek him. Those few days with Sheriff Warren had shown him how a man of authority should act. He had started learning without realizing it even as he'd sat in the dust cloud at the bottom of the hill with his useless Remington on the ground near him. When the man with the rope had asked if he could rough Joe up, the sheriff had threatened to throw a member of his own posse into jail if he touched Joe. Every moment he'd spent with Sheriff John Warren had added to those unrecognized lessons, and the actual lessons he'd been taught on that long ride had only reinforced them.

It was those deeply entrenched examples and words that now made Joe Armstrong the almost unanimous leader of the boys who wanted to return to the outside world as just men and not criminals.

The leaders of the two gangs were Furry Lundquist, who earned the name because he never shaved or even trimmed his mammoth beard, and Clem Jefferson. Clem was actually smaller than Joe but was regarded as the meanest kid in the whole school. It was beyond meanness, though. Clem had been in the school since he was eleven because he had killed his mother when she had chastised him, and he hadn't gotten any nicer, even under the benevolent conditions established by Warden Smith.

Clem and Furry didn't really get along, but each had eight followers and had reached an uneasy truce as they waited for the first of April, believing that they'd have free reign once Mister Phelps arrived.

They didn't realize that Mister Phelps would be bringing his own gang of thugs wearing guard uniforms.

The Warren sisters had barely entered the front door of their home and hadn't had a chance to take off their jackets when Minnie walked quickly from the kitchen followed by their father which surprised them all.

"Papa, why are you here?" asked Mary as she hung her jacket on the coat rack.

"Oh, I just came to talk to Cassie about something," he replied.

Cassie asked, "What is it, Papa?"

"Let's have a seat and we can talk."

"Alright," she said, looking at her father curiously.

After the girls were parked in their chairs in the main room, Minnie pulled out the two envelopes and said, "We received three letters from Joe this morning. We read the one to your father and in it, he thanked your father for all he'd done for him. We're just wondering if he explained why he felt he had to write the letter and thought he might have explained it either of the ones he'd written to Cassie or Bessie.

Bessie smiled and asked excitedly, "He wrote me a letter?"

"Yes. Here," she said as she handed Bessie her letter and gave Cassie hers.

Bessie opened her envelope and quickly read Joe's short letter as Minnie watched her face, seeing the obvious disappointment. She'd ask Bessie about it later as she switched her focus to Cassie. Cassie was always difficult for her to read. It was as if she was always playing poker.

As Cassie read, her normal poker face shifted from surprise to concern with furrowed brows as she finished.

She looked at her parents and said, "Joe says that they're going to be getting a new warden on the first of April and the old warden makes it sound like the new one is going to be much harsher than he was. Joe thinks that he won't be able to receive or send any more letters once he takes over."

Minnie turned to her lawman husband and asked, "They can't do that. Can they?"

"I don't know what the rules are for that place. It might just be that the new warden will start opening the mail under the excuse that they might be trying to plan an escape. There weren't even any fences when I dropped Joe off, but I wouldn't be surprised if they put them up again."

Then he asked, "Cassie, does he say who the new warden is?"

She glanced at the letter and replied, "Someone name Phelps."

John nodded and said, "That would probably be Bert Phelps. He was the assistant warden at the State Prison the last time I was there. If he's the one, Joe is in for a rough four years."

“Can’t you get him out of there, John?” asked Minnie.

“I’ll go and see Judge Madsen tomorrow, but don’t hold your breath. He’s so damned stubborn, and he’s never changed a ruling since he’s been on the bench.”

Minnie nodded and then stood and said, “I’ll go and start cooking.”

Mary popped up and said, “I’ll help, Mama,” then quickly followed.

“May I read your letter, Papa?” Cassie asked.

John was thinking about how to approach the judge and just held his letter out to her.

Cassie took the letter and read it quickly before handing it back and then standing and leaving the main room.

Bessie desperately wanted to read Cassie’s letter, but she knew if she asked to read it, she’d have to let her sister read her letter and she didn’t want that to happen. Bessie assumed that the reason Joe had told Cassie about the new warden was that she was the only one who’d been sending him letters. She wished she had started writing letters before Cassie did. Maybe she’d read it later. She knew where Cassie kept the letters.

Cassie sat on her bed in the room she shared with Bessie and reread Joe’s letter before folding it and returning it to its paper home.

She remained seated on the bed as she tapped the letter on her knee. She found herself in the biggest quandary of her life.

When she had first seen Joe in the jail cell, she had seen a sullen, defensive boy whom she'd seen as a challenge and had immediately decided to mount a concentrated effort to change his attitude. It was her way.

Then after she noticed his less-hostile behavior, she had just wanted to see how much he really had changed because of what he'd learned about his so-called brothers. She wasn't sure, but when she learned he was going to the reformatory for more than four years, she made her decision. He would be her boyfriend, and that would keep all the other boys away.

But now, after reading his letter, she saw that he had changed his attitude towards her, and it put her in a terrible position. She had been warming up to Joe through their letters over the past few months, but at the same time, Bessie had expressed an interest in Joe herself. Cassie had seen how Joe had been looking at her sister at the breakfast before he left and thought that her older sister was more suitable as a girlfriend because she was just a few months younger than Joe. She may not be ten any longer, but eleven was a far cry from fourteen.

So, when Bessie had written her letter, Cassie was convinced that the next letter she received from Joe would be much cooler. But instead, it was much warmer and even ended 'With Affection'. She was sure that he'd used the same closing that Bessie had used in her letter to him, and that made it worse.

She had watched Bessie as she read Joe's letter and thought she had seen disappointment, if not hurt in her eyes. Joe had written that Cassie could read Bessie's letter and not feel bad, so that meant his letter to Bessie hadn't been what her sister had expected. And that was the root of her dilemma.

Cassie loved Bessie. They'd shared a room for as long as she could remember and had always gotten along, despite their differences. Cassie knew that the differences were all hers, as Bessie was much like Mary and the other girls in school. One of the things that made them all alike and different from her was their interest in boys. Bessie, Mary, and their friends were always talking about boys, and that included the six girls in her year in school, too. Even the younger ones all seemed to be interested in boys.

But Cassie didn't want a boyfriend and Joe was the perfect opportunity to deflect the other boys' interest for four years. She'd been telling her father that she wanted to do something with her life that was truly important and not be tied down by being a wife and mother, and while that may be partly true, it was the other, most secret fear that kept made her want to have Joe as a distant, imprisoned boyfriend.

Her growing fondness for Joe didn't matter as he wouldn't be out of the reformatory until March of '79, but this Bessie issue was a problem. Her own interest was getting in the way of Bessie's, and that wasn't right. She didn't want Joe to get between her and her sister.

She knew that Bessie shouldn't read the letter in her hand and she really needed to talk to her father about what she should do. So, she slipped the envelope into her pocket and left the bedroom.

At the supper call, the first incident of the new atmosphere erupted as twelve-year-old Harvey Sanderson was leaving the chow line and heading for a table occupied by four of his friends, including Joe Armstrong.

There was a constant murmuring in the large dining hall as the boys were all talking about the upcoming changes when Mister Phelps arrived in two weeks.

Jimmy Twist, one of Furry Lundquist's gang, stood from his table, took two steps toward Harvey, and simply yanked his tray from his hands.

"Thanks, Harvey. I wanted seconds," he said loudly as he laughed.

Harvey turned and shouted, "That's mine!" but Jimmy acted as if he hadn't heard Harvey, sat the tray on his table and took his seat, and began eating Harvey's food.

As Harvey stood almost frozen at the theft of his dinner, Joe noticed that the two guards, who would normally have stepped in, were just looking at the blatant theft of a boy's supper. He didn't know why they chose not to intervene, so he stood, stepped away from the table, and approached Harvey.

"Go ahead and have mine, Harvey. I haven't eaten any yet."

Harvey glanced back at Jimmy and said, "Thank you, Joe," and walked to the table and sat down.

Both tables of boys expected a big fight, but instead, Joe just walked to the end of the chow line, picked up another tray and put an empty plate on it, some clean cutlery, and worked his way down the line as almost all of the boys watched.

Joe wasn't sure if the server would give him more food or not, but that wasn't the point.

When he held out the empty plate, the server, Howie Bristol, didn't bat an eye and filled it as he'd already done to another hundred and thirty-one plates.

His tray full, Joe headed back for his table. He was sure that the boys all expected him to throw the new food at Jimmy Twist in retaliation, but Joe just watched out of the corner of his eye to make sure that Furry's group stayed seated and took an empty seat at the table and began to eat his supper.

Jimmy Twist looked at Furry for guidance, but Furry was just as confused as Jimmy was. They had thrown a gauntlet on the ground and it had been ignored.

The two guards both smiled at the non-fight, not because of Joe's impressive decision to avoid the confrontation, but because both were trying to be among the four guards that would stay on the job after Mister Phelps arrived and didn't want any recent black marks on their records.

Joe knew that this wasn't the time or the place for a showdown with either of the gangs. A fight here could turn into a giant melee involving dozens of boys and there were knives and forks aplenty in the room. There probably would have been a few deaths, and he wasn't sure if his wouldn't have been the first. As Sheriff Warren had told him, don't let someone else pick the time and place for a fight if you could avoid it. He'd pick the time and place when he had to stand up to the bullies.

———

"Papa, could I come with you and talk?" Cassie asked.

Dinner and cleanup were finished, and her father was heading back to the jail to finish up some reports.

"Certainly, Miss Warren. I'd be honored to escort you," he replied and offered Cassie his arm.

She smiled at her father as she took his arm before they crossed the main room and left the house and stepped out into the warm air of early spring in West Texas.

Once they were on the street, John asked, “So, Cassie, can I guess this has something to do with the letter you received from Joe?”

“Yes. That and Bessie’s,” she replied as she hurried her footsteps to keep up with her father’s much longer strides.

“So, young lady, what is the problem?”

“When Joe was here, I told him that when he came back, he’d be my boyfriend.”

“I know. He told me eventually. He asked me if you were crazy at first, but I convinced him you weren’t. Is that what’s bothering you? Did he write in your letter that he really liked Bessie?”

“No. Why would you think that? Did he say he liked Bessie when you took him to the reformatory?”

“No. It’s just that Bessie wrote him a letter and your mother thought Joe had seemed to pay attention to her before he left.”

“Oh.”

Cassie lapsed into silence as they crossed the darkened street and stepped onto the boardwalk before the jail.

After the sheriff unlocked the door, he followed Cassie into the office and lit the lamp on the front desk. Cassie took a seat on the chair beside the desk as her father sat behind it, his report temporarily pushed aside.

"Do you want me to read the letter that has you upset?" he asked.

"Okay," she replied as she pulled the folded envelope from her dress pocket and handed it to him.

John didn't know what to expect when he pulled out her letter and read:

Dear Cassie,

We've just been told by Warden Smith that he will be leaving soon, and a new warden named Phelps will be taking over on the first of April. He also said that we should write letters now because I think he knows that the new warden and guards will be strict and not let us write anymore.

So, this will probably be the last letter you receive from me, and I may not get any more of your letters. I will miss them. Each day I would walk to the post office hoping to find one. I know that sounds silly because you are only eleven, but you really aren't, you know. Inside, I think you're a lot older than me.

I wrote a letter to Bessie and she said she wasn't going to let you read it, but if you could read it, it wouldn't make you feel bad.

I also wrote one to your father to thank him for all that he did for me. I want to thank you, too, Cassie. I know I told you I thought you were crazy at first, but I know that you're not crazy. You are special. A good special.

I promised your father and I will promise you that I won't let whatever happens these next four years change me back to being the stupid, angry boy that I was before. I will keep learning every morning until maybe I can read and write like you.

When I leave here in four years, I will come back to Warwick and if you still want me to be your boyfriend, I won't mind, even if you still have freckles.

With Affection,

Joe

His first reaction was one of surprise at the incredible advances that Joe had made in his writing in just six months. Aside from the crude script, he knew men who had graduated from school who didn't write this well. Joe must have put a lot of time into his studies.

After being impressed with the letter itself, he studied the content more closely and still had a hard time understanding why Cassie would be upset. Joe was obviously already thinking of Cassie as more than a freckle-faced, pigtailed little girl. He could understand why, too. If someone was just able to listen to what Cassie said without hearing her childish voice, they would think she was much older. Joe had already been gone for six months and was just reading what Cassie wrote and was seeing her as she really was, not just how she looked.

He found himself smiling because he recalled telling Joe that he pitied the man that married Cassie and thought that maybe Joe would be able to satisfy his youngest daughter's demanding nature.

John set the letter on the desk and said, "It seems that Joe wouldn't mind being your boyfriend when he gets out of that place, Cassie. So, what's the problem with Bessie?"

"I watched her as she read the letter Joe wrote to her and she seemed disappointed and sad. I don't want to read it or even talk to her about it because I don't want to make her sadder. Should I write another letter to Joe telling him Bessie should be his girlfriend? It would make her happy."

"Maybe it would, but would it make you happy?"

Cassie sighed and paused before replying, "Papa, I like Joe and everything, but that's not why I told him I wanted him for a boyfriend. I told him because he was going to go to reform school, and I didn't want him to turn bad."

"So, when he comes back in four years, you'd be happy to see him and Bessie together?"

After another, longer pause, she softly, but honestly replied, "No."

"Cassie, four years is a very long time and a lot can happen between now and then. You might meet a boy you really like, or Bessie might be smitten by another boy, too. I think that's much more likely. Just don't bring up the subject and we'll wait and see what happens. I don't believe sending another letter to Joe right now would get through anyway. We'll just have to wait and see if we get any more letters from Joe."

Cassie nodded and asked, "Papa, can you hold onto the letter? I don't want Bessie to read it because it would upset her."

"I'll keep it in my desk. I may use it when I see the judge tomorrow about getting Joe out of there, so if Bessie asks where it is, tell her I gave it to the judge. Okay?"

"Okay, Papa."

"Do you want me to walk you home?"

"No, Papa. I'll be okay. When are you going to show me how to shoot?"

"Not until you're thirteen."

"What if I start changing when I'm twelve and all those boys notice?"

John doubted if that was going to happen, but also knew that Cassie wasn't about to let it go, so he said, "Alright, Miss Warren, on your twelfth birthday, I'll show you how to shoot a pistol. I'll give you Joe's old Remington. Okay?"

Cassie grinned and stood, stepped behind the desk, and kissed her father on the cheek before she turned and waltzed out of the office.

The sheriff watched her go, shook his head for giving in so easily, but was still smiling when he folded the letter and slipped it into his pocket. He already knew he'd be showing it to Judge Madsen tomorrow morning.

He finally was able to pull some sheets of paper from the desk and begin his report on a late afternoon fistfight at the Lone Texan Saloon. Of the four saloons in town, it was the source of most of his headaches.

As Cassie returned to the house, she thought about her answer to her father about whether she wanted to see Bessie with Joe, and her answer surprised her. *Why did she say no, when just a short time ago, she wondered if she should let Bessie become his girlfriend?*

Cassie hadn't had any serious flirtations from any boys yet, unless you included the ones who pulled her pigtails, so she hadn't had to use Joe as her boyfriend shield yet.

She decided that her father was right, as he usually was. She'd just wait and not talk to Bessie about Joe, and if there was no more mail, Cassie was sure that Bessie would find a real boyfriend sooner rather than later.

———

Joe expected them to come after he was in bed. That non-fight in the chow hall had embarrassed Furry and his gang and he expected some form of retaliation. He knew that some of them had knives they had stolen from the kitchen and was expecting them to make use of their sharp weapons tonight.

There wasn't much light in the dormitory, and Joe lay awake on his bunk as assorted snoring and wheezing filled the large room. His only protection was his pillow, which he had laid on his torso under the blanket. He wasn't comfortable and hoped they'd come soon.

But they didn't. Joe was desperately trying to stay alert but kept drifting off until he finally fell asleep.

———

He awakened with a start and sat up quickly in his bunk. The room was still dark, but he didn't know what time it was, and his pocket watch was folded in the britches in the box at the foot of his bed, so he just lay back down.

His heart was still pounding as if he'd awakened after a nightmare and thought how silly he must be to be so worried about a nighttime attack. He was actually smiling to himself for his foolishness when he heard a "Sssh!" from the far end of the dorm and quickly turned his eyes toward the stairs at that end and picked up some shadows. He didn't know how they'd be able to navigate to his bed and was preparing his pillow for an expected stab when a better idea popped into his head.

He sat up quickly again and shouted, "Good morning, boys! Glad to see you!"

The whole dormitory sprang awake and the two upstairs thugs quickly turned and raced back up the stairs, cursing as they vanished into the darkness.

The general hubbub that resulted in his shout was quickly subdued when Joe said, "Sorry. I had a nightmare."

After a few grouses from the older boys, Joe laid back down, knowing he'd won this battle, but the war had just begun. The wild card would be when the new guards arrived with Mister Phelps. *Would he encourage the thugs or punish them?*

The next morning, shortly after his deputies arrived, Sheriff John Warren took the short walk to the county courthouse to visit Judge Madsen. The meeting hadn't lasted long, and his expected results were correct. Even Joe's letter didn't sway the judge. He didn't want the word to leak out among the criminal element that he was a soft touch. To make matters worse, he thought highly of Bert Phelps, the new warden. He told John that it was high time that the reformatory returned to its older, more disciplined methods.

Even though he'd expected Judge Madsen's response, it didn't make John feel any less downtrodden as he returned to the jail. He could have just let Joe go that first day and not even charged him with anything but knew he wouldn't have.

He had to do his job the right way or not at all. He knew the judge was doing his job as he saw it as well, so he really had no complaint.

He wasn't looking forward to telling Cassie that Joe was going to spend another four years in the reformatory. Even though he really did know his youngest daughter better than anyone else, even he didn't understand that a sudden return of Joe Armstrong was the last thing Cassie wanted.

April 1, 1875

The boys were expecting some kind of formal ceremony where Warden Smith introduced Warden Phelps, but the only indication of the new administration was the guards. There was an almost complete changeover among the guards with only four of the older guards still working in the reformatory.

But worse than just the new faces was that each of them now sported a new accessory to their uniforms. Hitched onto their right side from their belt loop was what only could be described as a riding crop.

The nasty-looking short whips were about two feet long with a heavy leather handle and a strap on the end to keep it on the user's wrist. Even the bullies looked at the newly armed guards with trepidation, and not a single boy in the reformatory believed the whips were there for show.

It was at the end of the first of the two lunches that Joe and the others finally got to meet Warden Bert Phelps.

They had gone through the chow line as usual but noticed that there were six guards in the dining hall rather than the usual two.

It was nearing the end of their thirty-minute lunch break that Mister Phelps made his grand entrance.

One of the new guards was standing beside the front door and suddenly barked, “Stand at attention!”

The unexpected command was obeyed, but slowly and in an awkward wave as the boys came to their feet with very few of them at anything close to resembling what the army would call the position of attention.

Warden Bertrand Edward Phelps strode into the room wearing what appeared to be a fancy version of the guards’ uniforms outfitted with an even fancier, silver-embellished whip. He wasn’t an overly tall man, about five feet and nine inches, but was stocky. He had a full head of graying hair with a bushy set of muttonchop whiskers and a matching full moustache. He had beetling brows with equally thick eyebrows that topped his piercing gray eyes. He had the aura of a commanding general and was obviously displeased with what his new army of young neer-do-wells regarded as being at attention.

He’d barely made it ten feet into the hall when he stopped, glared at the boys, and shifted his attention to the guard who had called the room to attention.

“Is this what I am to expect?” he growled as he pulled his silver whip from his side.

“I’m sorry, sir. I’ll make sure they do better the next time.”

“You’d better, Mister Tyler, or you’ll taste my lash.”

He then passed by the guard and stepped up to one of the largest boys in the reformatory, one of the indifferent crowd, a boy named Pete Hargrove.

He stuck the end of his whip into Hargrove's stomach and asked, "What's your name and how old are you?"

Pete stammered, "P-P-Peter Hargrove. I'll be eighteen in July."

"So, you think that you're so close to leaving here that you can get away with disrespect and laziness?"

Pete looked the new warden in the eye which was his first mistake and replied, "I ain't lazy. I didn't do nothin' wrong."

Warden Phelps, in a motion so quick as to be nothing but a blur to those watching, drew back his whip and snapped it loudly against Pete's left side. Then as he bent over in pain, the warden cracked his fancy whip once across Pete's back.

Pete was whimpering as he tried to cover up, expecting more strikes, but the warden wasn't even angry. He was just making a point.

He stepped away from a bleeding Pete and said loudly, "I am Warden Phelps. You will address me as sir or Warden Phelps. I do not believe that any of you have earned the right to return to our civilization as free men. You are all here because you have shown yourselves to be the refuse and castoffs of society, and I will do my best to ensure that once you leave these gates, you will no longer plague our society.

"You will address the guards as sir, and you will obey all orders immediately or suffer the consequences. You will notice that all of the guards are equipped with riding crops similar to mine. I find them to be very useful tools in maintaining order and discipline. Now you have seen the results of just a short display of the pain that they can inflict. Do not tempt me or the guards again. If you are sitting when I enter a room, you will come to immediate attention out of respect for my position.

"Tomorrow, you will all be put to work replacing the fences that had been taken down. Until that job is done, all other functions will be put on hold, including the morning classes. If you all behave yourselves and do as you're told, then you should notice no change in the administration of this institution. If you try to rebel, you will regret that decision."

His position clearly stated, Warden Phelps turned to the guard next to him, nodded, and then executed a military about-face and quickly left the room.

Once he was gone, the guard said loudly, "Finish your lunch in five minutes and clear the room for the next group."

The boys quickly attacked their food as none wished to be put on the new warden's bad list on the first day.

As Joe shoveled his lunch in as fast as he could, chewed once, and swallowed, he glanced over at Pete Hargrove as he ate and noticed the blood oozing onto his shirt. He was sure that the warden had used Pete as his example because of his size and age. He still wondered how the thugs on the second floor would be treated, and he was sure that Furry and Clem had the same question.

———

July 19, 1875

It had been more than ten weeks since Warden Phelps had made his speech to the boys and to Joe's surprise, he found that the thugs suffered more than the rest of the population, not less. The warden's speech should have been a warning to the gangs, but apparently hadn't had its desired effect on some of them.

As they put up the new fence in April, two of the members of Clem's gang tried to have four of the smaller boys dig the post holes that was their job. They thought they had gotten away with it because there wasn't a guard in sight, but soon found that it didn't matter when a patrolling guard saw them doing the lighter job of stringing the wire and the smaller boys digging the post holes. He made good use of his whip on the two thugs and they not only had to dig the post holes but weren't allowed to eat dinner.

The fence itself was only the first part of the construction. The post holes would support boards to seven feet and then would be topped by barbed wire. That fence took only a week and a half to build. Joe's job during that time was making nails in the smithy.

Once the fence was built, wagons began arriving with stones and mortar provided by the generous state of Texas. The labor would be provided by the boys. Joe's skills as a blacksmith were no longer required for nails, and he was put to work with the rest of the reformatory population in laying stones.

In the heat of the Texas sun, the wall didn't progress quickly enough to suit the new warden and the guards began to exercise their arms with their new whips to get the boys moving. Water breaks were allowed once an hour and limited to a single dip, but for some boys, it wasn't enough. During the month of June, four boys died from heat exhaustion and dehydration. So far this month, another three had died, but the wall was almost done.

The work in the smithy not only gave Joe an advantage in strength but prepared him to deal with the hard labor in the stifling heat. But even Joe found it exhausting work. He couldn't imagine how the smaller boys handled it.

Today, they were building the last twenty-four feet of construction and the boys were trying to get the job done today. It was almost a race to the finish when the reformatory had its first attempted escape since Joe had been there.

One of the members of Furry's gang, Willie Struthers, knowing that escape would be impossible once the stone wall was done, suddenly climbed the wooden wall and was clambering over the barbed wire as other members of his gang shouted their encouragement and surprisingly, none of the watching guards moved an inch to stop him.

He was halfway over the wall when a shot rang out, startling everyone, and the right side of Willie's chest suddenly popped like something was trying to get out of his shirt as he screamed. He fell back onto the side where they were working and writhed as everyone just stood staring.

Some of the heads, including Joe's, turned to the source of the gunshot and saw Warden Phelps standing at a window with a smoking Winchester in his hands as he looked down at the scene.

None of the guards seemed to care, nor did any of Willie's fellow gang members, so Joe finally trotted past one of the guards and the watching boys and soon reached Willie. He dropped to his right knee and turned Willie onto his back. He was breathing erratically, and blood was foaming at his mouth.

Joe simply didn't know what to do, so he turned to one of the guards and pleaded, "Can't you help him?"

He didn't wait for a reply but turned back to Willie as he gagged and choked, "Mama…" and died.

Joe reached to Willie's face, closed his eyelids, and was about to stand when he heard a short whistling sound followed by an immediate explosion of pain across his back.

"Sir!" shouted the guard who had swung the lash.

Joe was so shaken by Willie's death that he didn't understand his transgression and made it worse when he turned and asked, "What?"

He saw the second blow coming and compounded his second blunder by trying to block it from hitting his face when he lifted his left hand letting his wrist take the blow.

"Stand up!" the guard growled.

Joe finally realized just how bad things were for him, so he quickly popped to attention and said, "Yes, sir!"

"What's your number?"

"Eleven-fourteen, sir," Joe replied as he stared at the ground, not making eye contact.

"Well, eleven-fourteen, you just earned yourself another detail. You're gonna bury that escaping bastard all by yourself."

"Yes, sir."

"Go pick him up and follow me."

"Yes, sir," Joe replied and turned and dropped to Willie's body's side and slipped his hands under his chest and knees.

He lifted Willie easily, despite his bulk, and turned to follow the guard. The reformatory had a graveyard in back that was used for boys who died and had no relatives who wanted to claim them. It was surprisingly large, despite having only been there for seven years.

As Joe carried Willie along, he knew that there would be more punishment coming for his instinctive defensive action but had no idea what to expect. He, like almost all of the other boys, had tried to maintain a low profile since the arrival of Warden Phelps, and this was as high a profile as he could imagine.

The guard stopped at the southern edge of the cemetery and drew a box in the dirt with his boot and stepped back.

When Joe reached the spot, the guard said, "You bury him here and it had better be good and deep, too. I don't want to see any coyotes coming here to dig him up."

"Yes, sir," Joe replied as he set Willie's body near the gravesite.

Another guard appeared carrying a spade and tossed it on the ground without comment.

Joe had been working all morning and it was almost time for a lunch break, but he knew better than to even ask for a drink of water before he started digging. The water bucket was back near the construction area and they weren't about to let him leave to get his one dip of water.

He picked up the spade and rammed the tip into the dry Texas earth as the guard who'd hit him left to manage the other boys who had returned to building the last twenty-four feet of wall.

Joe glanced at the second guard and recognized him as one of the guards who were holdovers from Warden Smith's time but knew that each of them had quickly accepted Warden

Phelps' methods. If anything, they were more enthusiastic in meting out punishment than the other six who arrived with the new warden. They must have been trying to impress their new boss with a show of loyalty.

It took Joe more than two hours to dig Willie's grave, his own sliced cut from that lash stinging with his salty sweat, but he didn't notice the pain. The boys had gone to lunch in their two shifts and had all returned to finish the wall when he finally climbed out of the hole. He almost made another mistake when he thought about asking the guard if another boy could help him lower Willie into the hole, but instead, he slid Willie's body closer to the hole and dropped back down inside. Once he was deep in the hole, he had to dig two small steps into the side of the gravesite, so he could step up enough to reach the body.

He grabbed hold of Willie's corpse and slid it into the hole, thinking he'd be able to catch it in his arms, but he'd misjudged the effect of gravity and when he slid the body over the edge, it crashed on top of him, knocking him into the bottom of the pit he'd just dug. He collapsed into the grave, buried under Willie's already stinking, wet body. He almost screamed in terror but held it in check as he heard the guard start to laugh. Whatever revulsion he felt for having a dead body on top of him was shoved aside in disgust and hatred for the man who was so callous with what had happened that he could find humor in it.

Joe squirmed out from underneath Willie's body and was preparing to climb out of the grave when the guard walked to the edge and looked down at him.

"Take off his shoes, pants, and belt. His shirt is useless."

Joe replied with the expected, "Yes, sir," then bent over and began removing the shoes. He put them aside and had to undo the belt, slide it loose and unbutton his britches and slide them off. He wrapped the shoes and belt in the britches and set them on the ground outside the hole before clambering out.

“Now bury him,” said the guard as he picked up Willie’s pants.

“Yes, sir,” Joe said as he picked up the spade.

Joe didn’t know how he’d managed to say even those two words as his mouth was so hard and dry that his tongue didn’t want to work.

As he shoveled the dirt back into the hole, he finally felt the sting of the whip that had broken the skin on his back. He’d check the condition of his shirt when he returned. He knew he’d be denied dinner in addition to missing lunch, so he’d be pretty hungry by breakfast, assuming they let him have that.

When he finally made it to his bunk, he took off his shirt and found that it had been sliced neatly, but the blood had spread in a wide area around the tear. He had one other shirt, so he’d wear that tomorrow and drop his shirt at the laundry for repair. Laundry was one of the most detested chores that were assigned, just one step above latrine detail.

When the other boys began filing into the dormitory after supper, Lippy O’Reilly and Pete Spencer trotted over to his bunk and Lippy looked at Joe’s back and whistled.

“He hit you pretty good, Joe.”

“Trust me, I know. I hope it doesn’t get infected. I don’t think they can cut out a back.”

Pete and Lippy laughed and Joe asked, “Pete, do you think the warden will let us send any letters? Nobody wants to ask since he shut down the post office.”

“I don’t want to ask, Joe. I don’t have anybody to write to, anyway. Most of us don’t.”

“I know. Do you think that it’s even legal for him to do that?”

“I think he can do anything he wants.”

“Including shooting us from his office?”

Lippy glanced around and said in a low voice, “I think that it’s still murder. When I was in jail in Lubbock, this feller in another cell snuck out after the deputy left the door unlocked. He got as far as the front door and was leavin’ when he gets spotted and gunned down by some regular citizen. He figured he was okay, but they charged him with murder! They hanged him, too.”

“What was the man in for?” asked Joe.

“Would you believe for stealin’ a bunch of Bibles from the church? He said he wanted to start his own church.”

Joe and Pete both stared at Lippy, waiting for the punch line, but that was apparently it.

“Are you tellin’ the truth, Lippy?” Pete asked.

“Give me a Bible, and I’ll swear on it,” he replied with a giggle.

After the mild merriment subsided, some of the other boys approached to look at Joe’s scar and to tell him that he was really brave to go and try to help Willie, even though he was one of Furry's boys. Joe told them it was probably more due to stupidity than bravery not realizing that his dismissal of being called heroic made him even more respected.

There were four boys still around Joe's bunk when Furry, Clem, and their two gangs stepped down the stairway from the second floor, making the boys scurry away from Joe.

Furry led the group of thugs close to Joe, who made a point of not standing. They weren't guards.

The big, hairy brute of a boy stopped in front of Joe's bunk and said, "You didn't have to do that."

Joe looked up and replied, "Yes, I did. He shouldn't have been shot. He wasn't a coyote or a deer."

Furry tilted his head slightly and asked, "You're Joe Armstrong, right?"

Joe nodded but didn't reply.

"Well, Joe, me and the boys appreciate you buryin' Willie. We ain't gonna bother you anymore. I think we all got a bigger problem than each other."

"We've always had a bigger problem than each other, only it's worse now. We can't keep fighting among ourselves. We need to protect ourselves from the guards, and the best way to do that is for all of us to just wait them out. Unlike them, we all get out of here when we turn eighteen. They'll be stuck here. Let's not turn into targets."

Clem then said, "You're pretty smart, Joe."

"If I was so smart, I wouldn't have blocked the guard's second swing. That's going to cost me."

Furry then said, “I’ll pass the word. We’ll call a truce and we ain’t gonna give them guards any excuse to shoot another one of us.”

“It was the warden who pulled the trigger. He’s the one we really have to watch out for,” Joe replied.

Furry nodded and surprised Joe by offering his hand. Joe stood, shook his hand, and then had to shake the hand of all of the thugs. He doubted if they changed at all inside but knew that avoiding punishment was a powerful incentive.

———

Bessie had celebrated her fourteenth birthday, and to Cassie’s relief had been seeing Henry Fowler, the barber’s son, with whom she’d danced a lot at the social in March. The one that she’d mentioned to Joe in her letter.

She hadn’t asked to see Joe’s letter to Cassie, and once things began to simmer with Henry, rarely even mentioned Joe.

Cassie, on the other hand, was more concerned about Joe than before. Not receiving any letters from him triggered her powerful imagination into believing all sorts of bad things had happened to him, and if she’d actually known what had transpired, they probably would have been worse. She may not have wanted to have him back as a real boyfriend, but her fondness for the boy who wrote those letters outweighed her concerns about his return. If he did get out, that was a problem she could solve later.

Just two days after the death of Willie Struthers, she entered the jail and trotted past a smiling Deputy Sanborn to her father’s office.

The door was open, and Sheriff Warren had heard her footsteps and knew who was on her way to his office before Cassie appeared in the doorway. Only Cassie would visit him in his office.

"Yes, ma'am?" he asked as she bounced onto the chair before his desk.

"Papa, I'm worried about Joe. We haven't received a letter from him in almost three months and I spend too much time thinking of some horrible things that could have happened to him. I know it's only my imagination, but I can't turn it off."

"No, I suppose not. What would you want me to do?"

"Can you talk to the judge again?"

"No, sweetie. I know he'd just get even angrier. Judge Madsen is very strict and very stubborn."

"Can't you go over his head? You know, to the governor or something?"

"No, Cassie. I can't. I'm an officer of the court and I'm not allowed to fight a judge's decision."

"Could I write to him?"

John looked at Cassie's determined face and smiled before replying, "If you want to write letters to the governor of the state, you can do that, but don't hold your breath."

"Alright. I understand that it's probably futile, but I'll try," then she stood, smiled at her father, and added, "but who can refuse a freckle-faced girl's plaintive request?"

“Not me, ma’am,” he answered as she turned and left the jail.

John leaned back and almost pitied the governor.

Six days later, the governor’s administrative secretary, James Whitworth, opened Cassie’s letter, read the first four sentences, and tossed it and its envelope into the trash bin.

“Kids…” he muttered under his breath as he opened the next letter.

CHAPTER 4

January 11, 1876

Joe couldn't recall it ever being this cold in Texas before, and he was indoors with two furnaces and two braziers in the large smithy. Some of the boys were outside working with the horses or slaughtering some pigs, so he couldn't complain.

Since the murder of Willie Struthers, because to Joe, that's what it was, everything dropped into a routine of almost palatable tension. The boys all simply did their chores and apprenticeships without complaint or face the inevitable whip that always seemed to be within striking distance.

Of all of the restrictions placed on them, Joe found the lack of communication with the outside, specifically with Cassie, to be most oppressive. He was growing desperate to know at least something of what was happening in the outside world in Sheriff Warren's jurisdiction.

Mister Fletcher, their teacher, did tell them news of the greater outer world, but nothing more. Even in the classroom, the omnipresent guards had a stifling effect as questions that might be interpreted as offensive were avoided. That criterion engulfed a wide area, so unlike the classes held under Warden Smith's regime, the classroom now was almost exclusively a monologue by Mister Fletcher.

Joe still worked hard on his studies because he knew that he had a lot to learn if he wanted to serve justice on the Hogan brothers. He hadn't heard a word about them since Mister Phelps' arrival and as far as he knew, they all could be dead by now, but he doubted it. They were too mean, and with three different gangs being led by the brothers, too difficult to track.

The lack of information also caused some level of curiosity about what happened to the boys who left the reformatory when they turned eighteen, which included Furry Lundquist and Clem Jefferson. Shortly after Willie's murder, many of them, including Joe, expected some Texas Rangers or U.S. Marshals to arrive at the school and arrest Warden Phelps, but nothing happened. *Why wasn't the news of the murder and all of the deaths of the boys during the construction of the wall getting out?*

The new arrivals hadn't heard about anything that went on at the reformatory before they arrived either and the gossip among the boys was that after leaving the reformatory none ever made it as far as Gainesville.

Joe was working on a set of hinges for one of the barn stalls and didn't know that he had committed an egregious offense that morning because there wasn't immediate retribution.

Just after class had ended, Joe had approached Mister Fletcher, ensured the guard wasn't looking and asked quietly if it would be possible for him to post a letter for him in Gainesville when he went home for the weekend. Mister Fletcher hadn't answered, but shook his head slightly, which should have been a warning to Joe that someone was listening.

That someone was one of the newer boys, a fifteen-year-old named Zack Osterhaus. Unknown to most of the boys, some of the boys that had been sentenced to the reformatory after Warden Phelps' arrival had been promised more favorable treatment for spying on the other boys. Not all of the new ones were asked to act as snitches, but Warden Phelps screened their records and chose his spies well.

After Joe left the classroom that morning, Zack had meandered to Warden Phelps' office and told him that Joe was trying to get a letter out of the reformatory via Mister Fletcher.

Meanwhile, Joe, oblivious to the pending punishment, completed the work on the hinges and had his work evaluated and approved by Mister Vinton. His work over for the day, Joe cleaned up and left the smithy to return to the dorm for a short break before supper.

As he entered the main building, he was met by one of the guards, who stood with his whip in his hand, slapping it softly against his right thigh.

"Come with me, Armstrong. The warden wants to have a word with you."

"Yes, sir," Joe replied in his most servile tone, the untethered whip serving as a warning.

The guard surprised Joe by grabbing his shirt at the shoulder and marching him down the hallway as other boys gawked, knowing that Joe was in serious trouble.

Joe hadn't been escorted twenty feet when he guessed what this was about but couldn't understand how the warden had found out. The classroom guard wasn't close or even looking in his direction, and he knew that Mister Fletcher wouldn't turn him in because the teacher was under as much scrutiny as the boys. It had to be another boy, so as he was being manhandled down the hallway, he began trying to recall who was in the classroom and close enough to hear what he had said. There were only two, and it was most likely Zack

Osterhaus. He'd only been in the reformatory for three months and Joe didn't know him well.

But knowing who had told the warden didn't matter now as the guard shoved him into the warden's office and followed him inside.

Joe had stumbled after the last shove and almost fell headfirst into the warden's desk but caught himself before that added disaster.

The guard shut the door behind him and stood behind Joe who was the recipient of a hostile glare from Warden Phelps as he sat behind his desk.

The warden wordlessly stood then as he walked around his desk, he pulled his own, silver-tipped whip from his belt and stepped close to Joe's left side.

Joe kept his eyes straight ahead as he maintained his rigid attention position.

Finally, the warden asked in a low, threatening voice, "I hear that you are trying to sneak letters out of my reformatory, Mister Armstrong. Is that true?" and then accented his question with a crack of his whip on the side of his desk.

Joe replied, "I asked Mister Fletcher if he would post a letter for me, but he shook his head, sir."

"You know that any contact with the outside world must be approved by me, don't you, Mister Armstrong?"

"Yes, sir."

Warden Phelps put his lips just two inches from Joe's left ear and whispered, "You are a troublemaker, Armstrong, and you will be punished."

There was no point in saying anything, so Joe continued to stare at the wall behind the warden's desk when the first part of the punishment was inflicted in the form of the warden's special whip which suddenly snapped across the back of Joe's left thigh.

Joe grunted from the pain and buckled slightly but didn't give in to the anger or the temptation to strike back. Both would be fruitless and result in even much more severe punishment.

More punishment was soon meted out when the guard slashed his whip across the back of Joe's right thigh, with a similar reaction from Joe. He could feel his warm blood already flowing down the back of his legs but wasn't going to let them have the satisfaction of hearing him cry out in pain.

But the two quick lashes were only the beginning as the warden and the guard alternated striking Joe's thighs and then his back and buttocks. The whips whistled and cracked as they beat him as he remained more or less at attention.

Joe was trying to send his mind somewhere else, but the pain was excruciating, and he wanted to scream and break down in tears, but his overwhelming anger stopped him from doing anything more than gritting his teeth and grunting.

After sixteen total lashes, Warden Phelps finally stopped, and the guard followed suit. Joe didn't know how he'd remained on his feet and didn't know if he could walk as the warden stepped behind his desk and almost collapsed into his chair. Joe's eyes were wet, but he could see his own blood splattered on the warden's suit and the mess his blood made of his whip, and swore that the warden seemed to be excited about whipping him.

“Get him out of my office and throw him into solitary. Bread and water for two weeks.”

“Yes, sir,” the guard replied and grabbed Joe’s shirt again, and pulled him back from the desk.

Joe used every bit of the strength working in the smithy had given him to stay on his feet as he felt himself being half-dragged and half-walked down the hallway. He could see other boys’ faces as they saw his wounds and had no idea how bad they were to look at, but he knew how bad they felt.

The guard opened the door to the solitary cell and just let go of his shirt and pushed him inside before slamming the door closed.

There were four solitary cells, each one just six feet by four feet. There was what passed for a cot, but it was really just a few boards laying on the ground. There was one blanket and a chamber pot.

Joe collapsed onto the cot on his stomach, not wanting to have anything touch his back or thighs. He didn’t know if he’d survive this. The two weeks of solitary wasn’t the biggest problem. It was his injuries. He had no one to look at them or treat them and was sure that they’d become infected. Any infection would be a death sentence, and he’d witnessed several.

What really scared Joe was that this incredibly painful beating had been inflicted because he had asked if he could have a letter posted. He lay on his stomach with his back and legs in burning agony, unsure of what he could do to stay alive, but knew he had to keep breathing and then get stronger. He had debts to repay.

After he'd laid on his stomach for almost an hour, Joe rolled onto his left side and managed to pull off his britches and underpants and then take off his shirt. It was an enormously painful and lengthy exercise. Once the clothes were off, Joe laid back on his stomach and began to gently touch his injuries, grimacing as he found the broken skin and open muscle. He knew he had to keep them as clean as possible, another lesson from Sheriff Warren, and that meant he had to stay on his stomach for as long as he could.

The terrifying story of what had happened to Joe ripped through the reformatory, and the first question they all asked was: *what had he done to deserve such punishment?* Joe had been one of the best-behaved kids in the school, and for him to be whipped that badly, it must have been monstrous, but no one had seen him do anything. With Joe in solitary, he wasn't going to be able to tell anyone, and most of the boys believed, as Joe did, that he wouldn't be leaving that cell alive.

Warden Phelps' purpose for issuing such harsh punishment for such an innocuous transgression was simple. He was well aware that Joe Armstrong was one of the boys who was almost a model of what other boys should be. He'd read Joe's arrest record that Sheriff Warren had dropped off, so he knew that Joe wasn't going to cause any trouble. He wanted the rest of the population of the reformatory to understand that he wouldn't tolerate any violations, no matter how minor. Joe's beating was no more than an object lesson, and if he died, so be it.

———

The next morning, Joe was still lying naked on his stomach on his cot when his morning ration of stale bread crusts and water was left in his cell without a question of his condition. He had spent a fitful night, drifting in and out of consciousness. The pain seemed to intensify as the night went on, and even the cold of the night didn't numb the burning.

Joe turned his head and looked at the food out of his reach and knew he'd have to eat, or he'd hurry death's gruesome touch. He took a deep breath, rolled onto his right side, and then began a wiggling slide toward the bread. It took him almost three minutes to move the two feet to get to what passed for his breakfast.

He quickly ate the dried bread and had to raise his head slightly to pour some water down his throat. It soothed his parched mouth and throat and he wanted desperately to drink every bit but needed to use half of the water on his wounds.

When he was at least not so thirsty, he rolled back onto his stomach and poured some of the water on each thigh and almost cried in relief as the cold water rolled across the raw breaks in his skin.

He found that the blows delivered by the warden were deeper, probably because of those silver tips on his whip, but they weren't as bad as they could have been. If their hand whips had been true whips, those cuts would have been an inch or more into his flesh. They were deep, about a quarter of an inch, but Joe thought they'd heal as long as he could avoid infection.

Once his water was exhausted, he left the cup near the door and then had to try and use the chamber pot. At least all he had to do now was pee, which wasn't difficult. He didn't know how he'd manage the other end. He hoped for a few days of constipation.

His bodily functions done Joe lay on his stomach on his blanket with his torn, bloody clothes on the floor beside him. He reached over and slid his pants to him and removed his pocket watch from the pocket and wound the stem. He then read the carved script and the simple words strengthened his resolve to get past this and return to Warwick not as a bitter, angry young man, but as a man the Warrens would be proud to allow back in their home.

He closed his eyes and found himself not thinking about trying to get even with Zack for what he had done or even seeking vengeance against the warden or guard. He didn't even think about the painful, throbbing from his damaged legs, behind and back. Joe Armstrong let his mind work as he tried to imagine what Cassie Warren would look like without her freckles and pigtails and how her voice would sound.

Joe knew that it was far more likely that Cassie would have a real boyfriend when he returned, but she was all he had now. Cassie had become synonymous with hope.

Cassie was extraordinarily frustrated, even more than usual. Her letters to the governor had gone unanswered and neither her father, mother, or Miss Timmons at school could tell her who to write to other than President Grant.

She would have written a letter to the president but thought if the governor was going to ignore her letters, surely the President of the United States wouldn't care, either.

If her family had discovered what had happened to Joe, she wouldn't have had to write a single letter. Her father would be making a trip to Gainesville.

But no one in the Warren household suspected that Joe was doing anything more than studying and learning his trade as a blacksmith, so they went about their lives expecting him to return in three years and two months.

January 26, 1876

"All right, Armstrong, come out of there," the guard ordered.

Joe stood and shuffled past the guard with as much dignity as he could manage. His ripped, blood-stained clothes stunk something fierce, and Joe wasn't much better. His wounds had scabbed over and in the biggest of all miracles, hadn't become infected.

After his first week in solitary, Joe had pretty much remained on his stomach, and only after he managed to work his way to his knees and slowly stand, did he even get a chance to look at most of the backs of his thighs. The slices were red and angry with yellowish blue surrounding them, but he had expected a lot worse. There was no pus or other indications of the dreaded infection, and he hadn't developed a fever.

He made a point then of walking as best he could to keep everything from getting too tight. His stomach was growling constantly, and for the past two weeks, he had anxiously awaited his daily rations of bread. He, like most of the boys, didn't have any spare fat to burn, so he knew he was losing weight. If that wasn't enough, he was going through a growth spurt, so what little energy he could get from his food was used for that, which made him weaker than he'd ever experienced.

Now he was walking back to the dormitory, knowing he'd have to toss the clothes and get some hand-me-down replacements, which he would have had to do anyway because of the added two inches of height from the last time he'd gotten replacements. He'd need to replace his boots, and probably get stuck with some regular shoes, too. He'd miss his boots.

He reached the bunk and found Pete Spencer and Lippy O'Reilly sitting on their nearby bunks waiting for him. It was almost time for the supper chow call, and Joe was really looking forward to the food.

They both stood and trotted over to their slow-moving bunkmate.

"How are you doin', Joe?" asked Lippy.

"As well as I could expect, I think. I didn't get any infections, so I'll live."

Pete glanced around quickly and asked quietly, "Everybody's wonderin' what you did to get beat and sent to solitary. Did you sass a guard or somethin'?"

Joe shook his head as they continued to walk to his bunk and replied, "No. I did something much worse. I asked Mister Fletcher if he would post a letter for me."

As Joe opened his bunk box and took out his spare britches and shirt, Lippy asked in surprise, "Did Mister Fletcher turn you in?"

Joe was stripping off his shirt as he answered, "No, I'm pretty sure he didn't. I think I know who told the warden. I believe that some of the new guys are listening to what we say and then running to tell the warden. It's the only way he could have found out."

"*They're spyin' on us?*" asked Pete in a hushed exclamation.

"That's what I think. So, pass the word to guys you can trust, but be really careful. I wouldn't want to go through this again if one of the old-timers was one of his spies, too."

Pete and Lippy quickly searched the large barracks-like room, evaluating each of the boys as potential backstabbers.

Joe had barely finished changing when they had to go to the chow hall. The bottom floor went first and the second floor had their meals thirty minutes later. As they walked, one thing weighed heavily on his mind. He would have to sit down for the first time in two weeks and it would be painful. He would have preferred to eat standing up but knew that one of the guards would force him to sit anyway and probably give him another crack of his whip to make him do it.

As he went down the line, getting his food, he noticed that he was getting exactly the same amount of food as the other boys, but as the three boys on chow line duty spooned his food onto his plate, he could see genuine sympathy in their eyes. Each of them probably wished he could put a bigger helping onto his plate to make up for the last two weeks of deprivation, but none would dare risk undergoing what had happened to Joe.

Unknown to the boys, one of the guards had been told by Warden Phelps to look for that very thing. If Joe had received a teaspoon too much of anything, the boy giving it to him would have received an excessive amount of punishment, but not to the level inflicted on Joe. Joe was the example and obviously, it had worked.

Joe managed to sit down, and once on the bench, ate his food slowly, despite his stomach demanding the plate to be cleaned in seconds. He didn't want to throw up the first real food he'd eaten in two weeks.

The same guard who had followed his progress down the chow line now watched Joe to make sure none of the other boys shared their food with him. They didn't for the same reason that the boys in the chow line didn't give him larger portions. Every single boy, no matter how tough he believed himself to be, was now terrified of the warden and the guards.

If there was a pervasive mood of tension after the murder of Willie Struthers, it was magnified now and once word filtered around the reformatory of the warden's spies, the school became as silent as a library.

Joe wasn't excused from chores or his apprenticeship duties because of his injuries, nor did he wish any special treatment. He did exchange his clothes for longer pants and a better shirt. He also lost his boots and had to wear some particularly ugly work shoes.

Mister Vinton didn't comment on his absence as he entered the smithy and resumed work, but Joe could tell that the blacksmith wasn't happy with what the warden had done to him. Mister Vinton though, just like Mister Fletcher and the other craftsmen and workers that had boys as apprentices, served at the whim of the warden.

As Joe pounded a horseshoe into shape, he felt bad for Mister Vinton and the others. They had families in Gainesville and needed the jobs. They were no less prisoners of the reformatory than he was.

September 19, 1876

Buck Hogan led his three followers to the outskirts of the town of Horn Creek. It was an ideal target with no law and a small bank aching to be robbed. He didn't expect to get a big haul out of the job, but pickings had been slim over the past few months and they needed to make a score of any size.

His tactics had been modified since the Warwick disaster and now, he took a much simpler approach. He sent in two men with Winchesters from opposite ends of town and then the two robbers would ride in and enter the bank, grab the money and all four would ride away for a mile or so and set up an ambush for any posse that would form. They'd targeted two banks using the new method and it had worked easily, so Buck didn't see anything different about Horn Creek.

But Buck's choice of targets, which may have been ideal for any other day, was not a wise one today. As Buck's gang was preparing to take out the bank, Texas Ranger Corporal Pack Paxson was exiting the café with his three fellow Rangers. They had stopped at the town for lunch on their way south to Austin after trying to hunt down another Hogan gang led by Fred and Hank but had to stop at the Red River. Now they were about to confront Buck Hogan's gang, but hadn't realized it yet.

The first of Buck's Winchester men had ridden past the café to take up his position to the west of the bank while the other outside man had already stopped by the east side. Buck and his right-hand man, Johnny Lewis, had just passed the eastern Winchester man and were dismounting in front of the bank when Corporal Paxson and his Rangers exited the café. It only took him a few seconds to spot the obvious bank robbery attempt.

"Let's get to our Winchesters, boys," he growled as he stepped to his horse.

"I ain't got one of those girly repeaters, Pack. You know that," Ranger Nelson said as he walked quickly to his horse to retrieve his Sharps.

No one commented as they mounted their horses and pulled their rifles from their scabbards.

The outlook on the west side, Gene Allen, spotted the four Rangers as they mounted their horses and shouted, "We got trouble!"

His warning reached the ears of the eastern Winchester man as well as those of Buck and Johnny Lewis inside the bank as they faced off the cashier and two customers.

Buck made a quick decision and shouted, "Get out there and see what's going on, Johnny! I'll take care of this!"

Johnny Lewis nodded as he turned and trotted out of the bank with his revolver's hammer cocked.

Buck didn't waste a second, but in rapid order, shot the cashier and gunned down the two shocked customers.

With his Colt's barrel still oozing smoke, he raced behind the small counter, pulled the cash drawer open, and began stuffing bills into his pocket.

Outside, the gunfire had started when Carl Nelson opened fire with his Sharps at two hundred yards. He wasn't going to wait for those boys to shoot his fellow Rangers.

As Johnny Lewis exited the bank, he heard the loud roar of the Sharps and watched as Gene Allen was thrown from his horse when the powerful bullet smashed into the right side of his chest, even as he was trying to fire his Winchester at the fast-moving Rangers.

He only had his pistol but snapped off two quick shots at the lawmen as he ran to his horse to make his escape, not caring about Buck anymore. He had his foot in the stirrup when a .44 from Corporal Paxson's first shot slammed into his back, dropping him to the ground.

The last outside man, Elbert Finnegan, had fired four rounds at the Rangers, but had missed with all four and decided to make his break while he still had a chance, so he turned his horse to the east and set him to a gallop, his hot Winchester still in his right hand.

By then, Private Nelson had reloaded his Sharps and took his time to fire at the quickly retreating outlaw. He aimed at the man's lower back, knowing if he missed low, he'd hit the horse anyway. He'd rather it hit the man, but he had to be stopped.

He held his breath and squeezed the trigger. The long cartridge full of powder ignited, sending the .52 caliber missile across the three hundred and twenty yards before it struck right at the base of Elbert's back, making him drop his Winchester, then after two more strides of his horse, he slid off to the right and tumbled into the Texas dirt, making a good-sized dust cloud.

Inside the bank, Buck had heard the enormous amount of gunfire and knew his gang had come out worse in the exchange. It was time to get out before anyone came through the door.

Buck made one last, hurried search for anything valuable and then hurried to the back hallway and found a doorway. He opened the door slowly, checked for any spying eyes, and left the bank, closing the door behind him and walking quickly west down the back alley.

Once he was four buildings away, he cut between them and slowly stepped out into the town. He spotted the two Rangers examining bodies as two others approached the bank with pistols drawn.

He calmly walked across the street, selected a decent horse that was tied before the diner, mounted, and walked the horse out of town to the west without looking back.

Buck's heart was pounding as he rode, but still managed to keep his slow pace and his eyes focused ahead until he was almost a mile out of town. He then turned, saw no one behind him, and started the horse at a medium trot.

The road wasn't well traveled, so he'd have to find a way to disguise his trail, and they wouldn't even look for him until the horse's owner reported him missing.

But he didn't have that long of a delay when Corporal Paxson noticed the extra horse sitting in front of the bank. After a rudimentary scan of the saddlebags, he was convinced it belonged to a fourth outlaw, but there were no witnesses left alive.

He assigned two of his men to search the town, while he and Ranger Nelson rode west out of town because he knew that no one had passed them going east.

So, just twenty minutes after Buck rode out of town, the two Texas Rangers followed him west and soon picked up the fresh trail of a lone rider.

Buck had left the road after two miles and found a narrow but deep gully parallel to the roadway just fifty yards north. He had decided to follow his new tactics and wait to see if anyone was following, dismounted, and led the horse down into the gully.

Once inside the gully, he let the horse stand as he pulled his Winchester and removed his hat before using his knife to dig some holes in the wall of the gully. Once they were made, he stepped into the holes and slowly peered over the edge, not expecting to see anyone, but there they were. Two of the Rangers were riding out of town and were only two miles away now.

Buck wasn't sure if they'd seen him as they rode into the bright afternoon sun of early afternoon, but he had to assume that they had. He'd heard the deep roar of the Sharps, so he knew he was at a range disadvantage and a firepower shortcoming as well. His only chance was if they hadn't seen him.

They hadn't. The glaring sun had made both men drop the brims of their hats low to shield their eyes, so they could only see about six to eight hundred yards before them. The dry Texas ground that made up the road didn't allow deep hoofprints, so the trail left by Buck Hogan wasn't as pronounced as it might have been elsewhere, and that was going to be trouble for the lawmen.

Buck continued to watch as they continued to ride straight on the roadway, now only four hundred yards away. He cocked the hammer on the Winchester conveniently provided by the horse's owner, but still didn't expect them to ride within range.

"How far are we gonna trail him, Pack?"

Corporal Paxson lifted his hat's brim but shielded his eyes with his hand as he scanned the road ahead.

"We should've seen him by now. Let's give it another ten minutes and then we'll go back and get the boys."

"Okay, boss."

Buck had seen them talking but couldn't hear what they'd said at this distance. They were still riding and hadn't spotted where he'd left the road yet. He couldn't believe his luck as they passed within two hundred yards of his position.

He continued to focus on the Rangers when they came within range and slowly pulled the Winchester above the level ground and sighted on the closer of the two riders. Buck followed them with his sights locked, waiting for them to see his tracks leave the road. They were close now.

Pack suddenly shouted, "Damn it!" when he spotted the tracks turning north and swiveled his head to the right where he could see more easily.

The first thing he saw was a flash and a bloom of gunsmoke followed almost immediately by the crack of a Winchester.

Carl Nelson never even got his Sharps out of its scabbard before the .44 drilled into his chest, splintering a rib and then passing through his left lung and nicking the outside of his heart before leaving between two ribs. He fell awkwardly forward onto his horse's neck before sliding to the side.

Corporal Paxson was reaching for his Winchester as he snapped his heels against his gelding's flanks to urge him forward off the road and toward the shooter.

Buck was surprised by his aggressive move but had already pulled a fresh cartridge into the chamber and found the Ranger's decision to attack rather than flee made his second shot even easier. He took a second extra to aim and then fired as Corporal Paxson was just bringing his Winchester to bear.

His second shot caught the Ranger high, just above his breastbone but caused massive damage to his trachea and the critical blood vessels carrying oxygen to his brain.

His gelding continued to charge toward Buck as Corporal Paxson slipped from the saddle and fell, his right boot getting caught in the stirrup for a few strides before he dropped to the ground.

Buck didn't waste any time. He knew those other two lawmen would be after him soon, so he quickly led his stolen horse from the gully, gathered the gunbelts from the two Texas Rangers, and searched them for money, finding only eight dollars and ten cents. But before he dragged the bodies to the gully to drop them in, he removed their Texas Ranger badges and slipped them into his pocket. They might come in handy in the future.

He made a trail rope for the two horses, then after attaching it to his saddle, mounted and quickly trotted away from the scene. Now he had the advantage in firepower over anyone who might follow. He'd never fired the Sharps before but was gratified that the Ranger had two boxes of ammunition, which meant he had enough to use in practice.

As Buck rode away, he began to think that maybe bank robbery wasn't the best path to a comfortable life. With his new badges, he might be able to work a better scheme.

The word of the massacre at the Horn Creek bank spread quickly, primarily because two Texas Rangers were involved.

The name Buck Hogan was added to the reports and Sheriff John Warren received his three days later along with a new wanted poster for Buck Hogan. Like most of them, the poster had a vague drawing that could be most men, as was the description of the outlaw.

Buck Hogan just had no distinguishing characteristics. He had even cut off the flowing moustache that had marked the Hogan brothers. All of them had long since stopped wearing those distinctive brown leather vests, too. Buck Hogan would be a difficult man to hunt down now that he was alone.

October 9, 1877

Sixteen-year-old Joe Armstrong had already had to exchange his clothes again and was now the tallest boy in the reformatory and with his almost daily work in the smithy, he was also the strongest. If he'd wanted to be a bully, he could have ruled the place. Despite his calm, subservient demeanor, the guards regarded Joe as a threat and always watched him closely, expecting him to cause trouble after the lashing he'd been given over a year and a half ago.

But Joe had no intention of causing trouble. He had less than eighteen months to go before he walked out of the reformatory and wasn't about to give the warden any reason to inflict more pain. His wounds had healed, but he could still feel the scars with his fingers and was pleased that they were there to remind him of the warden's cruelty. When he finally left the place on March 11, 1879, he'd walk to the sheriff in Gainesville and file a criminal complaint against the warden for the murder of Willie Struthers.

Since July of '75 when Willie had been murdered, many theories had made the rounds to explain why nothing had happened.

Before, when Warden Smith had been in charge and there was no fence or wall, the boys who left the reformatory could be seen walking down the road north to Gainesville. Now with the wall, no one could see them as they left, so imaginations went wild.

They ranged from the logical reason that nobody really cared what happened inside the walls to the wildest of conspiracies, that the warden had killed and slaughtered the boys who were leaving and served them as food to the rest of the boys.

As the months slipped past with no contact at all from the Warrens, which he knew wasn't their fault, Joe began to believe that they had forgotten about him. It was only human nature to forget those who weren't there, just as it was for all the boys in the reformatory. They all had mothers and fathers at one time or another, yet had been either dropped off at an orphanage, become orphaned naturally, or had been shunned by their families for their behavior. No matter the reason, now they were all inside the four walls they had built. and the rest of society had forgotten they existed. To Joe, that was the real reason the warden had gotten away with murder.

Joe may not have understood why nothing had happened in the four years, but he knew that when he left, he'd tell anyone who would listen, and if they didn't act, he'd find someone who would.

Today, his chore was standing in chow line, doling out the food. The job itself wasn't difficult or stressful, but there was one danger. Each boy had to get precisely the same amount of food, so the server had to pay attention to what he was doing.

On his right, Sam Quist was ladling out creamed corn and must have not been paying attention when after he'd already dropped a scoop of the yellow mass onto Hank Bloom's plate, he didn't notice that Hank hadn't moved his away yet and poured on a second scoop.

Hank saw the error and quickly moved his plate, hoping the guard didn't notice, but before his plate had moved a foot, the guard stepped behind the line and approached Sam, who already began trembling in anticipation of his first stinging bite of the whip.

Joe knew he shouldn't do or say anything, but for some reason, knowing that Sam, an eleven-year-old who never should have been sent to the reformatory, was about to receive a lash, he finally had enough.

Sam had his eyes closed as the guard, without a word of warning, raised his whip and whistled it toward the back of Sam's right thigh.

As soon as that weapon was moving back to strike, Joe slid his own long right leg behind Sam and when the whip struck, it ripped into Joe's thick right thigh just above the knee instead.

The guard was furious, but Joe didn't say a word as he just turned his cold, hazel green eyes at the guard and left his bleeding leg where it was, still protecting Sam.

The guard hesitated for just a second, then lashed out and struck Joe's back before turning and leaving the line to go to his normal position.

Joe finally moved his leg from behind Sam and held out his ladle of mashed potatoes for the next boy.

The line began moving again as if nothing had happened. The guard had stopped at the second lash because he was actually afraid of Joe. Those eyes of his were threatening and he knew that if Joe Armstrong lost control, especially with that heavy ladle in his hand, his whip would be useless. He could go and tell the warden, but that would be committing suicide. He knew that none of the warden's snitches would tell his boss either. They were scared of the rest of the boys who had identified each of them, and they had to live with them. It was the widest Mexican standoff possible.

So, as Joe stood there quietly doling out mashed potatoes, he let the blood from his thigh wound flow. The blow to his back hadn't broken skin, and he wasn't sure if it had ripped the shirt either. The guard's conviction hadn't been behind the strike.

Every boy who had witnessed the extraordinary display of courage and rebellion had set it firmly in his memory, even the thugs who would later on become criminals. Joe Armstrong was a name they would remember.

November 7, 1877

Cassie opened her last birthday gift from her father and smiled. His wrapping hadn't been good enough to hide its shape.

"Thank you, Papa. Is there ammunition with it?" she asked.

"I have a dozen boxes of .44s in the office. You can use as many as you want."

"Can we practice with it later?"

"After your mother makes you eat some of your birthday cake, young lady."

Cassie grinned at her father as she held the Remington pistol and gunbelt in her hands. She'd been firing Joe's old Remington for two years now and was getting pretty good with it. Her father had even let her take a few shots with one of his Winchesters, but this was her pistol. She's asked for a Remington rather than a Colt because Joe's pistol was the same brand. She'd keep his gun with his mother's comb.

She's stopped writing her useless letters to the governor a long time ago and instead, once a week she'd write letters to Joe, anticipating his replies before she wrote the next. Bessie thought she was being foolish as the letters began to stack up.

Bessie had a real boyfriend now, having moved on from Henry Fowler. Now that she was popular, she had her choice of the boys at school and settled on handsome, tall, seventeen-year-old Kit Ryerson. He was the star athlete of the school and was widely thought of as the best catch in town. His father even owned the feed and grain store.

Cassie had long lost her freckles and even on her thirteenth birthday was showing the promise of fulfilling the belief that her father held that she would be the prettiest of his girls. She was still thin, of course, but that didn't stop a parade of boys from trying to become familiar with her, despite her prowess with firearms.

But Cassie had no intention of giving any of them the time of day, and Joe's position as her boyfriend was finally serving its intended purpose as she described Joe as big, strong, and handsome to any denied boy as further incentive to leave her alone. She was honest with herself that she was building up a largely imaginary relationship with Joe Armstrong. She had no idea what he looked like anymore at all, even after the first year. She just hadn't seen him very often. Now he was sixteen and would be leaving the reformatory in just seventeen months. *Would he even return to Warwick? Would he even remember her or her family?* Part of her wanted to see what he looked like and how he acted, but she dreaded that he might return and expect to really be her boyfriend.

Joe Armstrong was becoming an unusual combination of a fantasy knight in shining armor and the dark knight who would ruin her life, but that was still more than a year away.

March 11, 1878

Joe lay on his bunk that evening after supper and just stared at his pocket watch. He was amazed he'd been able to hang onto it, especially the first year he'd had it when he was much smaller. No one would dare take anything from him now.

One more year. In twelve months, he'd be walking out those gates, down the long access road, and then turning left on the road to Gainesville. By law, the state would provide him with fifty dollars, so he could last two or three months as he looked for a job, but he believed that the warden wouldn't give him a dime. He may not have believed that they were killing the boys who left, but that didn't mean they were following the rules either.

So, now the question would be how to get to Warwick? He'd already decided that was the only place he could go. It was a hundred miles and without any money, he'd have to get a job quickly. Luckily, he'd become a journeyman blacksmith and was now teaching the younger kids. He'd be able to work at the trade when he got to Gainesville until he amassed enough money to buy a horse and make the trip. Maybe he should take the train to Henrietta and buy a horse and saddle there.

He smiled as he realized that he was already imagining being free of the reformatory. After more than three years in this place, he was no fonder of it than when he'd first been dropped off by Sheriff Warren, and probably a lot less. Back then, Warden Smith had been in charge and it was positively benign, but now it was much more like a prison.

There had been about three or four beatings a month, but usually, it was the thugs who were punished and still bristled at being controlled. Most of the boys had retreated into shells of fear, waiting for the lash to whistle behind them. Even after the warden's canaries had been identified and shunned, there was still an overall lack of trust that was well deserved.

Joe himself hadn't felt the lash since the chow hall incident. Sam had thanked him later in the dorm room and apologized for making the mistake, but Joe had told him it was alright. It hadn't hurt that much because his skin was already scarred. Sam had believed him, but even Pete and Lippy knew it wasn't true.

Now he had just one more year to get through. His studies had reached a point where he had little else to learn from Mister Fletcher, so he used the time to read books in the library, which was in back of the classroom. The guards never objected, probably because they couldn't read that well anyway and there was no reason to confront the Armstrong kid for such a minor thing as reading.

As he looked at his watch, he slipped his fingers over the script and thought of Cassie. He wondered if she ever got to shoot a pistol as she said she would. He smiled as he thought of ten-year-old Cassie trying to get a grip on three pounds of steel in her small hands, but knew she was fourteen now and her hands were larger. She would be taller now, her freckles would probably be gone, and her hair would be in the ponytail she said she would wear. All he could remember about her is her dark brown eyes and light brown hair, so he worked those two traits into his imaginary Cassie.

Joe was sure that she'd have a real boyfriend by now, because her father had said she'd be prettier than Bessie, and although he couldn't recall Bessie's face either, he did know that he'd thought she was the prettiest girl he'd ever seen.

Joe was honest with himself enough to know that he was a tall, handsome young man with a big chest and broad shoulders that would attract young women once he was out of the reformatory, but for a reason he couldn't fathom, he wanted to meet Cassie before he even thought of another girl. Besides, when he got out in a year, he had scores to settle.

But still, the thought of seeing an almost grown-up Cassie Warren was one hell of an incentive to return to Warwick.

June 27, 1878

Earl and Glen Hogan were sitting before their campfire to discuss where they would go next. They had four other men with them now and had just committed a train robbery outside of Montague and cut into the Nations and headed west, knowing the law couldn't touch them.

They had wanted to do this job ever since they'd lost Drew, but after they'd broken up with Buck, Fred, and Hank, they didn't have enough firepower until recently. The train job was just a training lesson to see how they functioned as a group. That job had gone off even better than they had hoped, and the brothers felt it was time to revisit Warwick, just twenty-five miles southwest.

They believed that the method that Buck had used was a good one for bank robberies where the law was present, and they already knew the layout of the town, so it was a good idea. They had figured out the flaw in their last attempt when they had ridden in together wearing their matching brown leather vests. They had been spotted by the deputy and that had led to the disaster. This time, they'd run it differently.

So, as the fire crackled, Earl drew out the plan in the dirt with a weathered stick as the boys all watched. He even told them about what had gone wrong before, so they didn't repeat the mistake.

After almost an hour of talking and answering questions, the plan was set. Unlike the first time, they'd cross the river tonight and get closer to the town tomorrow and start drifting in one at a time in between the buildings.

This time, it would work, and Earl and Glen hoped that they'd kill every one of those damned badge toters.

———

The morning sun wasn't even halfway up, and the heat was already blistering the streets of Warwick, Texas.

Cassie had picked up a box of ammunition and was walking toward the eastern edge of town. She was wearing a pair of britches, which caused her mother no small amount of embarrassment. It wasn't that bad when she was eleven but now, she should be wearing at least a riding skirt as the britches showed too much of her curves. She was still thin, but she wasn't boy thin.

Cassie wasn't paying that much attention as she strode across the open ground, but as she glanced to find her target, she spotted a dust cloud coming from the north. The daughter of a long-time sheriff, especially one as smart as Cassie, understood a lot more than most girls, or boys, for that matter. She knew that there was nothing up north except the Red River and the Nations. There shouldn't be a cloud of dust coming from that direction because the road ran east and west.

She watched the cloud for another few seconds as they began to split up and she turned and walked back to town. She didn't run because she figured that if they were outlaws, they'd see her run.

Earl had seen Cassie in the distance, and when she turned, her ponytail flew out behind her.

"It's just some girl," he said to no one in particular.

He and Glen would handle the bank holdup and the other four would be the firepower and level the jail. This time, they'd walk their horses toward the sheriff's office and make sure that the lawmen were all down.

As he and Glen would be entering the bank, they kept their horses at a walk as the rest of the gang separated and would approach the town from the north but spread out, so they'd enter about two hundred yards apart.

Cassie, once she was past the first building, broke into a sprint and raced toward her father's office. She was leaving her own dust cloud as she tore down the street and hopped onto the boardwalk before rushing through the open door.

Deputy Sheehy spotted Cassie and was starting to smile when she shouted, "Deputy, I think there's a gang coming!"

He forgot about smiling, stood, and asked, “Why do you think that, Cassie?”

“I saw a big dust cloud coming from the north, and then they split up.”

Her father was in his office talking to Deputy Sanborn about an upcoming trial for theft when he heard Cassie and both men stood and quickly hustled to the outer office.

Cassie saw her father and said hurriedly, “I’m not being silly, Papa.”

“You’re never silly, Cassie. You head home,” he replied and he turned to his deputies and said, “Let’s grab Winchesters and get ready. We’re not going to be caught flat-footed this time.”

Neither replied as they stepped quickly to the gun rack and each took a Winchester and Deputy Sanborn grabbed a second rifle and handed it to the sheriff.

Cassie had already trotted out of the office and was heading home by the time the three lawmen left the jail.

Her father took a second to make sure she was going home, then said, “Dan, you start walking west, then cut north between a couple of buildings. Lou, you do the same to the east. If it’s a gang, they’ll be trying to get the bank, so I’ll stay in the middle. Cassie said they were coming from the north, so let’s hope they’re still there.”

“Okay, boss,” each man said before trotting off in opposite directions.

John felt an uneasiness about this. It was too much like that Hogan gang shootout.

He took off at a jog and didn't have to go far to find them as one of the shooters, his Winchester already drawn, was entering the space on the other end.

Both men were startled by the unexpected meeting and both quickly drew their Winchesters level. Neither had cocked their repeaters, so as they brought them up, each man thumbed the hammer back and quickly took aim, squeezing their triggers within a fraction of a second of each other.

The small space echoed with the sound of two Winchesters going off almost simultaneously. John Warren's shot arrived at his target a tiny part of a second earlier as it ripped the left side of the outlaw's face off when the bullet hit his left cheek and smashed into the thick bone skull behind it and ricocheted slightly, tumbling and taking flesh with it as it left.

Before the sheriff's bullet had reached its target, the outlaw's shot, which was much more inaccurate because it was taken from the back of a still-moving horse, slammed into the ground beside John.

Even as the small dirt volcano erupted, the horse panicked and twisted sending his rider to the dirt before the gelding ran back out of the small space as the sheriff ran behind him to see if more shooters were there.

The double shots were the catalyst for a chaotic burst of Winchester fire as both deputies emerged from between buildings and spotted three other men riding toward the town.

The three outlaws were pulling their Winchesters as the deputies opened fire.

Sheriff Warren emerged from the building and added his repeater's bark to the skirmish.

Earl and Glen couldn't believe this was happening again and both watched from horseback eight hundred yards to the northeast of the rifle battle.

"Do we go there and help?" Glen shouted.

"Wait a minute!" Earl yelled back, waiting to see who would be the next to fall.

The next to take a hit was another of the gang when Deputy Sheehy put a .44 into Roger Florissant that entered his left armpit as he tried to aim his Winchester. He dropped his rifle and fell face forward off his horse.

The last two men were facing bad odds, so one of them, Al Griffin, wheeled his horse to escape, but Deputy Sanborn's next shot drilled into his right side, just below his ribs, ripping through his liver and knocking him from his horse. He was still breathing when he hit the dirt but wouldn't be thirty seconds later.

John Peterman was the only one left and should have dropped his Winchester and thrown his hands in the air, but his internal fire was blazing, and he took aim at the sheriff, squeezing off his last shot as Deputy Sheehy's bullet shattered the right side of his skull, ending the fight.

Before he died, his .44 traveled the one hundred and forty-two feet to Sheriff Warren and slammed into his left ankle.

John screamed in pain and collapsed, dropping his Winchester as he reached for his leg.

Dan Sheehy took over and shouted, "Lou, go and get the doc. These others are all down. I'll stop John's bleeding."

Lou Sanborn nodded and raced off to get medical help for the sheriff as Deputy Sheehy trotted over to his boss and dropped to his heels.

"Boss, how are you?"

John grimaced and said, "He got me in the right ankle, Dan. Are there any more of them?"

Deputy Sheehy scanned the area and spotted two riders heading north at speed.

"There were two of them that got away, boss. I think these four were supposed to put us down before the other two robbed the bank."

"Sounds familiar, doesn't it, Dan?" he asked through clenched teeth.

"I know. I figured it was one of those Hogan gangs."

"We should've gotten those last two, but they're going to be back in the Nations soon."

As he'd been talking, Deputy Sheehy had removed his shirt and wrapped it tightly around the sheriff's boot. He wasn't sure if it was doing any good, but it seemed like the thing to do.

Less than ten minutes later, there was a good-sized crowd out in the open landscape north of Warwick as they lifted John onto a litter to take him back to the doctor's office.

After they'd gone, a shirtless Deputy Sheehy said, "Lou, let's get these horses and guns picked up. Art Bryson said he'd collect the bodies when he got his hearse harnessed."

"Okay, Dan. You'd better get a shirt on or you're gonna burn like one of the steaks my wife cooks."

Dan smiled, but couldn't make it to a laugh as he headed back to the jail where he had a spare shirt. As he passed the outlaws' horses, he stopped and looked at one of them. He'd never seen one like it before and was surprised that it was owned by an outlaw. It was all white with a tannish brown mark that covered his head and his ears.

He walked over and took the reins of the unusual animal and said, "Your new owner just got shot by your old owner, boy. John Warren is a much better man."

He then gathered it and the others before leading them between the buildings and across to the jail where he tied them at the hitchrail.

Two hours later, Minnie was sitting with her husband, holding his hand as he lay on their bed with his right foot wrapped in heavy bandages and laying on a pillow.

"How bad is it, John?" she asked for the fourth time.

"It's not good, Minnie, but it could have been worse, you know. A few inches higher and this bed would only be good for sleeping."

Minnie smiled at her husband and replied, "Leave it to you to be thinking such things at a time like this."

"I'm a man, ma'am. I think of such things all the time. You should be grateful that I only think of doing them with you."

She did laugh this time and said, "If you did otherwise, your foot is the last appendage you should worry about."

John then looked at his wife and said, "You know, if it hadn't been for Cassie, things would have been much, much worse. Most people wouldn't have paid any attention to that dust cloud, but that daughter of ours figured out what they were and warned us in time. She's a special young lady."

Minnie then surprised John when she said, "That's what Joe wrote in his last letter to her."

"I hope he's all right, Minnie. I want to be able to go out there in March and pick him up."

"If you do, it'll be because of that daughter of ours, Sheriff Warren."

Then she leaned over and kissed her husband before leaving the bedroom to find Cassie and thank her again.

March 10, 1879

Joe was returning from the smithy after his last day of work. Mister Vinton had thanked him for being the best apprentice he'd ever had and said he'd make a great blacksmith. Joe had just thanked him for teaching him and keeping him from cutting off any fingers or other valuable attachments.

His last day at the reformatory hadn't been any different from the last few hundred. No one had officially commented on his departure tomorrow, although almost every boy in the school over the past couple of days had shaken his hand.

The rule was that on the day a boy turned eighteen, he went to the warden's office, took back his paperwork that had been signed by the warden, was given his fifty dollars, and just walked out the door to make the long trek to Gainesville. Each of the boys had a card with all of their vital information, as well as transgressions and punishments issued, but the boys weren't allowed to see the cards and once they left, they'd be stored in the reformatory archives. Joe had always wondered what happened to the cards of the boys who had died, including Willie Struthers.

He entered the main building and was immediately confronted by a guard. Joe noticed that this time, the guard didn't touch him. He didn't even take out his whip either, at least not yet.

"Come with me, Armstrong," he said as he turned and walked down the hallway leading to the warden's office.

Joe followed, his only fear now was that the warden would somehow have found out that his real birthday wasn't March 11th at all, but it had been invented out of thin air by a clerk.

The guard opened the door and Joe was startled to see the warden already standing before his desk, and instead of a whip, he was holding a pistol.

Joe acted as if there wasn't any big change as he stood at attention. Maybe those tales about the boys being killed and then prepared for chow were true after all. He already made his decision that if the warden pulled back the Colt's hammer, he'd never get to pull the trigger.

The door closed behind him and Joe found himself alone with the warden. His heart was thumping against his ribs as he listened for that first click of the hammer being drawn back.

Instead, he heard the soft, but evil, threatening voice of the warden.

"Armstrong, you'll be leaving the reformatory tomorrow to return to a normal life. I expect that you will do just that, and no prison will ever see your face again. Do you think you'll do that?"

"Yes, sir," Joe replied without emotion.

"Good. I'm glad to hear it. Now I've had to do many things since I've taken over this job that I'm sure you think may have been too harsh. It's what I feel is necessary. Now before you reach civilization again, I want you to understand something.

"I know a lot of people who wear badges or black robes in this state. If you try to say one word about anything that happened in here, you'll probably be saying them to one of my friends. My friends like me, and they won't like you saying bad things about me. Do you know what will happen if you say one word, Armstrong? Within two weeks you'll either be hanged or slammed inside a much worse place than this. Do you understand?"

"Yes, sir."

"Now I could shoot you right now and no one would care. Do you understand that?"

"Yes, sir."

"So, let this be your final lesson, Armstrong. If you want to live anything resembling a normal life once you walk out those gates tomorrow, you'll forget all about this reformatory. No one cares about you worthless boys anyway. Don't be stupid. Even the biggest idiots that walked out of here understood the consequences of talking too much."

Joe didn't reply but kept his eyes focused on the back wall.

The warden returned to his desk, sat down, and laid the pistol on the desktop with the muzzle pointed at Joe's gut.

"So, tomorrow morning at ten o'clock, you will return to my office, pick up your papers and leave."

"Yes, sir."

"Dismissed."

Joe executed an about-face, opened the door, and walked down the hallway slowly, half-expecting to be shot in the back.

After making the turn into the main hallway, Joe wondered why the warden had made his threat today rather than as he was leaving tomorrow, and the answer popped into his mind even as the question was forming. He wanted to see if he'd tell someone else about the threat. He was sure that his spies were still watching and that some were still unknown to most of the boys, so he wasn't about to fall into that trap. Besides, he had never intended to tell any of the other boys about what the warden had told him. If he couldn't do anything to make things right, then it didn't matter if the other boys knew what the warden was doing.

After supper, he returned to his bunk and began sorting the few things he would take with him. He'd keep the clothes he was wearing because his other clothes were in the laundry. He'd take his pocket watch and his letters. He'd read Cassie's letters so often that the papers were all half separated at the folds. He could quote each word, and his only wish was that Cassie had ended her last letter as Bessie had ended hers, 'With Affection'. He knew it probably didn't matter, but it was Cassie, and his fantasies were all about the freckle-faced, pigtailed girl that had been his rock over the past four years.

And tomorrow, his new life as an adult would begin.

CHAPTER 5

March 11, 1879

Joe had finished his breakfast and wished he could have spent time with the other boys to shake their hands, but it was just another day for all of them.

He had gone to class for his last hours and when his pocket watch said 9:45, he stood, and despite the presence of the guard, walked to the front of the classroom and shook Mister Fletcher's hand, and thanked him profusely for all that he had taught him. Mister Fletcher just nodded, and Joe thought there was a tear in his eye as he turned and walked past the guard and out the back door of the classroom.

He walked down the main hallway and turned toward the warden's office. It was odd and surprisingly uncomfortable approaching the door without a guard present, but the guards all knew that he was no longer a resident of the reformatory and they technically had no control over him now.

Joe knocked on the door and heard Warden Phelps tell him to enter.

When he walked into the room, he wasn't surprised to find the revolver still on the desk along with some papers and an envelope.

"Have a seat, Mister Armstrong," the warden said.

Joe noticed the form of address and took a seat.

"Here are your papers, including the order sending you here. I've already signed them. This envelope contains the money that the state requires you be issued. Don't spend it foolishly."

Joe was more than just mildly surprised but didn't show it on his face as the warden slid the papers and the envelope across the desk and took the papers and the envelope, stood, and without a word to the warden, just turned and left the room, again half-expecting to be shot.

For the second time in twenty-four hours, Joe was able to breathe a sigh of relief as he turned out of the warden's office and instead of going to the main corridor, turned right again and entered the outer offices; the same ones he'd entered more than four years ago. The guard just glanced up at him but said nothing.

There was no gate just a doorway, but to Joe, it might as well have been the Gates to Heaven. He was free, and he was a man, not a boy.

Joe managed to maintain a calm face as his insides danced when he opened the door, stepped through the doorway, and closed it behind him.

He turned right and faced the long access road that was beyond the gate that they had built for the new wall. It wasn't locked, but there was a latch. He'd built the latch and the hinges for the door himself.

As he headed for the gate, he wondered if anyone would be waiting for him on the other side. He knew that there would probably be no one there, but he still had that deep hope that he'd see Sheriff Warren waiting for him with a horse and a smile.

He reached the gate, lifted the latch, and swung the heavy door wide, seeing an empty access road. His hopes sank as he closed the gate behind him and began to walk. He really didn't care if the warden was in his office with a Winchester pointed at him now. He knew he was being ridiculous in expecting anyone to be there but still, that hope had been burning brightly for a long time.

There was no shot from a Winchester just as there hadn't been any shots from the warden's pistol as Joe walked down the access road and realized how silly he was for following the access road and cut diagonally across the open ground, so he could cut some distance from his long walk.

It was four miles to Gainesville, and he should be able to get there by noon and buy himself a good lunch with the money in the envelope.

The money! He hadn't checked yet, so he quickly opened the envelope and pulled out the currency. There were five five-dollar bills. The warden had kept half the money. As the warden had told him yesterday, who could he tell?

But twenty-five dollars could still buy him lunch and some new clothes before he started looking for a job. He imagined there were at least two smithies in a town the size of Gainesville and surely, he could get a job at one of them.

Joe reached the road and began walking at a steady, but not tiring pace. It wasn't overly hot, but it was warm, and he had nothing to drink.

He'd been walking for twenty minutes when he spotted a carriage or a buggy coming south, so he stepped off the road and kept walking, deep in thought about what he could do about the warden's crimes. He really wanted to do something to protect boys like Pete and Lippy.

Joe didn't even pay attention as the buggy approached and then slowed. But when it stopped, he looked at the driver and a big smile crossed his face.

"Need a ride, son?" asked Sheriff Warren.

Joe turned to the buggy and stepped onto the road, "Hello, Sheriff. What's with the buggy?"

"My name is John. You're a man now, and I'll have to admit, you look like a hell of a man. I almost didn't recognize you. If there had been two young men walking north from that place, I'd have a bad time picking you out."

Joe was still smiling as he walked around the back of the buggy and stepped inside.

Once he was on the seat, he surprised John Warren and himself as well when he leaned across and embraced him as tears began to roll down his face.

John held onto Joe, feeling ready to bust loose himself as he wondered what had caused Joe to act this way.

It didn't last long, as Joe leaned back in the buggy and wiped his eyes.

"Sorry. I just thought no one would come."

John said, "Cassie wanted to come along, but her mother forbade her to make the long ride to Henrietta."

Joe felt his heart skip a beat or two as he asked, "How is Cassie?"

"You can ask her when we get back. Do you know that she's been writing letters to you every week?" he asked as he turned the buggy around.

"Why? They wouldn't let us send or receive letters."

"She knew that. She wrote a few letters to the governor to get a pardon for you but after he didn't reply, she just began writing letters to you instead. Bessie thinks she's crazy."

Joe laughed lightly as the buggy started north again and said, "I called her that at first, but I don't believe it."

"I know you don't. You'll be surprised to see our Cassie. She's taller now, almost as tall as me, about five feet and eight inches. She's still thin, but with those freckles gone, she's turning even prettier than I thought she would, and that was already something."

"Um…does she have any boyfriends, yet?"

John turned and grinned as he replied, "No, and it's not because they aren't interested. She just doesn't want any of them and has pretty much told the entire male population of Warwick between the ages of twelve and twenty to leave her alone because she had a boyfriend in the reformatory."

Joe smiled at the thought and remembered what he really needed to talk to the sheriff about.

"Sheriff…" he began.

"John," the sheriff interrupted.

Joe was uncomfortable calling him by his Christian name, despite being told to, so he just continued.

"When the letters stopped, it was because of a new warden named Phelps."

"I know, you put it in a letter to Cassie."

"Well, he was really a lot different from Warden Smith and issued a lot of punishment."

"I suspected as much. I knew about him when he was a deputy warden at the state prison."

"But could I ask you a question about something legal? One of the other boys gave me an answer, but I'm not sure he was right."

"Go ahead."

"The warden had the boys building a new stone wall around the reformatory and just as it was almost finished, one of the boys tried to climb the last of the lower, wooden wall and the warden shot him in the back."

John's head whipped over to look at Joe, then he asked, "He shot the kid?"

"Yes, sir. We all saw him do it from his office window with a Winchester. He still had the smoking rifle in his hands."

"When was this, Joe?"

"July 19th, 1875. I remember the day clearly."

"That's almost four years ago. Why haven't any of the boys who left the school since then reported it?"

Joe told him about Warden Phelps' warning yesterday and John just drove along listening in disbelief.

John then asked, “Would you be willing to testify to that murder despite the warning?”

“Yes, sir.”

They rode along in silence for a little while as John thought about how to deal with the problem. The warden’s warning wasn’t an idle threat. He did have a lot of contacts, but John thought they weren’t that far-ranging.

Finally, he said, “Joe, we’re going to have to take a train to Austin before we head back. Okay?”

“Yes, sir. And there’s one more thing. It’s not really important to me, but it could be to a lawyer.”

“What’s that?”

Joe pulled out his envelope and spread out the five bills.

“I thought we were supposed to get fifty dollars when we left as required by state law, but there was only twenty-five.”

John nodded and said, “You’re right, Joe. That could be almost as important as the murder charge to some of the bureaucrats.”

Joe then asked, “So, why are you driving a buggy?”

“Well, a few months ago, one of the Hogan gangs tried to hold up the bank using the same scheme that they used when you were with them. We shot the four gang members not named Hogan while the brothers ran back to the Nations. One of the four put a bullet through my left boot, and it shattered my ankle. It doesn’t work that well now, especially if I have to ride a long way, but I was lucky I didn’t lose the foot.”

"But you rode all the way to Henrietta, didn't you?"

John smiled and replied, "I wasn't about to miss picking you up, Joe. The whole family is waiting to see you again."

"Um, sher..., I mean, John, what about Bessie? I mean, in the only letter she wrote, she sounded as if she wanted to be my girlfriend, and I don't want to make her sad or anything."

"Don't worry about Bessie. She's being visited by a boy named Kit Ryerson. He's about your age and the girls all love him because he's a star boxer and wrestler. But looking at you, I think you could whip him. How on earth did you get so big?"

"I worked as a blacksmith for four years, but that didn't make me any taller."

"No, it didn't. But you need more clothes too, and you need to shave, too. I'm guessing that they didn't let you boys have razors."

"No, sir. Once a week, those that needed it were allowed to use one under the supervision of a guard, so most boys just let their beards grow. They only had six razors and they could really do some damage to your face."

"Well, we'll add a new shaving kit to your order. When we get to Gainesville, I'll send a telegram to my wife telling her I've picked you up and we'll be going to Austin, and then we'll do some shopping. Okay?"

"Okay."

As they entered Gainesville, John asked, "Joe, when we get to Warwick, what are you planning on doing?"

"I'm not sure yet. I can work in the smithy, but I know I have to go and find the Hogans and make them pay for what they did to my mother. I know I'm still nowhere ready to do it yet, though."

"When I took the bullet in my ankle, the doc thought he'd have to take off my foot, but I wouldn't let him. It healed but healed funny, which is why I can't ride a horse that well. They wanted me to hire another deputy after they couldn't convince me to give up the job. I've been holding off making that hire until I talked to you. It'll give you a source of income, and I could train you how to track and how to deal with them. I still don't believe it's a very smart thing to do. There will only be one of you and we don't even know where they are."

Joe asked, "If I become a deputy, after a while, can I just become like a bounty hunter, so I'm not limited by that stupid Red River border they keep crossing to get safe?"

John wanted to tell him no, but knew that it wouldn't change his mind, and not carrying a badge meant he could go wherever the Hogans went.

"It's a free country, Joe. A man can quit a job whenever he wants."

Joe nodded and said, "Then I'll be your new deputy, boss. I'll do whatever you need me to do but when I feel I'm ready, I'll go after those bastards."

John then asked, "What if Cassie asks you not to go?"

"She's only fifteen, boss. I know she's a lot older inside, but I haven't even seen her without her freckles, so she might change her mind about wanting me as a boyfriend."

John laughed as he pulled up to the livery where he'd rented the buggy and said, “Good luck with that.”

They both climbed out of the buggy and left it with the liveryman, who gave John a receipt. He was, after all, doing this as part of his official duties.

They walked to the diner before their shopping and John ate normally as he watched Joe demolish a huge steak in just minutes and didn't slow down even after the apple pie.

“Hungry?” John asked when they were finished.

“I'm always hungry, although I believe my stomach is close to exploding at any moment.”

John laughed and remarked, “Your vocabulary and grammar have improved remarkably, Joe. How is your reading and writing?”

Joe looked at the sheriff and said, “Well, shucks, sheriff. I still ain't got past figurin' out my letters and don't be askin' me about cypherin', neither.”

John laughed harder as he paid for their meal and took his receipt.

“I could have paid for that, boss. I have my money.”

“You aren't going to spend a dime of that. The money in that envelope is evidence. Don't worry about money, Joe. I may still collect receipts, but that shootout with the Hogan gang put five hundred dollars into my bank account, and I only got one of them.”

“Well, after I get my money back, I'll pay for things, too.”

"Maybe. Let's go and send that telegram."

Joe nodded and scooped the last biscuit from the table as they left the diner and headed out to the streets of Gainesville. He noticed how the sheriff limped slightly as he walked, obviously trying to hide the pain it caused him. Joe added that to the list of transgressions committed by the Hogans.

When they got to the Western Union office, John walked to the long side shelf and began to write his telegram to Minnie. He wasn't surprised when Joe pulled out a sheet and began to write as well. He was curious about what Joe was writing but knew who the recipient would be.

John carried his message to the telegrapher and paid his sixty cents as Joe stepped up behind him and gave the telegrapher his message, which conveniently came out to forty cents. John handed the man a dollar and then they waited while he tapped out the two messages.

MINNIE WARREN WARWICK TEXAS

PICKED UP VERY IMPRESSIVE JOE
NEED TO GO TO AUSTIN
WILL EXPLAIN IN LETTER
TELL CASSIE HOLD HER LETTERS

SHERIFF JOHN WARREN GAINESVILLE TEXAS

After handing John his message, he tapped out Joe's shorter note.

CASSIE WARREN WARWICK TEXAS

COMING TO WARWICK AS DEPUTY
HOPE BOYFRIEND POSITION STILL OPEN

JOE ARMSTRONG GAINESVILLE TEXAS

Joe knew that the sheriff was curious, so once the telegrapher handed him back his handwritten message, he just gave it to the sheriff who read it, smiled, and handed it back.

As they left the telegraph office, John said, "Be careful what you wish for, Joe."

As Joe and John were hunting for clothes for Joe in Gainesville, a messenger arrived at the Warren house and knocked on the door. He didn't have to wait long before Cassie opened the door, almost weakening Billy Hempstead's knees.

She looked at him for five seconds before he said, "Um…I have a message for you and one for your mother, Miss Warren."

"Thank you, Billy," she replied as she snatched the messages from his fingers and gave him a nickel before closing the door.

She shouted, "Mama, we have two telegrams," as she walked quickly toward the kitchen.

Bessie still went to school, more for the time she could spend with her friends than the education she really didn't need, and Cassie spent most of her time with her mother.

"Are they from your father?" she asked as she turned, wiping her forehead with her apron.

"One is. The other is from Joe," she replied as she held out her mother's message.

Minnie took her telegram and after reading the short message, she asked, "I wonder why he's going to Austin?"

Cassie didn't answer, aside from the rhetorical nature of her mother's question. She read the first communication she'd had with Joe in four years and it thrilled her more than she would have expected, and she felt guilty for it. But behind the thrill, was the ominous realization that the day she'd been dreading for four years was about to arrive. Joe Armstrong would be returning to Warwick.

When she looked up at her mother's curious face, Cassie held out her telegram and accepted her father's message.

Minnie quickly scanned the telegram and said, "Wow! That's a big surprise, isn't it? After four years without a single bit of communication between the two of you and he's asking if the position of boyfriend is still open."

"I know," was her short response.

"Well, my biggest question is why he's going to Austin."

"I'll bet it has something to do with what Joe told him about the reformatory. What else could it be?"

Minnie nodded and turned to finish baking her welcome home coffee cake but wondered how long it would remain uneaten. She could always feed some of it to Mary and her husband, Ned O'Neill, the same boy her husband had locked up for kissing her years before. Then Bessie would probably invite Kit Ryerson over, too. Bessie seemed fond of the boy but Minnie, despite trying to like him, never did. He seemed to care too much about himself and not enough about her daughter.

She wondered how Joe had turned out. For John to say he was very impressive in a telegram could mean many things. But in Cassie's message, he said he was going to be a deputy. John had held the position open for months now and said he'd only offer it to Joe if he thought he'd measure up. He must have measured up and then some.

Her other question was how would he measure up to Cassie? That was much more difficult for her to estimate. She had a difficult time understanding Cassie and when she'd seen Cassie read Joe's telegram, she thought her youngest daughter would be a lot happier.

———

After Joe left the store carrying a large bag with new boots, a Stetson, all new clothes, and his first shaving kit, he and John had supper at the hotel restaurant before going to their shared room.

Once inside, John said, "You can have the bed on the outside. I'll stay near the door. That way, if there's a fire, I get out first."

Joe grinned and replied, "I'll be out the window before you get the door open."

John laughed and dropped his saddlebags on his chosen bed before taking off his hat and hanging it on one of the hooks near the door.

Joe poked his mattress and said, "I don't know if I'll be able to sleep on anything this soft."

John was taking off his gunbelt as he asked, "How bad was it, Joe?"

Joe didn't reply but unbuckled his belt and let his britches drop as he took off his shirt. Once he had his shirt off, he turned to show John Warren his back.

The sheriff's eyes were enormous as he stared at the stripes across his back and legs.

"What did you do to deserve that?" he asked quietly.

Joe pulled up his pants and replied, "Most of it was when I asked the teacher if he could post a letter for me in Gainesville."

"Joe, tell me you're joking. Who did that to you? Was it a guard?"

"I was in the warden's office and he used his silver-tipped whip while the guard used his regular leather whip. You can still see the difference. The deeper ones were from the metal. There are two other ones that I took for a smaller boy who was about to be struck because he accidentally gave one of the boys a second helping of creamed corn."

John closed his eyes. He had no idea it had been this bad and felt incredibly guilty for leaving Joe at that place when he could have avoided doing it at all.

"I'm so sorry, Joe. I should never have left you there."

As he was putting on his shirt, Joe replied, "It's not your fault. You were doing what the law required you to do. If there is any fault in all this, it belongs to me for being so naïve, and to the judge for lacking humanity. You are blameless."

John was still finding it difficult to believe he was talking to the same boy he'd dropped off four years ago. He sounded better educated than he did, and he'd finished all of his years of schooling which was rare at the time, at least for boys.

"You've learned a lot, Joe."

"Maybe I've learned by reading so much, but those few days with you taught me much more and set me on the path I needed to choose. Do you know that I began learning when I was sitting in the dust at the bottom of that hill and you told a member of your posse that if he touched me, you'd throw him in jail? I couldn't believe you said that, and it began to open my eyes. It wasn't until I was lying in solitary confinement for two weeks with these gouges on my back and legs that I realized the value of what you taught me."

John sighed and asked, "They threw you into solitary confinement with those wounds being untreated?"

"Yes, sir. But I survived that and now I'm here talking to you. And I swear to God, I'll never disappoint you, Sheriff John Warren."

John nodded slowly and said softly, "I don't believe you ever could, Joe."

After their heartfelt talk, each of them used some of the hotel stationery to write a letter, both going to the same location.

John glanced over at Joe as he wrote and noticed what a neat hand he had now. It wasn't the soft, feminine script that Bessie or Minnie used, but closer to the precise handwriting that Cassie used. He wondered if it was because Joe had seen her handwriting, or if they were already that much alike. He had already seen many of Cassie's mannerisms and behavior in Joe in just the few hours they'd been together. Maybe he really was the only man that Cassie would ever marry. Time would tell.

At 9:20 the next morning, Joe and John boarded the southbound train to Austin. It was a ten-hour trip, and they wouldn't be arriving until almost eight o'clock that night, so they were able to talk a lot during the time they spent on the train.

John filled in Joe about what had happened with the Hogans since he'd been in the reformatory and all of the family news, centering on Cassie naturally. He went into detail about the gunfight with the gang that had crippled him, and how they'd discovered that the two Hogans that had escaped were Earl and Glen. He told Joe about Buck's loss of his gang at the hands of the Texas Rangers and how he'd managed to drygulch two of them and steal their horses and weapons.

Joe explained how Warden Phelps ran the reformatory and that the guards enforced even the slightest violations with the whip. He did admit that some of the methods controlled the bullying from the upstairs crowd, but the punishment delivered never seemed to vary by the severity of the offense.

It was only when he was talking about having to bury Willie Struthers that he finally mentioned something that he'd almost forgotten...the graveyard.

"Wait a minute, Joe. You said they just buried boys in a graveyard in back?"

"Yes, sir. We lost seven boys just building the wall from accidents or dying of thirst. We were made to bury them in back. When I buried Willie, I had to dig his grave, and then I accidentally pulled the body on top of me because I couldn't lower it down properly. The guard thought it was funny and made me take his pants and shoes so they could be reissued."

John felt his stomach curdle with the idea of having a dead body fall on you in a grave. He looked over at Joe and wondered how the hell anyone could get over such a thing, but when subjected to as many almost daily terrors as he'd been through, he only could hope that Joe hadn't grown immune to it.

By the time they reached Austin, John was emotionally drained listening to the horrors that had been inflicted on the boys in the reformatory, and what it made even more devastating was the almost casual way that Joe had told him. He knew that Joe was far from callous, because of how he'd wept when he first got into the buggy, *but how much damage had that bastard Phelps and the guards done to those boys?*

———

"Does it hurt a lot when you walk?" Joe asked as he and the sheriff strode along the Austin boardwalk toward the state offices.

"It's not pleasant, and it's really annoying with its clicks and snaps, but if I don't think about it, it's not too bad."

"We could have hired a carriage, boss."

"It's only half a mile, Joe. I need to walk some of the time."

“Do you think the attorney general will see us?”

“Either he will or one of his assistants will. What happens after that is the question. I doubt if Phelps has that many friends down here, but there’s always a chance he has a brother-in-law or something that I don’t know about. Just because someone doesn’t share a last name doesn’t mean he’s not kin.”

“I used to think I was a Hogan.”

“You’re a lot more of a Warren than a Hogan, but you should be happy being an Armstrong. I never was able to track down any more of the family, though.”

As they entered the state office building, Joe said, “I found one.”

John glanced at Joe and asked in surprise, “You found an Armstrong relative?”

Joe grinned and said, “No, sir. I found a family.”

John grinned back and checked the board, found the office of the Attorney General of the State of Texas and they both crossed the large foyer and entered the right-side corridor.

Five minutes later, they were being ushered into the office of assistant attorney general Sam H. Pell.

“Have a seat, gentleman,” the attorney general said as he stood behind his desk.

Mister Pell shared many of the physical characteristics of Warden Phelps, as both were average height but stocky with the same facial hair arrangement. But that’s where the similarities ended. Mister Pell’s eyes weren’t kind, but they were honest, searching eyes that hopefully reflected his inner nature.

Sheriff Warren and Joe took the only two seats in front of the desk as Mister Pell asked, “What can I do for you, Sheriff?”

“Mister Pell, over four years ago, there was an attempted bank robbery by the Hogan brothers in Warwick. We drove them off but caught and hanged one of them. During the pursuit, we found a thirteen-year-old boy standing on a hill shouting at us. He turned and fell down the hill and I had him restrained as we engaged the Hogans.

“The boy had been captured by the Hogan brothers eleven years earlier when they kidnapped two sisters to use as their personal prostitutes. Both women died within two years, leaving the boy to believe he was their youngest brother. It was only when he was in jail facing trial for murder that the Hogan brother that we had captured told him the truth about his mother. The Hogan was hanged, and the boy was sent to the state reformatory.

“That young man left the reformatory on Monday and is sitting beside me now. I am so impressed with him that when we return to Warwick, he will become my third deputy.”

“I heard about that robbery, but not the sentences. That’s the background, so what brings you to my office?”

John looked over at Joe and nodded.

Joe said, “When I first arrived at the reformatory, it was run by Warden Smith and even though it was still a reformatory, it was a place where we could learn and be good men when we left. Then he was replaced by Mister Phelps.”

The attorney general knew Phelps personally, so as soon as Joe began his story, he had an idea of what to expect. But all he was expecting were tales of beatings and cruelty, which weren't worth prosecuting. He'd actually been in several meetings where they had discussed Mister Smith's too-benevolent administration and wasn't surprised when Phelps was appointed to replace him.

His almost blasé attitude as he listened changed radically when Joe reached the story about the building of the wall and mentioned the deaths of four of the boys that first month.

"Excuse me, son. Did you say that four boys died and were buried on the grounds of the reformatory?"

"Yes, sir. There were four that month and three in July who died because of dehydration. That doesn't include Willie Struthers."

"Who was Willie Struthers?"

"Willie was one of the tough kids from the second floor. I think he was sixteen. He must have thought that once the wall was built, he'd have another two years of Warden Phelps and didn't want to wait that long. So, he tried to climb the temporary wall we'd already finished, and when he got onto the barbed wire, Warden Phelps shot him from his office window with his Winchester."

"Were guards there?"

"Yes, sir. They just watched him as he ran and jumped onto the wall. Any one of them could have stopped him from even reaching the wall. We figured that they knew the warden was there and were told not to intervene."

"How many of the boys witnessed the shooting?"

“About thirty.”

“And none of the ones who left the reformatory reported this?”

“More than half left in the time since the shooting. It was the nineteenth of July in ’75. Everyone wondered why the law never came to punish the warden for murdering Willie. Some figured he could do it legally and others thought that nobody really cared. Some thought that the warden was shooting the boys who turned eighteen as they left the reformatory. I didn’t find out how he kept it quiet until the day before I left.”

Mr. Pell asked quietly, “How did he manage to keep it and the other deaths quiet?”

Joe explained the warning and it reeked of the truth to the attorney general. It sounded like something Phelps would do. But shooting a boy in an almost premeditated fashion was beyond what he could believe.

After Joe finished his explanation of the threat, Sam Pell asked, “Do you know where the body is buried?”

“Yes, sir. I was forced to bury him myself.”

“Why did they have you do it?”

Joe explained what had happened after Willie was shot, and just as John Warren had felt sickened when Joe told how he’d been momentarily trapped under the corpse, Mister Pell felt nauseated himself.

“Were there any other murders after Willie’s death?”

“Not directly, sir. Some boys died when the guards or the warden whipped them too much, but they usually died a day or two later. Others died two weeks later because of the infections. I was lucky. I never got an infection."

"You were whipped?"

Before he could answer, John said, "Joe stand and take off your shirt."

Joe nodded and after he'd removed his shirt and turned to show Mister Pell his scars, he said, "The real bad ones are on my thighs. The deeper ones are from the warden because his whip had silver tips that cut worse."

The attorney general stared at the scars and said quietly, "You can put your shirt on now. What did you do to earn those scars?"

Joe was buttoning his shirt as he replied, "I asked our teacher if he could post a letter for me in Gainesville, and one of the other boys that the warden was using as a spy told him."

The lawyer's eyebrows peaked as he asked, "Why couldn't you just post a letter from the reformatory post office?"

"Mister Phelps shut it down. He said that we were planning on some kind of revolt."

"Alright. Go ahead and finish your story."

It took Joe another fifteen minutes as Mister Pell sat back and listened attentively with his fingers folded under his chin. This was much, much worse than he'd originally expected. The multiple deaths were murders but couldn't be proven. Willie Struthers' could be if his body was exhumed, but he didn't believe it was likely. What the young man was telling him was a political disaster. If this story hit the newspapers, heads would roll.

It was only at the very end of Joe's narrative that Assistant Attorney General Sam H. Pell saw a path through the political minefield.

"He only gave you twenty-five dollars?" he asked as he sat up quickly.

Joe already had taken out the envelope and had it in his hands as he replied, "Yes, sir. I have the envelope and the bills he gave me right here."

He held out the envelope to Mister Pell who took it and slid out the five bills.

As he examined the notes, he said, "I'll keep these if you don't mind. I'll have the treasurer issue you fifty dollars in accordance with the law and then I need to go and talk to my boss."

John then asked, "What are you going to do about this?"

"We have to get him out of there, but it is going to have to be much quieter than you'd probably like it to be. Let me go and talk to the attorney general. Stop and see my secretary outside and give him this note. He'll direct you to the office of the state treasurer."

Mister Pell quickly wrote out a note authorizing the disbursement and let it dry as he formulated his approach to the attorney general.

After he handed the note to Joe, they stood and before leaving the office, John said, "You know, Mister Pell, all of this could have been avoided if the governor had responded to any of the letters my daughter had written to him asking him to review Joe's sentence."

“She wrote a letter to the governor?”

“No, sir. She wrote dozens of letters to the governor. No one seemed to care.”

“I’ll mention that tidbit to my boss when I see him.”

Mister Pell shook the sheriff’s hand and when he shook Joe’s he said, “I’m sorry for all that happened to you, Joe. We’ll see if we can fix it.”

Joe just nodded as the three men left the room. Joe and John stopped at the secretary’s desk as Mister Pell hurried off to see his boss. The secretary read the note and escorted them to the office of the treasurer.

The assistant attorney general’s secretary talked to the assistant state treasurer’s secretary who took the note to the assistant accounting clerk in the next office. He filled out a voucher and gave it to the assistant cashier who put five ten-dollar notes in an envelope and had the assistant cashier sign a receipt. The process was then reversed with the receipt and the envelope of cash passing hands until ten minutes later, Joe signed the receipt and was handed the envelope of cash by the secretary to the assistant state treasurer. It was a model of bureaucratic efficiency.

After Joe put the envelope in his pocket, John asked the secretary, “What do we do now?”

“Come back with me until Mister Pell returns from his conference. It won’t take long.”

The three men then returned to the assistant attorney general’s office and each took a seat to see what, if anything, would happen.

As Joe sat next to Sheriff Warren, he stared at the floor, thinking about the meeting with Mister Pell. He had a sinking feeling that Warden Phelps was going to get away with murder. The attorney just didn't seem angry enough when he talked about Willie's murder. The outrage simply wasn't there.

Joe Armstrong was beginning to understand the difference between the law and justice.

They waited for another forty minutes while Joe and John sporadically asked and answered each other's questions about the possible outcome of the visit before Mister Pell returned with a dusty, tough-looking hombre who looked as if he'd just stepped down from a horse after a long, hard ride.

"Come into my office again, gentlemen," the assistant attorney general said as he passed.

Sheriff Warren and Joe both stood, followed the other two men and Joe closed the door behind him.

Once inside, Mister Pell sat behind his desk and indicated that Joe and John both sit.

Joe glanced at the hard man still standing who seemed to be staring at him before he took his seat.

"This filthy man that I brought with me is Captain Bull Raskin of the Texas Rangers. He wants to talk to you about a different matter when I'm finished. He's only interested in the reformatory issue as a possible job for another company of Rangers.

"After talking with my boss, we both agreed that if we prosecuted the warden for the murder of Willie Struthers, there would not only be the very good possibility that we'd lose the case but there would be a public outcry by the same people who insisted that he be placed in that position because of Warden Smith's failure to enforce discipline as they understood it."

As Joe began to protest, Sam Pell held up his hand.

"I know you disagree with that decision, Joe, but hear me out. Understand that a lot of folks believe that the reformatory is just a prison for boys and should be run like one. If we charge Phelps with the murder, it would be almost impossible for us to get a jury to convict him when all his defense attorney would claim was that a possible murderer was about to be set loose on society if the warden hadn't acted.

"Now we all know that it was murder, but I don't believe we'd stand much of a chance of conviction. The same applies to the other deaths while building the wall and after being whipped. But the fact that he was taking money that was supposed to be given to boys leaving the place is different. Those same men who would agree with Warden Phelps' treatment of the boys would want him hanged for taking the money that the state gets from their taxes.

"So, what we will do is go to the reformatory with your affidavit and with the affidavits of other boys who had recently left the school to show a pattern of embezzlement and have a talk with Mister Phelps. We'll use the murder charge as a threat to make him agree to pleading guilty to a three-year sentence for theft and embezzlement. He may believe that he'd be found not guilty of the murder, but it's a risk he may not be willing to take. Once he's out of there, we'll appoint a new warden and replace all of the guards. We can't send Mister Smith back there because of appearances."

Joe's temper was growing, but he held it in check as he asked, "Three years? That's all he'd get for doing what he did?"

"Three years in the state prison is a long time for most men, but three years for a man who had been the assistant warden is almost a death sentence."

Joe understood and just replied, "Oh."

Mister Pell then said, "This will all take some time for things to come together. I may need to contact you to return to Gainesville for a trial, but I don't believe it will come to that if we can intimidate Phelps. Men like him are nothing more than bullies who use their authority as a weapon. I think he'll cave. Right now, I need you to go to my outer office and write out your affidavit that my secretary will notarize."

Then he looked at John and said, "By the way, I mentioned the letters your daughter wrote to the governor to the lieutenant governor and he'll tell the governor this afternoon. Captain Raskin will want to talk to you after you finished writing the affidavit."

As they stood, Captain Raskin finally ended his silence as he said in a gravelly voice, "I'd rather talk to you boys first before you start writin'."

John turned to his fellow lawman and said, "We can do that outside, Captain."

He nodded and the three men exited Mister Pell's office to the outer office where the secretary had already prepared the necessary paperwork and had a pen and ink ready for Joe.

Sheriff Warren held up a finger to let the secretary know there would be a delay as the three visitors all took seats with Captain Raskin in the center.

He looked at Joe before saying, "I was headin' to talk to the attorney general when I bumped into Mister Pell who told me that you spent most of your life with the Hogan brothers. Is that true?"

"Yes, sir. I grew up with them, believing them to be my brothers. I only learned differently when the one that was going to hang, Drew Hogan, wanted to anger me by telling me the truth of how I'd come to live with them."

"So, you can identify each of the ones that are still alive?"

"If I can't, then no one can."

"That's what I figured. Now I don't know how much you heard about what those boys have been doin' since you've been in the reformatory, but they're playin' hell with the folks in northwest Texas. You can figure out how hard it is for us to track 'em down with as much territory as there is up there. They got a habit of goin' to ground either in the Nations or takin' a farmhouse and disappearin' for a while. What makes it worse is that they just don't stick out so much. Hell, one could be walkin' around in this place right now and I wouldn't know him.

"The worst of the bunch is the oldest, Buck. His gang was all wiped out by four of our Rangers in September of '76, but Buck got away and killed two of our boys. He took their horses and weapons and when we found their bodies, we found he had their badges, too. We spent another month lookin' for that bastard before we had to break off the chase. When we get a chance, we sent some men out there to check out reports, but we haven't found him."

Joe asked, "I already told Sheriff Warren that I'd be his deputy until I thought I was ready to chase them down. Then I'll resign from being a deputy, so I'm not limited by where I go. I want to get them all, Captain."

"I was gonna ask if you'd join us and help us find 'em, but can I guess you wouldn't want to do that?"

"No, sir. As good as the Rangers are, they still have to obey the letter of the law. As a bounty hunter, I can do what I need to do."

"Well, we kinda ignore some of those letters, but I'll tell you what. If you find 'em, you send a telegram to the closest Ranger company and they'll send you some help. I'll give you a list before you go."

"Okay, Captain. I appreciate it," Joe replied as he stood and walked to the secretary's desk to write his affidavit.

As Joe wrote, Captain Raskin and Sheriff Warren swapped information about the Hogan brothers, and each added valuable information that might put an end to their scourge.

Four hours after their meeting with Mister Pell, Joe and Sheriff Warren were on the northbound afternoon train to Henrietta. Even though it was a shorter distance as the crow flies, the railroad's tracks added another four hours to the trip they had taken from Gainesville to Austin, so they wouldn't be arriving until almost six o'clock in the morning.

Once they were underway, John finally asked. "Are you satisfied with Mister Pell's decision, Joe?"

"I'm not sure. I think he should hang for what he did, but I guess the law doesn't treat everyone fairly, does it?"

"No, it doesn't. You should never have been sent to that reform school. I can't tell you how many times I regretted leaving you there."

"No, that's alright. You had to do your job, just like Mister Pell has to do his. I just wonder if Warden Phelps will accept the deal. Why should he? He's got to know that if he gets sent to that prison he won't live long."

"He may be arrogant enough to believe that the guards he knew when he was assistant warden will protect him. We won't know for a few weeks, though. Mister Pell needs to track down some other boys who will provide him with affidavits about the money."

"Will they do it? Mister Phelps' threat was very real."

"They'll have two reasons to do it. First, they'll only be saying that they only received half of the money that was due them, and secondly, they'll get the extra twenty-five dollars."

Joe laughed and said, "I'd forgotten about the money."

"When we get to Henrietta, do you want to stay there a day to rest or ride back right away?"

"I'd rather start riding, but it's up to you, boss."

"I want to set out within a couple of hours, right after we have breakfast."

"Okay, but I'll pay this time. I have fifty dollars now."

"I accept your offer, Deputy Moneybags."

Joe laughed again and then just relaxed as he looked out the train window, saw his reflection in the glass, and rubbed his chin. He needed a shave already.

———

Sheriff Warren was snoozing on the bench across the aisle as the train hurtled north, but Joe was having a hard time sleeping although he had drifted off a couple of times. It seemed as if the trains stopped every two minutes to take on water or coal, but he knew it was at least an hour or so between stops.

There were so many things running through his mind now that he wasn't behind those walls any longer. Becoming Sheriff Warren's deputy was an easy choice because as much as he learned from him after just a few days, he was certain he'd learn even more over a few months. He expected to be leaving Warwick to chase after the Hogans before 1880 arrived.

Even before he'd listened to Captain Raskin talk about how difficult it would be to track them down, he was under no illusion about the enormity of the undertaking. He was even beginning to waffle about the decision to chase after them. Part of him really wanted to stay and work for the sheriff and start a new life. He'd be protecting people and stopping men like the Hogans. He barely had any memories at all of his mother and cursed himself for having such a weak mind.

But the still haunting memory of Drew almost endlessly describing what he, his brothers, and their father did to his mother and her sister was so branded into his mind that whenever he began drifting into letting his desire to seek retribution and justice for his mother wane, that memory renewed his resolve.

Mixed in among the thoughts of the Hogans and being a deputy were the recurring thoughts of Cassie. He thought it was silly that he wasn't afraid of chasing after a bunch of murderers at the age of eighteen, but he was scared to meet a fifteen-year-old girl. Because that was what he was. He was afraid to see her.

Joe could remember her voice more than her face, but it was her letters as brief and as few as they were, that had set her into his mind. Cassie Warren was all he had through those hard years in the reformatory. When he'd been lying on his stomach in solitary with those gouges in his thighs and back, it was thoughts of Cassie that kept the pain at bay.

He just didn't believe that it was fair to her to make her into such a critical figure in his life when he barely knew her. It was fine when he knew he wouldn't be seeing her for years, or even months. But now, it was just days away and he was scared.

The sheriff and Joe stepped down from the train almost exactly as the sun first began to peek over the eastern horizon, throwing exaggerated shadows across the roads and any other flat area.

"Where do we go now?" Joe asked.

"After I send a quick telegram to my wife telling her we are on our way, we eat some real food and then go pick up the horses. I packed some trail food for the ride back and if we push it, we can make it in one day."

"Really?"

"Sure. We keep the horses at a medium or slow trot, we'll get into Warwick in time for a late supper."

"Then let's get some breakfast," Joe said with a grin as they stepped off the platform and onto the boardwalk.

Thirty-five minutes later, the two men were walking to the livery where John had left the two horses. He was already smiling in anticipation of the surprise that Joe would have when they entered the big barn.

As they walked in, Joe had to wait for the sheriff to tell the liveryman to bring their tack so the horses could be saddled. As he stood in the barn his eyes were gripped by an almost white horse with a tan patch on his head that covered his ears. It was the most unusual horse he'd ever seen, so he walked to the gelding and began to rub his neck.

"You sure are a different boy, aren't you? You look like a pinto, but there aren't patches anywhere else."

The horse then turned to look at him and Joe was startled. He had blue eyes. He never knew horses could even have blue eyes.

"He's a handsome feller, ain't he?" asked the liveryman as he approached lugging a saddle.

"He sure is. What kind of a horse is he?"

John said, "He's what they call a Mexican hat pinto, and there aren't many of them around. Fred here offered me two hundred dollars for him."

Joe's head snapped around to look at the sheriff as he asked, "*He's yours?*"

"No, sir. He's yours," John replied with a grin.

Joe was too stunned to reply as his mouth just opened and stayed that way.

John laughed and began saddling his bay gelding as Fred threw a blanket over the pinto.

Joe recovered, at least enough to help saddle his new horse, and was so overwhelmed he didn't even pay attention to the Winchester in the scabbard.

As they were leading the two saddled horses out of the barn, Joe asked, "Boss, why did you give him to me? What about Drew's horse?"

The sheriff was painfully mounting, so he didn't reply right away but once in the saddle, he answered, "The pinto was being ridden by one of Earl and Glen's gang when they tried to rob the bank a few months back when I got shot in the ankle. Dan Sheehy saved him for me, but as soon as I saw him, I decided that you should have him. We sold Drew's horse in an auction."

Joe had mounted quickly, and they were already riding west when he noticed the Winchester in the scabbard but didn't say anything yet as he evaluated the pinto.

John watched with smiling eyes as Joe sped up, turned, slowed down, and put the smaller horse through all sorts of maneuvers before settling back next to the sheriff.

"You handle that horse really well for someone who hasn't ridden in five years, Joe."

"The horses that I was given were always the worst of the bunch, so I had to learn how to control them. This one almost reads my mind."

"That Winchester is yours, too. He was on the pinto, and the Colt and gunbelt in the right saddlebag are yours, too. It came from the same source."

Joe twisted in the saddle, opened the right saddlebag, and pulled out the gunbelt. He fastened it around his waist and snugged it down tight. He'd see if they could get some target practice in on the way back, but it wasn't that important yet.

He had time now.

Minnie had just closed the front door, quickly read the short telegram, and shouted, "Cassie, they're on their way from Henrietta."

Cassie rapidly finished washing her hands and grabbed a towel and waited for her mother to reach the kitchen.

When she did, Cassie asked, "When do you think they'll arrive? Tomorrow afternoon?"

"If I know your father, and I do, I imagine we'll be seeing them this evening."

"That's almost sixty miles from Henrietta. Isn't that bad for his ankle?"

"He takes his left foot out of the stirrup when it starts to hurt too much. I think he'll be fine."

Cassie nodded and said, "Mama, I have to confess that I'm really nervous about this."

"You'd be a fool not to be, sweetheart. Is there anything in particular?"

Cassie poured some coffee into two cups and handed one to her mother before they both sat down at the kitchen table.

"Mama, I've probably passed a thousand words in total to Joe, including those in the letters, and he thought I was crazy after the first hundred. I barely know him, and he barely knows me, yet he expects me to be his girlfriend."

"That's your fault, isn't it, Cassie?"

"Yes, I know it is but when I said that, it was because I knew he was going away and I thought he would need something, even if it was from a silly ten-year-old girl. I liked him, and I'll admit to being thrilled when I read his telegram, but I feel like such a phony. I'm not, well, I'm not Bessie."

"Would you want to be Bessie? She likes boys and seems awfully fond of Kit Ryerson. I know you've shunned every boy that's tried to invite you to a social or barn dance."

"I know I have, Mama. It's because I don't want to stay here. You know that, and Joe has been my shield since he left. I really never expected him to return."

Minnie was surprised by her reply and asked, "So, what are you going to tell Joe?"

"I don't know. Maybe he'll see what a child I am and just treat me that way. I guess I'm getting way ahead of myself."

"You are, but you surely don't think of yourself as a child. Do you? Your father and I haven't seen you as a child since you were seven years old."

"No, but he might. I suppose all I can do is wait and see."

"That's all we can do, sweetheart. Now let's make another coffee cake for your father now that we know he's coming home."

Cassie smiled, finished off her coffee, and as she stood, she said, "As long as Kit doesn't get any."

Minnie laughed and then said, “He ate almost all of the last one. He didn’t even leave any for Ned or Mary. That went over well.”

———

John pulled them to a stop around ten o’clock for a short break to let the horses rest and get something to drink. His ankle was bothering him, but he didn’t let it show as he dismounted.

Joe did notice the slight grimace when the sheriff had to put all of his weight on his left ankle and asked, “Boss, why don’t you get down on the right side?”

John led stepped onto the ground and stretched his back as he replied, ‘Because I’m not a lady riding sidesaddle.”

“I’ve seen men mount on the right side when they had to before.”

“Liar,” John said but with a smile.

“Can I ask you something, man-to-man?” Joe asked.

“Sure. You’re bigger than me, you know.”

Joe ignored the comment and said, “You saw Cassie just a week or so ago, and I haven’t seen her since she was ten. We’ve exchanged a few letters since then, but nothing in the past four years. I know you told me she’s pretty and everything, but I’m afraid that I’ve used the memory of Cassie so much while I was in the reformatory that I’ve created an image of her that will be hard to match.

“When I was in the worst of situations, not knowing if I’d live another day, it was the thought of Cassie that kept me alive.

The last thing I want is to hurt her feelings. I need to know what she expects of me. What does she really think?"

John rested his left hand on his horse's saddle seat as he replied, "If I knew what Cassie really thinks, I'd be as smart as she is, and I'm not. I don't know anyone who is, except maybe you. As to what she expects of you, well at least I have an idea in that department.

"Cassie has always been very frustrated by being a really smart person and a girl to boot. She believes with good cause, that she's trapped in a life where all she can do is get married and have babies. I think she wants to do something with her life. She told me when I returned from dropping you off that she felt bad for saying some of the things she did.

"She does like you, and I'm pretty sure she's done what you've done. She's imagined you as a tall, smart and handsome young man who could help her with her dreams. I don't think you'll disappoint her, Joe. But at the same time, I believe she's concerned about her own physical immaturity. She's tall and thin and sometimes envious of Bessie, who is shorter and more, well, more womanly in appearance."

"So, what do you think I should do?"

"You just let the future arrive and deal with things as they arrive just as you did in the reformatory and as you will when you go after the Hogans."

Joe nodded and said, "Thanks, boss. I think I can face Cassie now."

John laughed, mounted, and said, "You don't have any choice, Joe."

Joe mounted the pinto and was smiling as they set off.

"Mama, we have mail," Cassie said as she walked back to the kitchen where her mother was taking the new coffee cake from the oven.

As she stepped down the hallway, Cassie stared at the envelope addressed to her. The script was so neat and precise, she found it hard to believe it was from Joe, but his name was on the return address, so it had to be his handwriting.

She held out the letter from her father as Minnie set the coffee cake on the cooling rack and dropped the heavy gloves to the counter. After she felt the letter leave her fingers, Cassie sat at the table and waited for her mother to join her.

"Mama, look at the handwriting on my letter," she said as she slid the unopened envelope across the table.

"Oh, my. That is amazing, isn't it? He couldn't even read or write when he left here. I still remember those first letters he sent from the reformatory that were printed in childish block letters."

She handed the letter back to Cassie, who then slipped her finger under the flap and opened her letter, having no idea what to expect.

As Minnie read her letter, Cassie read:

Dear Cassie,

In a few days, after we go to Austin to see if they will prosecute the warden at the reformatory for murder, I'll be riding to Warwick with your father. It will be a long ride, but one that already fills me with some degree of trepidation.

I admit that I'm afraid of meeting you. That sounds silly, doesn't it? I know you're only fifteen and a girl, but I'm still scared. I'm scared because I don't know what to do. Obviously, I've never been around girls at all. I spent more time with you before I left than any other girl, and I surely didn't meet any in the reformatory.

But no matter what happens when I finally get to talk to you again, I want to thank you for the letters you wrote to me. In the darkest times, while I was in the reformatory, it was your words that kept me from falling into deep despair. It was thinking of you and imagining what you looked like and what your voice sounded like as you grew older that kept me going and calmed my spirit.

I still have your letters and will treasure them for the rest of my life.

I hope I don't disappoint you in any way, even if you don't need a boyfriend.

With Deep Affection,

Joe

Cassie reread the letter twice, still not knowing what to think. It sounded like a love letter, yet it didn't. For the first time that she could recall, she was perplexed.

Minnie had been watching her daughter after reading John's letter, and even though her husband's letter was two pages long, she had enough time to see Cassie as she read the letter for the third time.

"What's wrong, Cassie?" she asked.

Cassie didn't answer but slid the letter to her mother.

Minnie reciprocated and slid John's letter to Cassie. She only took a minute to read Joe's short missive and had no doubt what it meant, but found it hard to understand, too. She hadn't read any of the letters that Cassie had written to Joe and wondered if she had expressed any feelings for him. She knew that Bessie had written a letter that bordered on a love letter, but she wondered if Cassie had.

"Cassie, did you ever write to Joe expressing any affection for him?"

"No, Mama. Not like that. Bessie did, but I did write letters that told him he should study so when he came back, he could be my boyfriend. But I was ten years old, too."

Minnie sighed and said, "I guess we'll just have to see what happens. What did you think of what your father wrote?"

"It sounds like Joe had a pretty horrible time while he was there. Do you think Joe will tell us what happened?"

"I think so. He already told your father, but I think it's a lot worse than what he wrote. He only said that Joe was scarred."

"I hope he's not scarred inside," Cassie said as she folded Joe's letter and slid it back into the envelope.

"We'll know soon, but your father still describes him as an impressive, handsome young man."

Cassie slipped her letter into her skirt pocket and said, "I hope Bessie is satisfied with Kit after she sees Joe if he's like papa described him."

"If that boy comes here with your sister, you tell him that the cake is for your father and Joe. He doesn't get a bite!"

Cassie laughed and stood to help her mother clean the kitchen.

———

It was late afternoon, and they'd just had a longer break, including some of the jerky that John had packed. They hadn't had any target practice because neither wanted to take the time and then have to clean the guns.

Joe was thoroughly comfortable on the pinto and asked, "Does he have a name?"

"I'm sure he did, but we never got a chance to ask his owner. You may as well give him a new one."

"I'll think about it. How far out are we?"

"We're in my jurisdiction now, so I'd estimate another two and a half hours."

"Do you have a bed in the jail?"

John turned to look at Joe and replied, "We do, but why do you want to know?"

"I figured if I stayed there, I wouldn't have to pay for a room at a rooming house and I could pull night duty and give you and the deputies the night off."

"Joe, the county pays for your room and board. You get a room at Harrison's Boarding House and they pay the bill."

"I'd rather stay at the jail. I think I could be more help there."

John sighed and said, "We'll talk about it. You can stay there tonight, though. After Mary married and moved out,

Bessie and Cassie finally were able to get their own rooms and I don't have any space."

"I wouldn't want to stay there anyway, boss. You know, with Cassie and all."

"Oh, I didn't forget about Cassie. Trust me."

Minnie had the lamps burning, the coffee made, and leftovers still warming as she sat with Cassie, Bessie, and her beau, Kit Ryerson. He'd been eying up the coffee cake, but Minnie had let him know that it was for her husband, the sheriff. She hadn't mentioned Joe's return to Kit believing that Bessie had told him, but she hadn't. As far as Kit knew, they were all just waiting for Bessie's father to return. Cassie hadn't said a word since Kit had arrived as she ruminated about the imminent arrival of her erstwhile boyfriend.

Cassie felt even younger than her fifteen and a half years as she sat in the chair. Bessie and Kit were holding hands and Bessie's dress was filled out like a young woman's should be. Cassie didn't understand why it should bother her. She was still wrestling with the conundrum of Joe's return and how to deflect any interest he might have in her as a girlfriend.

"Are you sure papa's coming home tonight, Mama?" Bessie asked as she leaned forward slightly to see past Kit.

"I'm not sure, but I'd be surprised if he doesn't arrive within fifteen minutes. Does anyone want to place a small wager on it?"

Cassie finally smiled as she replied, "I'll take the next fifteen minutes after yours, Mama. I'll put in ten cents."

"Okay. My dime is on the next fifteen minutes. Bessie?"

Bessie glanced at the wall clock above the mantle and said, "I'll put a dime on nine o'clock to nine-fifteen."

Cassie glanced at the clock. It was five minutes after eight.

So, the three Warren ladies plus the one Warren lady caller, sat waiting as the clock ticked.

Kit was getting bored just sitting there with the aroma of the food still wafting from the kitchen. Having Bessie so close but only being able to hold her hand was annoying, too. All this because her father was returning from riding to Henrietta for some reason he hadn't even cared to ask about.

The clock read 8:25 when they heard boots stepping onto the porch and male voices talking outside.

The bet forgotten, Cassie snapped to her feet and absent-mindedly brushed down the front of her dress and began breathing rapidly.

Kit was going to stay seated, but Bessie had also risen as did Mrs. Warren, so he grudgingly stood as the door opened and Sheriff Warren entered, and the two men set their saddlebags on the floor.

Kit was then taken aback when he saw the second young man with the sheriff and noticed that he was taller than Bessie's father with broad shoulders and without any reason whatsoever, he was instantly jealous of the newcomer and saw him as a competitor for Bessie.

Cassie wanted to fade into the background when she saw Joe. He was more of everything that she had built in her imagination and that frightened her, but not for the usual reasons.

Bessie smiled at Joe and wished that Kit wasn't standing beside her. Joe Armstrong was the same age as Kit, but he was a man already.

It was Minnie who broke the ice when she walked quickly to Joe and said, "Welcome home, Joe."

Joe smiled at the sheriff's wife as he removed his new Stetson then said, "I'm pleased to see you again, Mrs. Warren."

Bessie then took three long strides, stopped beside her mother, and smiled at Joe as she said, "It's nice to see you again, Joe."

For just a fleeting moment, Joe thought he was looking at Cassie, and agreed with her father's assessment. She was stunning.

But her advanced female features quickly made him realize he was facing Bessie, so he said, "Hello, Bessie. How are you?"

"I'm fine."

Kit was annoyed with the attention Bessie had displayed to the newcomer, so he stepped beside Bessie, put his arm possessively around her shoulder, and said, "I'm Kit Ryerson, Bessie's beau."

Joe offered his hand and said, "Nice to meet you, Kit."

Kit smiled, took Joe's hand, and tried to crush it as he had with every other male whom he'd met and viewed as a challenger.

Joe was surprised by the attempt but literally didn't press the issue and just smiled.

After releasing Kit's hand, Joe turned to his left, surprised to see the younger girl still standing so far away. As soon as he saw those deep brown eyes, he knew without a doubt they belonged to Cassie.

He took one short step to stand three feet before her and said quietly, "It's nice to see you again, Cassie."

Cassie swallowed and replied, "Hello."

They both stood uncomfortably for barely two seconds when Minnie said loudly, "Joe, you and my husband need to get something to eat."

Joe turned and said, "Yes, ma'am," then watched as John hooked his arm around his wife's waist and walked down the hallway, talking as they did.

Kit then took Bessie's hand and followed them toward the kitchen.

Joe turned to Cassie and said, "After you, Cassie."

Cassie nodded and stepped quickly past Joe and almost trotted down the hallway.

Joe watched her rapid escape and guessed that he was off the boyfriend list and was relieved. It wasn't because Cassie wasn't pretty because she was very pretty. And it wasn't because she was fifteen and thin. It was because now, he could learn the job he had to do and leave when he was ready.

Cassie's reaction wasn't what Joe thought it was at all. She was simply afraid, but not of Joe. Despite all of her imagined images of Joe over the past four years, she hadn't made that one leap from boy to man.

Joe wasn't a boy any longer. He was not only a man but a big man, larger than both her father and Kit. He needed to shave and was so incredibly masculine, and she suddenly felt very much like the teenage girl she was. Her fear was that he might want her as a girlfriend anyway, and that simply couldn't happen. But she had felt the warm rush flow through her when she looked into his eyes and it had weakened her knees, and that moment had also weakened her determination to push him away.

As Joe began to slowly follow Cassie down the hallway, he did feel bad for scaring her because he had seen the fear in her eyes. He may have been relieved by her rejection, but that didn't mean he was pleased by it. The letters she had written to him had shown what she was like inside and it was that, even more than the imaginary Cassie he had pictured in his mind that had made him write 'With Deep Affection', to end his last letter.

When he reached the kitchen, he knew that regardless of how she felt about him, he would always regard Cassie Warren with deep affection.

"Take a seat, Joe," Minnie directed as she began spooning food onto their plates.

"Yes, ma'am," he replied as he took a seat beside Cassie, wondering if it had been left there for a reason.

He realized he hadn't hung his hat yet, so he just placed it on his lap. At least he'd left his gunbelt in his saddlebags. Joe intentionally didn't look at Cassie, so she wouldn't be uncomfortable. He'd have to talk to her, sooner or later, but maybe she'd get used to him being around after a few days.

Minnie placed the two plates of food in front of Joe and her husband, and Bessie put plates with slices of coffee cake before Cassie, Kit, and the two empty places.

Joe felt awkward eating when everyone else just had cake and coffee, but the sheriff didn't seem to have a problem and was already demolishing his dinner, so he began to eat, but not as quickly as his new boss.

"Joe, are you glad you're out of there?" asked Bessie.

Joe swallowed and replied, "Yes, ma'am."

Kit then asked, "Out of where?"

Joe looked at him and wondered how he could not have known the story at all. It was only four and a half years ago, after all. *Besides, how could he be spending so much time in the Warren home and not know about him? Were they so ashamed of him that they didn't talk about him?* He didn't believe it but had a hard time finding another reason.

John stopped eating and answered, "Joe was sent to the state reformatory near Gainesville after the first bank robbery attempt by the Hogan brothers. He's going to be my new deputy starting on Monday."

"He's a Hogan?" Kit snapped as he stared at Joe.

"No, he's not," John said forcefully as he glared at Kit.

Kit suddenly realized that he might have stepped on the sheriff's toes, and he didn't want to offend Bessie's father.

"Oh. Never mind, then," Kit said as he took a big bite of coffee cake.

After Kit's rebuff by the sheriff, Joe felt that he was causing more trouble by being here, so he just ate quietly while Minnie questioned her husband about the details of the murder investigation that had prompted the trip to Austin.

Joe kept his eyes down and after eating his food, just quietly sat drinking coffee while the sheriff explained what had happened.

"*He murdered a boy and he's going to get away with it?*" Minnie exclaimed.

"I'll explain it later, dear. But Joe and I both agree that justice will probably be served unless the warden avoids a prison sentence altogether."

"He'd better not," Minnie fumed as she took the two empty plates and set them in the sink, and replaced them with smaller plates and large slices of the coffee cake.

Joe began cutting into the coffee cake with his fork as his level of discomfort begin to rise. This wasn't what he was expecting on his first day back in Warwick. Everything seemed to be turned upside down.

He had just taken a sip of coffee when Bessie asked, "What time is it?"

It was such a simple question, but it turned Joe's evening around.

He slipped his hand into his right pants pocket, pulled out his pocket watch and opened the cover, and said, "9:20."

While he had it in his hand, he flipped the watch over and read the inscription carved into the silver back and lifted his eyes to the Warren family, and smiled.

He looked at Mrs. Warren when he said, "When I received the wonderful box you sent for Christmas that contained this watch and Cassie's delicious cookies, I was very happy, but even then, I didn't realize how lucky I was. It wasn't until a few months later that I began to realize that very few of the boys in that place had families that would want them back when they left when I truly understood how fortunate I was.

"I may have grown up thinking I had a family, but I had nothing. But now I have a family, and I'll never be able to thank you enough. Thank you for allowing me to be part of the Warren family, even if I'm still an Armstrong."

Minnie sniffed, smiled, and replied, "And we are very lucky to have you back with us, Joe."

Joe just nodded and took another bite of his coffee cake.

Kit then looked at Bessie and said, "I've got to get back. Will you walk with me?"

"Alright," she replied as she stood.

John was going to stand when Minnie looked at him and shook her head slightly. Bessie was almost eighteen now and it was only two blocks away.

Kit took Bessie's hand, and they exited the house through the back door.

After the door was closed, Minnie said, “Well, I may be wrong, but I believe Kit feels threatened by your presence, Joe.”

“I don’t know why he should. Was he expecting to be your deputy, boss?”

“He asked me about the job a couple of times, but just casually. I think my wife believes that Kit thinks you’ll try and take Bessie away from him.”

“I don’t think so, although he did try and break my hand when he shook it.”

John smiled and said, “I noticed. Why didn’t you snap a few of his bones? I know you’ve got a blacksmith’s hand strength.”

“A few years ago, when I was being escorted to the reformatory, a wise man told me not to get into fights unless you had to but when you did, try and make them under your terms. I took that to heart and expanded it somewhat while I was in the reformatory. I found that it’s easier to take some punishment to avoid greater punishment.”

Minnie asked quietly, “Was it bad, Joe?”

“There were a few times that will stay with me for the rest of my life, but others had it worse, including the boys who died from those whips.”

“Were you whipped?” she asked.

“I only received an extended whipping once, but I took a couple of lashes about a year ago, too. It still wasn’t as often as some of the other boys had to endure. It would be much worse if Warden Phelps gets away with it. What he did to me wasn’t as bad as what he did to some of the smallest and weakest boys. There's no way of proving that he murdered them with that silver-tipped whip of his, or if his guards did it on his orders, but he should have been convicted and hanged for shooting Willie Struthers."

Cassie finally spoke when she asked, "What will you do if he gets off?"

Joe stared into his empty coffee cup as he replied, "I'll get retribution for those boys after I find it for my mother and her sister."

John didn't comment and hoped that Mister Pell did his job. Going after wanted criminals was one thing but going after a warden who hadn't been charged with any crimes was something else altogether. At least he said after he found the Hogan brothers, so that might never happen. He still held out hope that Joe would settle into the job of deputy sheriff and stay, and that Cassie could help to change his mind, not realizing that it was the last thing his youngest daughter would want to do.

After listening to Joe's soft, compassionate voice and the emotions behind his words, Cassie had finally climbed over that summit of shock at seeing Joe, the man. He may be big and strong and needed a shave, but he was still the same person who had written to her, including the last letter she'd just received. She recalled that he had written that he was afraid of meeting her, yet it had been she who had been afraid, and now realized there was no reason to fear. He was still Joe, and she may not want him as a real boyfriend with the associated kissing and petting, but she liked him.

Joe then stood and said, "Well, I need to get over to the jail and get some shuteye. It's been a long ride and I'm sure my new boss doesn't want to hear any more of my ramblings."

The Warrens all stood and John said, “I’ll walk over there with you. I’ve got the key.”

“Thank you, sir. I’d hate to have to break a window to get into jail.”

John and Minnie laughed as John grabbed his hat from a peg, kissed Minnie on the cheek, and said, “I’ll be back soon, ma’am. I’ve been away from you for too long.”

“Don’t I know it, Sheriff,” Minnie replied and almost giggled.

Joe turned to Cassie and said, “Good night, Cassie.”

She smiled and replied, “Good night, Joe.”

Joe smiled back and turned to follow the sheriff, who had already begun to walk down the hallway.

Once they had gone, Minnie and Cassie began to clean the plates from the table and Minnie said, “You seemed awfully quiet tonight, missy.”

“I was just surprised when I saw Joe, that’s all. I didn’t expect him to be so, well, grown up.”

Minnie was putting the plates into the sink as she replied, “I bet he aged a lot more than four years in that place. He’s probably not even legally eighteen yet, but I think he’s a lot older inside. When we were walking down the hallway, your father told me that after he’d been whipped raw and then the warden threw him in solitary for two weeks. He saw the scars on his back and his legs, and he couldn’t imagine the pain that he’d been through.”

“Now he’s planning on chasing after the Hogan brothers when no one even knows where they are.”

"But he had one big advantage. He lived with them for most of his life. He knows their habits and what they look like. I'm much more worried about what happens if he finds them."

———

John had opened the office, showed Joe where the sleeping room was, how to find the privy out back, and was preparing to leave when he stopped and turned to face Joe.

"Joe, that comment you made about going after Warden Phelps if he gets off. You know that it might get you hanged if you did anything."

"Yes, sir. Only if you believed that I'd do something stupid enough that I could be charged with murder. Going after the Hogan brothers will be straightforward, but if I have to deliver justice for the murdered boys, then I'll do it legally."

John nodded and said, "You'll be a good deputy, Joe. I'm going to go and hunt down Bessie. She's been gone too long."

"Boss, what do you really think of Kit? I felt that Mrs. Warren didn't like him very much."

"I don't either, but it's not our choice. Bessie has been visited by four boys since she turned sixteen, and we're hoping that she moves on again."

"Is he any danger to Bessie?"

"No, I don't believe so. He's afraid of me."

"He should be," Joe said before he chuckled.

"Get some sleep, Joe. Tomorrow's Sunday, so sleep as late as you'd like."

“Yes, sir. Thank your wife for the coffee cake. I’ve never tasted anything so delicious in my whole life.”

“I’ll tell her, but you’d better expect more treats from her. She may not like Kit very much, but she really likes you.”

Joe smiled and replied, “I really like her too, boss. You are a lucky man but then, I think she’s a lucky woman, too.”

“Quit buttering me up, Joe. You’re not even a deputy yet.”

John left the office and turned left to try and find Bessie.

Once he’d gone, Joe quickly set about getting things ready for bed. He set his things on the small table near the bed and left his saddlebags on the floor. He just stripped off his shirts and pants and then, before he slid beneath the blankets, he ran his fingers over the long scars on his back, buttocks, and thighs, wondering what Cassie would think.

It was a silly thing to worry about, he told himself, she was only fifteen. She may not be afraid of him anymore, but in a few months, he wouldn’t be spending much time in Warwick, and it might be years before he finished tracking down the last of the Hogans. He didn’t think that she wanted him for a boyfriend anyway.

CHAPTER 6

Sunday morning broke sunny, but with a strong wind from the northwest, signaling a change in the weather.

Joe had been up for almost half an hour before the sunrise because he'd done so for more than four years. On the return trip with Sheriff Warren, he'd been awake and had just laid there rather than waking him. A couple of times, he thought his bladder was ready to explode by the time the sheriff had awakened.

He had a fire going in the heat stove to make some coffee as he shaved in a basin in the sleeping room. He was used to shaving in cold water and no mirror, but having a shaving mug, soap, and a brush was new and deeply appreciated. The new, sharp razor made short work of his tough beard and he only had three nicks, which quickly congealed. He knew he really needed to take a bath, so maybe he'd visit the tonsorial parlor tomorrow after he was sworn in.

He didn't have a hairbrush or a comb yet, so he just ran his fingers through his sandy brown hair and walked out to the front office to make the coffee.

Ten minutes later, Joe was sitting behind the front desk and began opening drawers. He found what he wanted in the middle left drawer and pulled out the stack of wanted posters.

He was sipping the coffee with the cup in his left hand as he flipped through the posters with his right. He had just taken the third poster from the stack when he found Earl Hogan's. The drawing wasn't even close, but the description was reasonable. He noticed that Earl had a four-hundred-dollar reward and was charged with six counts of murder, two armed robbery, and three rapes. His known associates were his brother Glen and two men named Red Victor and Tommy Johnson. The poster was only three months old. He guessed that the Hogans had to replace the four they lost when they tried to confront Sheriff Warren again.

He found Glen's right beneath it and had a five-hundred-dollar reward probably because of the additional murder, but he only had two counts of rape.

Red Victor and Tommy Johnson each had much smaller rewards of a hundred dollars each with just the two robberies. None of the men had anything that really stood out in their descriptions.

He found Fred's poster just above Hank's. Both men had four-hundred and fifty-dollar price tags on their heads for six murders, four robberies, and two rapes. They had no known associates. Joe noticed that neither of the drawn faces was anything more than generic. The artist even gave them close, beady eyes to make them appear evil but also made the image even less like the brothers.

It wasn't until he was almost at the bottom of the stack that he found Buck's poster. He wasn't surprised that it was the highest reward at seven hundred and fifty dollars, and it was more than a year old. He was charged with eight murders, including two Texas Rangers, in addition to the more mundane crimes of bank robbery and rape. Buck's drawing was closer to being accurate than the others, but still didn't really make him stand out from most men, nor did his description. He had no known associates, but the poster did say that he had two Texas Ranger badges.

He was putting the posters back in the desk when the door opened, and Joe looked up. He was greatly surprised to see Cassie enter the office.

“Good morning, Cassie.”

“Hello. My mother wants to know if you would be coming to church with us this morning.”

“No, I don’t think so. At least, not yet.”

Joe expected that she’d turn right around to leave, so she could join her family, but she didn’t.

Cassie walked to the front of the desk and sat on the chair before the desk.

“Aren’t you going with your family?”

“Not today. I told my mother that I might not be back. I needed to talk to you.”

Joe leaned back and said, “Okay.”

“I owe you an apology. Maybe more than one.”

“I can’t see any reason for you to apologize, Cassie.”

“Yes, there are. First, I wasn’t very friendly to you last night. I was almost rude, and I apologize for that. But that’s the easy one to explain. The other was when I told you that you would be my boyfriend when I first talked to you as you stood in that cell. I never had a chance to explain why I said it.”

Joe didn’t reply but just watched her eyes.

Cassie then explained, “I saw you behind those bars and you were only thirteen, so I told you that you were going to be my boyfriend for a silly reason. But then after you were gone and began writing back, I enjoyed our correspondence and I could see how much you were improving. I was proud of you. I stupidly gave myself credit for helping you, even though you were doing all the work. But once we could no longer write to each other, I began to think of you differently. As the years passed, I began to fantasize about what you would be like when you returned, and that was wrong."

Joe asked, "Why was it wrong? I used to do the same thing about you. I wondered if you lost your freckles and if you'd become as pretty as your father said you would. It's human nature, I believe, to try to imagine what someone looks like when we haven't seen them in years."

"It was wrong because of what I wanted, and it really wasn't a boyfriend in the traditional meaning of the word. I really didn't want a boyfriend like the other girls wanted one, and by claiming to have you as a boyfriend in the reformatory, I could keep the other boys from bothering me. Then I'd have a chance to do what I want to do.

"It seems as if the only thing a girl can do when she becomes a woman is find

some man who will marry her and make her have babies and be a housewife until she dies, and it makes me crazy. I have dreams that won't be found here. That's why I have to apologize. I feel as if I've lied to you all these years."

Joe exhaled as he looked at Cassie before saying, "Cassie, I don't mind that you used me as your protection from boys bothering you. What you did for me all those years is beyond my ability to express. If you want to keep telling the boys I'm your boyfriend to keep them at bay that's fine, but I won't act as one. Yet, I want to do something for you because I've become very fond of that freckle-faced girl who wrote those letters.

"Let me make you this promise. I just checked the wanted posters for the Hogans and the men that are probably riding with them. It's a considerable amount of money. If I'm successful at even getting one or two, the rewards should be more than enough for you to go to a school away from here and search for your dream.

"I'll set up a bank account here in town and have your father's name on it, so if anything happens to me, you'll still be able to get the money. When you're old enough, you go where you want and do what you want to do."

Cassie stared at him in silence. There were so many reasons for her coming to the jail, but his offer stunned her.

After almost thirty seconds, she said, "But that wouldn't be right. You'll be risking your life and all I've ever done is say stupid things and write you letters."

"Cassie, after I'd been whipped in the warden's office and thrown into solitary confinement, those letters and your spirit were all that kept me alive. I had to lie on my stomach to let the wounds heal, so all I could do was close my eyes and let my mind focus on something that would take away the pain, and it was always you, Cassie.

"It was imagining you without the freckles and trying to hear your new voice that made those two weeks pass and allowed me to walk out of that cell. I can never repay you for what you gave me. Those letters meant more to me than the bread and water they gave me. I read them so often the folds split open. So, let me do this for you. Let me give you your dream."

"But I don't even know what my dream is yet. Can't this all wait?"

"Of course, it can wait. I have to learn how to be a deputy, and that will take me a few months. We can talk a lot during that time, can't we? As friends?"

Cassie relaxed and smiled and replied, "Yes, I'd like that. Who knows? Maybe I'm all wrong and will be happy to be your girlfriend in the traditional sense."

Joe smiled back and said, "We can never predict the future, can we? Although your father was right when he said you were going to be prettier than his other two daughters."

Cassie blushed and protested, saying, "I'm just a skinny girl."

"I hear that half the boys in town don't think so."

"Well, they're going to have to get past my new boyfriend now."

"I'll take that as a challenge then, ma'am."

Cassie smiled and asked, "Can you come to the house and share breakfast with me? I'll make it for everyone else when they come back for church anyway."

"Is Kit going to be there?"

"Probably."

"Well, then I'd better join you, Miss Warren. I don't want him bothering my girlfriend," Joe said as he stood and plucked his Stetson from the desk.

Cassie rose and when Joe offered her his arm, she put her hand on his forearm and felt the hard muscle under his shirt as they stepped out of the jail and onto the boardwalk into the windy, sunny Texas morning.

As they walked across the street, Cassie felt less like a girl, despite her appearance, and with Joe's promise of only acting as her boyfriend, she felt safer and less concerned.

———

When the Warrens returned home from church, they found Joe and Cassie having post-breakfast coffee in the kitchen. What was remarkable was the loud laughter they heard as they entered the house.

Kit was escorting Bessie as they entered the house and he almost turned around to leave when he recognized Joe's voice, but then quickly changed his mind. He had to stay close to Bessie. He was convinced that Joe was only spending time with Cassie, so he could get close to Bessie, and he wasn't about to let that happen.

When Minnie and John reached the kitchen, they discovered what was making them laugh, and found it remarkable. Joe was telling Cassie stories about the reformatory that didn't involve cruelty or pain. There had been many instances of humor among some of the boys, usually at the expense of the guards or the bullies upstairs.

"How did church go, Mama? Was Reverend Kemper in good voice?" Cassie asked as she stood to help make them breakfast.

"Only if you like screech owls. How that man ever became a preacher is beyond me," she replied as she took off her Sunday cap.

Bessie still had her arm on Kit's as she entered, but smiled and said, "Mary and Ned are coming over in ten minutes or so, Cassie, so we need two more plates."

Joe stood to make room, took his cup of coffee and walked to the cook stove, and said, "I can help, Cassie. What do you need me to do?"

"Can you set the table?"

"Yes, ma'am."

He polished off the coffee and set the cup down near the sink in case he wanted more and began placing the necessary plates, saucers, cups, and flatware on the table.

Kit almost asked if he had learned how to do that at the reform school but managed to hold his tongue.

Joe could almost sense the hostility radiating from Kit but let it go. He wasn't important. He was beginning to wonder about Bessie, though. *Could she not see beyond Kit's handsome face?*

Once the table was set, Joe asked, "What next, Miss Warren?"

Cassie turned, smiled, and replied, "Can you make a fresh pot of coffee? We have two coffee pots."

"As you wish," Joe said as he bowed at the waist, eliciting giggles from all three of the Warren women.

As Joe was filling the second coffee pot, John said, "Good God, Joe! You're making me look bad."

"That, sir, is not my fault. Perhaps if you had been more amenable to providing assistance for culinary preparation, such a disparity would not have been noted."

Even John laughed at that response and Cassie said, 'Now you're just showing off."

"Just trying to impress my girlfriend."

John and Minnie glanced at each other with identical raised eyebrows. *What had happened when Cassie had gone to the jail?*

Bessie was happy for Cassie, although she didn't understand how they had become so friendly so quickly. Cassie was definitely still a girl and Joe was all man. But she loved her younger sister and had worried when she had been pushing so many boys away.

Kit wouldn't have believed that Joe was Cassie's boyfriend if Joe and Cassie had made love on the kitchen floor as they had breakfast. To him, it was all a show.

While everyone else was eating, Cassie said, "Joe, come with me. I want to show you something."

"Yes, ma'am."

Cassie left the kitchen and turned into what was now just her bedroom and Joe followed, leaving the door wide open to let her parents see them.

Cassie slid a wooden box out from under her bed, set it on the mattress, opened the lid, and stepped back so Joe could see the contents.

In a low voice, Cassie said, “These are all the letters I wrote to you while you were in the reformatory. My father said I should keep them.”

“How many are there?” Joe asked as he stared at the stacks of bound letters.

“One hundred and sixty-four. Once I decided to keep them, I dated each on the outside of the envelope. Do you want them?”

Joe thought about it and then replied, “Not now, but can you hold onto them? When I leave in a few months to go after the Hogans, I’d like to take them with me, so I can read them slowly and this time, I’ll be able to match them to the author much better.”

Cassie smiled and said, “That’s a good idea. Let me show you something else, too.”

She closed the lid and slid the box back under the bed before turning to her dresser and opening the bottom drawer. She pulled out her gunbelt and Joe’s old Remington and, after handing Joe his old pistol and buckling on her gunbelt, reached into the drawer and removed a small cloth bag.

Joe watched as she slid his mother’s hair comb from the bag and gave it to him.

“You said you’d cleaned it, but it looks almost new,” he said quietly as he examined it.

“Well, I did have four years to do it,” Cassie replied.

He then looked at her and asked, “Did you get to shoot when you turned thirteen, or did you talk your father into letting you shoot it earlier like you said you would?”

Cassie grinned and said, "I shot your Remington when I was twelve. This is my birthday gift when I turned fourteen."

"Are you any good?"

"I think so. Do you want to go out and have some target practice?"

"I'd enjoy that, Cassie," Joe replied and asked, "Can you hold onto the hair comb? I'd look kind of silly carrying it around with me."

Cassie accepted it from Joe, slid it back into its cloth bag, and returned it to the drawer and they left the bedroom and returned to the kitchen.

"Joe and I are going to do some target practice," Cassie announced.

John noticed the old Remington stuck in Joe's waist and asked, "You're not going to use that relic, are you, Joe?"

"No, sir. But I might try it out one of these days."

"Be careful it doesn't blow up in your hand when you do."

"I will," Joe replied and said to Cassie, "I need to get my pistol unless you don't mind sharing your Remington."

Cassie grinned and said, "I'd let my boyfriend share anything I have," then laughed as she began to walk out the back door.

After Joe had followed her outside and closed the door behind them, Minnie again looked at John with raised eyebrows. *Was that Cassie? She was close to giggling, for God's sake!*

Kit was just glad that Joe was gone as he and Bessie ate their breakfast.

———

Cassie only had the five cartridges in her pistol and the eight in the loops around her gunbelt, so it wasn't a long shooting session, but Joe really just wanted to see Cassie shoot and was surprised at how good she was. He hadn't seen that many shooters, except for the Hogans, but he knew that they weren't as good as they believed, and Cassie was probably their equal. He only took a single shot just to get the feel of her Remington. He'd have a lot of opportunities to shoot his Colt over the next few months before he had to use it in action. He needed even more practice with his Winchester.

After the short target practice session, Joe and Cassie just took a leisurely Sunday stroll and talked. Almost with each completed sentence, they uncovered more things that they wanted to discuss. The time flew by as their dialogue became more animated and expansive.

It was just past noon when Joe realized that they'd walked almost three miles away from the house and been talking for two hours.

"I think we need to get back, Cassie. They'll think I kidnapped you and took you to the Nations."

Cassie laughed and said, "No, they trust you. It's me they worry about."

They turned and began walking more quickly back to the house when Joe looked at Cassie and asked, "Are you sure you're fifteen, Miss Warren? I think they made a mistake on your birth certificate."

She laughed again and tugged on the front of her dress and said, “No, sir, there was no mistake. Trust me, I’m fifteen.”

Joe blushed, which ignited more Cassie laughter and then his as they took long strides to get back quicker. Joe was glad that she had long legs.

But they made the most use of the return walk to continue their conversation.

When they returned to the kitchen, they found that Kit and Bessie were gone, and so was the sheriff.

“Where have you two been?” asked Mrs. Warren.

“After we did our shooting, Joe and I walked and discussed things for a while. We were walking north and didn’t realize how far we’d gone. Where’s papa?”

“He received a telegram and rushed over to the office.”

“What was in it?” Cassie asked.

“I don’t know, but I think you should head over there, Joe.”

“I will. Thank you for the target practice and the conversation, Cassie.”

“Anytime, Joe.”

Joe trotted back out the back door and quickly left the back porch and headed for the jail. He couldn’t imagine anything that it could be that would involve him. Mister Pell was probably still in Austin or maybe looking for other boys to collect their affidavits, but it might have something to do with the Hogans.

Joe walked quickly from the Warren home down the side street and crossed the main street to the sheriff's office, entering just two minutes after leaving the kitchen.

The door was open, and he spotted the sheriff thumbing through the wanted posters as he crossed the threshold.

"What's wrong, boss?" Joe asked as he approached the desk.

Sheriff Warren didn't look up but said, "I just got a telegram from the town marshal in Greenwich that two men, believed to be Wally Fremont and Jackson Albers just left his town after stealing four horses from the livery. They were heading west, so they could be here pretty soon."

"Are they bad?"

"Not murdering bad, just common thieves and troublemakers. I guess they thought because it was Sunday and all the folks would be in church that no one would notice them taking the animals."

"Did you want me to get one of your deputies?"

"No, it's Sunday, besides Lou's Anna is ready to have her baby any day now. I'll tell Dan that we're riding east to see if we can run into them. Can you saddle our horses?"

"Yes, sir," Joe replied as he turned and left the office.

John stood, grabbed his hat, and headed out behind him, walking diagonally across the street to go to Dan Sheehy's place. His wife, Ellie, wasn't that far behind Anna in the baby department, so he was really glad to have Joe around, even if he wasn't a sworn deputy yet.

Joe had both horses saddled, their Winchesters in their scabbards, and had his Colt buckled around his waist before the sheriff entered their small barn behind the jail.

“That was quick, Joe,” the sheriff commented as he began to mount.

“I figured you’d want to get going, boss,” Joe replied as he stepped up.

They left the barn and turned east, the sun at their backs in the early afternoon.

Joe didn’t bring up his status as a civilian because he figured the sheriff was well aware of his lack of credentials. It really didn’t matter anyway. He considered himself a one-man posse supporting the sheriff, but just wished he had taken more target practice that morning. It had been a while since he’d shot either a pistol or a rifle. He didn’t ask why the sherlff had asked him to come along rather than his senior deputy but figured he must have a reason.

They rode east for almost an hour when they picked up a dust cloud on the horizon about four miles east. Ten minutes later, they could pick out two riders leading four horses, putting a brand on the two horse thieves.

“Well, there are our boys,” the sheriff said loudly.

“Why would they be coming into Warwick?” Joe asked.

“They probably think no one knows the horses are gone yet, so they can sell those horses quickly and then be on their way. They know that we don’t form a posse for horse thieves. Now we just need to get ready to chase them down if they bolt.”

Joe glanced over at the sheriff and noticed he'd moved his badge into his vest pocket. No sense in giving those boys any advance warning.

They were still more than two miles out, so the sheriff asked, "Tell me, Joe, what's going on with Cassie? She didn't say ten words to you last night, and today, you two are talking like an old married couple."

"I don't know, really. She came to the jail this morning and apologized because she felt as if she'd lied about needing a boyfriend. She said that she didn't want to get married and have babies but wanted to go away and live her life as she wanted. Then I told her that any rewards I'd get from getting the Hogans I'd put into a bank account in town and it would be hers, so she could go to a distant school and do whatever she wanted to do."

"And she agreed to that?" John asked loudly.

"No, not exactly. We agreed that there was a lot of time between now and then and we'd just talk. I guess it took the pressure off by telling her I would only be a pretend boyfriend, and now we just enjoy spending time together. She may be fifteen, but she's a real wonder."

John turned his eyes to the still-approaching dust cloud and just smiled. If those two weren't a perfect match, he'd never meet another.

Wally Fremont and Jackson Albers had spotted the sheriff and his single-man posse before they were spotted and had been watching them closely for the past ten minutes.

"What do you think, Wally?" Jack asked.

"I ain't sure. They're just ridin' and those Winchesters are where they belong, but I think we should be ready just in case."

"Alright, "Jack replied as he pulled his hammer loop from his Colt while Wally did the same.

It wasn't much of a move but to Sheriff Warren's trained eyes it was anticipated and noted.

"Did you see that, Joe?" he asked.

"No. What did I miss?"

"They both just dropped their right hands from their reins for a few seconds. They were pulling off their hammer loops, so they can draw quickly if they need to."

"I assume that if we did, they'd notice it too, wouldn't they?"

"They would. That's why we're going to continue to ride until we get within about two hundred yards and then we'll pull our Winchesters, cock the hammers and I'll let them know we're the law. If they run, we'll chase them down."

Joe replied, "Yes, sir," but wasn't sure that it was the right way to approach the pair.

John was pretty sure he could take both of the outlaws, but he wanted to see how Joe would react. It was a rare opportunity that these two had presented. He could go three months without any serious problems in the whole county and this was perfect. He doubted if either of them was a marksman, but even bad shooters could get lucky.

———

Wally was getting too tense as he was watching the two riders approaching. They were about four hundred yards away and they just had the look that said ‘law’ about them.

“I don’t like those two, Jack,” he said in a normal voice.

“Me, neither. Get ready to pull that Winchester.”

Wally didn’t reply but did pull his Winchester’s stock to make sure it wouldn’t stick. It was an unnecessary caution and gave Sheriff Warren and Joe an indication of their intentions.

———

Joe said in a voice just loud enough to be heard over their horses, “I did see that. It looks as if they’re preparing to use those repeaters.”

“You’re right, Joe. Good eye. This may be a bit uglier than I expected.”

Joe was watching the two men and knew that if both pairs of men pulled their Winchesters at the same time, it would be an even match, and he’d been told by the man riding beside him to never get into an even fight if you could avoid it. Joe wanted to avoid it. Shooting at moving targets from the back of a moving horse was difficult, and he questioned his own marksmanship already. He needed to even the odds. Then he looked at the four trailing horses and an idea popped into his mind, and there wasn’t enough time to explain.

So, as they closed within three hundred yards, Joe suddenly bolted the pinto off the road to his right at an angle as he pulled his Winchester, startling the sheriff and the two riders.

“Son of a bitch!” shouted Wally as he pulled his rifle.

By the time he had it out of its scabbard, Joe had circled in a loop and was charging at them with his repeater level, but not firing.

John immediately shouted, “Sheriff John Warren, drop your weapons!”, as he pulled his Winchester and cocked the hammer.

Joe waited until John’s shout and then when they both aimed their repeaters, he fired his first shot, aiming at the ground near the trailing horses. The animals were spooked by the gunfire and the resulting explosion of dirt at their hooves and yanked on the trail ropes, which jerked the riders’ horses just as they were preparing to return fire.

Sheriff Warren left the road on the other side but didn’t make as wide a loop as Joe had made, so he could cut them off if they tried to charge past on the roadway.

Jackson Albers managed to get a shot off at Joe as his horse was being yanked around by two of the damned trailing geldings making his shot go wildly wide of his intended target.

Wally’s shot at the sheriff was equally bad as his sights were bouncing all over the place. Joe fired twice more at the trailing animals’ feet, keeping them dancing and rearing as the two riders fought to control their mounts.

From less than eighty yards, Sheriff Warren shouted again, “Throw down your weapons, or the next one will be in your face!”

Wally tossed his Winchester down, expecting the sheriff to lower his Winchester, but John wasn’t about to do anything that stupid.

After Jackson dropped his repeater, Joe slowed his pinto to a walk and kept his Winchester trained on the two men while John did the same from the other side.

"Put your hands in the air!" John yelled.

Wally ran his tongue over his upper lip and put his hands high and Jackson did the same.

The gunfight was over.

Joe kept his carbine pointed at the men while the sheriff pulled their pistols from their holsters and said, "Okay, boys. Let's ride west just the way you were headed."

The two outlaws set their now calmed horses to a slow trot and rode into the sun toward Warwick while the sheriff sidled his mount next to Joe behind the trailing horses.

"Can I hope that you intentionally tried to miss, Joe?"

"I thought those trailing horses would be easier to spook and then they wouldn't be able to get a decent shot off. I haven't fired a rifle in years, and I wasn't sure about my accuracy, so I fired at the ground where I couldn't miss. The scheme just popped into my head so fast that I didn't have time to tell you. If we waited until two hundred yards, then we'd be in a standoff, and as a grizzled sheriff once told me, never get into an even fight if you don't have to."

John laughed and said, "He was a wise old geezer, wasn't he?"

Joe grinned and replied, "Yes, sir."

———

They reached Warwick an hour later and the sheriff locked them into the first cell and went to the desk, took out the stack of wanted posters, and pulled out those belonging to Wally Fremont and Jackson Albers. They were only a hundred dollars each, but neither was considered a ferocious criminal, either. Little risk, little reward.

"Well, Joe, it looks like you're coming into a couple of hundred dollars," the sheriff said as he slid the two posters across the desk.

"Boss, you take the money. I don't need it."

"I'll tell you what. We'll split it. You won't get your first paycheck for another month anyway."

Joe nodded and said, "I'll take your offer, sir."

"Good. Let's go back and talk to the ladies. I'm sure my wife is concerned."

"Don't you want me to stay with the prisoners?"

"Nope. They'll still be here when we get back. I'll send a telegram to the Greenwich marshal and let him know we have his stolen horses and the two men. It's a different county, so they'll pick them up in their jail wagon."

"Do we have one?"

"Sure. It's right next to the barn. Didn't you see it?"

"I did, but I thought it was a delivery wagon. I didn't see any bars."

As they left the jail, Sheriff Warren said, "That's exactly what it was in its prior life. It's a used delivery wagon. The county didn't want to splurge on some fancy rolling jail, so they gave us that one. We have to borrow the draft horses when we need to pick up some prisoners."

Joe walked alongside the sheriff knowing he had a lot to learn and needed a lot of target practice with his weapons.

The sheriff, on the other hand, was thoroughly impressed with the way Joe had handled the situation. He didn't get buck fever and start blasting away at the two men. He thought two moves ahead and when he made that sudden break, he had probably already decided to shoot at the ground near those trailing horses' hooves. It was a very impressive first performance. He was extremely pleased with his decision to hold the deputy slot open for Joe for more than one reason. Cassie was the other.

———

Bessie had returned to the house when they arrived, so there were about fifteen minutes of explanations of why they had to leave and what had happened on the road. John spared no amount of praise for Joe's performance, which turned Joe into almost a glowing red lamp for the duration.

Cassie had saved some lunch for Joe, so at least he was able to hide some of his embarrassment as he ate, but Minnie thought it was precious.

But as they were talking, Joe began thinking about the pinto. He was a handsome horse and was a great ride, but he was extremely noticeable, and after dealing with the horse thieves, he recalled that the sheriff had said that he'd been offered two hundred dollars for the rare Mexican hat pinto.

If he was going to be riding all over West Texas and the Nations hunting for the Hogans, he thought having such a distinctive animal would mark him easily and would also greatly increase the likelihood of horse theft. He decided he'd talk to the sheriff when he had a chance.

When the sheriff mentioned the rewards and that a hundred dollars would be added to the Warren bank account, Minnie was very happy with the news.

Cassie just glanced at Joe without comment, and she didn't seem happy, which thoroughly confused Joe. In fact, she said nothing during the half hour they spent at the house, baffling him even further. After their long and spirited conversations earlier, he had expected them to continue but obviously, he was wrong.

After their visit to the Warren house, Joe and the sheriff walked to the Western Union office where John sent the telegram to the Greenwich town marshal about the capture of the two horse thieves. He also sent telegrams to those who offered the rewards.

When they were leaving the telegraph office, Joe said, "I'll head back to the jail and stay with the prisoners. When do you think they'll send someone to pick them up?"

"Oh, I guess tomorrow or the day after. They just need to be fed and have their chamber pots emptied. They don't need to use the privy. When it's time to feed them, just go down to Rupert's and tell them you need two meals for prisoners."

"Yes, sir."

Joe waved to the sheriff as he headed back to finish his Sunday with his family while he walked to the jail.

After he'd entered and closed the door behind him, Joe looked at the two prisoners laying on the bunks and recalled when he was an angry boy behind those same bars and thought he was Joey Hogan. It was only four-plus years, but it was literally a lifetime ago.

He hung his hat on a peg and walked behind the desk and took a seat.

Wally Fremont shouted from his bunk, “Hey, Deputy, how about some chow?”

Joe didn’t turn, but smiled and replied, “I’ll get you fed in a little while,” not mentioning that he wasn’t a deputy.

As he sat behind the desk with his hands locked behind his neck, he tried to think of what he might have done to make Cassie so indifferent. He was fully aware that he had spent almost his entire conscious life in the presence of only men and boys, but even taking that into account, he simply couldn’t fathom Cassie’s behavior. She was just a very complex person and he’d never met anyone even within shouting distance of how her mind worked.

But her mind and personality that was confounding him now was also the same one that he found fascinating. She was the one who’d written those letters and mesmerized him when they had that long walk.

Later that night, as they lay in bed and finally had some private time, Minnie asked, “John, did Joe explain what happened when Cassie went to the jail? Last night, when you both arrived, Cassie acted as if you’d brought home some thug, but today it was as if she and Joe were old friends.”

John passed along what Joe had told him about what had been said when Cassie showed up that morning in the jail and about Joe's decision to set up a bank account for her to be able to pursue her dream of independence.

Minnie was surprised and a bit appalled by the idea and asked, "So, what was with the boyfriend-girlfriend comments? It was obvious to me that they got along exceedingly well, or am I wrong?"

John replied, "All the time I was with Joe, beginning on the trip to the reform school, I thought how much he and Cassie were alike in the way they thought. Even back then, I thought if anyone could marry her, it would be Joe."

Minnie replied, "But she said as recently as three days ago that she didn't want to get married and have children. She wanted to have her own life, and now Joe is making it possible that she could do that. It sounds as if he wants her to go away."

"I think he's just impressed with Cassie. We must remember, she may be smart, Minnie, but she's still fifteen and has a lot to learn. As she and Joe have already realized, they have time."

Minnie sighed and said, "I don't want to lose Cassie, John."

"You'll never lose her, sweetheart. I think things will work out."

"I hope so."

John pulled his wife close and hoped he was right.

March 18, 1879

It was one week after his release from the reformatory. Joe had washed, shaved, and emptied the prisoners' chamber pots, in that order, before going down to Rupert's to get their breakfast. He wasn't a deputy yet, and he didn't get one for himself, so his stomach was rumbling all the way back to the jail as he carried the tray of enticing food. The smell of bacon was driving him to distraction by the time he entered the jail.

After sliding the trays under the bars, he started a fire in the heat stove and filled the coffee pot with water.

He had just put the coffee grounds into the pot when Deputy Sheehy popped through the door.

"Good morning," Joe said.

Dan hung his hat and replied, "Morning. Are those our horse thieves?"

"Yes, sir. They've been pretty well-behaved."

Dan then grinned and said, "Which was more than could be said for Drew Hogan when he occupied Wally's cell the last time you were here."

Joe replied, "That's true," just before Deputy Sheehy stepped before him and shook his hand.

"Glad you're here, Joe. We really needed the help with the boss's ankle being messed up, Ned's wife about ready to have her baby, and my Ellie due just another month from now."

"I'm glad I could help, but I have a lot to learn."

"Tell me how you and the boss got those two," Dan said as he began filling his cup with fresh coffee.

As Joe began his explanation, Dan sipped the coffee and was pleased with Joe's effort. It was a lot better than the witch's brew that Lou Sanborn made.

As Joe talked, the two men in the cells understood that they'd been captured by a damned kid who wasn't even a sworn lawman yet, but that was about to change.

Joe hadn't finished telling the story yet when Sheriff Warren entered the office accompanied by his wife and Cassie.

"Good morning, boys," the sheriff said loudly as he hung his hat next to Dan's.

"Morning, boss," Dan replied.

"I brought my ladies along because they wanted to be here for the small ceremony when we make Joe a deputy and subject to my every whim, just like you and Lou, Dan."

"He's doomed," Dan said as he set his coffee cup on the desk.

Joe glanced at Cassie, who was already staring at him, but not smiling, which added a few more ounces to Joe's pounds of confusion concerning his non-girlfriend.

Lou Sanborn trotted into the office, distracting Joe and everyone else.

"Sorry I'm late, but Anna's seeing Mrs. Williams and she asked me to wait."

"Is it time?" asked Minnie.

“No, ma’am. Anna is just having some lady problems that she wouldn’t talk to me about.”

“I’ll go and stop by after Mister Armstrong becomes Deputy Armstrong.”

“Thank you, Mrs. Warren,” Lou said as he hung his hat.

“Now that everyone’s here, let’s get this thing done,” Sheriff Warren said as he took his last deputy sheriff badge from his pocket.

He had Joe recite his oath of office, pinned on his badge, and shook his hand.

His now-fellow deputies then lined up and shook his hand as well. Both of them had expressed their concerns to their boss when he had told them he was holding the new slot open until Joe left the reformatory. Neither of them had seen Joe very much, and both remembered him solely as the angry boy that had stayed with them for a couple of days four years ago.

They’d met him briefly yesterday and had been stunned by his size and even more so by his calm, almost professional demeanor. After hearing about his performance in the takedown of the two horse thieves, they were enthusiastic supporters of their new colleague.

After shaking hands with Lou, Joe received a buss on the cheek from Mrs. Warren before he noticed that Cassie was no longer there.

He didn’t have time to speculate when Dan Sheehy said, “Lou and I both appreciate that you’ll be staying here. It means we can spend more time at home.”

"I need to learn as much as I can. I'd appreciate anything that either of you can show me."

Lou said, "We'd be glad to help whenever we can, Joe, but right now, I'm going to go back to the house with Mrs. Warren and check on my wife. Congratulations again."

"Thanks."

Lou bustled out of the office with Mrs. Warren leaving Joe with the sheriff, Deputy Sheehy, and the two prisoners.

"I'll do morning rounds, boss," Dan said as he walked to the wall and pulled down his hat.

"Take Joe with you and show him how it's done," the sheriff said.

Joe grabbed his hat from the desk and followed Deputy Sheehy out the door.

———

When they returned from their rounds, they found the jail only populated by the two prisoners. Joe and Dan hung their hats and Dan went to the desk and picked up a note left by the sheriff.

He turned to Joe and said, "The boss has gone to Lou's apartment. His wife is having some serious problems with the baby."

Joe could see the strain on Dan's face, probably because of his own wife's pending delivery of their first child. John had told him that Dan's wife had a miscarriage two years ago, and he'd been nervous about this pregnancy.

"I'll take over, Dan," Joe said as he walked around behind the desk and took a seat.

"Are you sure, Joe? I mean, you're brand new."

"I'll be okay. I know where to find everyone if there's a problem."

Dan was already reaching for his hat as he replied, "Thanks, Joe. I'll be back when I can."

Dan jogged out of the office, leaving Joe officially in charge. It shouldn't have felt any different than it had before he'd been sworn in, but it did.

With the rush to go to see how Lou's wife was doing, Joe thought he at least knew where Cassie had gone. This was an entirely new phenomenon to him, watching people rush off to care for someone who wasn't even a family member. There had been times when he'd been growing up that his brothers had laughed when he'd been cut or once when he broke a finger. None of them cared at all, at least now he could understand why.

It was closing in on lunchtime when a wagon pulled up in front of the jail and judging by the lattice of steel bars on the sides, it was here to give the prisoners a ride back to Greenwich.

A few seconds after it had come to a halt, a deputy marshal, probably more than double Joe's age, entered the door and approached Joe.

"You got a couple of horse thieves for me, Deputy?"

"Yes, sir," Joe said as he stood.

Joe then pulled out a sheet of paper and a pencil and said, "I just need you to sign for them and I'll help you get them into your wagon."

The deputy marshal wasn't put off by Joe's request, so Joe assumed it was necessary. As the deputy filled out the sheet, Joe walked to the key ring, took it down, and opened the first cell.

"Let's go," he said to Wally Fremont, who stood and began to walk to the cell door.

Joe stepped back slightly, just in case he tried anything, but he didn't.

He and the deputy marshal locked Wally in the back and then a few minutes later, moved Jackson Albers in with him.

"You got those four horses they took?"

"Yes, sir. I'll bring them around," Joe replied and walked quickly behind the jail, put their makeshift bridles back on, and led them back to the jail wagon.

After he and the old deputy marshal tied them off, they shook hands and five minutes later the wagon was rolling back east out of Warwick.

Joe walked back into the jail hoping he hadn't screwed anything up. He checked the receipt and found it complete, even to the acceptance of the four horses. He wondered what the county's policy was on the two animals and saddles that the two horse thieves had been riding.

With no prisoners, Joe left the jail and returned to the corral in back to look at the two animals. Both were geldings, between six and eight years old. Neither had anything to really distinguish them, but they seemed healthy and hadn't spooked when he'd been firing in front of the four trailing horses.

He returned to the jail to wait for someone to return to verify he hadn't made any mistakes, believing it wouldn't be long and he'd be able to get some lunch.

He was mistaken on both counts.

By the time Joe finally checked his watch, it was 2:25, and there was still no sign of the sheriff or either deputy, so now he was becoming concerned. All of this childbearing was alien to him. He knew that it was a dangerous proposition for both the mother and child and the longer he remained alone in the office, the more he began to believe that there had been a serious problem for Deputy Sanborn's wife.

Ten minutes after checking his watch, a forlorn Sheriff Warren walked slowly through the doorway and hung his hat on a peg before stepping over to the desk and taking a seat.

He didn't look at Joe, but said quietly, "The baby was trying to be born but it was all sideways. There was nothing Mrs. Williams could do, but she tried. Anna died and then the baby died."

There was nothing Joe could say. He had never met Mrs. Sanborn and had barely met her husband. He felt awkwardly empty.

John then said, "Lou won't be in for a while, and I left Dan with him. I'll go back there in a little while."

Then he glanced at the empty cells and asked, "What happened to the prisoners? Did somebody come and get them?"

"Yes, sir. I had the deputy marshal sign a receipt for them and the horses," Joe replied as he slid the receipt to his new boss.

John looked at the sheet and then slid it back before saying, "Good job, Joe. I think you're going to have to hold down the fort a lot over the next few days."

"I'll do anything you need, boss."

John just nodded and exhaled sharply and said, "Life isn't very fair, is it, Joe?"

"It's all we have, boss."

John then snapped a quick look at Joe and asked, "Are you sure you're eighteen, Joe?"

Joe nodded and almost smiled, remembering that he'd asked Cassie the same question.

"Well, I'm going to go back and see how they're doing."

Any questions that Joe had planned on asking all faded into having no importance at all as he watched Sheriff Warren stand, take his hat, and leave the office.

———

When it was time for supper, Joe just walked down to Rupert's and had his meal there. Now that he had a badge, he just had to sign a chit. He could have paid for it with his fifty dollars, but they were all still in ten-dollar notes and he knew they couldn't make that much change.

He didn't see anyone else that day which surprised him, and he admitted, saddened him as well. He cleaned the office as much as he could and left the office. He made his night rounds, including stops in the town's four saloons. He thought it was funny because he knew that technically, he wasn't old enough to have a beer. He really wasn't eighteen yet, despite what it said on the birth certificate.

After he returned, he blew out the main office lamp and walked to the sleeping room, stripped off his clothes, and then just lay on top of the blanket in the dark room.

It had been a depressing first day on the job.

CHAPTER 7

His first full day on the job didn't start out much better when he had a good-sized nick on his jaw when he was shaving and had to hold a wet towel against it for a good ten minutes before it stopped bleeding and spent another ten minutes washing the towel.

After breakfast at Rupert's, he returned to the jail and started the heat stove. It was already warm outside, but he needed to make the coffee in case anyone else showed up.

The coffee was already made, and he'd finished a cup before the sheriff walked in and said, "Good morning, Joe."

"Good morning, boss. How is Lou?"

John walked to the desk and sat down in the chair before the desk and replied, "I just stopped by and saw him. He's doing better but has to arrange for Anna's burial. Dan is helping him a lot. They've been friends even before they were my deputies. They were in the same class at school and I swear they're closer than most brothers I know."

"Did you hire them at the same time?"

"Nope. I hired Dan because I already had one deputy. Six months later, the other one left to join the Texas Rangers so I hired Lou. Dan may only be senior by a few months, but it seems as if he's been on the job longer."

"How old was Dan when you hired him?"

“He was nineteen and right after I hired him, he married Ellie. Lou married Anna the same day that he was sworn in. It was kind of a double ceremony for him.”

John then stood and walked to the heat stove, poured himself a cup of coffee, and instead of going back to his private office, returned to the seat he’d just left.

“Joe, did you see Cassie at all after the swearing-in?” he asked before taking a sip of coffee.

“No, sir. I thought she had gone to help at the Sanborns. She was here for the swearing-in and then disappeared while we were shaking hands.”

“Cassie has been as silent as I’ve ever seen her, and I thought it might have been something that you told her because you seemed to get along so well.”

“I have no idea. I was confused when she wouldn’t talk to me yesterday after we came back with the two prisoners. I haven’t said a word to her since.”

John just nodded, took a long drink, and said, “You make good coffee, Joe.”

“I learned how to cook at the reformatory when we had cooking detail, but I’m not sure if I can cook for fewer than fifty.”

John smiled and stood and walked back to his office, topping off his coffee on the way.

Joe spent some time thinking about what he could have said or done to put Cassie in such a bad mood. She seemed so happy when they parted in the kitchen.

He finally shrugged, stood, and took his hat in his hands and after telling the boss he was making the morning rounds, left the office, and turned left on the boardwalk.

When Dan had shown him how to do the rounds, he'd pointed out each of the buildings, and told him who was the owner and which of their doors should always be locked. He'd shown Joe his and Lou's houses, and Joe glanced that way now. It didn't seem any different. There were no black flags, no hearse parked out front, and no wails were heard echoing from its windows. It looked like all of the other wood-framed buildings.

The streets were already busy with wagons, horses, and pedestrians, so Joe had to be careful when he crossed the crowded thoroughfare. After he had safely reached the opposite side, he turned and entered the bank.

Joe used forty of the fifty dollars to open a new account and had the last ten broken into singles and silver to make life easier. When he needed to deposit the hundred dollars for the reward, he'd have the sheriff added to the account.

As he was leaving the bank, he stopped on the boardwalk and wondered if that was what was making Cassie upset; his offer to give her the money so she could pursue her dream to be independent. But they had gotten past that when they had mutually decided that it was too far in the future to worry about, *so what had gotten her so upset that she had gone into a shell?*

Joe decided that if Cassie wanted to talk about it, she knew where to find him.

He finished his morning rounds, and on his way back to the jail, stopped at the small barn in back and shifted some hay from the barn to the corral. While he was there, he examined the two geldings more closely and thought they were better suited for law work than the pinto. He thought the mostly white horse might be the key to cheering up Cassie, so he stopped in the barn and checked out the handsome pinto. He hadn't given him a name yet, but if Cassie accepted him, she could have that honor.

After brushing down the horse, he left the barn and entered the back door of the jail. After closing the door, he cut through the sleeping room and turned into the sheriff's office.

"Boss…" he started to say when Sheriff Warren held up his hand and then wordlessly pointed to the front office.

Joe glanced that way and took six long strides down the short hallway spotting Cassie sitting in the same chair her father had occupied before the morning rounds.

"Good morning, Cassie," Joe said as he hung his hat.

"Hello, Joe."

He was about to ask why she was there when her father walked past, his hat already on his head, and left the jail, closing the door behind him.

Joe sat down behind the desk and just waited for Cassie to start the conversation.

"I've decided to accept your offer," she said quietly.

"Okay. That's fine. I'll be making the first deposit in the next few days. Is that why you haven't talked to me since Sunday?"

Cassie was avoiding eye contact, exactly as she had the night he'd arrived but replied, "Sort of. When you first told me about your idea, it seemed like such a distant thing that I was able to push it out of my mind. But when you and my father captured those two men, it suddenly became very real. It was very disconcerting."

"But you seem to be over that now. You said, 'sort of'. Was there some other reason?"

"Yes, but it doesn't involve you, at least not directly. It's my problem and I'll deal with it. I just wanted to let you know that I'll accept your offer."

"Alright. I understand. So, does that mean that I'm no longer even your pretend boyfriend and you'd rather not talk to me anymore?"

Cassie began wringing her hands, still staring at the floor as she answered, "I'm sure that we'll still see each other around. It's hard not to in a town this size and with you working for my father."

"But you'd rather I kept my distance. Is that it?"

There was a ten-second pause before Cassie replied softly, "Yes."

"I'll do as you ask, Cassie, but I won't be happy about it. I really enjoyed spending time with you. I think you're the most remarkable person I've ever met."

After she didn't say anything for twenty seconds, Joe asked, "Do I still get your letters to take with me on the trail?"

In that same soft voice, Cassie replied, "I burned them all this morning."

Joe had no idea why Cassie was so despondent, and thought he'd at least offer her the horse.

“Cassie, you know that Mexican hat pinto that your father gave me?”

“Yes.”

“I realized that it’s not a very good animal to use in law work or when I go hunting the Hogans. It’s too conspicuous and too valuable. I’d like you to have him. Is that alright?”

If Cassie was miserable before, she was worse now, but still replied, “Okay.”

Not seeing any change in her mood, Joe said, “Goodbye, Cassie.”

Cassie knew if she stayed another ten seconds, she’d burst into tears, so she just stood, said, “Bye,” and then almost ran out the door, slamming it behind her.

Joe was still staring at the closed door when Sheriff Warren entered, closed it normally, removed his hat, and walked to the desk.

“I saw Cassie run out of here like she was shot out of a cannon and then she was almost run over by a carriage. What happened?”

Joe leaned back looked at the sheriff and said, “I have no idea.”

The sheriff dropped onto the chair and asked, “What did she say?”

Joe replayed the entire conversation and when he finished, he hoped that John would be able to offer an explanation but was disappointed.

"I agree with your decision about the pinto, and I was going to give you both of those horses from the horse thieves anyway, but I have no idea what is bothering her. After Sunday, my wife and I thought you two were so alike it was spooky but now, I don't know what's going through her head."

"I thought you might know her a lot better than I do because she's your daughter."

"You would think so, wouldn't you? The odd thing is I know her better than her mother does. She's always talked to me, and I thought I understood her, but I must have overestimated myself. Cassie is the smartest, most complex person I know, and you're the second. When she showed up looking for you, I thought she'd tell you what was bothering her, but I can see I was wrong about that, too."

"I don't suppose there's anything I can do, but I told her that I'd limit any contact with her, so I will. I don't like it at all, but it's what she wants."

John exhaled and said, "Like I told my wife, she's still only a fifteen-year-old girl, and still has a lot to learn."

Joe nodded and said, "So, do I, boss."

John smiled at Joe and said, "At least I can help you with those things."

"Where can I get some target practice?" Joe asked.

"Away from Cassie's target range, I guess. Let's go south," he replied as he stood and grabbed a Winchester from the rack, and tossed it to Joe.

He then took a box of cartridges and a second Winchester and they left through the back door to do some shooting.

Cassie had reached her bedroom, closed the door, and dropped onto her bed, and began sobbing. She simply didn't know what to do. Joe had been the answer, then the problem, then the answer and the problem combined. Her decision to take his offer was a cowardly one, but the alternative was even worse.

Minnie had heard her return, the rush of footsteps, and the closing of the bedroom door. She walked quietly to the door and heard Cassie crying. She hadn't cried like that in years and wanted to tap on the door and talk to her, but this was Cassie, not Bessie. Whenever Bessie had broken down in tears, she had always found a comforting shoulder with her mother. But Cassie, on those rare occasions when she'd been upset enough to weep, had never explained to anyone what was bothering her. Even when she was eight, she thought it was important that she find a solution to her dilemma. Now for some reason, probably involving Joe, she was crying harder than Minnie had ever heard her before.

She finally sighed and turned and quietly walked back into the kitchen.

Five minutes later, she heard gunfire in the distance and guessed that Joe and her husband were engaged in target practice just by the cadence of the shots.

When John returned to the house for lunch, Cassie was still in her room, and John explained what had happened, leaving Minnie as confused as he and Joe were.

After the sheriff left to go back to work, Cassie left her room and had a quiet lunch with her mother. The only sign of her distress was in her red eyes.

Over the rest of the week, Deputy Sheehy worked sporadically as he continued to provide support as his friend deeply mourned the sudden, unexpected death of his wife and baby. Joe took on most of the burden of the day-to-day operations which he accepted eagerly as a learning experience.

There were only a few incidents in Warwick itself, all involving excessive alcohol use, and two of those were coupled with gambling.

On Thursday, when the reward vouchers arrived, he and the sheriff went to the bank to deposit them and Joe had Sheriff Warren added to the account.

The biggest surprise of the rest of the week was that Cassie had taken the pinto out several times for long rides and seemed to revel in the freedom.

Joe worked with the sheriff whenever he could, learning how to track, how outlaws thought, and how to defeat their tactics. Having lived with so many backward-thinking boys for a long time, he found it easy to understand criminal thought and behavior.

He was going through a lot of ammunition, and rather than have the county treasurer's office take notice, began buying boxes of .44s himself. He had three Winchester '73s now and still had Drew Hogan's Yellow Boy '66 model. He had four Colt '73s and the Remington that he'd used to ill effect on the hill trying to hold up the posse four years ago.

The town was already accustomed to hearing the daily gunfire south of town and most were actually comforted by the sound.

Joe had tried both of his new geldings and was pleased with them. While not spectacular in any way, they were competent and trustworthy. He even took some test shots from the saddle to see how each would react.

After a typical weekend where Joe had to break up three bar fights, tossing one of the combatants in the jail overnight, Monday arrived and so did Deputies Sheehy and Sanborn.

Joe had the coffee ready and was writing up a report on the second bar fight when they walked in together.

Joe glanced up at them and Lou seemed in a normal state, so he said, “Good morning, gentlemen.”

“Howdy, Joe,” Lou replied, “How’s business?”

“I had two bar fights on Friday night and another one on Saturday night, but nothing too bad. They were all too drunk to do much damage, but one of them took a swing at me, so I tossed him in a cell to sober up.”

Dan laughed and said, “I’ll bet it was Charlie Prebble. That boy just can’t tolerate his liquor.”

“That’s the name he gave me. He promised he’d behave himself if I let him go back to the saloon.”

“You didn’t let him go, did you?” asked Lou as he hung up his hat.

“No, sir, but I did spend a good half an hour cleaning up his cell after he left.”

Dan and Lou each took a coffee cup and were filling them when Sheriff Warren entered and didn’t appear to be surprised by having all three of his deputies present and accounted for.

After filling his coffee cup, the four lawmen engaged in a very unprofessional yet very casual conversation about anything not involving wives or babies.

"We hear all this gunfire all the time now, Joe. Is that you, or have the Comanches broken out of the reservation?" asked Dan.

"I had to fight off half the Nations while I was on my own, but I got some good target practice in while I was doing it, so it was worth it."

And that's the way Monday passed, with off-hand comments and rebuttals, joshing and counter-joshing, but no serious discussions.

Joe got his target practice done and was joined by his fellow deputies, who used county-supplied ammunition, and they had a community gun-cleaning when they were done.

At the end of the day, Dan and Lou left to return to their homes, and after they'd gone, Joe hoped that the sheriff would give him an update on Cassie, but he simply said, 'good evening' and left the office.

Joe walked down to Rupert's for dinner and then did the night rounds without any incidents.

When he returned to the jail, he sat down behind the desk and wondered if this was what he should expect until he was ready to go after the Hogans. He wanted to learn more.

April 17, 1879

Since Lou's wife's death, everything settled into that routine that Joe had expected. Aside from his daily target practice, he'd been reading the Texas law statutes and those of the county. He and the sheriff had spent a lot of afternoons out in the open country, where Joe learned what to look for while he was tracking men and how to avoid an ambush.

Things changed on Wednesday when a telegram arrived for Sheriff Warren and Joe Armstrong from the office of the attorney general.

SHERIFF WARREN WARWICK TEXAS

WARDEN PHELPS GONE
HEARD ABOUT INVESTIGATION
WARRANT ISSUED FOR MURDER AND EMBEZZLEMENT
LETTER TO FOLLOW

SAM H. PELL AUSTIN TEXAS

After reading the message, Joe said, "I suppose I shouldn't be surprised that he found out they were trying to get more affidavits, but I am surprised that they issued a warrant for murder and not just embezzlement after what Mister Pell said about the politics of the situation."

"So, am I," John said as he handed the telegram to Dan Sheehy just to satisfy his curiosity.

Joe said, "I guess we'll find out in his letter, but I doubt if Warden Phelps will be coming this direction. His best bet is to head south to Mexico."

"That would be my guess, too."

"Is this that warden who you told us about, boss?" asked Dan.

"That's him. We were told they'd charge him with embezzlement and throw him into the prison where his friendly inmates would greet him with open arms. I guess he figured out what would happen and skedaddled."

Dan handed the telegram back to Joe, who just stuffed it in his pocket. He supposed that it really didn't matter, but it still frustrated him. That cruel bastard was going to literally get away with murder. Granted, he'd be out of a job, but if he'd been taking twenty-five dollars from each departing boy for the four years that he was in charge, that would be a nice little bundle and Joe was sure he was skimming money from other areas, too. Ex-warden Bert Phelps could be just about anywhere and probably living pretty well, and Joe was pretty sure that no serious effort was being made to find him either.

———

After the telegram, the rest of the day progressed normally until just after noon when they had a visitor who asked to see the sheriff. After he'd spent a few minutes in the sheriff's office, he left the jail and Sheriff Warren walked out into the front office and looked at his curious deputies.

Sheriff Warren wasn't about to send Lou out on a job like this so soon, and he knew that Dan was concerned about Ellie after what had happened to Anna, so that left Joe which made him a bit queasy.

"That was Bill Benson. He's a ranch hand on the Rocking Z. He was on his way to town and when he passed the Chaney ranch, he heard some gunfire. Now the Chaneys and their neighbors, the Finleys, have been at each other since after the war. It's been quiet for the past few years, but it sounds like it's broken out again. Joe, I want you to ride out there and see if you can quiet them down. The last time I had a talk with them, they both promised to behave, but that was five years ago."

Joe nodded and asked, "How many men are on each ranch?"

"Both of them are family-run and only hire hands when they need to drive cattle. The Chaney ranch is owned by the widow Barb Chaney. She has two sons in their twenties, and each has a wife and kids. Jim Finley and his wife, Luella, have two widowed daughters and two sons in their teens. If I'd have to guess, I'd say it was the Finley boys who were causing the problem. Go there first and talk to Jim. Remind him of the promise he made to me five years ago."

"Okay, boss. How do I get there?"

"Just take the northwest trail. It'll only take you about four hours."

"I'd better be going, then," Joe replied, grabbed his hat and walked down the hallway, and exited the back door.

John watched him go and knew that both Dan and Lou felt as guilty as he did, but it was probably just going to be a tongue-lashing anyway.

Joe was riding one of the geldings, and after a quick stop at Lippett's Grocery for some jerky and crackers, headed out of town and turned northwest when he found the trail.

He'd only ridden a mile when he spotted a rider cutting cross-country, west to east. He knew the rider without too much difficulty and waved at Cassie as she fast trotted about half a mile in front of him. Either she didn't see him, or she didn't want to acknowledge his wave because she continued riding straight across his bow, and by the time he reached her tracks, she was a mile to the east and turning south toward her house.

The sun was halfway down on his left shoulder as he kept the gelding moving and his eyes busy, looking at country that looked vaguely familiar but then again, it usually did in West Texas.

On the Finley ranch, Earl and Glen Hogan, Red Victor, and Tommy Johnson were enjoying their dinner. The only ones still alive from the Finley family were the two widowed daughters, Patsy and Katie. The boys had been made to dig a big hole for their parents, and then they were shot and dumped in as well. Earl had Red and Tommy fill it in.

This was the second ranch they'd had to use since they had problems with those damned Indians. It was actually Red's fault when he'd taken advantage of a Choctaw woman who wasn't even that good-looking according to Glen. She had escaped and run back to her village, which had caused the Hogan brothers and Red and Tommy to hightail it across the Red River.

The first place they'd stopped was barely a ranch at all, but they'd stayed there a week and had been a bit frustrated by the lack of female companionship. The only problem with this place was that the area was positively crowded. There was another ranch just four miles north of this one and after all of the gunfire, there was some concern that they might have visitors from the other ranch, but no one had arrived.

They'd already enjoyed the favors of the two women and had put them to work feeding them now. They had ransacked the house and found a decent amount of cash, almost two hundred dollars. These folks must not believe in banks.

Earl thought that this haul was good enough that when they were finished in a few days, they might just go north to that neighboring ranch.

Joe spotted the barn first at about three miles and did a quick scan of the landscape for possible ambush sites. It wasn't likely, but he wanted to get into the habit. The boss had said he'd probably just have to give Jim Finley and his boys a warning, and he smiled at the idea. He was still a boy himself.

He was still snickering when he turned the gelding down the access road and was just fifty yards in when he froze and pulled the gelding to a stop.

It wasn't the quietness of the scene that caused him to pause, it was what he saw. There was a large, fresh mound of dirt just off to the side of the house. There was never any reason for turning earth there. It was right in the middle of the ground between the barn and the house, and it was still reasonably fresh.

Then as he scanned the ranch there was an oddity with the horses in the corral. It was hard to put a finger on it, but four of them didn't seem to belong with the others. They just looked different. It was as if the other horses in the corral were shunning the four.

As he sat in his saddle, he remembered the only letter he'd received from the sheriff when he was in the reformatory and he'd mentioned that the Hogans had taken over a ranch and murdered the entire family. Rereading letters dozens of times will let things like that stick in your memory. *But could this be the same thing or was his imagination playing tricks on him?*

Again, it was one of those early lessons that were all branded into his mind. Always trust your instincts.

Joe knew he didn't have much time with the sun already low in the sky. He didn't know if anyone was still alive in the family, nor did he know how many he'd have to deal with if the ranch had been taken over by the Hogans or anyone else.

First, he needed to get out of sight, so he quickly wheeled his horse around and trotted south, and then when the barn blocked the house, he turned back east to come up behind the barn.

As he rode, he had to come up with a way to be sure that he wasn't reading too much into those simple signs, and it didn't take long to come up with a solution. Those horses had saddles and they'd be in the barn. So, if he could get into the barn and check out the tack, he should be able to figure out if he was still sane or not.

Just three minutes later, he stepped down behind the barn and tied the gelding's reins to the pigsty. He slowly approached the barn's back door, took off his hat, and peeked through a crack, not seeing anyone inside. Joe opened the door, hearing a slight squeal, but not too bad, and walked inside.

It took him less than ten seconds to know that the ranch had been taken over by outlaws when he saw the four saddles stacked on a tarp. What made him so sure was that their Winchesters were all still in their scabbards.

He stepped over to the saddles and after a quick examination, he knew who was in the house. One of the saddles belonged to Earl Hogan and another was Glen's. Because all of the brothers were so close in size and had identical saddles, each of them had carved their first initial into the saddle horn and there was an 'E' on one and a 'G' on the other. He didn't care about the other two.

Now how could he deal with four murderers? He could ride back and get help, but he wasn't sure if any of the family was still alive in the ranch house. If he left, he wouldn't be able to get back until tomorrow and by then, it might be too late.

Joe reached for one of the Winchesters and was going to bury it and the others in the hay, but then had a better idea. He began cycling the repeaters lever, watching the cartridges fly out of the ejection slot and land on the tarp. When it was empty, he slid it back into its scabbard and repeated it with each of the other four. He then scooped up the mass of .44 cartridges and dumped them into his pockets.

After emptying their Winchesters, Joe slipped back out of the barn and when he reached the gelding, he began pulling the cartridges out of his pockets and dumping them into his saddlebags. Having live ammunition in your pockets during a gunfight wasn't a smart thing to do.

Now he had to figure out a way to get them out of the house and get them to try to use those repeaters. Their Colts with their shorter barrels had less range and their accuracy wasn't nearly as good. They could get lucky, though. He'd have to make every one of his shots count.

He mounted the gelding and reversed his looping ride back to the trail and made a second entrance down the access road a few minutes later.

It was important now that they see him and want to engage him at range, *but how could he do it?*

He walked his horse slowly toward the ranch house until he was about a hundred yards out. He hoped that the Finleys didn't have any long-range rifles in the house as he pulled the gelding to a stop, pulled his Winchester, and dismounted.

He then put his badge on his light jacket, hung his hat on the saddle horn, and shouted, "Earl and Glen, I know you're in there. Come out and meet me!"

———

Earl was about to grab the younger sister when Joe's shout passed through the open windows and entered the house.

"*Who the hell is that?*" he shouted as he bounced to his feet.

Glen grabbed his pistol as did Red and Tommy, and the women were forgotten.

"How would he know who we were?" Glen asked loudly.

"Let's spread out and see how many are out there," Earl said and added, "Red, you and Tommy sneak out the back and get ready to make a break into the barn and get our Winchesters. Me and Glen are gonna head to the front room and look through the windows."

"Okay, Earl," Red replied and he and Tommy opened the back door, did a quick scan for lawmen then went out onto the small porch, letting the door slam shut behind them.

Even at a hundred yards, Joe could hear the back door's loud bang and knew then that at least one of them was out back now. He cocked the rifle's hammer and took a few steps toward the house and angled closer to the barn to get a better angle and protect his horse from errant rounds.

Earl was the first one to reach the main room and scurried to the left to take a look out the window while Glen swung to the right.

Joe picked up movement in the house, but only from the right window. That meant that they were in the front and the back now, but he still didn't know how many were in each location or if any family members were still alive.

Earl loud whispered to Glen, "There's only one of 'em. He's got a badge, so he's gotta be a deputy from Warwick. Ain't that a hoot?"

"Why?"

"'Cause this will be payback for them hangin' Drew. They got our boys too, so it's about time we got this one."

"Oh, yeah," Glen replied and asked, "How do you wanna handle this, Earl?"

"We need our Winchesters to be sure, but I wonder how he figured out who we were. It's kinda buggin' me."

"If he knows we're here, it ain't gonna hurt any to find out by yellin'."

Earl chewed on his lower lip for a few seconds and replied, "Go ahead."

Glen stayed well away from the window and yelled, "Who the hell are you?"

Joe was a bit surprised by the shout, but yelled back, "The name's Joe Armstrong. I'm a county deputy sheriff. You boys come out now and I promise not to shoot you."

Glen snickered and turned to Earl, saying, “Can you believe the cojones on this hombre? He wants us to give up.”

Earl was thinking and ignored Glen. There was something about that name that was familiar, but he couldn’t put a finger on it.

Glen then shouted, “How did you know it was us?”

“I could smell you both from way down in Warwick. You boys need to take a bath.”

Glen snapped, “He’s one arrogant son-of-a-bitch, ain’t he?”

“Keep him talkin’. I’m gonna go and get our Winchesters with Red and Tommy. Once we open up, you stay here and make sure those women don’t try nothin’.”

“Okay, Earl.”

Earl then spun on his heels and quickly trotted back to the kitchen, glancing at the two women as he passed without saying a word. They were already terrified, and Earl didn’t have to add any more threats.

Once Earl was on the porch, he explained to Red and Tommy that when Glen had the deputy’s attention, they’d make a dash into the barn, grab their Winchesters and then face him down, three to one. He was off his horse, so he couldn’t run.

Drew shouted, “I can smell you, too, Deputy. You sure smell yellow to me! You ain’t nothin’ but a damned coward!”

The long delay between shouts made it obvious that Drew’s insults were meant to keep his attention, so he shouted back,

"You're right! You boys scare me to death!" while he watched the back of the house.

It was out of range, and they'd be running across his field of fire, so they'd be hard targets to hit. He wanted them coming towards him…with empty repeaters.

He'd never shot a man before, and he recalled his inability to even finish off that coyote. But this was different. These men wanted to kill him, and two of them had killed his mother. It was time for retribution.

When he heard Joe's shouted reply, Earl said, "Go!", and the three men made a dash across the open ground between the house and the barn, expecting a shot or two to head their way.

But after they arrived in the barn, they were almost giddy as they grabbed their Winchesters and then stood near the barn door.

Each man cocked his hammer, knowing their chamber was already loaded and not wanting to waste a cartridge. If they had, they would have discovered Joe's act of sabotage.

"Alright, follow my lead," Earl said before he stepped from the barn.

Joe spotted Earl's exit, quickly followed by the other two, whose names he couldn't recall from the wanted poster. He was surprised that they hadn't checked their weapons. He knew they hadn't had time to reload even a few cartridges, so he was sure that their Winchesters were useless.

Earl, Tommy, and Red spread about ten feet apart and began walking toward Joe, who stood his ground with his

Winchester's butt against his hip. He had the sun at his back, but it wasn't directly behind him.

Earl shouted, "How did you really know our name, mister?"

"I've known your name for a long time, Earl," Joe yelled back.

"We're pretty famous, but I'm askin'…" he began to shout when he realized that the deputy had called him Earl. Maybe he'd guessed that he was in charge.

He then continued his shouted question yelling, "I'm askin' how come you knew it was us who was here."

"Because you, Earl James Hogan, and your youngest brother Glen Lee Hogan both murdered a whole family about twenty miles east of here three years ago. Things like that stay in folks' memories."

Earl kept walking, now wondering how this damned lawman knew his and Glen's middle names. Nobody knew that. He was thinking so much that he failed to realize how close he was getting as the three men passed the house.

Glen had been wondering the same things but not as critically. He was just as curious about why Earl was still walking and not shooting. He was already within range.

"How'd you know our middle names, Deputy?" Earl asked as they closed to within eighty yards.

"I know more about you than those two idiots you have walking with you, Earl. You and your brothers and that bastard father of yours kidnapped my mother and her sister and used her for two years before she died. I'm going to kill you for that."

Earl stopped dead in his tracks bringing Red and Tommy to a halt as they saw Joe bring his Winchester level.

Earl recovered quickly from the shocked realization that the deputy was Joey and rapidly swung his Winchester's sights onto Joe, pulling the trigger when they steadied.

Neither Red, nor Tommy understood the significance of Joe's revelation but didn't need to know what it meant when Joe's repeater pointed their way, and both quickly readied their rifles to fire and squeezed their triggers.

Joe held his fire but had Earl in his sights as he watched their reaction when their trusty Winchesters failed them.

Each outlaw heard the same unexpected click as their hammers dropped within two seconds, but there wasn't time to realize the impossibility that all three would have a misfire at the same time and quickly cycled their levers to bring in a live cartridge.

Joe yelled, "They're empty, boys! I have all your cartridges! Put your hands in the air!"

He didn't expect them to surrender and had no desire for them to do so, but in those few moments of realization and decision by the three men, he believed he had the advantage, but he had forgotten about Glen.

Glen, like Earl, had been momentarily stunned by Joe's identity and his first thought was to go around the back and run around the other side of the house, so he could come at Joe from the flank while he was engaged with the others. But when Joe shouted that he'd emptied their rifles, Glen knew he had to protect Earl.

Glen cocked his Colt's hammer and walked quickly to the window just as Earl, Red, and Tommy tossed aside their useless Winchesters and started to reach for their pistols, setting off the fireworks.

The instant Joe saw their intent, he squeezed the trigger of his loaded Winchester, felt the pop against his shoulder as it spat its .44 from the muzzle, and was levering in a fresh round when Glen smashed a window pane and opened fire with his Colt.

Earl felt Joe's .44 slam into his gut like a hammer blow just as his Colt was coming free from his holster and both hands automatically flew to his stomach to try and staunch the flow of blood as he bent at the waist and then buckled and fell to the ground.

Red and Tommy were able to pull their pistols and were almost ready to fire when Glen's shot exploded from the house.

Joe had already planned on moving his sights to the next man on the right after hitting Earl and was taken off guard by Glen's shot, making him miss his second shot as Glen's .44 tugged him to the right when it ripped through his jacket.

He was levering in another round when Glen took his second shot just before Red and Tommy took their first shots. Joe was exposed to three shooters but didn't have any other option but to hope that he wasn't hit as he stood straight.

He then turned his Winchester's iron sights to the house and had the advantage of knowing that Glen was behind the window so, even if he couldn't see him, he had to be in that space. He fired as soon as his sights stabilized and brought in a new round and had to assume that Glen had been hit because he had two active shooters left standing before him.

Glen was just readying his third shot when he saw Joe's muzzle aim in his direction, yet despite the almost useless protection afforded by the dry wooden walls, he felt safe. When Joe's Winchester exploded in fire and smoke, he soon learned otherwise. His imaginary wooden shield had added just enough resistance to cause Joe's bullet to deflect slightly, so when the bullet drilled through the useless wood it barely slowed down, but after it crashed into his chest, it began tumbling, smashing ribs and mutilating tissue. Glen dropped to the floor, gasping for air as blood poured from the massive wound.

After their first shots, Tommy dropped to the ground to make less of a target and Red followed suit just a blink of an eye later. Once on their stomachs, they continued to fire.

From the moment of the first hammer drop to the time when Red hit the ground was less than fifty seconds, but the air around the two outlaws was already thick with gunsmoke.

Joe was now moving, sidestepping to his right as he kept his rifle on the two men. When each fired another round, one of the bullets passing Joe so closely he could hear the buzz pass his left ear. Joe fired at the left man's muzzle flare and reversed his sidestep and stopped.

Joe's shot at the flash creased the top of Red's skull before it slammed into the right side of his back, punching into the soft tissue and ripping through his renal artery. Red was unconscious from the head trauma and didn't feel the pain from the bullet strike on his back, so he died peacefully when the blood drained into his gut from the severed artery.

Tommy didn't notice Red's hit but knew he only had one more shot in his revolver and was torn between reloading the Colt or firing the last round.

"Red, how many shots you got left?" he asked loudly but received no reply.

Then he turned his head to see what had happened to Red when Joe fired the last shot in the gunfight.

That final bullet flew across the two hundred and twenty-six feet in just a fourth of a second and ripped into Tommy's left upper chest and followed a downward path tearing through vital lung tissues and blood vessels before it pushed through his diaphragm. Tommy couldn't scream in pain because he lacked the ability to move any air but simply collapsed onto the ground, shuddered, and died.

Joe stood motionless, his Winchester still aimed at the last two shooters, waiting for any signs of movement. He remained statue-like for almost a minute before his repeater's barrel slowly lowered and he exhaled his breath that he'd held longer than he realized.

He slowly began walking toward the carnage he'd inflicted, still not believing he'd been the cause of all the bodies. It was almost as if someone else had fired those shots.

Inside the ranch house, Patsy and Katie had moved into the bathroom and closed the door the moment Glen had left them alone. They'd stayed huddled together and had only been able to understand parts of the shouts from the men outside but when the bullets started flying, they dropped to the floor, still locked together as the gunfight escalated.

Now there was just silence, and they had no idea what had happened, so they stayed right where they were holding onto each other on the bathroom floor.

Joe reached the bodies of Earl, Tommy, and Red, but only looked at Earl's. He hadn't changed much in the past five years. His moustache was gone, but that was about it.

He spent almost a minute staring at the body wondering what he should be feeling. He felt empty and it bothered him. He should be either feeling some sense of satisfaction or revulsion but felt neither. He wasn't even sick over what he had done, which surprised him even more. He had almost cried when he had to shoot that coyote but now, after killing four men, he didn't feel a tinge of sadness.

He'd worry about that later and left the bodies, took his Winchester in his left hand, and pulled his Colt, cocking the hammer as he walked to the house to make sure that Glen was dead.

He carefully stepped onto the porch and listened for any movement inside. After not hearing anything, he approached the door and slowly swung it open.

Joe stepped inside and then quickly looked to his right and saw Glen's open, dead eyes looking back at him. A rush of eerie uneasiness passed through him before he took two strides to Glen's body, rolled it onto the floor, and closed his eyes.

He then shouted, "This is Deputy Sheriff Joe Armstrong! Is anyone here?"

Inside the bathroom, Patsy and Katie looked at each other and both burst into tears of utter relief at the sound of his voice and couldn't yell back.

Joe released his Colt's hammer, slipped it back into its holster, and after pulling the hammer loop in place, let out a long sigh. Those bastards had killed the entire Finley family. If he had felt any remorse at all for what he had just done, it wouldn't have existed now.

Joe walked over to Glen's body, pulled his gunbelt off, and was replacing the pistol when he heard noises coming from his left and quickly stood. He still had Glen's pistol in his hand but dropped the gunbelt and was preparing to cock the hammer when he heard a woman's voice.

"Deputy? We're coming out of the bathroom. Don't shoot!"

Joe was reaching for the gunbelt again when Patsy and Katie exited the bathroom and slowly entered the main room, seeing Joe picking up the gunbelt as he stood over Glen Hogan's body.

"Is he dead?" Patsy asked.

"Yes, ma'am. They're all dead. Are you all right?"

The sisters stopped just three feet into the room as Patsy replied, "We'll survive. They came here yesterday morning and killed our parents and our brothers. They used us like prostitutes and serving women."

"Ladies, I need to get that body out of the house and then round up the others. You can go into the kitchen and have some coffee while I do that. It'll take me an hour or so."

Katie then said, "Thank you, Deputy. They were going to kill us when they were finished with us, weren't they?"

Joe nodded and said, "Yes, ma'am, I'm afraid so."

"When you're finished, come into the kitchen and we'll fix you something to eat," said Patsy.

“I’d appreciate it, ma’am,” Joe said.

The sisters both turned and walked down the short hallway, leaving Joe to do his work.

It took him more than two hours to get the four horses saddled, the bodies loaded, and his own horse returned to the ranch house. He had searched all of the bodies before hanging them over the saddles, found a total of $248.55, and he guessed that most of it had been found on the Finley ranch.

With everything done and the sun setting, Joe finally spent a few minutes cleaning up at the trough before heading for the back of the house, stepping onto the porch, and knocking on the door.

Patsy opened the door and said, “You really didn’t have to knock, Deputy.”

“Yes, I did, ma’am,” he replied as he took off his Stetson and entered the house.

“Have a seat and we’ll get you fed.”

“I found this money on them, and I assume that they stole it from you,” Joe said as he set the cash on the counter near the sink.

“They found my father’s stash in our parents’ bedroom,” Katie said as Joe took a seat.

Patsy was scooping up the money and slipping it into her dress pocket as she said, “Thank you again, Deputy, but there’s more here than they stole, I think.”

“That’s okay, ma’am. It’s still not enough for what they did to you and your family. There’s never enough.”

Katie was putting food on the table before Joe and asked, "What's your name?"

"Joe Armstrong, ma'am."

"I don't recall seeing you before, and I would have remembered you if I had. Have you been a deputy very long?"

"About a month now, ma'am."

"And the sheriff sent you into this mess alone?" asked Patsy in surprise as she poured his coffee.

"No, ma'am. He wouldn't do that. He received a report of gunfire from a passing ranch hand and thought it was just a renewed feud between your family and the Chaneys. He thought all I'd have to do is talk to both families and everything would calm down."

"How did you know differently?" asked Katie as she and Patsy took seats at the table with coffee cups in their hands.

Joe explained the whole sequence of events but didn't go into the Hogan brother routine. Apparently, neither sister had heard what had been shouted back and forth and he didn't want the word to get out that he once thought he was a Hogan. It wasn't that he was ashamed of the connection, but he didn't want the remaining three brothers to know who he was, at least not yet.

As he finished eating, Katie asked, "Are you returning to Warwick tonight?"

"Yes, ma'am. I don't want those horses to have to keep the bodies on their backs all night."

She glanced at her sister, who nodded and asked, “May we come with you? I don’t wish to remain here tonight, and neither does Patsy. We have money, so we can stay at the hotel.”

“That’ll be fine, ma’am. The sheriff will probably want your statements anyway. I’ll go and saddle your horses as soon as I’m finished, and we’ll be on our way.”

Katie said, “We’ll get changed into something that we can wear to ride and pack some things while you do that.”

“That’s fine, ma’am.”

There was still a hint of light in the sky as Joe led the four body-laden horses out of the ranch while the two sisters rode alongside him, Patsy on his left and Katie on his right.

They kept the horses at a fast walk because of the trailers, so they were able to talk along the way.

Joe kept most of the conversation about them and their family, so he didn’t have to talk too much about his own background.

They were almost halfway to Warwick when Joe asked, “Are you going to go back to the ranch after a while?”

“No, we’ve already decided to sell it and stay in town. We’ll use the money to start a café, I think.”

“That would be nice. We only have Rupert’s, and their menu is already getting old.”

Patsy said, “If we do, Joe, you’ll never have to pay for food in our café.”

Joe turned to her, smiled, and said, “I don’t pay now, ma’am. The county does, and I sure wouldn’t want to let them get off the hook.”

Patsy and Katie both laughed lightly which made Joe feel enormously better for some reason.

It was almost midnight when they rode into Warwick’s darkened streets. The only lights were streaming from the four saloons and the hotel.

After Patsy and Katie dismounted in front of the hotel and took their travel bags, Joe said, “I’ll leave your horses at Madison’s Livery down the street. The sheriff’s office is right over there. Just show up when you’re ready.”

“Thank you so much, Joe,” Patsy said as she looked up at him.

“God bless you, Joe,” Katie added.

“Thank you, ladies. Good night,” Joe replied as he tipped his hat and led the six horses down the street.

Before going to Madison’s Livery, Joe stopped at the sheriff’s office, dismounted, and tied off his gelding and the two Finley ranch horses before heading to Sheriff Warren’s house.

He stepped onto the porch five minutes later and hesitated before knocking, thinking that maybe he should wait until morning to bother his boss, but he had no idea what to do with the bodies, so after a short deliberation he pounded the door.

Sheriff Warren wasn’t in proper dress to leave the bed, nor was Minnie, so the first one to leave her bed and walk to the door was Cassie. Bessie was still asleep.

She padded across the floor in her bare feet and when she reached the door before she unlocked it, she asked, "Who is it?"

Joe replied, "Joe."

Cassie thought about running back to her room and closing the door, but it was too late for that, so she unlocked the door and opened it slightly, not wanting Joe to see her in her nightdress, even if she was thin.

"What do you need?" she asked, almost harshly.

Joe bristled at her tone and replied, "Miss Warren, I have four bodies out in front of the jail. Could you advise your father that I need his assistance, please?"

Cassie blinked and asked, "*What?*"

Joe sighed and said, "Cassie, just go and get your father. I need his help."

Cassie left the door ajar and stepped quickly back across the main room and knocked on her parents' bedroom door.

"Papa, Joe's outside. He said he has four bodies and needs your help."

She heard a muffled but obviously shocked, "*What?*" from the other side of the door and then thumps and other sounds of hurried dressing before the door popped open and her father rushed past her.

Cassie, despite her still-fractured mood, followed.

Joe remained outside the house as he wasn't invited in and heard the commotion before the door was yanked wide open and Sheriff Warren said, “Come in, Joe. Tell me what happened.”

Joe nodded, removed his hat, and stepped into the dark room.

“Cassie, light a lamp,” Sheriff Warren said before he asked, “How did you get four bodies? Was it a range war?”

Joe stayed standing but closed the door as he replied, “No, sir. It was Earl and Glen Hogan and two others who had taken over the Finley ranch. They killed the parents and the boys and kept the sisters. The gang is all dead, I have their bodies in front of the jail, and I don’t know what to do with them. The sisters are in the hotel and will stop by in the morning to take their statements.”

Minnie was walking into the room closing her robe about her as the lamp flared into life. She had heard Joe’s incredible story and was aghast.

Cassie was appalled, and even more disturbed for her own reasons.

“Okay, Joe. Let’s head back to the jail, take care of the bodies and you can fill me in as we walk.”

“Yes, sir,” Joe replied.

“I’ve got to get my boots on first,” the sheriff said before he turned and walked quickly back to the bedroom.

Joe stood uncomfortably in the light from the lone lamp as both Minnie and Cassie stared at him.

Bessie finally wandered into the room in her nightdress and asked, “What’s going on?”

Before anyone could say a word, Sheriff Warren strode past the three women, grabbed his hat from the coat rack, and said, “Let’s go, Joe.”

Joe was only too happy to oblige and followed his boss out of the house leaving the Warren ladies all wondering what had happened. All Bessie was able to learn was that Joe had returned from an apparently simple job with four bodies that included two Hogan brothers and that the two surviving Finley sisters were in the hotel.

As they walked through the darkness, Joe explained what had happened but before he was even a minute into his narration, the sheriff interrupted.

“Why didn’t you return and get some help once you suspected they might be there?”

“When I saw what I thought looked like a big grave, I wasn’t sure if there were any family members still alive, so I felt I had to act quickly. I know it was a big chance, but I thought it was the best one I had at the time.”

“We’ll talk about that tomorrow morning. Keep talking.”

Joe had just reached the point of the gunfight when they reached the horses and, without examining the bodies, the sheriff began unhitching the four horses with the corpses and he and Joe each led two animals down the street.

Once they arrived at the mortuary, John said, “Stay here. I’ll go and wake up Art. He lives in back.”

“Yes, sir.”

After the sheriff disappeared in the blackness, Joe wondered if he was going to be fired for making that mistake and began to think it wouldn't necessarily be a bad thing. He'd be free to go after the last three Hogans and Cassie should be less worried about whatever he had done to cause her grief.

Forty minutes later, Joe and his boss were leading the empty horses to the corral behind the jail. Joe had decided to leave the Finley sisters' horses in the same corral, at least overnight. It would be crowded, but he wouldn't have to wake anyone else. He then realized he couldn't remember the sisters' married names even though they had told him their deceased husbands' names during the ride.

Once all six of the horses were stripped and settled and his story finished, the sheriff said he'd talk to him in the morning and returned to his house, letting Joe find his way into the jail. Despite all the excitement and work on the long day, Joe couldn't sleep. So, he lit a lamp and began to write his report.

When he finished almost an hour later, he lit a fire in the heat stove and walked back to the sleeping area, stripped and washed himself as best he could, and then shaved and dressed in clean clothes.

By the time he returned, the water was hot, and he made some coffee for himself, knowing that no one would be coming into the jail for at least four or five hours.

As he sipped his steaming coffee, he reviewed the day's events, looking at the many mistakes he'd made and the things he'd done right. It was about a fifty-fifty mix. He could have died in the exchange of gunfire and changed nothing, meaning the sisters would have died and nobody would have known. If he'd ridden back quickly, he could have returned in just ten or twelve hours with at least two more men and increased the likelihood of success.

He knew that he'd done it quicker and had better results than expected, but a lot of it had been luck. If any of those men had picked up his Winchester and cycled the lever to bring the hammer into position rather than just cocking the hammer, they would have outgunned him easily. Then he'd forgotten about Glen. What if he had one of the Finleys' Winchesters or a shotgun?

The more Joe examined the confrontation in detail, the more he understood his incompetence and unreadiness to stalk the remaining Hogans.

———

By the time the predawn arrived, Joe had finished the whole pot of coffee and had been out to the privy twice. Since his initial evaluation of his performance, he'd uncovered more mistakes and wrong assumptions and decided that he wasn't fit to be a lawman. He was a danger to the sheriff and the other two deputies.

He removed his badge, laid it on the desk, and slid out a sheet of paper to write his resignation after only a month on the job.

Joe had just signed the sheet when the door opened, and he looked up to see Sheriff Warren entering the office.

"Did you get any sleep at all, Joe?" he asked as he took off his hat and walked to the desk.

"I wasn't tired, boss."

"Writing your report?"

"No, sir. It's over there on the corner of the desk," Joe replied as the sheriff sat down.

Joe was suddenly embarrassed by the resignation sitting before him. It seemed a cowardly way to announce his decision.

"Then what's that?" his boss asked.

Joe exhaled sharply and answered, "It's my resignation, Sheriff. I screwed up a lot yesterday and I'm just not good enough to do this job. I'd just as soon chase after the Hogans now rather than get anyone else in trouble."

His boss stopped before the desk and said, "I'm not going to tell you that you didn't make some blunders, Joe, but we all make mistakes. I still make them which is why I took that bullet that almost took my foot off. But you also did some remarkable things yesterday. Things I wouldn't have expected from a seasoned lawman with ten years of experience. If you want to resign to chase after the Hogans, you can do that, but you'd be putting me in a bad situation."

Joe looked at his boss and asked, "Why would I put you in a bad spot?"

"Because, Joe, I held this job open for you for almost nine months and if you quit after only a month, I'll look like an idiot."

Joe laughed and said, "I suppose you're right."

"Of course, I'm right. Now rip that damned resignation up, put on your badge, and let's have some coffee before I review your report."

Joe did as the boss ordered, and they shared some coffee as the sheriff read Joe's report and the sun rose over the town of Warwick.

The early part of the morning was spent briefing Deputies Sheehy and Sanborn of the incident and clearing up the aftermath, including sending telegrams to those offering the rewards, going through the gang's possessions, and moving some of the horses, including the sisters' animals to the livery.

Although Joe was pleased that he hadn't resigned, he didn't feel he deserved the accolades that his fellow deputies showered on him. Those mistakes he had made still loomed large in his mind.

The rewards totaled a staggering twelve hundred and fifty dollars, all of which would be deposited into the bank account. That was already more than enough money to finance Cassie's education, no matter where she chose to go or how long she wanted to study.

Joe wasn't in the office when Katie and Patsy arrived to complete their statements, which was just as well, as both gushed with praise over Joe's performance and his gentlemanly treatment of them after the smoke had cleared. They told Deputy Sanborn, who took their statements, that they would be going to the bank to meet with the officer in charge of real estate to sell the ranch, and then they'd remain in town if there were any questions.

Skipping the night's sleep was catching up with Joe before noon and by lunchtime, he was barely able to stay awake but continued to work because he felt it was his mess and he had to clean it up.

Joe walked back into the jail after having his lunch at Rupert's and headed for the desk, not even removing his hat.

Sheriff Warren was talking to Dan Sheehy, took one look at him, and said, "Joe, go back there and get some sleep before you fall over."

Joe just nodded and shuffled past his boss and entered his sleeping area, finally taking off his hat and just tossing it aside, unbuckling his gunbelt and hanging it over the bed's foot post before collapsing face first on the mattress.

———

When Joe's eyes opened, it was dark, and it took a few seconds of disorientation to realize where he was. He rolled and swung his feet onto the floor and rubbed his cheek to get an idea of how late it was by the length of his beard, but it didn't help.

After sitting on the edge of the bunk for a few minutes, Joe stood and picked up his hat from the floor, walked out to the empty front office, and lit a lamp.

He dropped onto the desk chair and pulled out his watch, finding it was 10:20. He wound the stem, closed the cover, and slipped the watch back into his pants pocket. He was hungry but had no place to go to eat, so he stood and walked out the back of the jail and entered the small barn where he hunted down his saddlebags. It was a lot more crowded with tack now, so it took him longer to find them, but after almost three minutes of rummaging, he found his own set of saddlebags and took them back into the jail.

He sat down at the desk again and flipped open the cover to take out the jerky he'd bought before he left town…was it yesterday?

When he pulled out the bag of jerky, his leather pouch slipped out onto the desk. The pouch that contained his letters from Cassie.

Joe opened the bag of jerky, sat it on the desk, took out a piece, and stuck it in his mouth as he opened his pouch.

He began chewing the jerky as he slipped the stack of letters from the pouch that he could quote by heart. He took out the first letter, unfolded it, looked at the printed letters, and smiled. *Where was that innocent, freckle-faced, ten-year-old girl with the pigtails that asked him to be her boyfriend?*

He only read the first letter before folding it again, carefully replacing it in its envelope and returning them all to his pouch. He wished Cassie hadn't burned all the letters she had written to him in those missing years.

He ate more of the jerky and blew out the lamp and returned to the sleeping room. He wasn't really that sleepy, but he knew he had to get his own clock reset.

Joe did the morning rounds before making the coffee the next day as he tried to fight his way out of his downward spiraling mood. He should be almost buoyant after taking out two Hogans, rescuing the two Finley sisters, and getting a large reward, but he was on the downslope instead. He'd gotten past his mistakes and had learned from them, but it was now Cassie who was making him just plain grumpy.

He had the coffee made by the time Deputy Sheehy arrived, and when Sheriff Warren entered, they had already finished their first cup of the day.

"Good morning, gentlemen," their boss said as he walked across the office.

"Morning, boss," Dan replied.

As he passed, he said, "Joe, I need to talk to you in my office, please."

"Yes, sir," Joe replied, wondering what transgression he could have done in the last few hours.

Joe entered the sheriff's office as John was hanging his hat on a wall peg and after they each were seated, Sheriff Warren just looked at Joe, unsettling him.

"I have an important job for you today, Joe, that only you can handle."

"Yes, sir?"

"I want you to go to my house and talk to Cassie."

Joe blinked and asked, "About what?"

Sheriff Warren threw up his hands and replied, "It beats the hell out of me, and my wife doesn't have a clue, either. All we know is that she's been moping around the house and has been quieter than she's ever been in her entire life ever since the day we swore you in. Now if she won't talk to either of us, our last hope is that you can get her to tell you what's bothering her."

Joe asked, "What if it's me that's bothering her?"

"Have you done something that would set her off?"

"Not that I know of, boss."

John leaned back and stared at the ceiling for almost a minute before looking back at Joe and saying, "Then go over there and see if you can find out what it is. Cassie is just so hard to figure out and I think my wife is going crazy trying."

"Do you want me to go right now?"

"If you don't mind. Have you had breakfast yet?"

“Coffee.”

“That doesn’t count. Go to the house and tell my wife I sent you over for a proper breakfast. Then take it from there.”

Joe would almost rather face the last three Hogan brothers than try and find out why Cassie was so upset, but an order was an order.

“Okay, boss. I’ll head over there.”

“I appreciate this, Joe. I know it’s not an easy assignment.”

Joe stood, smiled, and said, “No, sir. It isn’t.”

He left the small office walked past his two fellow deputies, grabbed his hat, and headed out the door. As he crossed the street, he wondered how he would approach Cassie, expecting she’d see him and immediately leave. He decided he’d play his hand as the cards were dealt.

Three minutes later, he stepped onto the front porch of the Warren home and knocked on the door, not surprised in the least that it was answered by Cassie.

“Yes?” she asked.

Joe decided he’d go for broke and said, “Are you dressed for riding, Cassie?”

“Yes, but why are you asking?”

“Let’s go for a ride. Now.”

“What if I don’t want to go for a ride?”

"I didn't ask, Miss Warren. I said we are going for a ride, so just come with me and we'll saddle our horses and go for a ride."

Cassie looked at Joe and turned her head and shouted, "Mama, I'm going for a ride."

Minnie shouted from the kitchen, "Alright, dear."

Cassie stepped out, closed the door behind her, and stepped across the porch quickly, leaving Joe standing there for a few seconds.

He trotted after her and caught up with the fast-moving girl fifty yards past the porch steps.

"Okay, Cassie, drop this whole hostile act right now!" he said forcefully.

She stopped, whipped around to glare at him, and said, "Act? Is that what you think this is, an act?"

"Maybe not an act, but your behavior has been so bad that your father assigned me the job of finding out what's wrong. Personally, I'd rather get into a gunfight again, but this is what I was asked to do."

"Then why don't you just leave me alone and tell him that I wouldn't talk to you?"

Joe looked into her angry brown eyes and was surprised at what else he read behind the anger, and it shook him. It was fear.

He dropped his own act and said quietly, "Why are you afraid of me, Cassie? For that one day we talked and enjoyed our time together it made me anxiously await the next time.

But there wasn't a next time. I don't mind that you're angry with me, but it does bother me that you're afraid of me. Will you at least tell me why I scare you?"

Cassie's anger melted just as quickly as his command façade had crumbled and her brown eyes retained just the measure of fear and sadness.

"Walk with me. Please?" she asked quietly.

Joe nodded and Cassie turned and started walking east toward her shooting range. Joe walked quietly beside her with his hands folded on the small of his back.

"I know I've been acting miserably this past month, and it's not your fault and it's not anyone else's fault. It's all mine."

Joe didn't say anything as they strolled across the open ground, knowing that this was Cassie's time.

"Remember when I first told you that I wanted you to be my boyfriend? When you were locked up behind those bars?"

"Yes."

"I explained later why I did it and that's mostly true. I do feel frustrated about being kept here when I know I could do so much more, but even that wasn't the deep reason."

Cassie just strode beside Joe for almost a hundred yards in silence as she collected her thoughts. She had never told anyone what she was about to tell Joe, but she felt she owed him an explanation, much more than she owed anyone else.

"When I was six, my mother surprised us by announcing she was going to have another baby. My father, Mary, and Bessie were thrilled, but I was worried. Just a few weeks earlier, the wife of the butcher, Mrs. Clyde, had died in childbirth. As my mother's tummy grew larger, so did my worries. Then she started to have the baby and bad things began to happen. I could hear my mother's screams and I listened as Mrs. Williams began asking for help.

"I remember just lying on my face on my bed, crying and praying for my mother. Two hours later, I heard a baby cry, but there was still shouting and running around. I was absolutely terrified. Then suddenly, everything was quiet. There was no baby crying, no shouting, and I didn't hear my mother. I was sure she'd died. I was so despondent that I wished that I could die too, just to be with her.

"But a few minutes later, Mary came into the room and told me that our baby sister had died, but our mother would be all right. I was so happy, and then I felt terrible about being happy because the baby had died. My mother recovered, but couldn't have any more babies, and I was happy for her. But that lingering memory of the death of Mrs. Clyde and then almost losing my mother made me determined never to get married and have children. The thought terrified me."

Joe began to understand as they continued to walk further from the house, but he knew there was more to come. Specifically, his role in her sudden protracted sadness.

Cassie continued, saying, "But Bessie and Mary kept talking about boys and getting married as if it was inevitable. They couldn't wait to get older for it to happen, and I almost wanted to stay ten years old. Then you were arrested, and I thought if I told everyone you would be my boyfriend then, at least I'd have almost five years where I could push away any boys without my mother or sisters telling me to start down the path to becoming a woman and a wife."

Joe glanced at Cassie, whose eyes were still focused on the ground before her feet as they walked, so he said nothing.

"I wrote letters to you, not really expecting you to reply because you didn't know how to read or write, but when you did, I was surprised. I adjusted my writing to match yours and found you were learning even faster than I had. I was impressed and found myself thinking about you like a boyfriend, but the boyfriend I knew you would never be. If you came back in four years, I'd still be just fifteen and you'd be full-grown, so it wasn't a worry to me.

"Then you arrived with my father and I was shocked. You were more than just a big boy, you really were a man, and it scared me because you had written that last letter and still sounded as if you wanted to be my boyfriend. I thought about pushing you onto Bessie, even if she was going out with Kit, but as I listened to you talk that first night, I heard the same gentle, caring voice that I'd read in your letters.

"So, when we went to target practice, and you told me that we could delay the whole boyfriend thing for a few years while you hunted down the Hogans, I was able to relax. That was why we had such a wonderful time. It was the real me talking to the real you.

"But after you made that offer to set up that account, so I could find my dreams, it still seemed so distant and unreal. Then you earned that reward and suddenly that time was gone. It was happening now. That was bad enough and then Mrs. Sanborn died in childbirth the day you were sworn in and everything just crashed around me."

Joe said softly, "Cassie, I'm sorry for putting you in this situation, and I'll be more than happy to do anything you ask of me. Your father said that I'll be getting an enormous reward for taking down the four outlaws that had taken the Finley ranch, including two of the Hogan brothers, and that is more than enough for you to go to any school you want. Your life can be whatever you want to make of it now."

Cassie finally looked at Joe and said, "You don't understand my other problem, Joe. The one that makes any decision I make so painful."

Joe stopped and turned to face Cassie and asked, "What is that problem, Cassie?"

She looked at him with her brown eyes, no longer showing fear, and replied, "I've grown very fond of you, Joe. That's my problem. Don't you see?"

Joe was stunned and replied, "No, I really don't, Cassie."

"I can't go to find my dream and avoid getting married if I keep liking you so much. I've been avoiding you because I can't fall in love with you."

Joe finally understood and had to be careful with his reply, and even saying it saddened him.

"Cassie, I understand and as I told you before, I feel a deep obligation to you for what you did for me those four and a half years. I want you to find your dream and be happy. The money is there for you to use as a tool to fulfill your dream. If it means that we don't talk, I can do that without animosity. I have only one thing to ask of you?"

Cassie asked quietly, "Which is?"

"Be nice to your family. They're so worried about you and they don't deserve it."

Cassie nodded and replied, “I know, and I owe an apology to them. I promise.”

Joe simply said, “Good,” before they turned to go back to the house.

Cassie then asked, “Can we keep this just between us?”

“Of course.”

Neither spoke on the return walk but thought about the awkward agreement they’d reached.

For Joe, it meant that he’d be going after the three remaining Hogans sooner than he’d planned as he couldn’t spend all this time in Warwick with Cassie around.

Cassie’s thoughts were along the same lines as she began to think of a way to leave Warwick because she knew she couldn’t be around Joe. She had fibbed when she said she was worried about falling in love with him. She was already in love with him and hoped that distance and time could drive it away.

———

When Joe and Cassie finally returned to the house, she invited him for lunch, which he accepted because he believed it might be the last chance that he’d have to talk to her at any length, and he wanted to see how she’d be with her family.

They entered the kitchen just as Minnie was setting food on the table for her husband, and her parents both turned when she and Joe entered.

“Hello, Papa and Mama,” Cassie said with a smile, “Do you mind if Joe joins us for lunch?”

Minnie and John were both startled by the normal Cassie and Minnie replied, “No, of course not.”

“I’ll get it, Mama. You join papa and have your lunch.”

Joe said, “I’ll help you, Cassie. I’m not a bad cook, although we’ll need another ten pounds of potatoes. I’m not used to cooking for fewer than fifty.”

Cassie smiled and said, “Just divide by twenty-five, sir.”

Joe grinned and said, “Well, shucks, ma’am. Cypherin’ with big numbers ain’t easy.”

Cassie laughed lightly as she began to cut some beef.

John looked at Minnie and shrugged. He’d ask Joe when he got back to the office, but whatever he’d said meant that Minnie would be a happy wife tonight, and that was good news for him.

Joe didn’t understand how Cassie could act so naturally. He was just so happy to see her smiling and hear her laughter.

Cassie had used a mental trick she’d learned years ago and pictured a happy moment to lighten her mood before she entered the house. Joe’s natural humor had made it easier as she remembered the joy of their first Sunday conversation. But she knew that his wonderful personality would drag her into a somber mood when she was alone in her room tonight, knowing what had transpired in today’s talk.

———

On the return walk to the office, the sheriff asked Joe what he and Cassie had talked about that had made the big change and Joe lied...sort of. He told his boss that he’d told Cassie that the big reward would allow her to go to college and pursue her dreams.

John knew Cassie well enough to understand that Joe was only telling him part of the reason, and maybe only a small part, but it didn't matter. Cassie was happy and that was all that counted.

When they entered the office, Dan said, "A letter arrived for you and Joe from Austin, boss," and held up an envelope.

Joe was hanging up his hat when the sheriff said, "Let's find out what was going on with Mister Phelps," as he took the letter and opened the flap.

All three deputies were standing around their boss as he pulled out the two pages and read the letter.

Gentlemen:

We gathered eight more affidavits from boys who had left the reformatory during Mister Phelps' tenure as warden. Three received half of what was due and five received nothing at all. I arranged for them all to be compensated.

Once we had the affidavits, we sent a member of our staff, a young attorney named Barney Flanders to Gainesville to make the deal.

He arrived at the reformatory, and apparently, Mister Phelps agreed to accompany Barney back to Gainesville to see the judge and complete the plea bargain. They left the reformatory in Barney's rented buggy and about halfway between the reformatory and the town, Bert Phelps shot and killed Barney Flanders and hid his body in a nearby gully.

It was only when he'd been missing for a day that the sheriff sent a deputy out searching for him and found his body. By then, Phelps had stopped at the bank, emptied his account, and rode west out of Gainesville.

By the time we sent out the warrant notice, he had disappeared somewhere between Gainesville and Henrietta. Because this was a state issue, four Rangers were dispatched, but no trace of Phelps has been found.

Attached is the wanted poster we've issued for Bertram L. Phelps. Needless to say, he'll be hanged for this.

We sent a new warden to take over the reform school and replaced all of the guards. None of them were fired, of course. They were all sent to work at the state prison.

The new warden, John Martel, has already been advised, as have the new guards, that unscheduled, in-depth inspections will be conducted, and any abuse will be severely punished. The only real question is what constitutes abuse.

I apologize for this office for not affecting justice for the boys in the reform school, but hopefully, we will find and hang Mister Phelps soon.

Sincerely,

Sam H. Pell, Assistant Attorney General, State of Texas

John said, “No wonder they’re charging him with murder. He killed one of theirs,” then handed the letter to Joe while he examined the wanted poster.

Joe read the letter, gave it to Dan, and then accepted the wanted poster.

“That’s the most accurate drawing I’ve seen on one of these,” Joe said as he stared at the image of Bert Phelps looking out at him from the paper.

“I noticed. I guess when you’re important, they hire a real artist.”

Sheriff Warren said, “Well, let’s get back to regular work.”

Joe folded the letter and slid it back into its envelope, but left the wanted poster on the desk. Lou Sanborn opened the middle drawer and dropped it on top of the stack of posters.

Bert Phelps was wanted dead or alive.

Bert Phelps had been planning for the day when someone would arrive to arrest him since the day he took over as warden. He was actually surprised it had lasted four years and had been expecting them to come after him in half that time. He thought his threats to the boys leaving would be ignored by at least one of those young thugs a lot sooner. He just hadn't counted on the politics of the situation and the lack of concern for the boys that had been sent there.

The money he withheld from them was just a small fraction of what he'd been skimming from the budget allocated to running the reformatory. In the four years he'd been in charge, he'd amassed almost five thousand dollars. His bank account was only six hundred dollars because he didn't want anyone at the Gainesville State Bank to notice the larger amount of money.

His plan for escape was simple. Once he was arrested, he'd shoot whoever arrived to take him away and ride west out of Gainesville, leave via the well-traveled roadway to Henrietta, and halfway there, he'd ride south. Most men on the run would have ridden north to get to the Nations, but Bert was smarter than that. He knew that they'd be searching for him, and that meant they'd be watching the train stations, so he'd ride south until he reached a small burg without any law and sell the horse. He'd take the stagecoach across Texas and then take a train to go to California.

The other part of his plan was his makeover. Before he even left Gainesville, he'd shaved off his massive muttonchops and moustache and even trimmed his bushy eyebrows. Once he'd ditched his dark wool suit in favor of just canvas britches, a flannel shirt, boots, and a Stetson, he had no resemblance whatsoever to Warden Phelps. He'd never pass for a ranch hand, yet he surely didn't stick out as he would have, but shaving the facial hair did make him feel almost naked.

His only real problem was that he was now tied to the stagecoach schedules, and there were three different lines operating in the west part of Texas, which meant he'd suffer long delays in some of the towns. But it was worth the delays, knowing that no one would be looking for him on one of the seldom-traveled coaches. The spreading of the railroads was putting them out of business to the big towns.

Bert was sitting in the depot in Tiverton waiting on the driver to help harness a new team for the drive to Kingston, where he'd stay overnight before the next day's journey to Linder with its stop in the biggest Texas town on his journey, Warwick.

CHAPTER 8

Joe took extra care shaving that morning, not wanting too many nicks now that he and Cassie were talking again, even if they didn't search each other out. Now he had to learn much more and even faster if that was possible. He estimated that he'd be ready to leave by the end of summer. Then he'd take the bold risk of hunting down three notorious killers and any of their hangers-on.

But as he dressed, he thought about how much danger he'd been in since he arrived. It was a risky business. He was putting his shirt back on as he thought about that subject...risk. All of life is a risk, and sometimes the smallest of risks can cause the biggest danger, like a cut that becomes infected, or that simple walk across the street and getting killed by a runaway wagon.

The risks that he took as a deputy were higher than average, but not that much higher than a ranch hand when working a big herd. Going after the Hogans was a higher risk, but not necessarily the worst.

Cassie was right about childbirth being risky, though. So many women died having babies, but it was usually because of problems without having either an experienced midwife or a doctor around to help.

Sometimes even that didn't matter. According to Drew Hogan, his own mother had died in childbirth having one of the Hogan's bastards. Drew had said it was because they didn't care about her by then and just let her and the baby die. Joe knew he would never be sure if Drew was just saying that or it really happened that way, but it was one of the driving reasons for his desire for retribution. To allow his mother to just die because they didn't want to have her and her baby around anymore was beyond cruelty. It was savagely inhuman.

Once he was dressed, he walked out to the front office, started the heat stove fire, and put on the coffee. While the water was heating, he pulled out Bertram Phelps' wanted poster and looked at the picture. Those muttonchop whiskers, moustache, and thick eyebrows all dominated the face, and Joe tried to picture the face beneath the forest of hair. It was a difficult exercise. But as accurate as the picture was, it wasn't the hair that identified Phelps. It was his eyes. The artist had the eyes all wrong. Like most renditions, the eyes were set too close and were half-closed to appear menacing. Joe had seen those eyes hundreds of times and knew that he'd never forget them.

And there was something else missing from the description now that he looked at it more carefully. There were no distinguishing marks listed, but Joe knew that on the back of his left hand was a long, white scar. He'd whipped a boy named Eddie Green that first year and missed, striking his own hand. Eddie had received an extra series of lashes as punishment and been thrown into solitary where he'd died.

When the sheriff arrived, he'd let him know so they could send a telegram to Mister Pell and have the wanted poster updated.

As he was returning the poster to the drawer, the door opened, and Joe watched as Sheriff Warren removed his hat and ran his fingers through his hair.

"Boss, I was looking at Phelps' wanted poster and there's something missing. He has a long scar on the back of his left hand that wasn't listed."

"That's pretty important, Joe. Why don't you send a telegram to Mister Pell in Austin?"

"Yes, sir," Joe said.

Thirty-one miles east, Bert Phelps was boarding the coach for the five-hour ride to Warwick and after the change of horses, he'd take the four-hour ride to Linder.

Dan and Lou had arrived, so Joe turned over the desk to Lou and said, "I have to go and send a telegram to Austin. I'll be back in a bit."

Bert Phelps was getting annoyed listening to the constant ramblings of the fable-telling old man who seemed to have fought in every major engagement of the War of Secession. The man just didn't respect the need for silence. Phelps wished he had kept his silver-tipped riding crop. That would have shut him up.

Joe was writing his report about the theft of three cans of peaches by some boys from Lippett's Grocery. He'd found the boys, but they'd already eaten the three large cans of peaches and weren't in any condition to be incarcerated, so he warned them about conditions in the reformatory by showing them the scars on his back which had resulted in a chain reaction of upheaval. He'd then reimbursed Ed Lippett out of his own pocket, believing the boys had learned their lesson.

He was just finishing when Sheriff Warren walked out of his office, so Joe handed him the report without a word and watched his boss read it as a smile slowly formed on his face.

"Good job, Joe," he said as he handed him back his report and added, "I'm going to the house for lunch and now that Cassie is in a good mood again, would you care to join me?"

Joe knew he had no excuses, so he replied, "Yes, sir," and then placed the report into the box for filing.

He stood, grabbed his hat, and he and the sheriff stepped out of the jail.

They were crossing the street when Joe glanced at the Overland Stagecoach depot at the coach waiting for a new team to be attached.

The driver was having difficulty with two of the lead horses, so Joe said, "I'll catch up to you in a minute, boss," and then trotted toward the depot.

John just stood and waited as it wouldn't take long to help calm the animals.

Bert Phelps was preparing to board the stage again after his short rest break when he noticed the two lawmen as they left the jail and had turned his back to them, so they wouldn't be able to see his face, just to be safe. He was drinking out of a canteen as Joe walked to the coach.

"Need some help?" Joe asked the driver.

"I think I've got 'em now. I appreciate the offer, though."

Joe gave him a short salute, turned around, and began walking back to Sheriff Warren, glancing at the only passenger who was preparing to board as he passed.

After he was sure that the deputy was gone, Bert Phelps clambered into the coach and settled back in the leather seat, pleased that the two lawmen hadn't identified him. The coach rolled away from the depot less than a minute later.

The sheriff was talking, but Joe wasn't paying attention. There was something about that passenger that was tickling his brain and he couldn't come up with an answer. *What was it?*

They were almost to the house when his boss asked him a question that only partially filtered through his ears, "…that telegram?"

Then it hit him like a clap of summer thunder. The scar! That passenger who'd been facing the wrong way had a long scar on his left hand. He froze and looked at the sheriff.

"Boss! It's him! That was Phelps on the stage!"

John looked at him and asked hurriedly, "Are you sure?"

"Not completely, but I'm pretty sure."

"Let's get to the horses and saddle them up!" he exclaimed before they turned and raced back down the road leaving a dust cloud behind them.

It took them almost ten minutes before they were mounted and racing their horses down the main street of Warwick and soon left the town behind as they chased after the stagecoach.

The coach was a good two miles ahead when they started the chase, but it was traveling at a trot while Joe and the sheriff were moving faster and closing the gap quickly.

The brims on their Stetsons were bent back in the wind of the chase as they cut the gap to less than a mile and when they were just eight hundred yards back, the sheriff pulled his Winchester. Joe knew that both of them didn't need to have rifles, so he just kept his hands on the reins. He wanted to yank that bastard out of the coach himself.

As the gap closed even further, the driver finally noticed he had riders coming up behind him, but knew who they were even if they hadn't been wearing badges, and began slowing the coach, suspecting that they wanted to talk to his passenger.

Bert Phelps didn't notice the slowing speed, but when the two riders were within a hundred yards, he heard the added sound of the pounding hooves over the stagecoach's own noises and suspected that he'd been identified after all. He pulled his concealed Colt from behind his coat and cocked the hammer, unsure which side the lawmen would approach. But with two of them, they'd probably come on both sides. Bert chose to aim his pistol on the left side of the coach as the right side was closer to the side of the road.

Once they passed within a hundred yards, the sheriff replaced his Winchester and pulled his pistol. Joe still kept his weapons where they were stowed.

"Hold up!" Sheriff Warren shouted when they were closer.

As the stagecoach pulled to a stop, Joe swung to the left side and John to the right. Only as he was dismounting did Joe pull his pistol and slowly approached the left door.

The sheriff stepped down on the right side and cocked his pistol as he yelled, “You! In the coach! Come out with your hands empty and high!”

John’s shout was met with silence as Bert Phelps dropped to the floor of the coach in a crouch and pointed his pistol at the door facing Joe’s side.

Joe quietly approached the left side of the stage, suspecting that Phelps was waiting with a pistol. His only question was in which direction the muzzle was pointing.

The driver watched the two lawmen closing in and wished he could help, but there was nothing he could do.

The coach’s windows were blocked by curtains, so he couldn’t see inside, but Joe knew one thing for certain. He was less valuable than the sheriff. It was that realization that made him take the chance, but it wasn’t going to be a big chance. He’d give Phelps one shot, probably though the door and then he’d know where the ex-warden was when he saw the hole created by his bullet.

He was almost to the door when he said loudly, “You whipped me and threw me into solitary, you bastard. Now you’re going to hang.”

Bert Phelps then knew how he’d been identified and didn’t care about the other lawman as he began rapidly firing first through the door and then through the side panels.

Joe was stunned by the repeated fire as .44s blasted holes through the side of the coach. He dropped with the first bullet, but he was too late as Phelps’ second shot clipped the side of his left arm, spinning him counterclockwise as he fell.

Sheriff Warren didn't hesitate once Phelps began firing, and grabbed the door, swung it wide, and pulled his Colt's trigger. The bullet spun from his muzzle, traveling the four feet in an instant and blasting right between Bert Phelps' butt cheeks as he was still in his crouched position firing at the outside of the coach.

Bert screamed and tried to turn to get a shot at John, but the sheriff quickly cocked his hammer and fired a second shot that finished him off when it drilled through the left side of his chest under his ribcage and entered his heart. He stopped screaming and dropped to the floor of the coach.

Sheriff Warren then shouted, "Joe, are you okay?"

Joe was on the ground and grunted, "Yes, sir, but I took a hit."

The driver then clambered down from the seat as the sheriff ran around the back of the coach and spotted Joe on his back, blood pouring from his left arm.

The driver swung the door to the coach open, grabbed Phelps's travel bag, and opened it to take a shirt to wrap around Joe's arm. He snatched a shirt from the bag and saw wads of cash underneath.

He handed the shirt to the sheriff and said, "There's a lot of money in here, Sheriff."

John was wrapping the shirt around Joe's bicep and said, "Check on that bastard inside and make sure he's dead and we'll get Joe inside and you'll have to turn your rig around and head back."

"Okay."

Joe didn't understand what all the fuss was about and wondered why he was being put into the coach. Once he was on the coach's seat on his back, he kept wanting to tell his boss that he was okay and could ride back. But he was tired and decided it wasn't so bad to be in the stagecoach. Maybe a little rest wasn't a bad idea after all, so he closed his eyes and wondered when they were going to catch Warden Phelps. *He was getting away in the stagecoach, wasn't he?*

Joe heard strange noises that he couldn't understand. It sounded like banging and clacking. *Where was he?*

He opened his eyes and it didn't help. It was dark, and the noises weren't nearby. He slid his hands along his side and felt smooth cotton. He was in a bed, but where?

It took him another minute to remember he'd been shot and reached over with his right hand and felt his heavily bandaged left bicep. He tried to flex his arm, but it hurt like the devil and was stiff, too.

He concentrated on the sounds and then heard low voices. He couldn't understand what they were saying, or who was talking. The only thing he knew was that he was hungry and had to pee.

So, Joe sat up slowly with his head spinning. Once in a sitting position, he had to wait until everything stabilized which took a while. Then he swung his legs out of the bed, set his feet on the floor, and waited until he thought he could stand.

When he did, the room swayed, but he finally figured out where he was. He was in the sleeping room in the back of the jail. Even without much light, he knew where the door was, so he began a wobbling, unsteady walk toward the door.

He opened the door and stepped out into the night and after two steps, quickly undid his britches and felt the overwhelming relief of emptying his overly full bladder.

Even as he was relieving himself, he began to piece together what had happened. They'd chased after the stagecoach to get Phelps and he'd shouted something, and he'd been shot. He sighed, buttoned his britches, and stood looking at the stars. It was a cool night and the air was clearing his head, but there were still some blanks that Sheriff Warren would have to fill in.

He turned around and entered the jail again and passed through the sleeping room and when he opened the door to the rest of the office, he was bathed in lamplight but didn't hear anyone.

Joe slowly walked down the short hallway and stopped by the desk.

"What are you doing out of bed, Joe?" asked Lou Sanborn.

"I had to pee, or I'd die. What's going on?" he asked as he took the chair before the desk.

"How much do you remember?"

"It's kind of foggy. I remember chasing after the stage with the boss and then we split up, I shouted something and Phelps began shooting. That's all."

Lou leaned back and said, "After you were shot, the boss and the driver put you in the coach and they drove you back here and had Doc Gillespie fix your arm. He said you'd lost so much blood, there was only a fifty-fifty chance of you pulling through. He said you'd be out for most of the day. He just left an hour ago and said you were doing better."

"I heard noises. Was that him leaving? It only seemed like a minute ago."

"No, that was the boss and Cassie. She brought some food for us and then he walked her back to the house. He'll be back in a minute or so. The doc said you shouldn't be out of bed for another two days."

"I'm okay. What time is it, anyway?"

"I'd guess around ten o'clock or so."

"Why don't you go home, Lou? I'll take the desk."

Lou snapped, "What home?"

Joe said, "I'm sorry, Lou. I didn't mean to be so thoughtless."

Lou sighed and said, "No, it's my damned fault. I shouldn't be so touchy. I know you didn't mean anything by it."

Before Joe could say anything else, the door opened, and Sheriff Warren asked loudly, "What are you doing out here?"

Joe turned to look at his boss and replied, "I'm okay, boss, but I sure am hungry."

"I don't care how hungry you are, you're going to get your behind back in that bed right now. I'll bring you something to eat in a little while."

Then he looked at Deputy Sanborn and said, "Go home, Lou."

Lou stood, picked up his hat, and said, "Yes, sir."

Joe watched Lou walk past him out of the office before he rose and shuffled to the back room, leaving the door open for light and the sheriff.

Once he was sitting on the bed, he asked, “What happened after we got there, boss? I can’t remember it very well.”

After filling in Joe’s blanks, John continued with the aftermath. Once he’d been told what had happened, the rest of the action became clear in his mind.

“The doc said you were lucky and unlucky at the same time. The bullet took out a good chunk of your upper left arm, but it was clean. He had to use a lot of thread to close it up, but he said because you’re young, it should heal in a few weeks.”

“I’ll be okay, boss. It’s my left arm, anyway.”

“We’ll talk about that tomorrow. But after we took care of you and dropped off Phelps’ body, I sent a telegram to Mister Pell in Austin letting him know that the bastard was dead and that we’d recovered all of his money. I wasn’t sure what he’d want to do with it because part of it was the state’s money and part of it was Phelps’ own money. Anyway, I got a reply a couple of hours later and he said to keep it because he didn’t want the headache of dealing with it. So, I deposited it in your account.”

“Boss, you should have kept the money. I didn’t do anything.”

The sheriff didn’t argue, but asked, “Joe, why did you yell at Phelps? You had to know he was in there with a pistol.”

“I knew. But I was unsure of which way he was preparing to shoot. I figured I could get him to aim in my direction once I let him know who I was. Then when he fired, I’d be able to see where the bullet exited the coach and fire back. But I made a mistake when he began peppering the rest of the coach and the second shot got me."

"Okay, but why would you want him to shoot in your direction? Did you want to be the one to shoot him?"

Joe sighed and answered softly, "No, sir. It was because I didn't want you to get shot if he was aiming at your side of the coach. That's all."

John looked at Joe but didn't ask any more questions.

Joe finally asked, "How is Cassie?"

"As you might expect, she's pretty upset. Just to let you know, she saw the scars on your back while you were being taken out of the stagecoach. She knew about them, of course, but I guess seeing them added to the shock she had when she saw you being carried into the doctor's office."

Joe didn't want to see her upset, so he said, "Boss, forget about the food. I can wait until breakfast. I'll put on a shirt and get some sleep."

"Are you sure, Joe?"

"Yes, sir."

"Okay. I'll see you in the morning then."

"Thanks for getting me out of there, boss."

John just nodded, stood, and left the sleep room, leaving the door open. He blew out the lamp and left the office.

After the door closed, Joe just sat on the bed for a while thinking about Cassie. This was virgin territory for him. No one had ever cared about what happened to him since he was four years old, and it made him feel guilty for making her distraught.

After fifteen minutes, he laid back down and closed his eyes forgetting about the shirt. He was asleep five minutes later.

"Joe?"

The soft voice startled Joe into almost instant wakefulness as his eyes popped open and he found Cassie's brown eyes looking at him less than two feet away. His surprise was compounded when he realized that he'd forgotten to put a shirt on.

"Cassie. How are you?" he asked.

"I'm fine, how is your arm?"

"It's okay. Um, is your father here?"

"No. No one is here yet. I came over before anyone else to see you."

"I need to put on a shirt. Can you wait for me out in the front office?"

"I saw your scars, Joe. I didn't know they were that bad until I saw them. I guess in my mind, I thought they were like getting a switch and you have a welt that goes away after a few days. He really hurt you, didn't he?"

"He hurt a lot of boys, Cassie. Some of them died because of that whip of his."

"But he's gone now. You and my father caught him. My father told me that you wanted him to shoot at your side of the stagecoach and not his. Why did you do that?"

"I made a mistake, Cassie. That's all."

"No, it wasn't a mistake. Was it? I can tell that you're not telling the truth. Why did you do it, Joe?"

Joe sighed and answered, "Because he is important. He's the sheriff, and he has a family to take care of. I'm just a new deputy with no responsibilities. I am expendable."

"And you believe that?"

"Yes. It's not anything noble or even debatable. I didn't try and get shot, but I did make that mistake thinking he'd only fire once. If I'd been smarter, I would have just had my cocked pistol aimed at the door and when that first bullet passed through, pulled my trigger. I screwed up, Cassie."

"You're eighteen, Joe. You're not invincible and you don't know everything that you need to know. Maybe you never will."

Joe smiled and said, "This from a fifteen-year-old who knows everything."

"I never said I know everything, Joe, and you know it. I know that I'm incredibly ignorant and need to learn so much more. It's just that my not knowing things won't get me killed."

"Cassie, I'd love to continue this conversation, but I need to go use the privy. So, could you wait for me in the outer office? Please?"

"Alright," she replied as she stood and quickly exited the sleeping room, closing the door behind her.

Joe needed to wash and shave, but thought that Cassie wouldn't give him the time, so after making a hasty exit out the back door and returning and quickly putting on a shirt, he opened the door and entered the front office.

Cassie was sitting at the chair before the front desk, so Joe sat behind the desk, and asked, "Cassie, why did you come by? I thought we'd try to ignore each other."

"Because I do care about you, Joe, and you were shot. You're only eighteen and when I saw all those scars and that new wound, I thought I'd try and talk you out of going after the Hogans."

"The new wound won't change my mind. I still have to get the Hogans."

"Why? Why can't you just let them go? Is vengeance so important to you?"

"Vengeance is a harsh word. It sounds like a base, thoughtless desire for inflicting harm for real or perceived damage. What I seek is retribution, Cassie. To me, it's based more on justice than a visceral reaction. If the Hogans were just the murdering monsters that they are, I could let it go, but there is more than that. I didn't tell you what is driving me because of the nature of what Drew told me in that jail cell right behind me. Trust me when I tell you that it's more than enough justification."

"Will you tell me now?"

Joe looked at her and wasn't sure he should after she had confessed her reason for not wanting to get married.

"Cassie, I don't think you want to know. I don't want you to get upset."

"I'm already upset, Joe. Tell me."

Joe glanced at the door hoping for someone to arrive and interrupt, but he didn't get his wish.

"Alright, but if I tell you, I'm not going to make it any prettier than it is."

"I wouldn't want that."

"You should because of what you told me the other day. The reason you don't want to get married. You don't want to hear this."

Cassie's brown eyes bored into him as she said, "Tell me."

Joe blew out a breath and said, "I was told this by Drew Hogan the night before he hanged. He wanted to hurt me as much as he could before he died.

"You know that my mother and her sister were kidnapped by the Hogans during the war when I was two years old. There were seven of them back then, including the six brothers and their father. They turned my mother and aunt into common wives, to keep the house clean, do their laundry, and cook for them. They also raped them repeatedly, sometimes just lining up in the hallway.

"After they'd been there almost a year, my mother's sister killed herself when she discovered she was pregnant. My mother was warned that if she tried anything like that, they'd throw me down the well. So, she became the sole object of their attention before she became pregnant. They continued to use her as her belly grew and when she began to have the baby, they just took her out to the barn, left her there, and closed the door.

"Drew said that when they went out there a few hours later, they found her dead and her dead baby girl lying on the floor. He said that they all laughed because it was just another girl."

Joe was watching her horrified eyes as he told the story and hoped he hadn't gone too far.

He then said, "Now you understand why I didn't want to tell you. But my mother and sister would probably still be alive if they hadn't been left in that hot barn alone. It wasn't childbirth that killed my mother, it was those soulless bastards named the Hogans."

She finally asked softly, "Why did they let you live?"

"Drew said it was because when they first kidnapped my mother and her sister, their father, Alex, said that I was a boy and I might be useful. Then after my mother died, most of them wanted to get rid of me again, but Buck said that I might be useful when I grew up because I looked so different. Drew and the others put up with me because Buck was in charge. I guess they thought it was funny after a while when I thought I was their brother and I was too stupid to notice the differences."

"I'm sorry for what happened to your mother and her sister, Joe. I understand now."

"I'm still not sure I should have told you, Cassie. I know how frightened you are about having a baby, and I thought it would make it worse."

"It doesn't. I'm still afraid of the idea, but what happened to your mother wasn't the same."

"No, it wasn't."

She nodded, turned, and slowly walked across the floor, and left the jail.

Joe still thought it wasn't a good idea to tell Cassie what Drew had told him. He didn't doubt the truth of it, but it was a brutal story and one worthy of seeking retribution on the Hogan brothers.

Cassie walked back slowly. The combination of being terrified when she heard that Joe had been shot and seeing his scars all across his back was bad enough, but now hearing about his mother's death had added a new layer of fear.

Joe was clean and shaved when the next arrival entered the jail in the form of Deputy Sheehy. He was surprised to see Joe at the desk and the coffee already made. It was as if he hadn't been shot at all.

"Good morning, Dan," Joe said.

"Morning, Joe. What are you doing behind the desk? Weren't you shot yesterday?"

"I can't use my left arm much, but I'm okay. I can do desk work and do the rounds."

Dan hung his hat and asked, "The boss said you could do that?"

"Not yet, but I'm sure he'll think it's okay."

"I wouldn't bet on it."

Dan was pouring his coffee when Joe's breakfast arrived, but it wasn't being carried in by Cassie. Bessie brought the tray into the office, as her father held the door open.

"What are you doing behind the desk, Joe?" the sheriff asked.

"Just waiting for my breakfast, boss."

"Good morning, Joe," Bessie said as she smiled and set the breakfast tray on the desk.

"Good morning, Bessie. How are you?"

"I'm fine. Did my father tell you my news?"

"No, ma'am," he replied as he snatched a strip of bacon.

"Kit and I are going to be married on May fifteenth."

"Well, congratulations, Bessie. Am I invited to the wedding?"

Bessie giggled and replied, "Of course you are, silly. After we get married, we'll be moving into our own house just two houses down the street from our house. Kit's father bought the place yesterday after I agreed to the proposal."

"Now that's handy," Joe said as he began to wolf down the much-needed food.

In between bites, he glanced at his boss who was smiling at Bessie, which surprised him because he didn't think that Sheriff Warren approved of his soon-to-be son-in-law.

"How is your arm?" Bessie asked.

"It's okay. The doc did a good job."

“Well, you take care, Joe. I’m going to go back to the house now. We have a lot of planning to do.”

“I’ll bet. Thank you for breakfast, Bessie.”

“You’re welcome, Joe,” she replied and turned and floated out of the jail.

After she was gone, Joe looked at his boss and asked, “That was sudden, wasn’t it?”

“We thought so. Minnie tried to get Bessie to push the date back at least a month or so, but she wanted to get married right away.”

Joe just nodded before biting into a biscuit, wondering if wanting to get married right away was the same as needing to get married right away.

He finished his breakfast before Lou Sanborn entered the jail and was the first one not to ask why Joe was at the desk. He expected to find him there after talking to him last night.

Joe then said, “Boss, I can mind the desk and do rounds at least. It’s not that bad.”

“Joe, you can sit at the desk, but you are not doing rounds. What if you have to break up a barfight?”

Joe was satisfied with his partial victory and replied, “Okay, I’ll just handle the desk.”

The sheriff then called his two healthy deputies back to his office to give them assignments leaving Joe at the desk sipping his coffee, determined to get his arm working better as quickly as possible. He knew he’d have to wait until the sutures were removed before he did any serious work at restoring the arm to full strength, and he knew just where he could do it, too.

The next few days, including Sunday, Joe spent at the jail, taking walks that were like rounds, but not enough to draw the wrath of the boss. He read more state and local statutes and visited Rupert's for his meals. He bought some more shirts and britches and had his fast-growing hair trimmed by Al Crandon, the barber.

Cassie hadn't visited since that one right after the shooting, but he wasn't surprised. He probably scared her away for good when he'd told her the story of how his mother had died. Granted, he hadn't gone to the Warren home since then but that was because he figured they'd be busy getting ready for Bessie's wedding.

On the last day of April, Cassie finally showed up after everyone had gone for the day, probably passing her father on his way back to their home.

Joe was at the desk, reading the county statutes when the door opened, and he saw her enter.

He closed the book and said, "Hello, Cassie."

"Hello," she said as she walked across the floor and sat down.

"Been planning for Bessie's wedding?" he asked.

"We all have, and that's what I wanted to talk to you about."

Joe was expecting some deep soul-searching revelation but was soon disappointed.

“The money you have in the bank. You said I could use it to go to school or anything else I wanted.”

“Yes, I did. Are you leaving?”

“No. Not yet at least. I was wondering if I could use some to buy a new cookstove for Bessie as a wedding present. It’s expensive, almost two hundred dollars, but the one in the house now is broken and it can’t even hold heat that well.”

“Of course, you can. It’s your money, Cassie. Just tell your father to take whatever he needs. I don’t even know how much is in there. There should be plenty after those vouchers were deposited.”

“You don’t know? That warden had over five thousand dollars in his travel bag. My father took out money to reimburse the stagecoach line for the damage and deposited the rest.”

Joe was astonished. The sheriff hadn’t said a word about how much it was. He thought it might be a couple of hundred dollars, but as soon as Cassie said the amount, it made sense. But it was too much for him to have.

“Cassie, your father should have kept that money. He has a family to support. Go ahead and get the stove for Bessie but see if you can get him to move the money to your family’s bank account. You always had a way to get him to do anything you wanted.”

“I’ll order the stove, but I’m not going to have him move the money, Joe. That’s yours because you were the one who identified him, and you were the one who got shot. Don’t try to argue with me, either. You’ll lose.”

Joe was sure that she was right, so he said, “Okay. Just make sure it’s a good stove and if you want to buy her anything else, go ahead.”

“The stove is more than enough.”

Joe leaned back and asked, “Cassie, what do you think of Kit?”

She scrunched up her face before replying, “I don’t like him at all. My mother and father don’t either. I think it’s because he’s so full of himself. When Bessie is talking, he’s staring off somewhere not paying any attention, and when he talks, it’s always about himself.”

“He must have some positives.”

“All of them are on the outside, I think.”

Cassie then paused, looked down, and said, “I applied to go to a preparatory school in Dallas. If they accept my application, I’ll be leaving in September.”

Joe was stunned and somewhat saddened by the news but couldn’t let it show.

“That’s wonderful, Cassie. How long is it?”

“Two years. Then I’ll be able to go to college. It’s what I always wanted to do, but I only found out about the school a few days ago. I didn’t know how to get ready for college before that. That’s the real reason I haven’t stopped by. I was afraid to tell you.”

“So, you’ll be gone for two years and you’ll go to college for four more years?”

“Yes,” she replied in a whisper.

“Have you decided what you want to study yet?”

“No. I’ll do that at the preparatory school.”

“What’s it called?”

“Carlisle’s School for Young Women.”

“When do you think they’ll reply?”

“In a few days, I think.”

“It’s the first step to achieving your dream, Cassie.”

“I suppose. Well, I need to get back to the house. Thank you for letting me buy the stove, Joe.”

“You’re welcome, Cassie,” he replied.

She smiled weakly, stood, and walked out of the jail.

Joe stared at the closed door after she’d gone. Cassie would be leaving in a few months for six years. He felt so completely empty inside even though she would still be in Warwick for another four months.

He didn’t bother opening the statute book again but walked out of the back of the jail, saddled one of his two brown geldings, and rode east out of town, not intending to go anywhere. He just needed to ride.

———

Joe returned after sunset and rode to the back of the jail, dismounted, and then unsaddled and brushed the horse. It was awkward with one arm, but he got it done.

He walked in the back door made sure the jail was empty and just sat on the bed for a few minutes. The ride had served its purpose in clarifying his thoughts. Cassie was fifteen and had her own dreams that she'd had for years. He was just a means to an end. For that brief time, he thought that maybe she'd changed her mind, but apparently not.

So, he'd fall back to his primary goal of finding the remaining three Hogans. Fred and Hank were making news periodically as they had paired up and hadn't added any non-Hogans, apparently deciding to keep their evil-doing in the family. The last report had them somewhere outside of San Antonio. Buck was the mystery. Nothing had been heard from him since that day when his gang had been wiped out by the Texas Rangers and he'd made his escape…not a word.

The way things had been working out so far, it was almost as if Warwick was a magnet to the Hogans, not to mention Phelps. He had stumbled onto Earl and Glen just a few miles from town and then Phelps passed through town, just to be caught. He seriously began to wonder if Fred and Hank wouldn't just show up, especially with all of the news about Earl and Glen's deaths.

He had also spent some time thinking about Kit and Bessie. He strongly suspected that Bessie might be in a motherly way already. She and Kit spent a lot of private time together just since he'd been here. He'd run into Kit on several occasions, some of them at the Warren home but mostly when he was making rounds. They just passed a casual greeting and never exchanged more than a few sentences even when they were in the same room at the Warrens for over an hour.

Joe just felt a serious amount of hostility from Kit for some reason. He finally thought it might have to do with Bessie somehow. He liked Bessie, and they were friendly, but that was all. Kit must have seen it differently. Maybe that would change after he and Bessie were married, but Joe doubted it would. He'd seen Kit's type too often at the reformatory, and they were always in the group of boys that should have been in prison rather than the reformatory.

With his mind somewhat settled, Joe lit a lamp and opened the statute book.

CHAPTER 9

May 15, 1879

It was the day of Bessie and Kit's wedding and the Warren home was a disaster.

Joe, who'd had his sutures removed two weeks earlier and had been doing volunteer blacksmith work to build up his arm strength, was helping with setting up the wedding which was going to be held at the Warren house.

The new stove had been installed in the new Ryerson house and Bessie hadn't known about the gift yet, which took an amazing amount of deception. Cassie had also stocked the kitchen with flatware, cookware, and a set of china, obviously changing her mind after telling Joe that the cookstove was enough.

She'd been accepted to Carlisle's School for Young Women and would be leaving at the end of August. Joe had gotten that bit of news from his boss as Cassie had thrown herself into helping with the wedding and hadn't had any time with Joe at all. At least, that was the excuse she gave.

At ten o'clock, the Reverend Wilcox arrived to perform the ceremony, and everyone stood as Sheriff Warren escorted Bessie into the main room. Joe had to admit that Kit was almost a picture-perfect groom, but Bessie was much more impressive. She was prettier than he'd ever seen her before and was almost jealous of Kit for getting to marry her.

Bessie walked on her father's arm to the fireplace where Reverend Wilcox and Kit waited. After John gave Bessie's hand to Kit, he stepped back and took Minnie's hand.

Joe glanced over at Cassie as she stood with her sister Mary and her husband, Ned. All of them were focused on Bessie, as they should be. Joe tried to see Cassie as a bride and couldn't. Maybe she really never was meant to be one. She was every bit as pretty as Bessie but still thin. She looked so much like a teenaged girl, except in her eyes.

Joe finally sighed and turned and watched the ceremony.

It wasn't long or overly flowery but still, by the time it ended, Minnie and Mary were in tears, but Joe noticed that Mrs. Ryerson, Kit's mother wasn't crying. He was her only child, so this was her only opportunity to weep at a wedding involving one of her own, yet she remained dry-eyed.

Cassie wasn't weeping but looking at Bessie with curiosity. Joe wasn't sure if the curiosity was because of Cassie's questioning of her sister's choice in husbands or her possible condition.

The bride and groom kissed, and everyone applauded, even Cassie. The newlyweds then were congratulated by the guests and for once, Kit didn't try to break Joe's hand. Not that he stood a chance of doing it anyway. Joe kissed Bessie on the cheek, as did all of the other men and most of the women in attendance before everyone settled down to have some food and drink. It wasn't a meal, but hand food, punch, and coffee.

Joe didn't seek out Cassie as she seemed to be avoiding him, probably because she didn't want to tell him that she'd been accepted at the preparatory school and would be leaving. She must not have expected her father to spill the beans.

So, after he'd had two cookies and a cup of coffee, Deputy Joe Armstrong left the house and walked back to the jail. Somebody had to be the face of law enforcement on a Thursday.

After Joe had gone, the others continued the mid-week festivities and by late afternoon, everyone walked from the Warren home to escort the newlyweds to their new house. Once inside, Bessie saw the new cookstove and accessories and squealed with delight, and hugged Cassie. Cassie then explained that Joe had made it all possible, and when Bessie began looking for Joe to thank him, they finally realized he was gone.

“I wonder where he went?” asked Bessie.

“Probably back to work,” Cassie replied.

“Will you tell him how grateful we are for the gift? I'm going to be busy,” Bessie said with a laugh.

“I will,” she replied and asked quietly, “How are you feeling, Bessie?”

Bessie smiled slightly and whispered, “Morning sickness is annoying.”

“When are you due?”

“Just before Christmas.”

“I'll be in Dallas, but you'll let me know how you're doing, won't you?”

"Of course, I will. They don't let you out for the holidays?"

"They do, but not long enough for me to make the long trip both ways."

"Well, I'll write to you often."

Cassie kissed her sister and gave her a hug. By the time she returned to Warwick next summer, Bessie's baby would be six months old.

———

After returning to the jail for a while, Joe left the office and walked to Yancy's smithy to do some work. His arm was getting better, but it still hurt when he used it and the strength wasn't there yet.

Once there, he took off his gunbelt, hung it on a cast iron hook he'd made for that purpose, took off his outer shirt, and began to work. He'd bought some undershirts before he started his blacksmith rehabilitation. Yancy didn't even acknowledge his presence anymore when he was busy working some iron. Joe just arrived and started working.

Joe had a flat piece of glowing iron in a set of tongs in his left hand that was about to be flattened into the start of a set of large hinges for a barn door when a horse flashed by on his left, leaving a cloud of dust.

Joe left the glowing metal on the anvil, dropped the tongs and hammer and turned, snatched his gunbelt from the hook, and ran out onto the street. He turned and saw the rider pull up to the jail, dismount, and enter the office. He was moving too fast for Joe to know who he was.

He was almost to the office when the man popped back out the door and looked both ways. Joe still didn't know who he was.

"I'm Deputy Armstrong. What's the problem?" Joe asked as he reached the door.

"Rustlers. We tried stopping them, but they shot Henry and then took off. They rode east. There were four of 'em."

Joe strapped on his gunbelt and said, "Okay. Stay here. I'll go and get more help and then we'll go get your rustlers."

"Okay."

Joe crossed the busy street, jogging toward the Warren house, not knowing that everyone was two houses down.

Luckily, Cassie was leaving the house to go find him before he turned to go to the Warren home, spotted her, and changed direction.

Before she could ask why he'd gone or wonder why he was wearing a sweaty undershirt, he said loudly, "Cassie, tell your father that a group of four rustlers shot a ranch hand and are riding east. I'll go back and get some horses saddled."

Cassie didn't hesitate, but shouted, "Okay," before turning and trotting back to the house.

Joe reversed his course as he ran back to the jail where he enlisted the ranch hand's help in saddling three horses. They were almost finished when Sheriff Warren arrived with Dan and Lou.

The ranch hand, who gave his name as Bob Cass, gave the sheriff the details as Joe mounted one of his geldings. He'd made sure that he'd saddled one of his animals. The only one he didn't saddle was Dan's. His wife was due any day now and she hadn't been able to attend the wedding.

Sheriff Warren noticed the horse selection and agreed with Joe's choices. He sent Dan into the jail for three Winchesters and Lou went inside to get their gunbelts that weren't appropriate for a wedding.

Just twenty minutes after the rider passed the smithy, the three lawmen and the cowhand rode east out of Warwick at a fast trot.

As they rode, Joe kept looking at Bob Cass. He knew he'd only been in town a few months, but he didn't recognize him. The ranch hands usually showed up at the saloons on Fridays or Saturdays, but he didn't remember seeing him at all. He could have been a new hand, which wouldn't have been too out of the ordinary.

He was riding behind the sheriff and the ranch hand with Lou riding on his left. Then as he was pondering the man's identity, he noticed something that was really out of the ordinary. The man's hammer loop was now off. When they started the ride, the loop had been in place. None of the others could see it, and he hadn't noticed when the man had popped it free, either.

Joe loosed his own hammer loop, pulled his Colt, cocked the hammer, and pointed it at the man's back as Lou looked at him with big eyes.

Joe shouted, "I've got my Colt cocked. Put your hands in the air! Now!"

The sheriff's head whipped around as the cowhand thought about pulling his pistol but that damned deputy was just twelve feet behind him, so he put his hands in the air and shouted, “What the hell you doin’, Deputy?”

“Lou, can you take his pistol?” Joe asked as he kept his sights on the man’s back.

Sheriff Warren called them all to a stop and asked, “What’s going on, Joe?”

“Have you ever seen this jasper before, boss?”

“No, but there are always new faces showing up. What made you draw on him?”

“When we started riding, his hammer loop was in place. If you look now, it’s off. I think he’s leading us into an ambush.”

John turned to the phony ranch hand and asked, “What ranch is your brand?”

“I’m with the Rocking W.”

“Then Phil Johnson will vouch for you when we get there and ask him?”

“Of course, he will.”

“Then we’d better go to the Double B because that’s where he’s the foreman. Lou, get him off his horse and tie him up. Then we’ll ask him kindly what his intentions are.”

After the man was on the ground and trussed up like a Thanksgiving turkey, Sheriff Warren pointed his cocked pistol at the man’s crotch and said, “Talk to me, mister before my finger gets tired.”

He didn’t answer and Joe asked, “Boss, do you want me to get your whip?”

John turned to Joe and didn't bat an eyelash before replying, "I'm getting a real hankering to use that thing again, and we're far enough out that no one will hear him scream."

Joe looked at the man sitting on the ground and pulled his shirt over his head, turned, and said, "He did this to me when he found me sleeping on the job."

The man's eyes grew wide at the deep slashes and then he swallowed and said, "I'll talk. I'm with Babe Frick. He wants to get to the bank, but you got too many lawmen in town, so I was supposed to get you all out of there."

John snapped, "He's going to try and rob the bank right now?"

"Just before they close. They're swinging around to the north right now."

"How many?"

"Three, including Babe."

"Damn!" John swore and said, "Get him on his horse and let's get back as soon as we can. Joe, you bring him back. Lou, let's get those bastards before they can get into town. I don't want lead flying all over town."

The sheriff and Lou mounted quickly and raced back west while Joe pulled the outlaw into his saddle and mounted, took his horse's reins, and set off at a fast trot, wishing he could join the sheriff.

He watched the sheriff and Lou ride diagonally cutting northwest across open country to cut off the outlaws and glanced back at the outlaw to tell him his boys were going to die when he saw a smirk on the man's face.

He whipped his head back and looked south of town and saw a dust cloud in the low sun. It was about two miles south of town and about three miles from where he was.

"Son of a bitch," Joe swore under his breath and looked back at the receding horses of Sheriff Warren and Lou.

He pulled his Colt and fired one shot into the air, keeping his eyes on his boss. When John turned to see why Joe had fired, Joe began gesturing wildly with his pistol to the south.

Sheriff Warren and Lou then shifted their direction and turned south as Joe pulled his horse to a stop, dismounted, and tied the outlaw's horse to a bush. He then yanked the man onto the ground, pulled his rope from his saddle, and wrapped it around him until he was cocooned in the heavy hemp. He tied it off and mounted, pulled his Winchester, and set off at a gallop to make up the distance.

The shot he'd fired alerted Babe and his two other gang members, but they could only see Joe as the town blocked the sheriff and Lou.

"Looks like we got trouble, boss."

Babe weighed the odds. There were four lawmen in Warwick, but he wasn't sure how many were still in town or how many had fallen for his ruse. Either way, it was going to result in a gunfight. It may as well be with only one of them.

"Let's get this one and when we're finished with him, we'll see if the others are in town or Billy got them outta there."

The three outlaws then changed their direction from north to northeast to meet Joe head-on.

Joe picked up the change and at first, didn't understand why they'd done it, initially thinking they were trying to rescue their fourth gang member. He thought they could see Sheriff Warren and Lou both riding almost due south now along the eastern edge of town.

But they hadn't seen the other two lawmen yet as they pulled their rifles. They were concentrating on Joe now, but if they'd looked to their left, they would have spotted the oncoming threat from the north.

It was a three-pronged convergence that would meet about a mile southeast of Warwick.

Joe had his Winchester cocked and his horse slowed to a medium trot as the gap closed to less than five hundred yards. He still couldn't understand why the three outlaws weren't aiming at the sheriff and Lou who were closer than he was.

Sheriff Warren wasn't about to look a gift horse in the mouth as he and Lou spread apart enough to give them room. They were just two hundred yards from the three outlaws' left flank and still there was no indication that the bad men knew they were there.

Babe had his other two men spread apart as they all had their repeaters' sights on Joe as he closed to within three hundred yards. None of them seemed to think it was odd that a single deputy was so stupid as to continue to ride straight at them by himself.

When Joe passed within two hundred yards, Babe opened the skirmish when he fired, attempting to unhorse the approaching deputy. It was then that he and his partners discovered their fatal mistake when John and Lou opened fire from just eighty yards and were actually slightly behind the outlaws now, at about their eight o'clock position.

The sudden sound of rifle fire from their left caused chaos among the three outlaws.

Joe was forgotten as two of them wheeled to face the new threat. The third was already on the ground, having taken the sheriff's first shot in the neck.

But when they turned, they left their right flank exposed to Joe, who opened fire at just over a hundred yards.

The two outlaws had been rapidly firing at the two lawmen when Joe's first shot arrived and smashed into Babe's left side, just below the ribs. The .44 just penetrated into his stomach before it lost its energy.

Joe continued to fire as did the sheriff and Lou. Bullets were tracing through the air as a giant cloud of gunsmoke covered the scene.

Babe continued to fire despite the bullet in his gut. Joe's fourth shot ended his fight when it struck the right side of his chest and punched clear to his heart.

The last mounted outlaw never had a chance to surrender when two .44s, one from the sheriff's Winchester and one from Lou's found their marks in his chest, and he flopped back over his horse's rump onto the ground.

Then just eighty-two seconds after that first shot, it was over. The lawmen slid their rifles back into their scabbards and Joe trotted his horse over to his boss.

"How'd you see them, Joe?" Sheriff Warren asked when he was close.

"I was going to tell the one we captured how stupid he was, and he was smirking like he'd pulled one over on us. So, I began looking to the south and saw them coming. I still can't figure out why they didn't see you coming."

"It doesn't matter, I suppose. We'll start getting this crowd on their horses while you go and get that one into town."

"Yes, sir," Joe replied before turning his horse back northeast to pick up the only living member of the gang.

Three hours later, the sun was setting, and Joe was the only one left in the jail with the prisoner. The gang was wanted in a neighboring county for murder and robbery, so the sheriff decided they'd let them try the man and hang him there. Joe convinced his boss that this reward should go to him and Lou. He had enough, and the sheriff didn't argue.

He'd managed some supper when he had to go to Rupert's to get some food for his prisoner but was still a bit hungry. He was drinking coffee and writing his report when the sheriff entered the office, took off his hat, and sat down.

He smiled and said, "That was a wedding day that won't be forgotten."

"No, sir. I wouldn't think so."

"I hope things stay quiet for a while now. We've had too much excitement since you've been back."

"Do you think I'm attracting them somehow?"

Sheriff Warren grinned at him and said, "Maybe."

Joe laughed as the sheriff stood, gave him a short wave, and left the jail.

Joe leaned back, finished his coffee and despite the absurdity of the idea, wondered if there might be something to it.

The prisoner was picked up two days later and Joe was able to return to normal duties. He continued to work at the smithy when he could, and his left arm was improving rapidly.

The next major event was when Dan's wife, Ellie, went into labor on May 21st, and before the sun went down, presented Dan with a son he named John William.

Dan stayed home for three days but was glad to get back to work, complaining about the lack of sleep and constant attention required by his newborn son.

Joe had heard more rumblings about the whereabouts of Fred and Hank, but nothing specific. The last ones placed the pair further west, around Fort Griffin, which was still a good hundred and fifty miles south. It looked as if the magnetism of Warwick didn't attract the brothers as much as he'd thought.

After the incident with the Babe Frick gang, there were no shootouts in the county that involved the lawmen, but they were still busy with routine law enforcement.

The summer was nearing its end and Cassie's departure was imminent which seemed to depress her and had surprised her parents.

Just a week before she was scheduled to take the eastbound coach, she entered the jail, knowing that only Joe was there.

Joe was in back brushing down one of his horses when she arrived, so he was surprised when he entered to find her sitting at the desk.

"Good evening, Cassie. This is a pleasant surprise," he said as he sat down.

"It may be a surprise, but it's not pleasant."

"What's wrong? Are you having misgivings about going to that school?"

"No, it's Bessie. I'm worried about her, Joe. I'll be leaving soon, and she hasn't said anything, but I think Kit is hitting her."

Joe should have been shocked at the news, but he wasn't even surprised as he asked, "Does your father know?"

"I don't believe so. I haven't said anything to him because I'm just guessing. I can't see behind her dress to look for bruises, but when I hugged her the other day, she winced. I asked her what was wrong, and she said that everything was fine. But since then, I've watched her closely and she grimaces and seems to be uncomfortable when she tries to sit down."

"It's not because of her pregnancy?"

"No. I'm sure of that. But if he hits her, the baby might be in danger. Joe, can you do anything?"

Joe rubbed his palms together as he thought. *What could he do?*

"I'll tell you what, Cassie. I'll pay her a visit when Kit is at work at his father's store. I'll talk to her and make my own judgement. Okay?"

"But what if you find that he's beating her?"

"Legally, there's nothing I can do, but that doesn't mean I can't do something as a man."

"I would be very grateful, Joe. Bessie is such a sweet person. Maybe you should have married her instead of Kit."

Joe was surprised by her comment but didn't let it show and said, "I'll see her tomorrow morning."

"Thank you, Joe."

"You're welcome, Cassie."

She smiled at him and stood and left, leaving Joe puzzled and in a bit of a dilemma. If she was right about Bessie, that could lead to all sorts of problems.

Her casual remark about Bessie being better off if she'd married him rather than Kit had really disturbed him. What had driven her to make that comment? Joe was no closer to figuring out Cassie than he had when he first saw that ten-year-old freckle-faced girl, but if she was right about Bessie being hit by Kit, then he'd have to do something. Beating a woman was bad enough, but when she was with child, it was demonic.

He'd see for himself tomorrow.

———

The next morning, Joe made his rounds, passed the Warren house and continued to Bessie's new home. It was a nice house, smaller than the sheriff's, but seemed to be well-built. He stepped onto the front porch and knocked politely on the door.

It was almost nine o'clock, so he expected that only Bessie was in the house. He was wrong.

The door swung open and Joe found Kit scowling at him.

"What do you want?"

Joe paused for a few seconds and replied, "Cassie said you were having trouble with the new cookstove and asked me if I could take a look at it."

"There's nothing wrong with it."

"How would you know, Kit? You don't cook. Let me ask Bessie."

Kit shrugged his shoulders and said, "Come in," then turned and headed back into the main room.

Joe followed and had to commend himself for coming up with the quick fib about the cookstove but knew he couldn't ask Bessie about anything other than the appliance with Kit around.

Bessie was in the kitchen looking tired but smiled when she saw Joe.

"Good morning, Joe. What brings you by?"

"Cassie said your cookstove was having a problem with the vent pipe."

She glanced at the stove and said, “Not that I noticed.”

“Maybe I misunderstood. Was there anything else that she could have meant?”

“Not with the cookstove. Would you like a cup of coffee while you’re here?”

“I wouldn’t mind. The boys already finished the pot back at the office.”

Kit had never moved from the hallway entrance and leaned against the door jamb as he watched Joe pour himself a cup of coffee.

Joe remained standing as he sipped his coffee and tried to give Bessie a quick scan for bruises, but her dress had long sleeves and a high collar, so any bruises would have to be high on her neck, and there weren’t any.

“How is your baby?” Joe asked.

“She’s doing fine,” Bessie replied, her obvious joy on the topic reflecting in her eyes.

Joe smiled and asked, “Are you sure she’s a she?”

“We don’t have boys in the Warren family,” Bessie said before she giggled.

Joe laughed before Kit snapped, “You’re a Ryerson now, not a Warren. You’re gonna have a boy.”

That’s when Joe saw it. It wasn’t much, and it wasn’t a grimace. Joe saw fear in Bessie’s eyes. She was afraid of offending her new husband.

Bessie quickly looked at him and replied, "That's right, Kit. I'm sorry."

Her husband grunted and cut in front of Joe and poured his own cup of coffee.

Joe was going to ask Kit why he wasn't working but didn't. Joe had felt the added hostility in Kit's glare when he and Bessie were talking, and he finally realized that Kit suspected that Joe wanted Bessie.

Joe took one last long swallow of coffee, put down the cup and said, "Well, I've got to get back to my rounds. Thanks for the coffee, Bessie, and I'll have to ask Cassie what I got wrong. I know it had to be me because Cassie doesn't make any mistakes."

Bessie smiled and said, "You're welcome anytime, Joe. And Cassie most surely does make mistakes. I think going away to that school is one of them."

"It's her dream, Bessie."

"I'm not sure she knows what her dream is, Joe."

Joe nodded, tipped his hat to Kit and walked past him, down the hallway and out of the house.

He turned onto the street, but rather than returning to the jail, he headed down the Warren house's walkway.

He stepped up onto the back porch and knocked.

A few seconds later, Minnie opened the door, saw Joe and smiled as she said, "Come in, Joe. What brings you around at this time of day?"

"Oh, I just thought I'd come and talk to Cassie. I won't be able to have the opportunity much longer."

Minnie turned to call out to her daughter when Cassie entered the kitchen as Joe was closing the door.

"Hello, Joe. Do you want to go for a walk?" she asked.

"I'd enjoy that, Cassie," Joe replied and opened the recently closed door.

As they were leaving, Minnie said, "If you elope, I wouldn't object."

Joe laughed and waved as he and Cassie left the house, crossed the street and began walking east out onto the open ground.

"Well?" Cassie asked.

"I didn't get to talk to her much because Kit was there."

"In the middle of the morning?"

"I know. I should have checked to see if he was at work when I did my rounds. Anyway, I made up some story about you telling me to check the cookstove pipe, so I could at least see Bessie. I didn't see any evidence of her being struck, and she never winced or grimaced, either."

"So, you don't believe me."

"I didn't say that. She was wearing a dress with long sleeves and a high collar, so all I could see was part of her neck. She didn't move much, and she didn't sit down, so I wasn't able to see her react to any pain. But when I asked her about her baby, Bessie said it was a girl because Warrens always had girls and it seemed to offend Kit. He reminded her that she was a Ryerson now and she was going to have a boy. He said it in a very brusque, almost threatening manner. And that's when I saw obvious fear in her eyes. She's afraid of him, Cassie."

"So, I'm not wrong? He's beating her?"

"My opinion is that you're right, but what to do about it is the question. He's legally entitled to discipline his wife, so he's not breaking the law. That means I'll have to come up with something else."

"You can do it, Joe. I know you can," Cassie said hopefully.

Joe wasn't sure he could as they continued to walk.

After walking for another fifty yards in silence, Cassie asked, "Joe, after I'm gone, will you take care of Bessie?"

"What do you mean, Cassie? She's married to Kit and she's the sheriff's daughter. I'm nothing but an onlooker here and after you leave, I won't even be here much longer."

She stopped and looked at Joe, asking, "You're leaving?"

"Probably within a month or so. I told you I would as soon as I felt ready. That gunshot wound slowed me down, but I'm ready now."

"But Bessie will need you. She's so sweet and precious and that bastard Kit is going to hurt her and her baby."

"No, he won't, Cassie. I'll make sure of that before I leave."

"But if you leave, what will happen to Bessie?"

Joe asked sharply, “What is with your sudden obsession with Bessie? I told you that I’d make sure that nothing happened to her and I will.”

“It’s just that Bessie is, well, Bessie needs someone to care for her, especially if you take care of the Kit problem. You don’t think you can just make him stop, do you?”

Joe exhaled sharply and said, “No. Men like that have an anger inside them. If I was to threaten him, he’d take it out on Bessie. If I beat him senseless, he might even kill her. Not intentionally, of course, but she’d still be just as dead.”

“You’re going to have to kill him, aren’t you?” she asked quietly.

“Unless I can come up with another answer. I’ll talk to your father about it.”

“Okay,” she replied as they continued to walk east.

After a few more steps, Cassie asked, “If Kit is gone, will you marry Bessie?”

Joe stopped and turned to face her as he said, “No, Cassie. Bessie has your parents and Mary and Ned to help her. I’ll be gone.”

“Why? Is your obsessive hate toward the Hogans so great that you don’t care what happens to Bessie and her baby?”

Joe was growing incredibly irritated with her seeming obsession with paring him with her pregnant sister to the point of throwing that accusation at him, so he had to pause to get his emotions in check before he could answer.

He finally replied, “You know better than that, Cassie. I told you about what they did to my mother and her sister. I’ll make sure that Bessie is safe and happy before I go. That’s the best I can do.”

Cassie didn’t answer but turned and began walking quickly back to the house. Joe let her go and followed at ten feet wondering why Cassie seemed so determined to marry him off to Bessie.

After Cassie had turned to go to her home, Joe continued across the street and headed for the jail.

He entered an empty office which initially surprised Joe until he realized that it was lunchtime. He walked to the back of the office, expecting to find the sheriff’s office empty as well, but found the sheriff at his desk writing some report for the county.

Joe stuck his head in the doorway and asked, “John, could I talk to you for a minute?”

Sheriff Warren noted the use of his Christian name which Joe rarely used, and replied, “Sure, Joe. Come on in.”

Joe closed the door, which was another eyebrow raiser for the sheriff, before sitting down.

“Last night, Cassie stopped by with a disturbing concern. She didn’t tell you because she wasn’t sure, so she asked me to go do some of my own investigating, and I just did.”

“Was it about Bessie being hurt by Kit?”

Joe was taken aback and said, “Um, yes. You knew?”

“Minnie suspected it first and then she told me about it, and I watched Bessie more closely, and I agree with her. I never saw any physical injuries, but she always was well covered, and Minnie felt she'd be opening a can of worms just by asking. What did you find?"

"Nothing physical because she was dressed the same way, but when Kit corrected something that she said with a real bite behind it, I saw genuine fear in her eyes before she apologized."

"What did she say that made him angry?"

"I asked how the baby was and she said she was having a girl. Kit told her otherwise."

"That was what made him mad?"

"Yes, sir. But if he is, we have a problem, don't we?"

"Sometimes it's hard to be wearing this badge. He's not breaking the law and if you or I did anything, we'd be in the wrong, legally at least. You understand that problem, don't you?"

"Yes, I do, and I told Cassie that I'd find a solution somehow."

"Do you have any ideas, Joe?" the sheriff asked with the same hope in his voice that Cassie had when she had asked.

"One, but it's not going to be pretty and it has all sorts of consequences."

"Can you enlighten me?"

"I want to force Kit into a fight. I'm pretty sure that he believes that I'm either in love with Bessie or plan on taking her away from him. I think it won't take much to push him into a serious confrontation."

"You think a fistfight would straighten him out? You've got to know better than that, especially after spending those four years in the reformatory. Men like that don't change."

"No, sir. I don't expect him to walk away, and that's what makes it messy."

John was a bit stunned by the casual way Joe effectively said he'd beat Kit to death, but asked, "Messy?"

"What if Bessie really does love him? What if we're wrong? Even if we're right, I'd still be a deputy sheriff and that would make the whole office look bad, and we'd lose our credibility. You've spent all your time as sheriff building up respect for the office and it would all be gone in an instant."

"You're right, it would."

Joe then said, "Boss, next week Cassie is leaving, and there's no longer any reason for me to stay here. Everyone knows I was planning on leaving to chase after the Hogans, so no one will be surprised when I resign. After you have my badge and everyone in town knows I'm leaving, I'll stop and make my goodbyes to everyone and light Kit's fuse. I'll want witnesses to prove it's an evenly matched fight, though."

"Joe, that's just not right. It won't be fair to you at all."

"Life isn't fair, boss. Bessie doesn't deserve to be hurt, and she has a baby that needs protection, too."

John sighed. He didn't have any other answers and he wanted Bessie safe.

"Okay. I suppose I'll have to live with that."

"You'll have to let everyone know that Bessie was innocent in all this. I don't want anyone to get the impression that we were having an affair."

"No, that's not a problem."

"Okay. Can Mrs. Warren somehow get a reading on Bessie's feelings toward Kit?"

"I can already give you an answer to that. Bessie was having coffee with Minnie two days ago and she mentioned that she'd made a big mistake even letting him call on her."

Joe nodded and said, "Alright, boss. I'll keep thinking on how to get this done, but there's something that's bothering me that you might be able to answer."

"Ask away."

"It's Cassie. We went for a walk and after I explained what I'd found, she seemed determined to marry me off to Bessie if I did what she expected me to do. Why would she do that?"

"She did? Now that comes as a surprise to me. I have no idea at all. I'll ask my wife, but she talks to Cassie less than I do."

"I don't want her going to Dallas not understanding how I feel about her."

"How do you feel about her, Joe? I always thought that you two were as closely matched as any two people I know, but all this boyfriend-girlfriend talk seems to bounce all over the place."

Joe smiled and said, "It is odd, isn't it? I've loved Cassie since before I left the reformatory and that feeling has only gotten stronger. I'll never want to marry another woman."

"Then why in God's name are you letting her go to that school?" he asked in exasperation.

"I have to let her go. If I somehow convinced her to stay and wait for me to finish with the Hogans and then marry her when I returned, for the rest of her life, she'd wonder if she'd made a mistake and given up her future. I believe that letting her go to the preparatory school to discover what the world is like outside of Warwick is critical for her. I know I'm risking losing her if she discovers that her new world is everything that she hoped it would be, but I have to let her make that decision."

John leaned back and said, "I hope you're not making a big mistake, Joe."

"So, do I, John."

Joe left the sheriff's private office and returned to the front desk where he took a seat. He hadn't really lied to him about why Cassie wanted to leave because he still thought it was one of the reasons she was going. But after thinking about it for a while, he believed the Bessie marriage comments were Cassie's attempt to permanently end any chance that she would have to marry him because of her fear of childbirth. Whatever the reason, it still hurt.

———

Joe saw Cassie only occasionally over the next couple of days but made a point of seeing Bessie more than usual. Each visit was with Kit present, and Joe ensured he always made Bessie laugh at some time during his visits. His only concern was that he was making it more dangerous for her.

He was also getting very fond of Bessie. She was no longer the easily impressed teenager, despite her age of eighteen. Bessie had matured mentally, maybe because of her pregnancy, marriage, or the stress that Kit was putting on her. Whatever the reason, Bessie was a much more pleasant person to be around.

Cassie was preparing for her departure and had arranged for her father to watch Sommy, her pinto, the name derived from sombrero, and in one of their too-infrequent meetings, she gave Joe her Remington pistol to use while she was in school. He didn't mention that he now had four Colts, but when he left carrying the Remington, for the first time since he'd arrived in Warwick, he felt he was losing Cassie forever.

August 26, 1879

Cassie's eastbound stage was due to leave Warwick at ten o'clock, and Joe remained in the office at the desk. For all his brave talk about Cassie having to make her own decision after sampling the world outside of her home town, he was disconsolate. He had remained in the jail because he was worried that he might change his mind at the last second, grab Cassie, kiss her and beg her not to go. *What a scene that would be!* Not only would it be embarrassing to Cassie, it might ruin his plans for Kit.

The entire Warren clan was at the depot along with the other two deputies. Everyone had assumed he'd be there, but he'd already told the sheriff why he would mind the desk.

So, as the driver brought the coach to the front of the depot, Deputy Sheriff Joe Armstrong stood at the window of the office watching Cassie kiss her sisters and mother goodbye and hug her father. She never even looked at the jail before she clambered into the stagecoach with one small travel bag while the porter loaded her two large travel bags into the boot.

The driver snapped the long reins, the coach lurched forward and then rolled quickly away, leaving a large crowd of well-wishers waving as it left town.

Joe exhaled and turned, walked to the desk, took a seat and pulled out the stack of wanted posters.

In the dusty, rocking stagecoach, its only passenger had her face buried in her hands as tears flowed down her wrists onto her dress. Joe hadn't even been there to say goodbye.

The sheriff, Dan Sheehy and Lou Sanborn all arrived back in the office a few minutes later, just as Joe was setting aside the two posters for Fred and Hank Hogan. The one for Buck was so old that there was no need to take it with him.

On the trip from the depot to the jail, Sheriff Warren had informed his deputies that he'd asked Joe to stay in the office because he was expecting an important telegram, so they didn't ask about his absence as they hung their hats.

"What do you have there, Joe?" asked Lou.

"Two of the three Hogan brothers. My arm is feeling pretty good, so I'm thinking that it's time I went after them."

Dan grinned and said, "It doesn't have anything to do with your girlfriend leaving, does it?"

John was going to interrupt, but Joe smiled at Dan and replied, "Nope, but I'll admit it was a factor."

"Do you have anything about them, Joe?" asked Sheriff Warren.

"Only that they're operating in Texas. That narrows it down to a quarter of a million square miles, so I should find them in a few days."

Lou and Dan both laughed as their boss left the front office and returned to his own knowing that Joe was miserable, but setting up for his departure and his confrontation with Kit.

With Cassie gone, Joe began to do some serious preparation for his departure. He outfitted one of his four horses with a pack saddle and bought supplies that he'd need for an extended chase. He didn't think he'd even find his first hint of the whereabouts of Fred and Hank unless they were identified committed a crime.

Joe was ready to begin his search, but first he had the Kit issue to resolve.

A couple of days after Cassie had gone, he'd paid a visit to Bessie and found the first physical evidence of her mistreatment when he found a welt on her left cheek, probably from a recent slap. She had downplayed the injury as her own foolishness in trying to swat at a wasp with a belt. Kit had confirmed her story, but Joe knew he couldn't delay much longer.

On Monday, September 8th, Joe sat at the desk having his usual morning coffee when Lou and Dan both entered the office.

"Morning, Joe? Coffee ready?" Lou asked.

Joe hoisted his cup and replied, "Nope, just didn't feel like walking all the way to the privy," then took a big sip, creating the expected loud guffaws from his fellow deputies.

Sheriff Warren walked into the office as they were laughing and asked, "What's so funny?"

"Joe made yellow coffee this morning," Lou replied before laughing at his own humor.

Joe then said, "Boss, I need to leave. I'm going to give you my badge today."

Even though they expected Joe to be leaving shortly, his announcement startled Lou and Dan.

John replied, "I understand, Joe."

"I'll stay on the job for the rest of the day, though."

The sheriff then said, "Joe, before you go, I'd like to have a farewell party at the house. It won't be a big affair, just coffee and some cake."

Joe smiled and said, "I'd like that, boss."

"How about tomorrow at noon? I'll talk to Minnie and set it up. We'll have Mary, Ned, Bessie and Kit there, too."

"I'll look forward to it, boss," Joe said with a smile.

The sheriff slapped him lightly on the back as he passed to go to his office with the plan to help Bessie set in motion.

As he entered his private office, Sheriff Warren closed his door, hung up his hat and took a seat. He felt sickened by what he knew would soon happen. There were so many things about this that made him nauseous. Joe's departure had always been expected, but John thought he'd be around longer.

Joe might get hurt or even killed himself. He'd seen Kit box and knew he was the best he'd ever seen. Joe was strong as an ox, but John didn't know if he understood how to fight. He was outstanding with his pistol and Winchester, but neither would come into play tomorrow.

If Joe somehow managed to put Kit down, then there would be a firestorm from his father and accusations that Joe and Bessie were having an affair. His only proof was to have Doctor Gillespie examine Bessie, ostensibly for her pregnancy and find the evidence of her being beaten.

Behind it all was his concern for Cassie. Before she'd gone, John knew that she was surprisingly unhappy about it. She said she needed to discover what she was missing, but John believed she'd be missing what she'd already discovered.

Minnie knew what was going to happen with Joe and Kit and was just as torn about it as he was but knew that Kit had to be stopped. She had held out hope until the last second before Cassie boarded the stagecoach that Joe would run from the jail and get her to stay, and suspected that he hadn't because of what he needed to do with Kit.

John had told her what Cassie had said to Joe about marrying Bessie, and it had startled her. Now she wondered if Cassie wasn't serious. She just couldn't understand that girl.

The morning rounds were complete. and Joe sat behind the front desk.

“Are you coming back, Joe?” asked Dan as he and Lou tossed a .44 cartridge back and forth.

“I’m not sure. I have no idea how long it’ll take me. I think the boss should hire a new deputy. You boys need the help.”

Lou caught the cartridge and lobbed it in a high arc to Dan as he said, “We’ll be okay, Joe. I think the boss should leave that slot open.”

“It’s up to him. Are you both coming to the farewell party? Mrs. Warren makes one hell of a coffee cake.”

“We’ll be there, Joe, even if there wasn’t any cake,” Dan replied and returned the cartridge to his gunbelt loop.

“I just wanted to let you both know that I learned a lot from both of you while I was here. I still have a lot to figure out, too.”

“Hell, Joe, we didn’t show you a damned thing,” Lou said.

Before Joe could reply, the sheriff entered from outside and said, “You boys all coming to Joe’s little ‘get-your-butt-outta-my-town’ shindig?”

All three deputies laughed as they stood, grabbed their hats and followed their boss out of the jail and onto the main street of Warwick.

Lou and Dan were in a good mood, but Joe’s stomach was churning at the idea of what was about to happen. Like the sheriff, he was keenly aware of Kit’s boxing ability. He hadn’t seen him box but had heard dozens of comments about his skills in the ring, even from Cassie. His own fights, and they weren’t many, were more bull rushes and swift combinations. He hadn’t been in a real fight in three years. His only advantage was that the fights he was in were always against bigger opponents.

He was about the same height as Kit, but probably outweighed him by thirty pounds, which might be a disadvantage as it could make him slower. No matter what, it was too late to stop it now. He knew that he could just ride away, but he'd promised Cassie, and didn't want Bessie to be hurt anymore.

They entered the already crowded Warren house and Joe was greeted by Ned, who shook his hand and he got a peck on the cheek from Mary before Minnie gave him a big hug and a longer kiss on the cheek.

"We're going to miss you, Joe," Minnie said, "but now that you're here, let's have some cake."

Joe glanced at Bessie and smiled as he followed Minnie. She hadn't said anything, much less given him a kiss on the cheek, and Joe understood why as Kit had her by the left arm. Joe guessed that his frequent visits had made Kit even more possessively jealous, which was their purpose.

The group made it into the kitchen where Minnie began handing out plates with slices of cake. The coffee was self-serve.

"I made two cakes, Joe. One is going with you," Minnie announced loudly as the hubbub grew a little louder.

"Thank you, ma'am. I'll probably eat the whole thing before I camp for the night," Joe replied causing general laughter.

Joe was smiling as he began to eat his cake, but he was getting more nervous by the second.

"Where are you going first, Joe?" asked Lou as he poured his own cup of coffee.

"I think I'll start in Texas," Joe answered, generating more laughs.

Joe thought that he'd have to hug and kiss Bessie to get Kit to explode, but that turned out to be unnecessary.

"You're really kinda stupid, aren't you, Armstrong?" Kit snarled, quieting the room instantly.

Joe set his plate down and turned to Kit.

"Excuse me? What's stupid about making a joke? Or are you such an idiot that you didn't understand?"

Kit then stepped provocatively close to Joe and glared at him as he spat, "Who are you calling an idiot? I'm not the one who got sent off to the reformatory. You shoulda gone to prison or been hanged with that brother of yours."

Dan Sheehy then tried to intervene by pulling Kit back from Joe, and that was a mistake.

Kit's right fist flew in a sharp jab into Dan's chin, knocking him back four feet before he whipped back around and faced Joe with both fists ready.

Minnie shouted, "Stop it! I won't have this in my house!"

Joe had his opportunity laid before him as he said, "You must be even dumber than I thought. You just struck an officer of the law. I'm not a deputy any more, Ryerson. Do you want to try it with me?"

"Anytime."

“Outside,” Joe growled and stepped past Kit, half-expecting him to try a sucker punch, but he didn’t. He trusted his boxing ability.

Joe exited the back door, crossed the porch and walked east, where he and Cassie had begun their meaningful conversations. He could almost feel Kit stalking behind him as he strode across the ground.

When he’d gone fifty yards he turned and was somewhat surprised to see Kit removing his shirt. Joe wasn’t sure if it was to try and intimidate him with a display of his physique or he didn’t want to get Joe’s blood on his shirt.

Joe had always been hesitant to take of his shirt in front of people, but this had to be an exception. So, as Kit was undoing his last button, Joe just ripped his shirt open, the buttons flying across the dirt. It wasn’t for show. He just didn’t want to be caught by a right cross while he was unbuttoning his shirt.

Both men tossed their shirts aside at the same time.

Kit was a well-muscled young man, but Joe was almost scary with thick, coiled muscles from years working the forge and anvil. He was facing the crowd, so no one could see his long scars on his back as he clenched his fists, waiting for Kit to make the first move.

“C’mon, you bastard, let’s see what you’ve got,” Kit said with a sneer.

Joe correctly suspected that Kit was waiting for a lunging punch that he could deflect easily and hit him with an uppercut.

But even as he realized what Kit was trying to do, Joe understood he'd almost have to let Ryerson take the shot. Joe knew that he had a power advantage over Kit, but he was short on speed, so he'd have to absorb some punches.

Joe took one quick step inside and threw a left cross, surprising Kit when it struck his ribs as he'd been watching Joe's right.

Joe had been surprised himself as he thought Kit was going to block it and he wished he had put more into the punch, but when Kit grunted, he knew he'd done some damage.

Kit quickly recovered and blasted a left jab into Joe's face, catching the left cheek, but Joe was already moving backwards, so Kit's jab didn't have the impact it could have. His quick follow-up right uppercut had more effect when it landed in Joe's gut, just under his diaphragm.

Joe blew out some air as he grunted, and Kit unleashed a series of fast jabs to Joe's face and neck.

Joe felt the blows and knew that he'd keep losing if he stayed where he was, so he quickly pirouetted on his left foot and swung his right fist as hard as he could into Kit's left rib cage. It was a massive blow, and Kit cried out in pain before he tried to counterpunch with his own crushing shot when he smashed a right into Joe's chest, but he'd already lost a lot of his power after Joe's devastating right.

Joe felt the weaker punch and knew he had to follow up quickly with another heavy body blow. So, just as Kit's right hand was being drawn back, Joe unleashed a hard left to the right side of Kit's chest, smashing the same ribs that had been damaged with his first punch, and hearing another cry of pain from his adversary.

Kit should have just called the fight and walked away, but he still thought he could beat Joe and that was all that mattered to him. *He was a boxing champion, for God's sake! He couldn't lose to this bastard!*

Joe wouldn't have let him leave anyway and knew what he was going to do now was nothing less than murder, but he felt it had to be done.

He stalked Kit, his fists tucked under his chin, waiting for his chance.

Kit began a series of fast, weak jabs at Joe as he watched him close, looking bear-like in his slow, weaving walk.

"You, bastard!" Kit screamed and let loose with a surprisingly powerful left jab that snapped Joe's head back when it connected with his chin.

Kit thought he saw his opening and was drawing his right hand back for a more powerful punch when Joe's right suddenly shot out, smashing into Kit's face, knocking teeth out of his jaw as bones crumpled under his fist. Before Kit could fall to the ground, Joe ripped an even more powerful left into the side of Kit's head, snapping his head to the side before Kit dropped to the ground with blood pouring from his mouth.

Joe was bleeding from his mouth and his swollen eye, but as he unclenched his hands, he simply walked to his button-less shirt, picked it off the ground and walked back to Kit to see his condition.

He was blubbering in pain as he lay on the ground, so Joe had failed.

He looked at the sheriff and said, "Sheriff Warren, I think we need to get him to the doctor."

John nodded and then Dan and Lou helped Kit to his feet and helped walk him away, his shirt still on the ground.

Bessie was about to follow when she looked at Joe and said softly, “Thank you, Joe.”

“No, Bessie. I may have made it worse for you. He beats you, doesn’t he?”

She just nodded and then said, “I’ve got to go to the doctor and see how he is now.”

“I’m sorry, Bessie,” Joe said.

Bessie looked at him as if to reply and turned and hurried after the deputies and her husband.

John stepped over to Joe and said, “You tried, Joe.”

“It’s not enough, John. Bessie confirmed that he’s been beating her, so somebody will have to help her.”

John nodded and said, “How are you, Joe? You’re bleeding.”

“I’m all right. I need to wash, though.”

Minnie picked up Kit’s shirt and then she and John followed Joe to the house. It was then that Minnie finally saw Joe’s scars and grimaced at the sight, pleased that it had been her husband who had ended the life of the man who had put them there.

After he’d cleaned up and put on his open shirt, Joe returned to the jail to finish packing, while the sheriff went over to the doctor’s office to see how Kit was doing.

As he was changing into a shirt with buttons, he heard the front door open and expected that the sheriff had returned.

“Joe Armstrong? Are you in here?”

Joe recognized the voice of Ron Ryerson, Kit’s father, and knew it was time for the firestorm to erupt. So, he just sighed and walked out of the sleeping room into the main office.

“Yes, sir?” Joe asked.

“Joe, I just left the doctor’s office. The doc doesn’t know if Kit is going to make it.”

Ron wasn’t armed, so Joe didn’t know what to expect and didn’t reply.

Mister Ryerson took off his hat and slowly began walking toward Joe as he said, “I want to apologize for what he did. Everyone told me what had happened and how he’d picked the fight with you thinking he could beat you easily. He’s always been so pleased with himself that he thought he could get away with anything, and it’s all my fault.”

Joe was stunned as he slowly lowered himself into the chair behind the desk.

“I always bragged to everyone how good he was with his fists. He was such a handsome boy and I thought he’d grow up to be a good man. I ignored all of his faults until he was sixteen and I found out that he’d been slapping his mother around. My wife!”

He then dropped into the chair before the desk and continued.

"I confronted him, and he asked what I would do about it. I'm ashamed to admit that I did nothing, just as he expected. I did make sure that he didn't hurt my Beatrice anymore, but it wasn't enough. Then he began seeing Bessie Warren. She was such a sweet, lovely girl that I thought it would change him, and it seemed that way. For months he was nice to my wife and I had hope that he would become the man I expected."

But then, I noticed that when Bessie came over, she seemed afraid of him. My wife noticed that she seemed to be in pain and suspected that he was beating her. Is that why you did what you did?"

Joe nodded.

"Is Bessie okay? I'm so ashamed that I did nothing to stop him. He might have killed that baby. He might have murdered our grandchild!"

Joe sighed, then said, "She's all right. It seemed that almost everyone knew what he was doing to Bessie, but no one could stop him. He was entitled to beat her according to the law, so I was going to stop him illegally. I thought I'd have to do something to get him angry enough to fight me, but I was wrong. He wanted it worse than I did."

"Didn't you know he was a boxing champion?"

"Yes, I knew."

"Weren't you afraid he might kill you?"

"Yes."

"And yet, you still went through with it?"

“Someone had to, Mister Ryerson. Besides, Cassie asked me to.”

“Well, thank goodness for Cassie Warren. What happens if he lives?”

“Then he lives. I can’t shoot him, as much as I’d like to do it. If she returns to live with her parents, Kit would be legally able to walk into the house and drag her back home.”

“I know. I suppose that means that all we can do is wait.”

“Yes, sir.”

Mister Ryerson rose and shook Joe’s hand, turned and left the office.

Joe watched him leave and wondered why some men will turn their sons into monsters by being hard on them and others, like Mr. Ryerson, turn theirs into beasts by being nice to them. He’d seen both kinds in the reformatory.

He finished dressing and as he was returning to the sleeping room to finish packing, Sheriff Warren walked inside accompanied by Deputy Sheehy.

Joe was tucking in his shirt as he turned and said, “I was just visited by Mister Ryerson.”

“I know. He said he was coming by. He told me that he knew what Kit was doing and now he hoped his own son would die.”

“That’s what he told me.”

“Maybe I’m lucky to only have daughters,” John said.

“Bessie might argue the point. How is she doing?”

"She's at home with Minnie. She didn't wait long at the doctor's office. I stopped by the house and told her the prognosis. It's almost as if everyone wants Kit to just go away."

Joe just nodded, still feeling guilty for what he had done.

John asked, "Are you leaving tomorrow morning?"

"No, I'm going to get the horses ready to go and leave this afternoon."

"Joe, why don't you wait until tomorrow?"

Joe said, "I don't feel like staying here anymore."

John nodded, finally appreciating how hard it must have been on Joe to do what he had done. He kept forgetting that Joe was still only eighteen. He'd had a hard life, but he was still part boy inside. Having to shoot bad men who were shooting at you was one thing, but having to beat a man almost to death, even if it was in a fair fight, was totally different.

Three hours later, Joe had his pack horse and his best gelding saddled and hitched in front of the Warren house. He had his wrapped coffee cake as he prepared to make his real farewells to the Warrens.

He hugged and gave a kiss to Mary and to Mrs. Warren. He shook Ned's hand and then faced Bessie.

"Bessie, after you have your little girl, be sure and tell Cassie how wonderful it is to be a mother. Let her hold her niece and understand how incredible it is to bring new life into the world."

Bessie smiled and said, "I will. I'll tell her that you love her, too."

Joe nodded but said, "I don't think it matters to her, Bessie, but all we can do is wait for tomorrow to arrive."

Then he hugged Bessie and kissed her gently on the lips.

Finally, he turned to Sheriff Warren, his mentor, his boss, and as far as Joe was concerned, the father he never knew.

He took his hand and just held it as he said, "I've called you many things since that day you threw me into your cell. I've called you sheriff, sir, boss, mister and probably a few worse things in those first couple of days. But before I go, I want to tell you that more than anything, I've wanted to call you father. You've helped me more than any man has ever helped his son, and for that, I can never thank you enough."

John couldn't reply but nodded and embraced Joe in a bear hug. They two men remained wrapped tightly for almost a minute before Joe let him go and turned, picked up his cake and left through the back door.

No one in the kitchen could speak even after the sounds of eight hooves faded away.

Joe Armstrong was gone.

CHAPTER 10

November 7, 1879

It was Cassie's sixteenth birthday, a day she'd been anxiously awaiting since she was just a young girl. Now she was celebrating it away from her family and worse, away from Joe.

She'd received letters from home about what Joe had done for Bessie and that Kit had died three days later. She was so happy for Bessie but wondered why Joe had gone after the Hogans anyway. She thought he'd stay and marry Bessie as she'd asked him to. Granted, she really didn't want him to do it but thought that it was best for both of them because Bessie needed someone, and Cassie knew she could never get married.

What did surprise her was that Bessie was going to get married again, but not to Joe. She was going to marry Lou Sanborn at the end of November.

What was depressing her, even more, was that she hadn't heard a word from or about Joe after he'd gone. She knew he had her address, but the only mail she received was from her parents or Bessie.

The school itself was nothing like she had expected. There were just so few schools that educated young women beyond high school, especially in Texas. She should have done more research, but it was too late now.

She hadn't been there three days before she discovered that the school was to educate young women in the social graces to prepare them for marriage to wealthy husbands. More than that, she found quickly enough that she didn't fit in, and not because of the same reasons that had made her an oddity in her old school in Warwick. Here, she was a hick and an unpolished outsider, and the refined girls let her know it almost immediately.

There were no academic lessons beyond calligraphy, and she knew she should have turned right around and headed back home, but two things kept her at Carlisle's School for Young Women. First, she had never backed down from any challenge. Second, she didn't know that Joe had gone and not stayed and married Bessie until she'd been there three weeks.

Cassie resolved to stay at least until the end of the school year. She had already used a hundred and twenty dollars of Joe's money to pay for it anyway. There would be other costs as well, some of which made her physically uncomfortable. The most noticeable example was when she had to buy and learn to wear a corset. That particular lesson had been most embarrassing for Cassie because she not only had never worn one, she didn't have the need or the figure for one. Even the few younger girls seemed to have more curves than she did.

So, here it was her sixteenth birthday, and Cassie was miserable when she should be enjoying some of her mother's cake with her sisters back in Warwick.

As she was walking back to the room that she shared with three other girls, she stopped at the central student office and went to her box. There was an envelope inside, so she slipped it out of the box and dropped it into her dress pocket, not even looking at the address. She wasn't even in the mood to read a letter from her parents.

Cassie walked into her room and plopped on the end of her bed as the only roommate who was present at the moment, Elizabeth Curran, looked at her.

"Isn't your birthday today, Cassie?" she asked as she set down the book she was reading.

"It's my sixteenth if anyone cares," she replied morosely.

Seventeen-year-old Elizabeth flopped back onto her bed and asked, "Have you ever been kissed, Cassie?"

"No. I suppose you have, though."

"Of course, I have. I've kissed four different boys and two I even let feel my breasts."

Cassie wanted to throw something at her but instead, didn't reply at all. She decided she may as well see what news her parents had included in her letter and slid it from her pocket.

She absent-mindedly looked at the return address and gasped. It was from Joe!

Elizabeth saw Cassie almost ripping an envelope open and asked sweetly, "Oh, is that a letter from your boyfriend?"

Cassie replied, "Yes, as a matter of fact."

Elizabeth then said, "I'm sure it is."

Cassie ignored her and read:

My Dearest Cassie,

I'm writing this letter to see if I could time it to arrive on your sixteenth birthday. Before I wrote this, I reread the letter I received some time ago on my fourteenth birthday from a girl who wanted me as a boyfriend.

I've been searching for the Hogans now for more than two months, and have only a few rumblings, but not much more.

How is life in the big city? Are you learning a lot? I doubt if those teachers know anything more than you do, and I'm sure that you're the only girl in that school who can put a .44 through the six-inch bullseye at fifty feet with a pistol.

I'm sure that you heard about what happened with Kit after you left Warwick. I don't know if I'll ever get over that enough to return to the town. It still weighs on me more than I expected. It doesn't make much sense sometimes and other times it does.

On my way south, I stopped at Lickville to see the wrecked farmhouse again, and when I went to the diner to get something to eat, I talked to a man who heard my name and asked me if I was related to Zeke and Agnes Armstrong. I told him I was their son and he explained that he had served with my father during the war and gave me more information about my parents. It wasn't much, but it helped me get a better picture of them.

Cassie, I believe I owe you an explanation for not being there when you left Warwick. I was standing in the jail, watching out the window as you climbed into the coach. I wanted to see you off badly, but I had to stay away, just as I had to let you go to Dallas. It was because you had to have the chance to find your dreams and if I hadn't let you go, you would resent me for the rest of your life.

Realized dreams rarely meet expectations, but for you, Cassie, I hope that they do. It is only if you are truly happy when they are fulfilled that I will be happy with my decision to watch you leave.

With the Greatest of Affection,

Joe

Cassie closed her eyes and sighed. At least now she understood why Joe hadn't seen her off.

As she laid her letter-gripping hand onto the bed, Elizabeth giggled and asked, "What's the matter? Did your imaginary boyfriend find another girl with a bosom?"

Cassie opened her eyes, turned to Elizabeth, and said, "No, he's out hunting outlaws, and as soon as he's gotten the last three of them, he's going to come here, take me home, and then he'll marry me."

Elizabeth laughed and said, "Your imaginary boyfriend is a tough man, is he?"

"He's much more than that. He's the best man I've ever met."

"I'm sure he is," Elizabeth said as the other two girls who shared the room entered.

Elizabeth gleefully told both of them about Cassie's big, handsome imaginary boyfriend, giving them a case of the giggles.

Cassie didn't care, nor was she about to let them read Joe's letter. She was now impervious to their snide little jokes about her. But as happy as the letter made her feel, when she had lied to deflect their barbs and said that Joe was going to marry her, it resurrected that somnolent fear, shackling her good mood.

Thirty-four days after sending the letter to Cassie, Joe was walking his pack horse into the town of Fire Bend just before noon. He needed to get new shoes for both horses while he had some lunch. He'd learned that two men matching the vague descriptions of Fred and Hank had robbed a stagecoach just fifteen miles north of the town two weeks earlier and he was seeking more information.

He'd hunted down four such reports over the past three months and run down the suspects only to be disappointed. He'd captured half of them and had to shoot the other four, but none had been a Hogan. Granted, the reward money that had been wired to Sheriff Warren in Warwick was enough to make him a successful bounty hunter, but that wasn't his reason for hunting the men.

He left the horses at the livery and after having a filling but not overly tasty lunch, he walked to the stagecoach depot to find out what had happened.

"Afternoon," he said as he entered the ramshackle building.

"Howdy, young feller. What can I do for ya?" asked the ticket master/porter and probably the station manager and janitor.

"You had a stage robbed a couple of weeks ago and the driver reported that it was probably the Hogan brothers. Can you tell me anything more than that?"

"You huntin' 'em?"

"I've been chasing them for a while. I got two of them up north of Warwick."

"Good luck. Those two have taken three of our coaches in the past six months, but the law don't seem to care. I guess we're too small for them to pay attention."

"Where did they stop the stagecoaches?"

"Well, the last one was northeast of town, about twelve miles. The one before that was northwest of here a half-day's ride. The first one they stopped was way up north a day's ride or so."

"And all of them were within six months?"

"Yes, sir."

Joe nodded. This was the best lead he'd ever had, assuming that it was the brothers, and he was beginning to doubt if it was them.

After picking up his newly shod horses, Joe left town heading along the same road as the last robbery. It wasn't much of a road, but that worked to his advantage as it wasn't well-traveled. He followed the trail left by the last day's stagecoach and kept riding.

He pulled out his watch to check the time, smiling at the inscription as he always did. The watch gave him a better idea of how fast he was moving, and the distance traveled.

There had been a good, soaking rain three days ago which meant that their tracks were probably long gone, but that wasn't going to dissuade him. From what the station manager had told him if they were still in the area, they'd be northwest of where he was now, and it was just a question of where they could be holed up. He should have asked before he left town.

If it was the brothers, they were being smarter in their decisions about their crimes. Robbing stagecoaches usually didn't attract the interest of the limited law in this part of Texas unless someone was shot. The paying customers would complain mightily, but nobody would bother chasing after the thieves.

Joe estimated he'd ridden ten miles or so which was close enough and turned left off the road and headed northwest, looking for any buildings.

As he rode across the uneven ground, he wondered what he would do if it was the Hogans. He was sure their dispositions hadn't improved, even if their criminal behavior had altered. He didn't know if they were laying low before they moved on to bigger and more profitable crimes or if they were just playing it safe. Either way, he knew he had one big advantage. Neither of them had seen him since he was just a boy. He remembered when he had caught up with Earl and Glen. They had been shocked when they discovered who he was, and he'd actually gotten a bit bigger since then. He also needed a shave and a haircut. He hadn't cut his hair since he left Warwick.

The sun was low in the sky when he first spotted a building breaking up the horizon about three miles ahead, and it wasn't anything like he'd expected. It wasn't a farmhouse or a ranch house, it looked like a mansion. There were outbuildings and a large barn, too.

Plantations like this one were rare in this part of Texas. He imagined that before the war, someone from East Texas had moved out here expecting to start the plantation on almost free ground. He was probably the son of a plantation owner and was given enough money and slaves to get the operation started.

It either failed immediately because of the soil or a little while later because of the war. Either way, it hadn't been worked in a long time.

The closer he drew to the big house he began picking up other signs to identify what he'd found. It was an abandoned cotton plantation, or at least an attempt to establish one. He could see rows of plants, most little more than sticks in the ground with a few white puffs on some of them. The barn and outbuildings were all in a dilapidated state and the big house was in worse shape. The roof was partially down in the front and the wraparound porch was collapsing in places. It would probably be nothing but a heap of wood in another year or two.

But there was smoke coming out of the chimney in the back of the house, which meant it was occupied. He doubted if it was the original owner, though. If they had enough money to build the place, they'd have enough to leave. Whoever was in there was either squatters or a family of slaves that had been brought in to work the place and had no place to go after they were emancipated.

But the smoke was there, and he began to think that there was another possibility, one that was never far from his mind. It might be that Fred and Hank were there.

He was just a half mile from the house when he pulled the horses to a stop as he thought about how he might approach the place. He gave the possibility that it was the Hogans less than twenty percent, but that was a good enough number to be cautious.

He dismounted and detached his trail horse and led him to one of the failed cotton bushes. It wasn't much of a hitching point, but it was the closest one available. After tying off the packhorse, he returned to his gelding, mounted and swiveled in the saddle, opened the right saddlebag, and pulled out Cassie's Remington pistol. He slipped it into his heavy coat's right pocket and unbuttoned the coat to give him better access to his Colt. Satisfied with his level of firepower, he nudged the horse forward.

Joe swung the horse northwest to head for the access road, so he could approach the house as if he'd been coming from the road, not cross country. He had no idea why he thought it was necessary, it just seemed appropriate.

He was almost to the access road when he heard a loud bang from a slamming door at the back of the house. He turned his gelding to the east and set him at a fast trot, paralleling the access road toward the house.

When he was almost to the house, he spotted a woman running from the house about sixty to seventy yards away struggling to run because she was carrying a child. He was about to shout that he wasn't an outlaw, believing she had seen him coming and been scared when he was stunned to hear the crack of a pistol from the back of the house.

The woman turned wide-eyed to look at the house but continued to run. The shooter had missed. Then he heard cackling laughter and a voice shout, "You missed, Larry!" but before he could even get his Winchester out of his scabbard, another shot rang out and the woman arched her back, took one more half-stride and collapsed.

He was sick as he drew his Winchester and heard, "Whoeee, Bo! That was one helluva shot! Let me try now!"

He still didn't have them in sight, but they should have heard his horse's hooves slamming into the dry ground if he could hear their shouts. He had to stop them from killing the child.

Larry took his pistol shot as Joe was cocking the hammer to the Winchester, and he knew he'd waited too long as the ground near the youngster exploded in a blast of dirt and dust.

Joe didn't want to waste his first shot, so he shouted, "You bastards! Shoot me!"

The two outlaws hadn't even registered the sound of hoofbeats because they were concentrating so much on their targets and no one ever came here anyway except those stupid squatters that showed up two days ago and were now nothing more than target practice. But Joe's shout got their attention.

Larry yelled, "Son of a bitch!" before he took four steps along the run-down porch and stuck his head around the corner of the house to see who was there just before Joe fired his Winchester at the expected head.

The .44 slammed into the wood just four inches above Larry's head, and he jerked it back before turning to get back into the house.

Bo had seen the corner of the house blast apart from the shot and hadn't wasted any time running into the kitchen as he heard the hooves getting closer.

Larry's first hurried step to reach the relative security of the house was placed onto one of the many weakened boards that made up the porch and his sudden placement of the full two hundred pounds of his weight onto that one spot was too much for it to support. There was a loud crack as the board lost its integrity and his foot crashed through the porch into the three feet of crawl space beneath.

He didn't break any bones, but the sudden plunge by one leg into the porch, left Larry in a vulnerable position as Joe cleared the corner of the house and spotted the outlaw's predicament. Larry hadn't lost control of his Colt, but Joe wasn't about to give him a chance to use it and fired his Winchester at thirty yards. But he'd hurried his shot and the bullet raced past Larry and slammed into the porch ten feet behind him.

Larry's leg was still in the hole in the porch, but he was able to turn enough to get Joe in his sights as Joe was working his Winchester's lever. He fired his Colt, cocked his hammer, and fired again. Both shots missed as was shooting at a fast-moving target in a stressful situation.

By now, Bo had realized that Larry was hung up somehow on the porch and was debating about going out there amid all the gunfire and decided, whether from cowardice or from good tactical thinking, to go out the front of the house and come around behind the shooter.

That left Larry alone to face Joe, who had fired his second shot and this one was closer, but he missed again as the .44 buzzed past Larry's left ear. The two shooters were now only fifty feet apart. One was on a moving horse and firing a rifle and the other was in a more stable position but trapped in a hole in a porch using a pistol. It made for an unusual gunfight that neither seemed to be able to finish.

Bo was trotting down the long hallway to reach the great room in front when the shooting in back suddenly stopped.

Larry had taken another shot at Joe who had finally brought the horse to a stop, but his bullet went wide as he was surprised at the rifleman's sudden halt.

Joe fired his now stable Winchester and the .44 spun across the thirty-eight feet and kept spinning as it drilled through Larry's chest and left his body without losing very much of its energy.

Larry fell over backward, his leg still trapped in the porch as blood poured onto the dry wood.

Joe didn't have time to check on the woman as he quickly dismounted, glanced at Larry, set his Winchester on the porch, and pulled out Cassie's Remington. He hesitated about going into the back door because he expected that Bo might be just inside with his pistol ready to fire.

He heard the child crying in the distance, but nothing else. He was still debating whether to go through the door when he heard the squeal of hinges as the front door opened, and the debate ended. He didn't repeat Larry's mistake and placed his steps more tentatively on the boards of the porch, but soon reached the inside of the house.

He didn't take time to examine the place, but as he walked, he kept his eyes focused on the glassless windows, hoping to see Bo as he walked down the side of the porch.

But Bo wasn't on the porch. he was on the ground outside the porch. He and Larry had lived there long enough to not trust the aging wood, a lesson that Larry must have forgotten in his haste to escape Joe's Winchester.

Joe was halfway down the hall and was able to see the open front door. If he was going to see Bo on the porch, he should have spotted him already, so he quickly reversed course and headed back to the kitchen.

Bo saw Joe's horse just standing there and for a moment thought about just riding away, but he couldn't leave his partner who might be wounded. Besides, he wanted to kill this bastard.

Joe had the Remington's hammer cocked as he slowly exited the back door and then had to choose which side to face. He'd been looking through the windows on the south side of the house, so he took the better odds and faced north.

Bo was almost to Joe's horse on the south side of the house when he spotted Joe's Winchester lying on the porch. He stopped and did a quick count. He'd taken one shot at the woman and one at the kid, so that left him only three live rounds in his Colt. He could take time to reload all his cylinders, but the Winchester was just twenty feet away and he'd have at least another ten shots. He decided to get Joe's rifle, then made the dash for the gun, expecting the gun's owner to be inside the house.

Joe really was being tugged to go and see if he could help the woman and her child, so he took a glance that way to see if she was moving. His head was turned just enough, so when Bo's shadow appeared on the ground before he arrived, Joe had enough time to turn his pistol to the south just as Bo appeared with his left hand outstretched as he reached for the Winchester's stock while he gripped his Colt in his right.

Joe took that extra fraction of a second to lead Bo before he squeezed the Remington's trigger. The pistol erupted in flame and smoke and the deadly missile spat from the muzzle and slammed into the left side of Bo's chest, just below his outstretched arm.

He screamed and spun to the ground, his Colt striking the ground first, burying the muzzle in the ground as his finger jerked the trigger back. The expelled .44 had no place to go as the pressure from the burning gunpowder tried to ram it out of the rifled barrel, but the monumental pressure exploded the pistol, showering yards of West Texas with hot metal. Bo's right hand blew backward as he felt the sharp pieces slamming into his body, but the pain didn't reach him as he died just six feet from his partner.

Joe had been shielded from the exploding weapon by Bo's body, so he just remained standing, Cassie's Remington smoking as he held it low, and pointed at the porch.

He slipped it into his pocket and left the porch and trotted to the woman and her child. She hadn't moved after the shot, so she might be playing possum, but Joe didn't think so.

When he arrived, the child was pulling at her hair crying, "Mama! Mama!", and it only took Joe a few seconds to realize that she was dead.

Joe picked up the child, unsure if it was a boy or a girl because of the long, light brown hair. He guessed he or she was between two and three years old, and his stomach recoiled thinking that those two bastards were going to use him for target practice.

Joe did a quick check and then said, "Okay, mister. It looks like I have work to do. I'll bury your mama and then I'll get you something to eat. Those two can rot out here, for all I care. Let the critters eat them."

The little boy was staring at his mother's body on the ground and reaching for her as he kept crying, "Mama!"

Joe turned with this squirming cargo and walked slowly back to the house, stepped onto the porch, and went inside. As much as he hated doing it, he entered one of the empty rooms, and sat the little boy on the floor and sat next to him.

“Son, I’ve got to go and bury your mama right now. I don’t want you to go wandering anywhere, so I’m going to have to leave you in this room. Okay?”

The little boy’s bright blue eyes looked into his hazel green eyes and kept saying, “Mama.”

Joe exhaled and took off his Stetson, set it on the floor before he stood, took off his heavy coat, folded it, and laid it near the hat. He set the boy on the jacket after removing the pistol and left quickly before the boy could scurry out of the room, closed the door behind him, and headed out to the yard to do the dirty work.

He walked to the barn to see if he could find a spade, and when he opened it, he found four horses inside the ready-to-collapse structure. Two were in poor condition and when he checked, found that they were unshod, but still had the holes where there had been nails. They probably belonged to the woman and her husband, wherever he might be. They were probably squatters who had seen the house and wandered inside, not knowing it was occupied as a hideout by the two unidentified stagecoach robbers.

He found four saddles, two of them in as bad condition as their horses. The other two were well-maintained, and Joe assumed they were the property of the two deceased thieves.

When he spotted the spade tossed in the back of the barn, he noticed that the leading edge of the spade wasn’t rusty, which meant it had been used recently. He was pretty sure the bad men hadn't used it and imagined they had the woman bury her husband.

So, when he left the barn with the spade, he did a quick search of the grounds, and found recently turned earth just a few feet behind the barn, probably because it was softer there. He began to dig the hole just a few feet away, probably going deeper than she had.

As he dug, he recalled the last time he'd done this, back at the reformatory, and for a few turns of the spade, couldn't remember the name of the boy who'd been murdered by Warden Phelps. The memory of the body falling on him was etched deeply into his memories, but the name escaped him as he continued to toss dirt out of the hole.

He was almost done digging when it came to him: Willie Struthers. He couldn't remember his face at all, and that had only been a few years ago.

Joe climbed out of the hole. It wasn't six feet deep because he didn't want to have a repeat of being covered by a dead body. He stuck the spade into the pile of freshly turned earth and headed for the woman's body.

When he got there, he finally turned her over and saw the face of the boy's mother. She looked younger than he was. She was Cassie's age and already had a toddler, so she had to have gotten pregnant when she was fourteen or fifteen. She was a small woman if he could call her that and her dress was paper thin. She was wearing nothing underneath the dress, which confirmed her status as a squatter.

But even as he picked her up, feeling like a child in his arms, and began to walk to her gravesite, Joe thought that despite her destitute nature, she showed incredible courage to try to escape and save her son's life. He didn't doubt that the bad men had been using her after killing her husband, and that may have been the real reason for her decision to run, but he wanted to believe it was her mother's protective instincts that had driven her to make the dangerous decision to escape.

Joe reached the grave, set the body on the edge, and climbed into the hole. Unlike Willie Struthers' burial, her light weight, his increased size and strength, and the slightly shallower hole made laying her to rest in the bottom effortless.

Once she was in place, Joe clambered back out, grabbed the spade, and quickly began filling in the hole, not looking at her body.

As soon as he was finished, he just walked away, believing he didn't have the right or the words to give her peace. He entered the barn, leaned the spade against the wall, and, before entering the house to see the boy, picked up his Winchester, slid it into the scabbard, mounted his horse, and rode out to where he'd hitched his pack horse.

Two hours later, with the bodies of the two outlaws dragged out a hundred yards into the sorry excuse for a cotton field and his horses unsaddled, Joe sat with the little boy at the kitchen table. The table and two chairs were the only real furniture in the place, probably stolen from someplace else by the robbers. He'd found their bedrolls spread in two of the rooms on the first floor and sets of saddlebags nearby that contained their spare clothes and other necessities. Joe didn't venture onto the second floor, knowing he'd probably find himself on the first floor if he wasn't careful.

The boy was eating a mix of beans and canned beef that Joe had mashed together and warmed in the kitchen's fireplace. He had surprised Joe when he had taken the spoon he'd been offered and used it to scoop the food into his mouth. Joe only had water to give him, but he didn't seem to be demanding milk.

The boy had stopped crying for his mother by the time Joe returned from burying her and had seemed to accept him as his protector already. Now he had to decide what to do with him. Joe had no idea how to care for a child but didn't want to leave him in some town, either. He knew what would become of the boy. He'd be stuck in some orphanage, and that led him to recall the startling fact he'd discovered at the reformatory when he had found that more of the boys inside had been in orphanages than had families. He looked at the eating boy and felt an obligation to him and his mother.

It didn't take him long to conclude there was only one place for the boy. He'd take him to Warwick and to the Warrens. John had always joked about only having daughters, and Joe believed that his own treatment by the sheriff was largely due to the lawman's desire to raise a son. Even if the Warrens didn't want the boy, which he doubted, he'd find a way to take care of him. He'd make sure that this boy learned earlier the things he didn't learn until he was thirteen.

That night, as he lay on one of the outlaw's bedrolls and the little boy snug in the second, already asleep, Joe knew he'd have to drop his hunt for the Hogans and just head home. He had a greater responsibility now.

Joe and the boy had been on the trail for four days now and he was on familiar turf as they were just a couple of hours outside of Warwick.

He'd built a secure riding chair for the boy on one of the Hogan's horses and was trailing his packhorse and the two brothers' horses. The other two he'd just let go into the open ground, but he left the barn doors open in case they wanted to return.

He'd done a thorough inspection of the dead plantation before he'd gone and found no evidence at all as to the identity of the boy's parents or the two outlaws. He hadn't seen the father, of course, and his mother was so young he doubted if there was any record of his birth anyway.

Joe hadn't given him a name because he didn't believe he had the right and had called him 'son', 'boy', 'sir', or 'little man'. The boy had warmed up to him considerably on the trip and Joe had become very fond of him as well, even after he'd peed on his coat. He'd learned a lot about taking care of children on the four-day ride, mostly by making mistakes, but the boy was eating well and seemed healthier than when Joe had first found him. But in a few hours, he'd be leaving the child and was surprised that it saddened him.

When he turned down the main street of Warwick, it was late afternoon, and surprisingly warm for the middle of December, even for Texas. Rather than ride to the sheriff's office, Joe turned his tired horses to the right and walked them to the Warrens' home, pulling up to the front of the house and dismounting just two minutes later.

He hitched his gelding and walked back to the Hogan horse with the boy sitting in his modified, belted seat. Joe undid the belt and the little boy reached out with his arms to be plucked from the saddle.

"Let's go and meet Mrs. Warren, son. I'm sure she'll be impressed with such a strong man as you."

The boy smiled at Joe as he grabbed onto his neck and Joe began striding down the long walk, having a wild assortment of feelings as he approached the porch.

He climbed the three steps, crossed the porch, and knocked. As he waited for the door to open, Joe tickled the boy's tummy to get him to laugh, which he'd grown accustomed to doing. At first, he did it to make the boy forget his mother's death but found that his laughter made him laugh inside as well.

The door opened and Joe smiled at a still very pregnant Bessie and said, "Hello, Bessie."

Bessie's face lit up as he saw Joe and said, "Joe! You're back!"

"Yes, ma'am, and I brought my little friend here with me. May I come inside?"

"Oh, yes. Of course. You shouldn't have to ask, you know," she said as she swung the door wide and stepped aside.

Joe entered, removed his hat, and waited for Bessie to close the door.

"Still carrying around that little girl?" Joe asked.

"She's still there, who's your little friend?"

"Is your mother home?" Joe asked.

Bessie didn't have to reply as Minnie had heard his voice and dropped her husband's soaking shirt into the laundry tub and trotted down the hallway, shouting, "Joe!"

Joe smiled as she ran into the room and stopped when she saw Joe carrying a young child.

Joe then set him down, and he just grabbed onto Joe's right leg as he stared at the woman.

"Who's that?" Minnie asked.

"If you and Bessie will have a seat, I'll explain."

Bessie didn't need any excuse to sit down and was the first to find a chair. Then after Minnie was seated, Joe told the story.

Both women were staring at Joe with tears rolling down their cheeks long before he finished and when he finally ended his narration a few minutes later, neither could even speak.

"I couldn't leave him in some town, Mrs. Warren. They'd put him in an orphanage if he was lucky. I wanted something better for him."

Minnie asked softly, "Are you going to raise him yourself, Joe?"

"No, ma'am. I was hoping that you and your husband wouldn't mind doing that. I know it's asking a lot, but you are the best people I've ever met, and I think it would give him his best chance at a good life."

Minnie felt her heart ready to explode as she almost begged confirmation when she asked, "Do you mean it, Joe? You want me and John to adopt him?"

"I'd help any way I could, Mrs. Warren, but that's what I'm asking."

Minnie looked at the bright blue eyes staring at her from beside Joe's right knee and asked, "Did you give him a name?"

"No, ma'am. I thought if you agreed to raise him, that would be yours and your husband's choice."

Minnie rose and approached the boy, who shied away slightly.

Joe felt him slide behind his right leg, so he bent over picked up the boy, and said, "Son, this is Mrs. Warren, she's going to be your new mama."

The boy looked at Joe and asked, "Mama?"

Joe nodded and pointed to Minnie and said, "Mama."

Minnie was smiling with her entire face as she gazed at the toddler, and the little boy finally reached out his arms to her. She slowly accepted the boy into her own arms as she began to softly cry.

Then she looked at Joe and asked, "Do you mind if I tell John?"

"Not at all, Mrs. Warren. I'll just head over to the jail and talk to him about what I've been doing, but I won't mention the boy."

She sniffed and smiled as she replied, "Thank you, Joe," and then kissed the boy on the cheek.

Joe smiled at Minnie and glanced at a still-weeping Bessie before turning and leaving the house to go and talk to the sheriff about what he'd been doing the past few months. He hoped that the boss was just as happy with the boy as his wife seemed to be. Then once that was settled, he'd restock his supplies and head south again.

Joe mounted his gelding and led the other three horses out to the main street and as he walked them the short distance to the sheriff's office, he was greeted by the folks he passed as if he were a prodigal son. He guessed that none of them blamed him for Kit Ryerson's death after all.

He dismounted in front of the jail, hitched his gelding, crossed the boardwalk, and opened the door.

"Joe!" shouted Lou Sanborn before Joe even set one boot into the office.

"Howdy, Lou," Joe replied.

By the time he closed the door, Sheriff Warren and Deputy Sheehy both boiled out of the sheriff's office and he barely had time to hang his hat on a peg before all three lawmen were shaking his hand or slapping his back.

"What happened, Joe? Did you find the Hogans?" asked Dan.

"Not yet."

"Joe, grab a cup of coffee and tell us what happened," the sheriff said.

"Yes, sir," Joe replied as he removed his coat, hung it on another peg, and picked up his cup.

They were all crowded around the front desk as Joe reviewed the search and the constant frustration of trying to track down the Hogans. He told them about all of his five non-Hogan showdowns and what had happened to the young woman but didn't mention the boy, as he had promised Mrs. Warren.

When he finished, there were all the expected questions, but after the first few, the sheriff exercised his authority.

"Okay, boys. That's enough. I'm sure Joe's a bit whipped after that long ride and needs some rest."

Then he turned to Joe and said, "Joe, I've deposited all of the rewards that have been coming in."

"Thanks, boss. I've got a few extra horses and guns outside that I can leave with you."

"Okay. We'll all help you get those horses unsaddled. You can put them in the barn and corral in back and then, Mister Armstrong, you will come with me for dinner. I want to surprise my wife when I bring you home."

"Thanks, boss," Joe said as he stood.

Forty minutes later, after the horses were clean and brushed down, Joe and John Warren were walking to his house.

Joe said, "Boss, I'll be here for a day to get my supplies and the horses reshod then I'll be leaving again."

"Joe, why don't you stay? You've probably traveled almost a thousand miles and haven't even seen any of them. They'll be caught sooner or later."

"I can't give up. It's not just because of what they did to my mother anymore. After what I found at the Finley ranch, I feel that I have to stop them from hurting other people. Even if I don't find them, I'm preventing other bad men from doing evil."

John nodded, knowing he wasn't going to win the argument.

Joe then asked, "How's Cassie doing at the school?"

"She seems okay. We don't get as many letters as we expected, and she's not exactly gushing about the place, but she's still there."

"I hope she's happy."

"I think she should have stayed, Joe."

Joe didn't answer as they stepped onto the porch and Joe followed Sheriff Warren inside, waiting to see his reaction to the surprise that would be toddling around his home.

"Minnie, I have a guest!" John shouted as he crossed the main room.

"So, do I," Minnie replied loudly from the kitchen.

John believed he had the bigger surprise as he and Joe walked down the hallway, as he expected Minnie's guest to be Bessie.

It was, but Bessie had a little boy on her lap and was feeding him bits of sugar cookies as he entered. John was momentarily stunned and confused by the unknown boy's presence, so he looked back at his wife.

"Um, Joe is back. Who is the little boy?"

"Joe brought him when he returned. He's going to be our son, John."

The experienced lawman was more flummoxed than he'd ever been in his life as his head jerked from Minnie, to the boy and Bessie then back to Joe as he searched for answers.

It was Joe who provided them when he said, "The woman that those outlaws shot was his mother. She was running from the back of the house and they must have been chasing her with their pistols. One shot her, and the other was trying to shoot the boy. I couldn't leave him there, boss. I felt obligated to him and thought that if you and Mrs. Warren raised him, he'd be the luckiest little boy in Texas."

John then turned back to look at the boy and asked, "What's his name?"

Minnie answered, "What do you want to name our son, John?"

John may no longer have been flummoxed, but he was still somewhat shaken as he said slowly, "Our son."

Minnie slowly walked to her husband, put her arm around his waist and whispered, "Yes, John. Our son. The boy that I was never able to give you."

John smiled at Minnie and said, "I was very happy with our daughters, Minnie, but having a son is pretty special."

"Then thank that big oaf behind you that you treated like a son from the day you found him on the back of that hill."

John turned and embraced Joe, saying, "Thank you, Joe. You'll never know what this means to me."

Joe just nodded before John looked at Bessie and asked, "Can I hold him?"

“I hope so, I’m not very comfortable for some reason.”

John laughed and then took one long stride, plucked the boy from Bessie and looked at him as he continued to munch on the cookies.

The boy had grown accustomed to new people by now, so he wasn’t afraid of John, and even poked his new father’s nose, making John laugh, which he then mimicked.

Joe knew he’d made the right decision and walked to the stove to pour himself some coffee.

Dinner was filled with conversation about everything that had happened in Joe’s absence and he’d been surprised by some of it. Lou Sanborn’s marriage to Bessie was the biggest surprise because Lou or Dan hadn’t said anything about it when they were in the jail. Maybe they wanted Bessie to spring the news on him.

They told him about the new café that had opened called Katsy’s Kafe, and it didn’t take long for Joe to figure out who the owners were. He vowed to sample their menu when he had a chance.

John said he and Minnie would need Joe to accompany them to Judge Madsen’s offices tomorrow, so he could explain the boy’s status which would allow them to adopt him. They’d already decided on naming him Michael James, which was a relief to Joe who hoped that any form of Joseph wasn’t used. The boy needed his own life.

Bessie and Minnie both tried to talk him into staying, but their arguments fell as flat as the sheriff’s.

He returned to the sleeping area in the back of the jail before ten o'clock that night and just undressed and collapsed onto the bunk.

The next morning's meeting with Judge Madsen had been a waste of time for Joe as he wasn't asked a single question, which made sense. The judge had sent him to reform school, so why would he trust him now? But he approved the adoption, of course. There were many more parentless children than parents willing to adopt them.

After the hearing, Joe spent the rest of the day preparing for his morning's departure. His two horses were being reshod as he made several trips lugging his full panniers to the sleeping room at the jail. He had lunch at Katsy's Kafe and was unable to pay for his food, although he was allowed to tip the waitress.

His last meal in Warwick was at the Warren home where he withstood one final attempt to make him stay, but Joe knew he had to leave. As much as he enjoyed being with the Warrens, being around them only reminded him of the Warren that wasn't there. Joe believed she was happily finding her dream in Dallas.

"I'm not going to wear this thing!" Cassie snapped as she held the corset out before her.

"You have to wear it, Cassie, even if you don't have anything to fill it," Elizabeth said before she giggled.

“We all have to be properly corseted and gowned for the Christmas gala, even if you don’t have a boyfriend,” Mary Anderson said.

Cassie sat and dropped the hated undergarment on her bed alongside the four petticoats she was expected to wear under that hideous red gown. She had to pay some of Joe’s money for all of it, too. She’d have to wear her hair up and properly held in place with hairpins and a fancy hair comb. She’d been to all of the classes on how to prepare herself for the soiree, and had fumbled through each of them, to the amusement of the other girls.

Then there was the dancing, and that was the worst of all. They’d had classes on dancing since she’d arrived, and although she had actually done well, she had hated every note and each step. The reason she hated it so much was what was expected of her when they held the annual gala. There would be boys at the gala, and she had been told by the headmistress, Miss Hampton, that she would dance with them or face discipline.

The other girls were all excited about getting to dance with boys, many of them with their own boyfriends, and each of them hoped the dancing would lead to additional touching. But the thought of having one of the boys touch her gave her the willies. Granted, she’d be wearing white kid gloves and wouldn’t really feel his skin on hers, but the idea that he could slide his hand just slightly and touch something that he shouldn’t made her nauseous.

The gala was close to becoming the final push that would make her leave, but she thought if she could get past this, then she could deal with anything else they would throw at her.

So, as she sat on the bed, surrounded by her Christmas gala wear, Cassie closed her eyes and thought about Joe. He was still her greatest dream and yet at the same time, her greatest nightmare. She missed him terribly but knew seeing him again might lead to what she feared the most…marriage and pregnancy.

But thinking of Joe always brought that other fear. *What if he'd been shot by the Hogans or some other malcontent?* She'd never see him again and that possibility could crush her spirit.

Cassie was a mess and she knew it. She just had no way out of any of it.

December 20, 1879

The band was playing and most of the girls were dancing already as Cassie stayed sitting in her red gown, corset and petticoats. Her hair was piled atop her head, she was wearing makeup and had rouge on her cheeks as she sat at the table with her kid gloves watching the couples float across the floor. Cassie felt like either a matron or a whore. Maybe both.

Miss Hampton had already told her that she had to dance with the next young man who asked, and Cassie knew that she couldn't delay any longer. She'd been asked three times already and told each of them that she was waiting for her boyfriend to arrive.

As the last waltz ended, she thought she'd have a reprieve, but just as the band struck up another melody, a boy of her height approached her and bowed, as required.

"May I have the honor of this dance, miss?" he asked.

Cassie managed a weak smile and held out her gloved hand as an affirmative reply, as required.

The boy took her hand and after they'd stepped out onto the floor, he put his hand on her waist as she picked up her skirt with her left hand and they began to dance.

Cassie caught Miss Hampton watching her with a small smile, so she turned to the boy and smiled at him, as required.

"What's your name?" he asked.

"Cassie Warren."

"I'm Randolph Hardesty."

"Do they call you Randy?"

He chuckled and replied, "No, they don't. My father owns the Hardesty Flour Mills, and I can never be called anything other than Randolph. What does your father do?"

"He's a sheriff."

Randy missed a step and recovered before he replied, "Oh. I see. How old are you?"

"Sixteen."

"Really? I'm eighteen and ready to make my mark in the world," he replied.

Cassie didn't want the conversation to continue, but what she wanted didn't matter as Randolph continued to talk, mostly about himself and his father's wealth that he would inherit someday. Even Cassie, with her limited experience with boys, could see that Randolph was trying to impress her for some reason.

The dance ended, and Cassie thought that with her dancing requirement satisfied, she could return to her seat, but Randolph didn't release her hand and when the music began again, she felt obligated to dance.

Randolph was infatuated by Cassie's pretty face and her lower societal class. He and his friends believed that girls like Cassie would go to the school to try and move up the social ladder and would do anything for boys like Randolph, so he wanted to see just how much that would be.

To Cassie, this was nothing more than an annoying situation that would soon be over.

Cassie was on her third dance with Randolph and he had already suggested that he could give her things that she'd never expected to possess and hinted that he would like to know her better.

Cassie was pretty much ignoring most of what he said, but still thought of him as a boy, and not a problem.

"Don't you have a boyfriend?" Randolph asked.

"Yes, I have a boyfriend. He's really big and strong, too. He's out chasing outlaws and couldn't be here."

"So, you're alone here in Dallas?"

"Yes, I suppose."

"That's a shame. A pretty girl like you shouldn't be alone for the holidays."

Cassie blushed slightly, and with her rouge, it made her more attractive to Randolph. He'd been to more than one of the soirees at the school and knew their true purpose, even if Cassie didn't. He thought she was ready for the next step.

The dance ended and Randolph said, "Let's go and sit down, Cassie."

Cassie turned and headed for the same seat she'd had before, but Randolph guided her to another table on the opposite side of the room where the light was dimmer. After she took a seat, he surprised her when he sat close beside her and was more surprised when Randolph's shoulder was pressed against hers and there was no room for her to move any further.

As she looked at the other tables on the shadowy side of the room, she noticed that all of the boys and girls were most assuredly sitting close together, and more than half were actually kissing. Right there in the open! She turned to look for Miss Hampton to see if she was aware of it, but instead found Randolph's face just inches from hers.

"This is nice, isn't it, Cassie?" he asked, "This is where dreams are made, you know. All of these pretty young women waiting for the right young man to come to dance with them, and maybe more."

Cassie asked quietly, "What do you mean, maybe more?"

He leaned even closer, almost conspiratorially, and whispered, "You know, don't you? All of you come here looking for that wealthy boy who will fill your closets with fine things and give you servants to do all of the menial things that women hate to do. That's why you all learn how to please us. Haven't you learned yet, Cassie?"

She was about to ask to leave when she felt his hand drop onto her lap, startling her. If she had been anywhere else, she would have shouted or yanked his hand away, but this was all so alien to her, she just sat unmoving, not knowing what to do. It seemed none of the rules that applied back home worked here.

She finally caught sight of Miss Hampton who was looking right at her and smiling! *Why didn't she rush over with a yardstick to stop all of this boy-girl contact like Miss Timmons back on Warwick would have done long before now?*

When she didn't react to his hand on her lap, Randolph thought he was home free, so he said, "You know, you're so pretty, Cassie, I'd like to kiss you. Can I kiss you?"

Cassie wanted to push him away, but she couldn't. She was completely confused and out of her element. *Why wouldn't Miss Hampton do anything?*

She closed her eyes trying to settle her mind, which triggered more action by Randolph.

He took her nonresponse and closed eyes to mean yes, so he leaned over and kissed her on her lips as his right hand searched beneath her petticoats for something interesting.

Cassie was startled when she felt his hand behind her bare neck and his lips touch hers and didn't notice as Randolph began pulling her dress and petticoats up. For a young woman who'd never even so much as held hands with a boy before, having one kissing her was a mammoth shock, and it released an unexpected, unrealized rush of physical desire in Cassie.

As Randolph continued to kiss her before sliding his lips to her neck. She found herself thrilled by what he was doing to her as her eyes remained closed and she reveled in the new sensations. Once that first release of desire had struck, Cassie slid into a dreamworld that had Joe kissing her, and placed her gloved left hand around his neck, pulling his head closer, her newly experienced sensations overwhelmed her defenses.

Randolph was very good at what he was doing, and soon found Cassie's thigh and slid his hand along the inside making her gasp as his lips were still sliding across her neck with her hand behind his head.

Cassie never wanted Joe more than she wanted him now, and when Randolph's hand slid deeper under her dress she whispered, "Joe."

Randolph lifted his head slightly from Cassie's neck slightly and whispered, "I'll make you forget all about Joe."

Cassie was so enraptured in her freed lust she almost missed what he said, but when 'forget' and 'Joe' filtered into her hormone-controlled mind, her eyes flew open, she pulled her right hand from behind Randolph's head and then realized where his right hand was.

She pushed Randolph's shoulder away to get his lips from her neck and snapped, "Take your hand out from under my dress. Now!"

Randolph was taken aback but was too far along to give up so easily, thinking Cassie might be playing hard to get, and replied, "I will not. You're not fooling me, Cassie. You want me to bed you and we can do it right here if you wish, but I can take you back in your room if you're a shy girl."

His comment shocked her as much as his hand still lying atop her stockinged thigh, but Cassie was no longer confused or thrilled. She was Cassie Elizabeth Warren, the girl who shot her own .44 caliber pistol.

She slammed her knees together almost snapping Randolph's forearm and then released them and pushed his hand out with her left arm as he winced and cursed under his breath.

"Now get away from me!" she exclaimed, distracting the other couples who were progressing well beyond kissing.

Then Randolph made the cardinal mistake of raising his right hand to put Cassie in her place. But Cassie was too quick for him and with her back to the wall and both hands against his chest, shoved him hard.

Randolph's eyes registered the shock of being hurled away from the girl he'd just been kissing and flew awkwardly onto the dance floor onto his back with his arms outstretched trying to slow his slide.

Cassie bounced out of the seats quickly and with dozens of formally dressed boys and young women, the few women chaperones in their gowns and bouffant hairdos, Miss Hampton, and the musicians and servers all watching, Cassie Warren took two long strides to Randolph, swung her right foot from under her red, petticoated gown and slammed it into Randolph's still aroused manhood, as required.

Randolph screamed as he grabbed for his nether regions as Miss Hampton shot to her feet and stormed over to Cassie.

"Miss Warren! What have you done! How dare you ruin this evening!" she shouted as she strode across the dance floor.

Cassie turned to the headmistress and replied loudly, "What I did was to stop that boy from taking advantage of me, as you should have done!"

“You aren’t worthy to be in this school, Miss Warren! Go to your room and I will talk to you later!”

“No, you will not talk to me later,” she said as she began pulling hairpins from her tall hair and tossing them on the floor, “I made a big mistake in coming here. I thought this was a school that prepared young women for college, but it was far from that. Where I come from, this would be nothing less than a fancy bordello and you, Miss Hampton, would be what you truly are, the madam who procures women for men. You make money from both sides, so that makes you even worse.”

Miss Hampton was livid as she snapped, “You keep quiet and leave my school!”

“Oh, I’m leaving,” Cassie replied, “and I’m returning to my home where I belong.”

Then as her eyes passed the gowned girls who were all staring at her, she said, “You all joked about my not having a boyfriend, and you were right. I don’t have a boyfriend. I have a real man who loves me and when I return, I’ll marry him. We won’t live in a fancy house and ride carriages to elegant soirees, and I’ll be doing laundry and cleaning, too. But we’ll ride and go shooting together, and we’ll be happier than any of you will ever be. I’m going home to my Joe.”

Cassie glared at their staring faces as she pulled the hair comb from her hair, let it fall to her back and with her dignity restored, walked gracefully from the silent dining hall, turned down the hallway and disappeared.

Miss Hampton watched her leave and after fifteen seconds of silence, turned to the band and said, “You may resume playing.”

The band leader tapped his baton, and the music filled the dance hall, but only two couples continued to dance as Randolph writhed on the floor, still clutching his crotch. The couples who were amorously engaged returned to kissing, but the boys were all more reticent about progressing beyond that as the image of Cassie's kick was still vivid in their minds.

Cassie heard the music start again as she entered her room and took the two large and one small travel bags from the storage closet and set them on her bed before she began to disassemble her massive wardrobe.

As she undressed, she was digesting all that had just happened. She was embarrassed and ashamed that she had let it go that far but understood why she hadn't stopped him earlier than she had. Bessie had told her how wonderful it felt when she had been kissed and touched in private places, but Cassie thought she was immune from such feelings. Once Randolph started kissing her, it had awakened those dormant longings within her, and she'd been stunned by their power. She had been overwhelmed by her own lust and it had surprised her. She wasn't prepared for any of it.

As she stepped out of her petticoats, she began to review what she had said, not only to Miss Hampton, but to all of the other girls in the room. She had said she was going back to Warwick and marry Joe. She knew she had said it to push back all of those snotty, snide remarks they had all said about her, but she knew she couldn't marry Joe. She didn't even know where he was anymore.

Yet, when that smarmy Randolph slid his hand on her thigh and had his lips on hers, she wanted it to be Joe who was doing it. She knew for certain that the desire was very real. She did want Joe to kiss her and touch her but knew that could that never happen without progressing to the point where it could result in her pregnancy.

She tossed the last of her petticoats onto the floor and had to work to remove the hated corset, half expecting either Randolph or Miss Hampton to enter as the fought to pull out the strings. But she was able to finally toss the whale-boned straight jacket onto the petticoats and take a deep breath. For all their taunts about her not having anything to fill the dreaded undergarment, Cassie knew that she wasn't nearly as thin as she'd been just a few months ago. She wasn't as bosomy as Bessie, especially after she became pregnant, but she wasn't so girlish anymore either.

She quickly slipped on a camisole and hurriedly dressed in some normal clothing before wiping the makeup from her face, which took longer than she'd expected.

After pulling on her normal shoes, Cassie began to pack. It was probably already ten o'clock, and it wasn't a good idea for a young girl to go out into the streets of Dallas that late, but she thought she was safer out there than inside this bordello school, so she began to pack.

She had both large travel bags packed and as she packed the smaller bag with her toiletries and other necessities, she realized she only had two hands. But she was the sheriff's daughter from Warwick now and began to fashion a shoulder strap out of one of her belts.

Cassie was almost finished when she heard steps outside, giggling, and then the door opened.

Elizabeth was startled to see Cassie still there and wearing daily clothes. She'd expected to find the room empty. Standing behind Elizabeth was her very anxious boyfriend, who Cassie noted, was a pimply-faced boy that was even smaller than Elizabeth, who was three inches shorter than Cassie.

"Oh, you're still here," Elizabeth said.

"I was just trying to figure out how to get to the hotel."

Surprisingly, Elizabeth's boyfriend provided the solution when he said, "Just go to the parking area and ask for the Simpson carriage. Tell my driver, Harold, to take you to the Metropolitan Hotel and then return."

Cassie replied, "Thank you," then hoisted her modified travel bag to her shoulder, grabbed both of the larger bags and left the room, letting the short boy close the door so he and Elizabeth could do whatever they planned on doing.

As she lugged the travel bags down the hallway, she noticed other girls leading boys into their rooms, which sent a chill up her spine. She hadn't been far off in her accusation to Miss Hampton when she'd accused the headmistress of being a madam.

Twenty minutes later, Cassie was entering the Metropolitan Hotel as Harold, the Simpsons' driver, carried the two large travel bags into the lobby and left them beside the desk and tipped his cap and quietly left the hotel.

After getting her room and having the porter take the bags upstairs, Cassie was finally able to relax and was almost giddy when she found the room had an attached bath with hot and cold running water.

After a long, hot bath, Cassie returned to her room and slid beneath the quilts and blankets. She had a lot to think about as she closed her eyes.

The next morning, a corset-less Cassie checked out of her room and half-expected Randolph or a lawman to be waiting for her in the lobby, but neither was there. She had breakfast in the hotel restaurant before walking to the train depot, checking the schedule and buying a ticket for the westbound train which was leaving at 10:10 that morning.

She sent a telegram to her father letting him know of her departure and that she'd be arriving on tomorrow evening's stagecoach.

At half past ten, she was sitting in her seat on the train as Dallas began fading out of sight and she vowed she'd never do anything so foolish again. She'd learned a lot in the past few months, and none of it was her classroom studies.

Last night, she had laid awake for more than two hours before succumbing to sleep. During that extended, undisturbed rumination, she made several determinations. The most obvious was that she loved Joe Armstrong. The others were not as clearly defined. She realized that it wasn't necessary for her to leave her family to find her dream, but still needed to clarify what that dream was.

It would be a long trip to Warwick, and that would give her more time to see if she could solve her problem, and maybe understand what she really wanted out of her life.

Randolph may not have been in the lobby waiting for Cassie, but he was not about to let the humiliation of what she had done to him go unpunished. As Cassie was waiting on the platform for her train, Randolph was angrily blaming Carlisle's School for Young Women for allowing such a non-compliant girl to attend the institution.

His father, Arthur James Hardesty, was appalled that such an inappropriate response could have occurred right there in a roomful of upper crust young people. He knew that there would be whispers and snickering at his and Randolph's expense and he was going to nip it in the bud.

So, as Cassie's train was rolling out of Dallas, Mister Hardesty arrived at Carlisle's School for Young Women before Miss Wilhelmina Hampton closed it down for the holidays.

He had expected to be able to browbeat Miss Hampton, but the headmistress was already in a defensive and hostile mood when he arrived for the same reason that he was in an offensive and hostile mood, and the meeting went badly.

Before he left, Mister Hardesty threatened a lawsuit, which would never be filed as gossip of Cassie's punishing kick and diatribe filtered through the community, was picked up by a newspaper reporter who then quickly investigated what really happened at the school. His front-page story about the immoral behavior encouraged by Miss Hampton quickly resulted in the school's closing before the young women were scheduled to return to classes.

On Saturday evening, a resolved Cassie stepped out of the stagecoach and was greeted by only her father, which surprised her.

"Where's mama?" she asked as her father took her travel bags from the driver.

"She's at home with your brother," he said off-handedly.

"Bessie had her baby!" Cassie exclaimed and quickly corrected herself and said, "Wait. He'd be my nephew, not my brother. Are we talking about Bessie's baby?"

They had begun to walk along the boardwalk when her father replied as he grinned, “No, Cassie. I mean your brother. Bessie hasn’t had her baby yet.”

Cassie was flummoxed as she walked beside her father trying to understand what had happened. Her mother surely hadn’t been with child before she left, so it was a bit of a mystery.

“How did that happen?”

“Joe brought a little boy back with him a few days ago and we adopted him.”

“*Joe’s here?*” she exclaimed, her heart almost bursting with excitement.

“No, he left the day after the adoption. He hadn’t found any of the Hogan brothers yet.”

“Oh,” she said in disappointment and asked, “How did he find a little boy?”

“We’ll tell you everything when we get home. What made you decide to leave the school?”

“It wasn’t what I expected at all. It was just to prepare young women to marry wealthy young men. I should have done more research before going.”

“You can tell us about it when we introduce you to your brother. It’s good to have you home, Cassie.”

“I’m glad to be back too, Papa,” she said as she smiled.

Even as they turned to go into the house, Cassie knew that none of her family would ever know what had happened to drive her out of the school. That information would only be given to Joe, provided she ever got to talk to him again.

———

Two days later, on Christmas Eve, Cassie was in Mary's house helping her with decorations when Lou burst through the front door and shouted, "Mary! Cassie! Come quickly!"

Both women turned, and Mary asked, "What's wrong?"

"It's Bessie. She's having her baby!" he yelled and stood waiting as both women rapidly donned their coats.

"How long has it been so far?" Mary asked.

"Just an hour or so, but Mrs. Williams says it's going very fast."

"That would be a blessing," Mary said as she and Cassie followed Lou out the door.

Cassie was holding Mary's hand as they entered the house and she could hear Bessie's cries from the front room.

"Who's inside with Bessie?" Mary asked.

"Your mother and Mrs. Williams," Lou replied as John walked into the main room from the kitchen.

"We made two pots of coffee," John said before turning back down the hallway.

Cassie glanced at the closed door and heard all the noise inside and felt her stomach flip. The old fear was still there, despite her resolve and reasoning on the return trip.

When they reached the kitchen, Cassie took a cup and filled it with coffee before taking a seat at the table. Her father sat across from her with little Michael on his lap. She'd only known her new brother for a little more than a day but was already very fond of him. He seemed to like her, too. She smiled at the little boy as he waved at his new sister.

They talked and had coffee for three hours, as Bessie's cries and sobs filled the house. Mrs. Warren and Mrs. Williams came out of the room periodically to tell everyone how things were progressing, and that Bessie was doing fine. Lou was the only one in the room who appeared frightened.

It was just before midnight when they heard the miraculous sound of a baby crying and everyone stood, except for Michael, who was already asleep in the main room.

They all anxiously waited for the official news, and after another five tense minutes, a smiling Minnie Warren stepped into the kitchen and announced, "Bessie is the mother of a beautiful little girl. She's doing fine."

The room was filled with smiles and congratulations to Lou, who, although he wasn't the biological father, had every intention of being the baby's real father. John commented about another girl being born to a Warren, although she was now a Sanborn.

Minnie led Lou to Bessie's room to see his wife and new daughter about thirty minutes after her first announcement, and after ten minutes, she returned with him and said, "Cassie, Bessie wants to see you."

Cassie wasn't sure why Bessie would want to see her so soon, but nodded, stood and followed her mother to her sister's birthing room.

Inside, her mother and Mrs. Williams both stepped aside to let Cassie pass.

Cassie approached the bed and looked at her sister's sweating, but joyful face as she held her baby to her breast letting the tiny girl have her first nourishment.

"How are you, Bessie?" Cassie asked softly.

Bessie looked into her sister's brown eyes and smiled as she said, "I've never been so happy, Cassie. Look at her. Isn't she perfect? I wanted you to meet your niece and understand the immeasurable joy I'm feeling right now. I can't come close to describing it. I know that you've been worried about having a baby, but it's too wonderful to just throw away. This is life, Cassie, and she's here because I carried her inside me."

Cassie didn't know how Bessie had found out about her fears, but it didn't matter now, so she leaned over, kissed her sister on her damp forehead and gently touched the baby's back before stepping away and saying, "I love you, Bessie. Thank you."

"I love you too, Cassie," Bessie said as she continued to smile at her younger sister.

Cassie then smiled at her mother before leaving the room and gently closing the door behind her. She was going to go to the kitchen but turned instead to the main room. She wanted time to think. The sight of Bessie's radiant face had touched her deeply.

She slowly sat on the couch in the darkened room and saw the sleeping Michael beside her. Bessie's obvious joy after she had experienced all those hours of agony had surprised her. She'd always equated childbirth with only pain and death. Yet Bessie had seemed positively rapturous as she lay on her bed with her new daughter at her breast. *Was having a baby worth all the pain and the months of walking around with that massive bulge in your belly?*

Cassie then remembered how Dan's wife was after she had her baby, rather than thinking about Lou's first wife's death in childbirth. Ellie Sheehy had the same happy look on her face and that was two days after the baby was born. Cassie had never seen a woman who had just given birth until she saw her sister.

Cassie sat for almost forty minutes as she reshaped her whole outlook on being married and having babies. Yes, it was a risk, but all of life was a risk. Right now, the man she loved was out in the middle of nowhere risking his life trying to find the Hogans. *Which risk would have a better ending?*

The final exclamation point to her musings was when Michael stirred and saw Cassie sitting beside him. She smiled at the small boy, who then crawled onto her lap and rested his blonde head against her chest. As she laid her hand softly on his head, he said quietly, "Mama."

The feeling that had come over her at that moment was indescribable, just as Bessie had told her that the joy she felt was beyond words. He may not be her child, but Cassie Elizabeth Warren was no longer afraid of having one of her own baby and she wanted it to be Joe's.

CHAPTER 11

May 17, 1880

Joe was almost to the southern border as he rode into Uvalde. In the past six months, he'd tracked eleven different leads to the Hogan brothers and captured or killed seven outlaws. He'd been wounded once, taking a .41 caliber bullet from a Remington derringer in the left side of his back. He hadn't searched the bastard who shot him and had put a .44 through his neck before he could cock the small pistol for a second shot. The bullet had hit his left shoulder blade, so it hadn't hit his lung, but it took a while to heal properly and added a new scar to his back.

This lead was taking him just to the west of the town, and he was so discouraged by now that he doubted every clue he had found. This was no different. Two men, matching the vague description of the Fred and Hank Hogan had been playing a card game in a saloon in Uvalde and according to witnesses, had instigated a fight by accusing the dealer of bottom-dealing before they stole the money from the other players and those at the other four tables as well. It was a pretty good haul, but no one had chased after them. It was just another hazard to those that frequented saloons and brothels. It was the almost instantaneous nature of the report that piqued his interest as much as the descriptions. It had happened just the night before he arrived in town.

Joe hadn't shaved in three days and his hair was almost as long as Cassie's now. He needed to change that and would have if he had stayed longer in Uvalde or any other town. But as soon as he got a lead, he'd leave to chase it down.

He was an hour west of Uvalde traveling on the road and was so accustomed to the chase now that he scanned for ambush locations automatically. This lead was so fresh that he wouldn't have been surprised if the two men hadn't gone that far from town.

But even after two breaks to rest and water the horses, he hadn't seen any signs of the two men and almost wished for an ambush.

Late that afternoon, he walked his horse and pack horse into the small town of Bitter Springs. At least they were honest when they named the place. He'd been to a lot of towns that had names that made them sound like paradise on earth but were little more than hell holes.

Bitter Springs, on the other hand, had a horrible name but appeared prosperous for a small town.

As it had become his routine during his long search, his first stop was at the livery to drop off his horses to get them fed, watered and have their shoes checked. He'd gone through a lot of horseshoes on this pursuit.

After leaving his animals, he asked his perfunctory, "You haven't seen a couple of strangers ride in over the past day or so, have you?"

"You the law?" the liveryman asked.

"I used to be a deputy sheriff up in Warwick, but I've been hunting the Hogan brothers for a while. They killed my mother."

"I can appreciate your doin' it then. We had two fellers show up last night and they ain't gone yet. Their animals are over there," he said as he pointed at the back two stalls.

"I don't know what they'd be riding now, but I know what their saddles would look like."

"Well, c'mon, son, and I'll show 'em to ya," the liveryman replied as he waved Joe to the back of the barn.

Joe followed him into the darkness and when he pointed him at the shelves of tack, it didn't take Joe fifteen seconds to know that he'd found two of the Hogans. Carved on one of the saddle horns was an 'H' and another had an 'F'.

"See the ones you're lookin' for?"

"Yes, sir. That's Hank Hogan's saddle right there, and Fred's is next to it."

"Well, I'll be snockered. You gonna go and face 'em down?"

"You have any law in town?"

"No, sir. If we have a problem, we go to Sheriff Lee back in Uvalde."

"Okay, I'll handle it. You don't know where they are right now, do you?"

"Well, a good guess would be one of the three saloons. We only got one church, but three saloons, and each one of 'em still does better business than that church."

"That's not unusual," Joe said as he thought about how to approach this.

Joe had developed several strategies for taking on more than one shooter, including using both hands. He'd had to expend a lot of ammunition practicing with his off hand, and it still wasn't nearly as good as his right, but it was still better than most gunmen with their right hand.

But this one was important. It was the Hogan brothers.

He still only wore a one-gun rig because two-holstered gunbelts marked him as a threat, whether it was an outlaw or a lawman looking at him. He didn't like to attract unwanted attention.

Joe slipped one of his six spare Colts into his waist in back behind his black vest and left the livery, walking west into the sun. As he walked, his eyes scanned every other human being he spotted, even the women. He could see the church at the end of the road, its steeple and cross highlighted by the low sun, but this wasn't a time for praying.

The first saloon, The Rusty Bucket, was across the street, so he continued on the south side of the road and soon reached the next one, Wooly's Place, and entered the batwing doors. After letting his eyes adjust to the shadows, he scanned the clientele. There weren't many at this time of day, and he wasn't sure if he could have picked them out in a crowded bar, but none here attracted his eye, so he turned and continued along the boardwalk, entering The Q Ball Billiards Parlor just a minute later.

Again, he looked around the room and found no Hogans among the customers.

That left The Rusty Bucket across the street unless they were elsewhere. Not finding them in either saloon had seemed to in keeping with his long, frustrating search. *Why would they be in the first place he looked?*

As he approached the last saloon, he slowed down knowing there was a good chance they were inside. He knew even without a two-gun rig that he stood out, for his size if nothing else. Now with his long hair, he was much too noticeable.

But that couldn't be helped as he stepped onto the northern boardwalk and then walked through the batwing doors without stopping as he had in the other two places.

The Rusty Bucket was more crowded than the others, and rather than scan the room, Joe took long strides across the floor and stopped at the bar.

"Beer," he said as he pulled out a nickel and dropped it on the bar.

The bartender nodded and filled a glass and let the head flow over the sides as he slid it to Joe and took the nickel.

Joe then walked to an empty table, sat down carefully with the Colt stuck in the back waist of his britches, and then finally began to examine each of the other patrons.

His eyes first took him to the two poker tables as the Hogans had used that ploy back in Uvalde, and he had no problem identifying both Hogans as they sat with their backs to the wall to prevent anyone from slipping in behind them. Each brother had his own table and were facing him less than thirty feet away.

He spent another couple of minutes just casually looking around the bar, but mainly keeping watch on the Hogans as they played the game.

Eventually, he had to order a second beer, but still waited. Probably the most valuable lesson he'd learned in the past year was patience. Haste in gunfights was always a bad thing.

He had just ordered a third beer and had been following both poker games, which wasn't unusual. It was usually the sole source of entertainment in small town saloons, unless one's purpose was to imbibe enough alcohol to not care about entertainment at all. He had both of his pistols laying on his thighs as he watched.

Then it was like a door suddenly slammed open when Hank Hogan, on the right-side table, stood suddenly and threw his cards down.

"You cheatin' son of a bitch!" he shouted as he went for his pistol.

Almost at the same moment Fred stood and pulled his Colt, cocking the hammer and stood facing the others.

Joe dropped his hands to his Colts, cocked the hammers, slipped his fingers under the grips and his index fingers in front of the trigger guards. He was ready, and now he just needed to wait for the opportunity.

"What are you talkin' about," the player across from Hank shouted and started to stand.

"Sit down, mister! I watched you dealin' from the bottom of the deck for ten minutes now, and it's time to call you what you are. You ain't nothin' but a cheater."

"You're lyin' and you know it. Hell, you're winnin' more than I am."

"All of you boys are in on it, so why don't you just put your cash on the table before I get an itchy trigger finger."

By now both tables of card players had already concluded what this really was. Both men had stood at the same time and they even looked alike. This was a robbery and nothing more, but the two thieves had their guns drawn and cocked and there was nothing any of them could do.

Joe had turned his chair slightly clockwise to face the two poker tables, but there were men in the way, and he didn't want to shoot someone else just to get to the Hogans. He slipped his index fingers to lightly touch the triggers as he felt they'd be needed soon.

The men began shoving all the money into the middle of each of the tables and Fred shouted, "Empty your pockets, all of you!"

Then Hank swiveled his pistol around the room and shouted, "All the rest of you empty your pockets and put the cash on the table in front of you."

Then he looked at the bartender and added, "You, barkeep, take that scattergun out from behind the bar and pull out the shells and toss 'em on the floor."

The bartender tried to think of a way he could fire at the two men, but he'd hit too many patrons with the spread of pellets, so he did as he'd been told and after tossing the shotgun's shells to the floor, left the useless weapon on the bar.

Joe released his hand from the Colt on his right thigh and pulled out his fairly large wad of cash and set it on the table near his beer, so he wouldn't be noticeable before sliding his hand back under the table and taking hold of his pistol again. He was surprised that as experienced criminals as they were, the Hogans didn't have all of the men either stand with their hands raised or at least have them put their hands on the tables. Maybe that would come shortly.

They seemed to have a different plan as they had each man, after emptying his pockets, leave his pistol on the table if he carried one and then stand behind the bar. Once each table was cleared, they moved the cash and silver to the one table with a tablecloth.

Joe was sitting at one of the back tables, and once the two poker tables were empty of players, he had a clear shot.

Hank was facing him as Fred cleared off a table, so Joe said loudly, “Hank, you haven’t gotten any prettier with age and neither has Fred.”

Fred whipped his Colt around to face Joe, but Joe didn’t wait for either to fire as he pulled both triggers and the table exploded as the twin .44s blasted through the cheap wood and reached the two Hogans almost instantly. Fred took a grazing wound to his left shoulder and Hank wasn’t hit, but the suddenness of the two shots, made him flinch and jerk his trigger.

Joe was rising from the chair immediately after firing and had his hammers cocked just before Hank could draw his hammer back.

Joe fired again, and this time both bullets traced across the room and slammed into a Hogan. Hank’s wound was almost instantly fatal, as his abdominal aorta was blown apart by the gut shot and he felt to the floor. Fred’s wound was still a fatal shot, but a slower killer when the .44 drilled through his right lung after shattering his sixth rib and leaving his body and punching into the wall behind him.

He collapsed to the floor and began gagging as he choked on his own blood.

Joe approached the two Hogan brothers and said nothing as he holstered his Colt and slid the Remington into his waist.

The gunsmoke filled the barroom as he just stood and watched Fred breathe his last.

He then turned and said, “This is Fred Hogan and that’s his brother Hank. Both are wanted men, dead or alive. I’m going to get them on their horses and head back to Uvalde. Could I get some help, please?”

The men who just moments before were about to lose all of their cash were more than ready to provide whatever assistance Joe required, as he returned to his table, picked up his cash, stuffed it back into his pocket and finished his beer.

Except for the lost table, the saloon hadn’t suffered too badly, but Joe gave the barkeep twenty dollars for the damages. Joe would be making a lot more from the rewards on the Hogans.

He didn’t get out of Bitter Springs until almost seven o’clock that night, but he wanted to get back to Uvalde and get rid of the Hogans’ bodies.

Joe made better time going back than he did on the ride west because he knew where he was going and how long it would take to get there, but he still didn’t arrive until after ten o’clock. He hunted down a deputy and explained what had happened, just so he could get rid of the bodies.

Once they were dropped off at the mortician, Joe dropped off the four horses at the livery, got a room at one of the two hotels and within ten minutes of entering the room was sound asleep.

Six days later, Sheriff Warren walked to his house for lunch and asked his wife, "Where's Cassie?"

"She's over at Bessie's with Michael. Why?"

"I just received two vouchers for Joe that I need to deposit."

"Two more? It's the only way we even know where he is. Where was this one?"

"Uvalde. What makes this one special was that it was for two of the Hogan brothers."

"He finally got them? Do you think he'll be coming home now?"

"I don't know, dear. I just wanted Cassie to know."

"I'll fix your lunch and you can go to Bessie's house and tell her."

John kissed his wife and left the kitchen and the house. He didn't want to tell Minnie that he was beginning to believe that Joe would never return to Warwick. His lack of contacts indicated that he'd given up on Cassie and probably believed that she'd given up on him. If only there was some way of letting him know that Cassie was home and desperately wanted to see him again.

November 3, 1880

Joe hadn't given up on Cassie at all, but believed she was still at school and had found her dream. But he was about to give up trying to find Buck Hogan. He had searched for almost a year now, and as tenuous as the leads had been for Fred and Hank, Buck had left no trail at all. Texas was enormous, but Joe began to think that Buck had left the state entirely and gone west. It was the most likely reason for his total disappearance.

He had worked his way east and then north and was now in of all places, Gainesville. He had even ridden past the reformatory on his ride north. It didn't look any different, and he wondered if the boys were being treated any better.

Joe rode into town and after leaving his two horses at the livery and getting a room, walked to the barber shop and got the full treatment to feel human again. He then bought himself two complete outfits and threw out his old clothes except for his boots, hat and belt.

He was eating his dinner at the hotel restaurant when he had to decide what to do next. He really wanted to ride to Dallas to see Cassie but knew it would only make her either angry or sad, and he knew it wouldn't be possible for him to leave her again. It had been so painful the last time when she left.

Joe sighed as he sipped his coffee. He had thought that the longer he was away from Warwick, the thoughts about Cassie would fade, but if anything, they had strengthened.

It was a lot like when he was in that reformatory as he'd ridden around much of Texas hunting for the Hogans. He had used his imagination to try to envision what Cassie would look like now. He was well aware of the enormous physical changes that teenagers went through and he hadn't seen her in a long time now. She could be a taller version of Bessie by now, and that had generated a new concern, beyond his original worry about losing her to her dream. What if she'd gotten over her fear of having a baby somehow as she slid into womanhood and then met a young man who swept her off her feet? He simply didn't know but knew who would know, and they were all in Warwick, Texas.

But beyond that, he really did miss the Warrens and was curious to see how Michael was growing. When he'd gone, Bessie was still pregnant, but her baby would almost be a year old by now.

It was only then that Joe fully realized how long he'd been gone. The time had dribbled past, one day at a time as he sat in the saddle, crossing open territory looking for the Hogans. There was one left out there somewhere, *but was it worth the rest of his life to find him?* He'd wasted more than six months after finding Fred and Hank without a whisper of where Buck was. He hadn't even had any more gunfights or captures because he was just looking for clues, not men.

By the time he was eating his apple pie dessert, he'd made up his mind. He'd ride to Warwick and see the Warrens. Maybe he'd see if he could get his deputy job back, but it had been over a year since he left the first time, so Sheriff Warren had probably replaced him already. It didn't matter, he just wanted to go home.

———

The next morning, a clean-shaven, freshly trimmed Joe Armstrong departed Gainesville heading west. Because he wasn't taking the train or a stagecoach, he wasn't tied to a schedule. He'd arrive in three days and smiled knowing that Cassie would be celebrating her seventeenth birthday in Dallas as he was with her parents in Warwick.

He'd read all of her letters dozens of times each during his ride around Texas and could quote most by heart, but her first letter, as faded and sorry state as it was, was still his favorite.

The ride from Gainesville to Henrietta wasn't familiar because he'd only taken the train between the towns and even the terrain past Henrietta wasn't recognizable yet, but the closer he rode to Warwick the more landmarks he identified.

He'd camped out twice on the trip and was only about a half-day's ride to Warwick when he mounted on the seventh of November. He'd taken extra care when he shaved that morning in the cold water, but he knew he'd have time to heal the two nicks.

For the first time in almost a year, Joe spotted the outline of Warwick in the distance and he smiled at the sight. It was a bit odd that he should consider the town his home. He'd spent less than six months living in Warwick, but everyone he cared about was there. Everyone except the one he cared about the most.

Joe regretted not sending her at least another letter on her birthday, but he wasn't sure of what Cassie's interests were anymore. At least he'd find out how she was doing soon.

Sheriff Warren left his office with his hat in his hand and as he reached the front office, looked at his son-in-law and asked, "Are you coming, Lou?"

"Yes, sir," Lou said as he scratched his signature on a report and stood and followed the boss out the door, grabbing his hat on the way.

"What did you get Cassie for her birthday, boss?" Lou asked as they stepped out into the street.

“Not what she wants, I don’t think, but I picked up a new Winchester ’76 that I think she’ll like.”

“What does she want?”

“If you don’t know you haven’t talked to her in the past few months.”

“Oh…that,” Lou said as they headed east, “but she sure helps Bessie a lot with little Jo.”

“I think part of it is because she can say ‘Jo’ so much without anyone asking questions,” John said with a light laugh.

Lou was laughing as he looked down the street and asked, “Boss, is that who I think it is about a half mile out?”

Both lawmen stopped as John lifted his eyes and said, “How on earth did he time this? We haven’t seen him in almost a year, and he shows up on Cassie’s birthday?”

“How did he find out she’s here? Do you think he went to Dallas?”

“I don’t know, but you head back to the office and tell Dan he’s coming, but don’t let him say anything about Cassie. I want you and Dan to take care of his horses. I’m sending Cassie over without letting her know. Okay?”

Lou was grinning as he said, “Okay, boss,” then turned and jogged back to the jail.

Joe had seen them before they saw him and assumed that Lou had been told to let Dan know he was back, and maybe hand over the jail to the new deputy. But the job didn’t matter as he kept smiling while he closed the gap to the sheriff, who was standing there with his own smile, waiting for him.

"Howdy, Sheriff Warren," Joe said loudly as he brought his gelding to a stop.

"Joe, you are a sight for sore eyes. Why the hell didn't you at least write to us? We didn't even know if you were alive anymore."

"I'm sorry about that. I have no real excuse. Are you headed home for lunch?"

"I am. Why don't you drop off your horses at the office and tell Lou and Dan to take care of them? You can clean up a bit and come join us. You won't believe how much bigger Michael is now."

Joe's smile had never faded as he said, "I can't wait to see the little feller. I'll head over there and clean up. I'll be over in about twenty minutes or so."

"I'll have my wife make some more lunch for you."

Joe then asked, "Before you go boss, have you heard from Cassie? How is she doing at that school?"

John then realized that Joe didn't know Cassie was just a couple of hundred yards away and replied, "She is a happy girl, Joe," changing the tense of the verb intentionally from 'will be' to 'is' to keep the secret.

Joe nodded but felt sick inside. He knew he'd always told her that he wanted her to be happy, but he wanted to be the one who made her happy, not some damned school for young ladies.

"I'm glad to hear it, boss."

"We'll see you in a little while and you can meet Bessie's little girl."

"She was right, then. She did have a little girl after all."

"Yup, she named her Josephine Anne, but everyone calls her Jo. I'll let you figure out why."

Joe managed a smile, still thinking about a distant, happy Cassie and said, "I'm looking forward to seeing her. I'll head over to the jail and be finished as soon as I can."

John waved and began walking at a brisk pace back to the house.

Joe walked his horses to the sheriff's office as Dan and Lou stood out front wearing grins.

Despite the news about Cassie, Joe couldn't help but grin when he saw his two friends.

He pulled to a stop and dismounted as they quickly descended from the boardwalk and began shaking his hand and slapping his back.

"You're looking pretty tired, Joe," Dan said, "It's about time you came home."

"It's good to be back."

"The boss said we should take care of your horses, so you could clean up before joining us in his home for lunch," Lou said.

"I appreciate it. How's Bessie and your baby, doing, Lou?"

"They're doing great, and Bessie's due again in April. Dan's Ellie is going to have another baby, too."

Joe congratulated them both as they took the reins of his geldings and he entered the jail. It hadn't changed much since he'd been gone. They added a bigger gun rack, probably because of the new guy. Joe walked back to the sleeping room, hoping the new man wasn't back there, but it was empty.

He took off his shirt to clean up and began trying to imagine who the sheriff would have hired. He could only think of one or two men that might work.

"Why do I have to go to the jail to get it?" Cassie asked her father.

"It's too heavy for me to lug back here."

"Then how am I supposed to move it?"

John should have known that Cassie wouldn't have just happily trotted to his office to retrieve her birthday gift, and now he was running out of answers.

"You'll figure that out when you see it."

Cassie eyed her father suspiciously and started to tell him that his answer made no sense at all, but finally just sighed and said, "Alright."

She then turned to her mother and said, "I'll be back in a few minutes, Mama," before leaving the house through the back door.

Once she was gone, a very curious Minnie asked, "I thought you bought her that new Winchester?"

"I did, but the present she really wanted is waiting for her in the jail."

Minnie's mouth dropped open as she exclaimed, "*Joe's back?*"

John grinned and hugged his wife as she began to laugh and cry at the same time.

Cassie wondered what the big mystery was as she strode along the road. She would be getting birthday gifts in a little while, but all she really wanted was an envelope. She'd been hoping that she would have received a birthday letter from Joe, but nothing had come. For so long, she'd pushed him away for the silliest of reasons and now that she wanted him so badly, he was somewhere out in the vast empty spaces of West Texas. Her old fear of motherhood had long since been displaced by the real fear that Joe may be dead or never return to Warwick.

She crossed the street and headed for the jail.

Joe had finished washing and even combed his hair and was about to put his shirt on when he heard the door open and footsteps cross the front office floor. He guessed it was the new deputy, and his curiosity was piqued, so he opened the door to the sleeping room and froze.

Cassie had passed through the main office to go to her father's private office for her mystery gift when the door at the end of the hallway opened and she quickly stopped and stared.

“Cassie?” Joe asked quietly, still stunned by her unexpected arrival.

An equally shocked Cassie replied softly, “Joe?” almost not noticing his bare chest.

Joe forgot about the shirt in his hand as he began to walk slowly toward her.

Cassie couldn’t move as she felt her heart pounding and her breath quicken.

When Joe was just a foot away, he stopped and asked quietly, “Why aren’t you in Dallas? I thought you were in school.”

“I left before last Christmas. I was even here when Bessie had her baby.”

Joe realized he’d missed seeing her by just days, and he was beyond frustrated with the thought.

“Why…” he began before Cassie asked, “Can we sit down and talk, Joe? Please?”

“Yes, of course. Do you want to use your father’s office? It’s more private.”

Cassie was about to agree but then replied, “Let’s sit in the sleeping room.”

“Alright.”

After letting Cassie pass by, Joe walked behind her and left the door to the sleeping room open rather than risk scaring her.

Cassie then closed the door and took a seat on the bed while a mildly confused Joe pulled the straight-backed chair close to the bed and took a seat and realized he was still bare-chested.

"Oh, excuse me, Cassie," then began to put his shirt on, but she put her hand on his arm to stop him.

"No, Joe. It's fine. Could you turn around and let me see your back?"

Joe was now more curious than confused as he turned to face the back wall.

Cassie stood and saw the still prominent scars across his back and began to trace them gently with her fingers.

Joe added a whole herd of new feelings to the confusion and curiosity as he felt her touch.

She noticed the new scar from the derringer's bullet and rested her fingers on his shoulder blade.

"You were shot again."

Joe had to focus on her voice before replying, "I stupidly turned my back on a man I thought I'd disarmed, and he shot me from ten feet with a derringer. It was at a steep angle and it went through enough muscle before it hit my shoulder blade, so it wasn't too bad."

"You could have died if he'd shot lower, Joe," Cassie said quietly as her fingers stayed in contact with the latest scar.

"But I didn't, Cassie."

She sat back down and said, "You can put your shirt on now, Joe."

Joe quickly donned his shirt and turned as he began buttoning the front before he sat down. He had almost lost his breath when he had seen the physical changes in Cassie since he'd seen her last, and the fact that she had touched him made him believe that she'd undergone even bigger changes inside. He only hoped that the original Cassie, the one he'd grown to love, was still there.

Cassie looked at his perplexed hazel green eyes and said, "Joe, I'm going to explain some things and I don't want you to interrupt me until I'm finished. Okay?"

"Yes, ma'am," Joe replied, seeing the old Cassie, his Cassie again.

"That school that I went to in Dallas wasn't what I expected it to be. There are so few colleges that accept women and even fewer preparatory schools for young women who want to go to college, and that one was the only one I could find. I should have done more research before applying, but I needed to get away from you. I told you why."

Joe really wanted to say something but abided by her request to remain silent as she continued.

"When I arrived, it didn't take long for me to realize what it really was. It was a school to prepare young women to become proper wives for wealthy young men. I was appalled, but I stayed, hoping that they taught other things as well, but they didn't. Everything was focused on all the skills needed to be a proper lady. I still should have left the place, but my arrogance and stubbornness made me stay.

"On the last day of classes before the Christmas holiday break, we were required to attend a gala. You wouldn't have recognized me in my red gown with my hair put up and wearing petticoats and even a corset and makeup. I was determined not to dance, but Miss Hampton, the headmistress, threatened disciplinary action if I didn't. I was wearing gloves, so I didn't think there would be a problem when I finally danced with a boy. He was your age, but he was still a boy.

"After a few dances, he guided me to the dimly lit section of the dining hall, and I noticed that many of the couples were already engaged in kissing and fondling, which surprised me. I was confused that the headmistress and the chaperones allowed such a thing, Then when I had my eyes closed, the boy began kissing me and I was shocked at first but then, I'm ashamed to admit, I found it thrilling. He began to touch me in places that I had never been touched before and I let him because I was so excited. But in my mind, it wasn't that boy that was touching and kissing me, it was you.

"When I realized it wasn't, I made a scene and left the dance hall, returned to my room where I changed, packed, and then left. All that night and on the way back to Warwick, I had to wrestle with what had happened and what it meant to me. I knew even before I left to go to the school how much I loved you and now, I realized how much I wanted to be with you but was still afraid of what would happen."

Joe was torn between anger at the boy who had taken advantage of Cassie and his relief that she had been able to fend him off. It was buttressed by the confirmation that she loved him. The explanation so far had solved the mystery of why she was able to touch him, but she wasn't finished.

"When I returned," Cassie said, "I found that you'd just left again after dropping off Michael and I was heartbroken, but

Michael helped soothe the pain. Then Bessie had her baby girl and less than an hour after she was born, Bessie called me into her room, and I saw how joyful she was to be a mother. It wasn't some fable that I'd been told. I saw her face, Joe. Then when I went back to the main room, I sat and thought about my fear for a long time. Then Michael woke up and crawled onto my lap. I was holding him when he just said, "mama", and my heart melted.

"I'm not sure if my fear is completely gone, Joe, and I'm still not sure where my dream lies, but I'm not going to have my fear rule my life any longer. For the past year, a much stronger fear has taken over my thoughts completely because I didn't know where you were or even if you were still alive anymore. Now that you're back, I just wanted you to know that more than anything else for my birthday, I wanted to be your girlfriend. Your real girlfriend, not some pretend girlfriend who used you as a shield for all those years. I want you to love me as much as I love you."

Joe looked into her brown eyes and waited for some sort of signal for him to speak, but all they did was look into each other's eyes.

He finally decided that the best answer wasn't with words, so he stood and shifted to the bed, put his arm around her, and kissed Cassie.

Cassie may have experienced being kissed before, but this was totally different as she felt Joe's love blended with the passion of his kiss and threw her arms around his neck, and pulled herself closer.

It was Joe's first kiss and he found the same sensations as Cassie had with hers only much more deeply because he was kissing the young woman he had loved exclusively for years. He had loved her as a freckle-faced girl with pigtails who had written to him and as a skinny girl who walked with him across the Texas landscape. Now he was kissing the woman he wanted to be with for the rest of his life.

When they slowly pulled apart, Joe asked, “May I say something now?”

Cassie was trying to catch her breath and gasped, “Yes.”

“I’ve loved you for years, Cassie, and I’m sure that you understood that because it was what frightened you away. I’m never going to let you go again. If you want to leave to pursue your dream again, I’ll come with you. Whether we get married or not, doesn’t matter. We still have time. You’re only seventeen and even though you’re far from the skinny girl you used to be, there’s no rush.”

Cassie’s eyes joined her lips in a smile as she looked at Joe just inches from her and said, “You noticed, did you?”

“It’s kind of hard not to, ma’am. I’ve got my arms wrapped around you and you’re a lot softer than a skinny girl.”

“Joe, I want so much to marry you, but can we take some time to be together like we should have been since you first returned?”

“I think that’s a good idea, Miss Warren. For as long as we’ve known each other, I believe we’ve spent about a day and a half in each other’s company. I may turn out to be very annoying.”

Cassie laughed and kissed him again just out of pure joy.

After the shorter kiss, she said, “My father told me my birthday present was in the jail and it was too big for him to carry back to the house. He was right.”

"I didn't expect to find you here, so I didn't bring you anything."

"You have to be joking, Deputy Armstrong," Cassie said as she leaned back.

"I'm not a deputy anymore, ma'am. Who did your father hire, anyway?"

"The last new deputy he hired was you, and he held the job for you if you ever returned. I'm sure that Dan Sheehy and Lou Sanford will be very happy to have you back to share the work."

Joe grinned and replied, "Then let's go to your house and see everyone."

"Can I have one more kiss before we go? It is my birthday, after all."

Joe stood and took her hands until she was standing before him, wrapped his massive arms around her, and picked her from the floor before he kissed her as they had the first time.

Cassie would have been floating even if her feet were on the floor.

Ten minutes later, the couple entered the Warren home and were greeted with a big round of applause with some laughter mixed in as the main room was filled with the entire extended family, who all soon learned of the new, and not unexpected relationship between Joe and Cassie.

John and Minnie were both surprised they weren't getting married tomorrow, but Bessie understood. She hadn't learned of Cassie's fear of motherhood from Joe, but from Cassie herself, just not from being told in so many words. Bessie, despite her almost frivolous manner, was very perceptive of her younger sister's feelings.

They spent the rest of the day talking to everyone as Joe met the older Michael, who hadn't recognized him, and little Josephine. He was also introduced to Dan and Ellie Sheehy's little boy, John.

Joe had been told by his boss that his original oath was still in effect and he could pick up his badge in the morning.

After they all shared Cassie's birthday cake and coffee, she was presented with her other birthday gift, the shiny new Winchester '76, which made the three deputies jealous and pleased Cassie even more.

It was past dinnertime when the house was emptied of everyone but the elder Warrens, Cassie, Joe, and Michael.

Michael was in his room playing with Cassie's empty Winchester box as the adults sat at the table just drinking coffee.

"How long are you going to stay, Joe?" Minnie asked.

"I'm here to stay, Mrs. Warren. This is my home."

"What about Buck?" John asked.

"I never was able to even find a clue to where he'd gone. I think he's probably in California by now, or he could even be dead."

"So, the long hunt is over?"

He looked at Cassie, smiled, and replied, "Yes, sir. I found what was really important right here all along."

Cassie slid her hand onto Joe's and smiled back as she said, "This has been a wonderful birthday."

Minnie then asked, "So, when is the wedding going to be?"

Cassie turned to her mother and replied, "When we're ready, Mama."

John looked at Joe with arched eyebrows and Joe knew he'd have to explain tomorrow.

"Well, I'm going to head back to the jail. I still have to unpack."

Cassie grinned and said, "I'll bring you breakfast, Deputy Armstrong, so you'd better be all clean and shaved when I get there."

Joe stood, smiled at Cassie, and replied, "Yes, ma'am."

He then waved to the sheriff and Mrs. Warren before leaving the house and returning to the jail.

As he did the last of his unpacking, he wondered just how this new relationship would work. The new Cassie had the old Cassie with a whole new layer of confusion on top, but he had to admit, it was a very interesting layer.

As promised, Cassie arrived at the jail just after sunrise the next morning with Joe's breakfast and sat it on the desk before corralling him and throwing her arms around his neck, and kissing him.

After the well-appreciated start to his day, Joe sat down with Cassie and was pleased that she'd brought two breakfasts, so they could eat together.

"I'm going to have to buy one of those new Winchesters to keep up with you, Cassie," Joe said before shoveling a big forkful of scrambled eggs into his mouth.

"You'll have to buy some more ammunition, too. My father only bought a single box of the .45 center fire Winchester cartridges."

Joe grinned at Cassie and said, "I'll bet there weren't too many girls in that school that would know that."

Cassie smiled back and said, "They'd be horrified to even think of something as beastly as a gun."

"And to think that Dallas is still in Texas."

Cassie laughed before Joe said, "Cassie, I did some thinking last night about us, and one of the many topics that crossed my mind was where we would be living. I have a lot of money in the bank and what I'd like to do is have a house built across the street from your parent's house. I'd buy the lot, maybe two or three, and have a house built the way we wanted it. You, your mother and sisters could decide on the furniture and decorations. We have the time, and it would be a wonderful thing to do together. What do you think?"

Cassie was surprised that Joe had already thought of it because even she hadn't reached that level yet.

"But what if we don't get married?"

"I still need someplace to live. The sleeping room is wearing thin."

Cassie then agreed with Joe that it would be a good project for them to do together and said, "Let's do it."

“Good. We’ll go to the bank to find the lots and then we can stop at Philby’s Construction today and start things going.”

Cassie found herself already enthused about the house, so she smiled and said, “Come to the house and get me when you’re ready.”

“Yes, ma’am,” Joe replied as he snapped off a bite of bacon.

By the end of the day, Joe and Cassie had purchased three lots across from the Warren home and then visited Philby’s to select a design for the house. That took them over two hours as they pored over existing designs and made modifications. Joe added a large barn on the southern lot, and by the time they left $1660 poorer, Cassie was excited with the idea of their new home.

Construction would take six weeks, and Joe had totally left the furnishings and everything else to Cassie. He’d added her to the account when they were buying the lots, so she was free to spend whatever she wished to fill the house as she and her mother and sisters saw fit.

While the house and barn were going up, Joe did buy himself a new Winchester and six more boxes of ammunition for him and Cassie. They spent hours shooting their new repeaters just half a mile behind their new house and were able to monitor its progress as they honed their skills.

More important than either the house or the target practice was the time that they were now able to spend together without any emotional or mental barriers. As John Warren had suspected when they were both children, two people could not have been more closely matched than Joe Armstrong and Cassie Warren.

They became closer and even more deeply in love with each minute they spent in each other's company, and their private time together only tightened the grip each had on the other's heart, even though they had amazingly managed to avoid reaching that final act of love.

The house was completed on February 4th, 1881, as colder than normal weather had interrupted construction twice in January and then Cassie, along with the other female members of the sheriff family, including Ellie Sheehy, set about converting the new structure into a home. The two pregnant women, Ellie and Bessie, limited themselves to decorating while the others set up the kitchen and furniture locations.

It was the first house in Warwick with hot and cold running water, and even though it still had a privy out back, they had installed a newfangled water closet in the downstairs bathroom.

Joe had been prohibited from entering the house while it was being furnished and decorated, not that he objected.

There had only been one serious incident involving gunfire since Joe's return and it hadn't involved Joe until the shooting was over.

On New Year's Eve, just after sunset, a set of rowdy ranch hands from the Rocking W decided to have a shooting contest and were firing their pistols at the church's bell across the street. As the gunfire scattered the few nearby citizens, one of the hands, Max Norton, claimed victory when the bell clanged with a ricocheted .44. One of his fellow cowpokes, Johnny Voorhees disagreed, and an argument ensued. An argument between drunk, armed ranch hands, no matter the reason, was never a good thing.

Sheriff Warren and Lou Sanford had been returning to their homes when the gunfire broke out and both had turned and raced to the west side of town as the argument began. Dan was already home with his wife but was quickly preparing to leave.

Joe and Cassie were returning from a walk behind their new house and still chatting when they heard the unexpected gunfire, and Joe raced to the sound.

By the time the sheriff shouted at the boys to drop their weapons, Johnny had already shot Max in the leg and the group quickly realized that things had gotten out of hand.

As the two lawmen reached the scene, the ranch hands were all tending to Max's gunshot and all they could do was direct them to Doc Gillespie's house to get the wound treated. Joe and Dan arrived as Max was being carried by his friends, including the shooter.

No charges were even filed as they all admitted to being overly filled with whiskey.

The house was ready for occupancy on the 12th of February and Joe finally entered his new home holding Cassie's hand just after noon.

"You did a wonderful job, Cassie," he said as he marveled at the new place.

Cassie was all smiles as they walked from room to room receiving Joe's compliments.

When they reached the big bedroom, neither commented on the large bed that took up much of the space as the subject of marriage hadn't been mentioned at all since their new relationship had begun.

Joe was appreciative of the rows of books in the library/office and noted how many were textbooks and was sure that Cassie had ordered them to fill in the gaps in her insatiable quest for knowledge.

They were in the well-appointed kitchen, sitting at the new table when Cassie asked, "Are you going to move in now?"

Joe had hoped that he'd be moving in with Cassie, but her question implied that she wasn't ready yet, so he replied, "Yes, ma'am. I'll move my horses to the barn first."

"The pantry and cold room are all stocked, too."

Joe nodded and smiled at her before he said, "It's a beautiful house, Cassie."

"Yes, it is."

Joe finally asked, "Cassie, that first day I returned, and we had that talk in the sleeping room, I thought you'd gotten past your fear of having a baby, but it's returned, hasn't it?"

"Yes, but it's not nearly as bad as it was before. I think I'll be over it soon."

Joe was more than worried because Bessie was due soon and if anything bad happened to her sister, Cassie would simply be lost again.

"You're waiting for Bessie to have her next baby, aren't you?"

"I don't know, Joe. I really don't."

Joe didn't want to push it anymore, so he just replied, "That's alright, Cassie. I'll always be here for you, no matter what."

She smiled at Joe and put her hand on his as she said, "Thank you, Joe. I do love you so very much."

"I love you, too, Cassie."

After another minute of just eye contact, they stood and left the house. Joe needing to move his horses, tack and his clothes and other personal items from the sleeping room at the jail. He didn't have much in the way of clothing but now, with all the closet space and dresser drawers, he'd be able to buy some more.

They walked back to the Warren house holding hands as they always did now but this time, they walked in silence, each fully aware of the subtle change that had just happened when the marriage/baby blockade resurfaced.

Joe didn't want to admit how anxious he'd been in waiting for Cassie. She was so exciting to him and he'd been in agony almost every time they'd spent private time together. Now he knew he'd have to curtail such advanced levels of fondling as he wasn't sure he'd be able to stop much longer.

Cassie was acutely aware of Joe's discomfort because she had the same problem and had almost succumbed to her own desires on more than one occasion, and surprisingly it had been Joe's concerns for her that had prevented them from reaching the inevitable conclusion. She had loved him even more for that afterwards but knew how much it had affected him. Cassie was angry with herself and her inability to get past her fear.

After kissing Cassie almost chastely and returning to the jail to begin his move, Joe could see no other way out of the dilemma other than to keep his hands off of Cassie until she was ready to marry him. He kept telling himself that she was still only seventeen, but her personality and mind were so much older than that, it didn't seem to matter how old her body was.

———

That afternoon after helping Joe with moving the horses, tack to the new house, Sheriff Warren, Dan and Lou joined Joe for the first coffee made on his new cookstove.

"Now that you've got the house, when are you and Cassie going to get married," Dan asked after taking his first sip.

"We haven't decided yet," Joe replied.

"You'd better make it soon or Bessie will be having our third before you and Cassie have your first," Lou said with a grin.

Joe just smiled back and took a long drink of coffee so he didn't have to say anything.

"They did a great job on the house, Joe," Sheriff Warren said.

Joe nodded and said, "I think it's perfect."

"I like your gun room, too," Dan said.

"Believe it or not, that was Cassie's idea. Between the two of us, we have seven Winchesters and eight pistols."

Dan laughed and said, "You two have the sheriff's office outgunned."

Joe nodded and took another sip of coffee.

"Minnie is planning on having a new house party tomorrow, so that'll be our lunch," John said.

"Cassie mentioned it."

John wanted to ask more personal questions, but not in front of Dan and Lou, so he held them in abeyance as the conversation slipped back to work-related things, and one of them caused a major upheaval in Joe and Cassie's plans, as tenuous as they were.

Dan Sheehy made an innocent comment that kicked over the pebble that would soon grow into an avalanche.

"I just got this story yesterday. Did any of you hear about that town marshal down in Mesquite Creek who shot his own mayor?"

Sheriff Warren asked, "Mesquite Creek has a marshal?"

"Yes, sir. For a while, I guess. Anyway, the story I got from this kitchenware drummer who came from there was that this marshal was out doing his night rounds and saw someone running behind the general store, pulls his Colt and chases after the shadow. According to the drummer, the marshal shouted a warning and the man didn't stop. He fired and killed the man only to find out he was the mayor and owner of the general store. The drummer said that the townsfolk suspected that the marshal just wanted to have his way with the mayor's wife, but nobody could prove anything."

"I hadn't heard about that. When did that happen?" Lou asked.

Dan replied, "About a month or so ago, I think."

Sheriff Warren said, “It’s out of our jurisdiction anyway. Do you recall that marshal’s name?”

“Um…Alex Carson…no that’s not right. It was really short and began with a ‘C’.”

The other three lawmen began bouncing one-syllable names beginning with that letter off of Dan, and there weren’t many: Cox, Cook, Cord.

“Clay?” Lou asked, and Dan smacked the table, saying, “That’s it. Alex Clay.”

Joe sat back and looked at his new ceiling. *What was there about that name that sounded so familiar?* He’d never been to that town, so he knew he’d never heard the name before.

The other three men were still talking about the story as Joe tried to think why it would tickle his memory. *What was it?* He even forgot about the Cassie dilemma as he tried to solve the riddle of the marshal’s name.

John was the first to notice Joe’s distracted silence and asked, “Joe, what’s wrong?”

Joe didn’t turn to look at the sheriff but replied, “It’s that name. It’s banging around in my head like a wild ricochet that won’t stop, and I don’t know why.”

“Alex Clay? I’ve never heard it before, maybe it was while you were at the reformatory,” John suggested.

Joe thought about it for a few seconds but that didn’t seem to fit any of the boys.

Then Lou said, “It’s one of those good names that has two first names put together.”

Joe suddenly had his connection and his eyes quickly snapped back to the other lawmen.

"I know why that name was bothering me."

John asked, "Well, are you going to tell us?"

"I think the marshal is Buck Hogan."

Dan asked quickly, "What gave you that idea?"

"When I was growing up believing I was a Hogan brother, I never noticed how different I was from the other brothers, but one of the things that reinforced that belief that I was a Hogan was my name. They called me Joey."

"And what is the significance of that?" Lou asked.

"Their father named each one in them in succession with a four-letter name following the alphabet. They used to joke about his plan to have twenty-six boys. He had names for each one all the way to Zeke. Buck was the oldest. The second brother died when he was just a few months old. Then there was Drew, then Earl, Fred, Glen, Hank and I was called Joey. I assumed that Izzy had died."

Dan said, "I still don't understand what that has to do with the marshal."

"Their father's name was Alex, and the boy who died was Clay."

John asked slowly, "You don't believe that it's a coincidence?"

"It could be. But remember a few years ago when his gang was killed to a man by the Texas Rangers when they tried to rob a bank, but Buck escaped. He then ambushed two of the Rangers who chased after him. He took their horses, guns and their badges. The Rangers were mighty upset about what he did and spent a long time looking for him, but he'd just disappeared. Texas is one mighty big place to try and find one man. If he had those badges, he could go to some small, out-of-the-way town and just become the law."

John said, "There's only one way to find out."

"I have to go down to Mesquite Creek."

"Joe, we can just wire the Texas Rangers to go in there and check him out. They want him as badly as you do."

"Boss, I'm the only one who can recognize him. Remember Captain Raskin when we were in Austin? He wanted me to join the Rangers because no one else could pick him out. I need to do this."

John sighed, but nodded and said, "You'll take Dan with you, or Cassie will never forgive me."

"Thanks, boss. We'll head out tomorrow."

"No, you'll leave the day after tomorrow. I'm not going to be made the focus of my wife's ire for letting you spoil her little party tomorrow."

Joe smiled and said, "Yes, sir."

"Alright. That's settled. Let's let Joe figure out how to deal with the marshal. Even if he's not Buck Hogan, it'll be interesting to hear the true story of why he shot the mayor."

After another couple of minutes discussing the likelihood of Joe finding the last Hogan, the four lawmen disbanded leaving Joe alone in his new house.

He was beginning to make himself his supper when he wasn't surprised to hear the front door swing open and slam shut followed by hurried footsteps down the hallway.

He didn't turn around but said, "Hello, Cassie."

Cassie stopped, put her hands on her hips and said, "My father told me you are going after Buck Hogan."

"Yes, ma'am. He may not be him, but I'm pretty sure he is."

"I thought you were going to stay with me and give that up."

Joe finally turned to face her and said, "Cassie, this isn't the same thing. I'm not going on an extended search. I'm riding with Dan down to Mesquite Creek about a day's ride away. If the marshal is Buck Hogan, he won't even know me. I'll have the advantage and Dan will be with me."

"But you could get killed!" she exclaimed.

Joe stepped closer to Cassie, took her hand and they took seats at the table.

"Cassie, each day we wake in the morning could be the last day of our lives. We could get killed by walking across the street or get bitten by a rattlesnake or struck by lightning. There is risk in almost everything we do. Yes, I know there's risk in going down there, but it's actually a much lower risk than what I've been doing for the past two years. I should have died in that solitary cell in the reformatory, or when I took the derringer shot in my back, but I didn't.

"Right now, Bessie is taking a risk to have her second baby, so is Ellie Sheehy. You worry about having a baby because you might die. I don't deny that it's risky having a baby, but the rewards are enormous. What rewards will I get for risking my life to go after criminals? Sometimes there are monetary rewards, but no amount of money can match the reward you would have when you feel your baby growing inside you.

"In a few days, I'll be facing my own risks but I'm only thinking about the rewards I'll receive when I come back and see your face again."

Cassie softly replied, "I'm sorry, Joe. I'm being selfish, aren't I?"

"What I believe isn't important, Cassie. It's only what you believe."

Cassie nodded and after a short pause, surprised Joe when she asked, "Can I stay here in our home tonight?"

Joe asked, "Are you sure, Cassie?"

"Yes," she answered quietly.

———

Joe had been planning on sleeping in the bedroom next to the large bedroom, but that night, after all of the lights were out, he slid under the new quilts of the big bed before Cassie slid in beside him in her nightdress.

She curled in beside Joe and he put his arm around her, feeling her softness.

"Why did you make this decision, Cassie?" he asked quietly.

"Because I'm afraid you might not come back, Joe. I know that the odds are much better this time but now, it seemed so much more important. I wanted to be with you."

He kissed her on the forehead, but just enjoyed the closeness that they shared, which astonished him. He didn't know why he wasn't pawing at Cassie as he had expected to be, but he just had an overwhelming feeling of concern for her.

Cassie was waiting for something to happen, but just as Joe did, she felt the almost oneness of just being with him as she was pressed closely against him.

After almost twenty minutes of silent, warm thoughts, Cassie was the first to drift off to sleep and once Joe heard her rhythmic breaths, he kissed her again and let himself fall asleep.

No comments were made in the Warren household when Cassie returned in the morning and she doubted if her parents would have believed that nothing had happened anyway. When she had awakened in Joe's arms. She had kissed him on the lips and then slipped out from the bed left the room while he slept. She'd used the new water closet and as she was leaving the bathroom, Joe had passed her to use the facilities. He had kissed her quickly before entering the small room and she'd returned to the bedroom to dress.

That night that they'd shared without any of the tension that having sex might have produced meant more to each of them if they'd consummated their relationship. Cassie was now determined not to let Joe leave without giving herself to him, but her plans were soon to be interrupted.

Shortly after the home opening party, Ellie Sheehy went into labor at around three o'clock in the afternoon. Mrs. Warren notified Mrs. Williams, the midwife and Cassie offered to help as Bessie was just another month away herself.

The sheriff and Joe were in the sheriff's office with Michel as Dan paced in his main room with his friend, Lou waiting with him.

"Boss, I'll go down there by myself," Joe said as he leaned the straight-backed chair on its back legs.

"Joe, you can wait until after the baby is born and Lou can go with you."

"Bessie's too close, boss. I'll be fine. I have all of the advantages."

"And what about Cassie, Joe? What if she's pregnant?"

"She can't be pregnant. We haven't done anything that could cause that condition."

"You're kidding! She spent the night there last night, didn't she?"

"In our big bed, but we just held each other before we fell asleep."

If anyone other than Joe had told him, he wouldn't have believed it but said, "I'll never understand Cassie as well as you do, Joe. Is there some reason for the delay in getting married?"

Joe thought he may as well tell him as Bessie seemed to know anyway.

"Cassie is afraid of having a baby. It's that simple, but it's really complex, too. Everything about Cassie is complex, which is one of the reasons I love her so much. Your daughter will never be boring."

"She never has been. What time are you leaving?"

"Tomorrow morning. I'm all packed and should be able to get there before sundown."

"Okay, Joe. I don't have to tell you how careful you need to be with him. Buck was always the worst of the bunch."

"I know. It might not be him after all."

John nodded but didn't believe it. He was sure that Joe was right.

Ellie Sheehy gave birth to a little girl at a little past three the next morning, and Cassie visited the new mother and her daughter just ten minutes after Dan had. Despite the long labor, she was greeted by a beaming Ellie and her fear was again pushed aside.

As she left the room, she wondered how long before it returned, and prayed it never would. She wanted to marry Joe and make him as happy as he made her.

Joe rode out of Warwick heading southwest before dawn, wanting to get to Mesquite Creek before the sun was down.

Cassie had planned on going to see him before he could leave but hadn't risen until Joe was already fifteen miles out of town.

Once she realized he was gone, she began moving her things into the big bedroom in the new house.

———

As he kept the gelding moving at a medium trot toward Mesquite Creek, Joe had a lot on his mind. Cassie was always first but now, he had Buck Hogan to think about.

Buck was going to be harder than the others because he was all too aware that Buck, for whatever reason, was why he was still alive. All of the Hogans had acted friendly and maliciously to him at times, and Buck was no exception. But Buck was always considered the leader of the brothers and was the meanest and cruelest.

Joe hadn't seen him in more than six years now and doubted if he'd changed at all. If he was the marshal of the town, he'd probably murdered the mayor rather than just having shot him by mistake because Buck found it so easy to kill.

The miles passed faster than he expected as he let the horse move while he tried to come up with strategy to deal with Buck. First, he had to think of what Buck would do and discovered that he had no idea. Buck had always been a planner, and Joe hadn't seen how he reacted when those plans went awry except for the one job he'd been on.

In this case, Buck wouldn't have any plans, he'd be reacting to whatever Joe did and that was what was making this harder.

The small town of Mesquite Creek showed up sooner than Joe had expected. Either he'd underestimated the distance or ridden faster than he thought but whatever the reason, he spotted the settlement just after three o'clock in the afternoon and slowed his gelding as he approached.

It wasn't as small as he anticipated, either. He'd seen smaller towns in his long search throughout Texas, and guessed it had something to do with the potash deposits that were in the area.

He had his Colt around his waist under his coat and in his pocket, he carried a .31 caliber Remington Model 1858 Army with all six chambers loaded and with fresh percussion caps on the nipples.

In his left pocket he had a broken, cheap hair comb that Cassie had given him with the old Remington when they set up the new house. Having the items with him when he met Buck Hogan was important to him.

His hand was in his left jacket pocket, feeling the hair comb to build his resolve if he confronted the last Hogan. He tried to remember all of Drew Hogan's vitriolic harangues about his mother, too. He wanted to hate Buck Hogan as much as possible when he entered Mesquite Creek.

Joe turned his horse onto the town's only street and didn't take long to spot the town marshal's office. It was nicer than he'd expected in such a small town, but it didn't matter as he headed for the jail and pulled up.

He dismounted and after tying off his horse, moved his badge to the outside of his coat. He knew the town was out of his jurisdiction, but it still had some positive effects that might make the difference.

Joe took in a deep breath, opened the door and was disappointed when he saw the man behind the desk. It wasn't Buck Hogan.

"Can I help you, Deputy?" the man asked.

"I was just heading down to Preston and heard this story back at the office and figured I'd stop by and get the particulars."

The man laughed and said, "I can tell you what I heard, but you'll be wantin' to talk to Marshal Clay when he gets back."

Joe was relieved that he hadn't made the long ride for nothing and asked, "When do you expect him back?"

The man snickered and said, "Knowin' our marshal, I'm guessin' about another twenty minutes or so. He's busy talkin' with the widow Johnson if you know what I mean."

Joe had a good idea, so he asked, "Mind if I wait?"

"Nope. In fact, if you're gonna stay, I'll head on back to the shop. Just tell him when he gets here that Fred found his missin' horse."

"I'll tell him. Are you Fred?"

"Yup. Fred Winters."

Fred then grabbed his hat and was whistling as he left the office.

Joe then took off his own hat and set it on the desk before sitting behind the desk and scanning the office. It didn't have any cells, but there was a small room that the marshal probably used. He then put the hair comb under the hat and leaned back in the chair to wait.

He wondered, if the marshal really was Buck, why he stayed here. It had been more than four years since the Rangers had killed off his gang and he'd made his escape. If it hadn't been for the story about killing the mayor, he might have believed that Buck was trying to go straight.

Joe waited for more than half an hour and the sun was getting low in the sky as he began to wonder if the marshal was going to return at all.

Five minutes later, he heard heavy footsteps just outside the door, and when it swung open, Buck Hogan walked through the doorway, saw Joe, and closed the door.

"Who are you?" he asked as he hung his hat on a wall peg.

Joe realized his coat had flipped open, so he closed it and showed Buck the badge before replying, "Deputy Dan Sheehy from Warwick. I was just passing through and figured I'd stop by."

Buck looked at him for a few seconds and took off his hat.

"Fred said to tell you he found his horse."

"Okay. Now why'd you stop by?"

Joe supposed he should make small talk to put Buck at ease, but he couldn't do it.

He slipped his right hand into his pocket and gripped the old Remington as he slowly lifted his hat from the desk with his left hand and set it aside.

“This is why I stopped by.”

Buck looked at the hair comb and then at Joe before he asked, “What the hell is that? It looks like something women stick in their hair.”

“It is. It’s an old hair comb that a friend of mine found when we were searching the ruins of an abandoned farmhouse about four miles east of Lickville.”

“Lickville?” Buck asked. The town meant nothing to him.

“Yes, Lickville. It had been owned by a young woman who lived there with her sister. She had a two-year-old son with her. They were kidnapped by a bunch of brothers and repeatedly raped until one committed suicide when she got pregnant and the second woman, the one who owned this hair comb, died in childbirth a year later.”

Buck swallowed but still hadn’t made the connection between that skinny thirteen-year-old boy and the rugged man sitting at his desk.

“So? What’s that got to do with me?”

Joe tightened his grip on the Remington and said in a low voice, “Because, Buck, that woman was my mother.”

Buck’s eyes bulged as he stared at Joe and asked, “Joey?”

Joe pulled the Remington from his pocket and cocked the hammer.

“The name is Joe. Joe Armstrong. That was my mother’s name, or don’t you remember?”

Buck may have been shocked, but he wasn't panicked as his mind raced to gain time and an advantage.

"Joey, you gotta remember that I was the only reason those other boys didn't throw you down that well, and I never took your mother, either. Not once. I didn't have to, see. I had a girl down in Hinkley that kept me satisfied."

"You didn't stop them, though, did you?" Joe asked as he stood.

"How could I? They weren't gonna listen to me, not when it came to women. You got a woman, Joe?"

"Yes, and I hear that you shot the mayor to get his wife."

"That's a damned lie. I shot the bastard 'cause he was beatin' her. You can even ask her. Her name is Millie and she's a good woman. Come on, and I'll prove it to you."

If there was one argument that Buck could have used to throw Joe off in his desire to find retribution for his mother, Buck had chanced on it, and he could see it in Joe's eyes.

Joe almost let him turn to leave, so he could prove that he'd helped the woman, but then he almost smacked himself in the head. This was Buck Hogan he was talking to, not some considerate defender of women. He recalled all of the stories he'd heard, from the McPherson farm massacre to the murders of all of the people in that bank where his gang had been wiped out. Buck Hogan was the worst kind of man.

Buck saw Joe's fire return and he knew his argument had gone flat, so he glared at Joe and said, "You think that popgun is going to do any good, Joey? You couldn't even shoot a damned coyote with that thing. You think you can shoot me, face to face?"

Joe stared back at Buck and said, “I killed Glen and Earl, then Fred and Hank face to face, why shouldn’t I be able to kill you?”

Buck felt his rage boil inside him as he said, “You killed my brothers, you bastard?”

“Every last one of them, Buck. Now undo your gunbelt buckle and let it drop.”

“You think I’m stupid enough to let you take me back to get me hanged?”

“Either that or risk getting a bullet through your chest, Buck. But that’s all life is, isn’t it? Risk?”

Buck had already made his decision and was bracing for being hit by Joe’s shot. Knowing it was a smaller caliber pistol, and if he moved just enough, he’d be able to get his Colt drawn and fired before Joe could bring his sights back in line.

Joe could see Buck thinking and knew that he was going to make his move soon and suddenly regretted having the old Remington in his hand. So, he suddenly switched it to his left hand and was reaching for his Colt when Buck dropped and leapt to his right.

Joe fired with the old Remington and the .31 caliber bullet ripped down the barrel, crossed the eight feet and whistled past Buck who was yanking his Colt out as the Remington’s slug punched through the jail’s eastern wall.

Joe knew he’d missed as he brought his Colt free of his coat and cocked both pistols’ hammers at the same time while Buck was bringing his Colt level and cocking his hammer.

Joe fired both pistols at the same time that Buck fired, filling the small office with loud echoes and smoke as two bullets raced east, and one went west.

Joe felt the Buck's .44 slam into his coat and somehow didn't hit his chest as he was turning to get away from Buck's muzzle.

Joe's .44 missed high, but the smaller .31 penetrated Buck's left eye and drilled into his brain killing him almost instantly.

Joe had cocked both hammers again but soon realized they weren't necessary as he stood and looked at Buck's face. The bullet hadn't exited the back of his skull, so he knew it was the .31 caliber from the Remington that had killed him.

Then he looked to find out why his chest hadn't been hit. He'd felt the punch of Buck's .44, but when he looked at his jacket, he saw that his deputy sheriff's badge had a long, deep gouge across the face, and the badge itself was bent in half and almost split in two. He must have been turning when the bullet struck, at least enough to change the bullet's path.

Joe then picked up his mother's hair comb, slid it into his coat pocket and said quietly, "Mama, if you're looking down at me now, tell me I did the right thing. It seemed so simple when I was just a boy and on my way to the reformatory, but now that they're all dead at my hand, I need to know that you are at peace now. It's the only thing that would make this all right."

There was no reply from his mother, so he exhaled and walked past Buck's body and stepped out onto the boardwalk. There were a few townsfolk across the street looking at him, so he waved.

"I'm Deputy Sheriff Joe Armstrong. The man you believed to be Alex Clay was really Buck Hogan, a notorious murderer. Could I speak to someone in charge?"

Three of the men crossed the street, including Fred Winters, the man who'd found his horse.

When they reached him, Joe explained what had happened and not surprisingly, they seemed to be relieved that their marshal was no longer alive.

They removed Buck's body, and Joe said he'd stay the night before leaving tomorrow.

He sent a telegram to his boss and then a second to Cassie. Then when he left his horse at the one livery in town, he found Buck's horse and the saddle with the 'B' carved in the saddle horn.

After dinner, before he went to his room, Joe returned to the marshal's office and went through his desk drawers, looking for something and finding them in the bottom right drawer. He took out the two Rangers badges and slipped them into his left pocket with his mother's hair comb.

A little past eight o'clock, Sheriff Warren walked to Joe's new house and knocked on the door.

Cassie trotted to the door and swung it wide, knowing it had to be her father with news about Joe.

"Is he all right?" she asked hurriedly before her father could even greet her.

He held up the telegrams as he stepped inside and said, "He's fine. He'll be home tomorrow night."

She didn't ask another question as she ripped the two sheets from his hand and as he stood by, she read the one to her father first.

SHERIFF JOHN WARREN WARWICK TEXAS

BUCK HOGAN DEAD
WILL RETURN TOMORROW

DEPUTY JOE ARMSTRONG MESQUITE CREEK TEXAS

She quickly flipped to her telegram and read:

CASSIE WARREN WARWICK TEXAS

I LOVE YOU

DEPUTY JOE ARMSTRONG MESQUITE CREEK TEXAS

Cassie looked at her father with a smile and tears in her eyes as she said, "I guess he didn't want to spend too much money on telegrams."

"I guess not."

"Papa, can you tell Mama that we're going to be married on March 11th?"

John nodded and hugged his daughter and kissed her on her forehead before saying, "It's about time."

She smiled as tears continued to slide across her face and said, “No. It’s the right time.”

Her father smiled at Cassie, turned and left the house, hearing the door close behind him before Cassie began to dance across the floor, as required.

———

Joe had heard the full story of the mayor’s demise from Mrs. Johnson, his widow. Of course, she was never even admonished by her husband, much less beaten, and was grateful that the marshal was dead.

He left town after breakfast leading Buck’s horse and saddle. He kept a fast pace and with two horses, was able to swap off, so he expected to arrive before four o’clock.

———

Cassie was bouncing all over the new house in preparation of Joe’s return. She wanted everything to be perfect, including herself. She’d taken two baths, shampooed her hair and brushed it until it was almost too shiny.

It was almost four o’clock and she was running out of things to do as she kept glancing out of the southern window hoping to see Joe ride into town.

But Joe was coming from the southwest, so when he did ride into Warwick a little past four o’clock, he rode straight to the sheriff’s office, pulled up in front and dismounted.

He stepped through the door and found Lou and the sheriff in conversation at the front desk. They stopped talking and looked at him.

"Welcome back, Joe," Sheriff Warren said, "How bad was it?"

Joe didn't reply but walked to the desk and tossed his badge onto the surface.

The sheriff picked up the mauled piece of steel and whistled before he asked, "Was that a .44 that did that?"

"Yes, sir. I knew I'd been hit, but it didn't even penetrate my coat. I do have a nice black and blue mark on my chest, though."

"You can tell us all about it tomorrow," John said as he handed the badge back to Joe.

"I've got Buck's horse and saddle outside."

"Take them back to your new barn for the night."

"Okay."

Joe then turned to leave and as he was opening the door, the sheriff said, "Oh, and happy birthday."

Joe looked at him curiously and replied, "Thanks," before walking outside and mounting his gelding wondering what John had meant.

He walked his horse and the Buck's trailing gelding down the street and headed for his new barn.

Cassie saw him coming and felt giddy as she readied for his imminent entry into their home, so she could tell him of her decision to finally put all of her fear behind her. This time, she swore that it wouldn't return and there was only one way to make sure that it didn't.

Joe unsaddled both animals and put their tack on the long shelves he'd had built into the walls. He took a few more minutes to brush them down and as he was working, he wondered if he should wait until tomorrow to go and see Cassie. He wanted to get cleaned up after the long ride, but he really wanted to see her.

After he left the barn, he noticed that there was smoke coming out of the cookstove pipe and he knew who was cooking. It had to be Cassie. How he'd missed the smoke on the way past the house didn't matter as he jogged across the yard, bounced onto the porch and without knocking, threw open the back door.

Joe and Cassie then looked into each other's eyes as Joe kicked the door closed behind him.

"I'm back," he said quietly as he took off his hat and tried to hang it on a peg near the door but missed letting the Stetson bounce off the lacquered floor.

"I got your telegram," Cassie replied barely above a whisper.

Joe removed his jacket and let it drop to the floor, making a big clunk as the old Remington struck the wood.

"I missed you, Cassie," he said as he unbuckled his Colt and lowered it onto his jacket and stepped out of the pile toward her.

Cassie took one step closer to Joe and took his hands in hers and said, "I told my father that we'll be married on March 11th. Is that alright?"

"That's what he meant when he said, 'happy birthday' as I was leaving the jail, and I had no idea what he meant."

"But is that alright? You know, for getting married?

Joe stepped closer and asked, "Do you want this, Cassie?"

Cassie didn't answer but turned kept his hand tightly in hers and led him down the hallway to the big bedroom.

Once inside she began unbuttoning his shirt and drew it apart and began to kiss his chest before looking up at him and saying, "Make love to me, Joe. Now. Please?"

Joe wanted her in the worst way but needed more confirmation and he asked, "Are you sure, Cassie?"

Cassie put her arms around his neck and whispered, "Yes, Joe. It's my dream."

———

March 11, 1881

The wedding was held in the Warren home and attended by the entire family, including the Sheehy family and the Sanborns.

Joe's witness was, of course, John Warren, the bride's father, so he was standing alone as he waited for Cassie to be led into the room by his best man. Cassie's witness was her ready-to-deliver sister, Bessie, who was sitting as she waited for the bride.

When John walked in with Cassie on his arm, Joe smiled. She wasn't wearing a bridal dress or even a gown, Cassie was wearing a riding skirt and blouse, but at least she wasn't wearing her Remington on her waist.

What she was wearing that surprised Joe was a cheap hair comb that no one could tell was broken because the tines were hidden by her long brown hair. Others may have wondered why she wore it at all, but Joe knew.

That first night that they'd been together, and Cassie's fears were finally erased, Joe had told her about what he'd said to his mother in that marshal's office in Mesquite Creek. He had said he wished there was some way he could have known if his mother was at peace for what her son had done.

Cassie was now giving him that confirmation. She had put her fears behind her with the act of love they had shared, and now she wanted him to put those concerns he had about what he had done behind him.

The new life that they were starting together today would have no regrets. Neither of them could predict what problems may arise in their future, but as Cassie took Joe's hand to begin the ceremony, each of them knew that no matter what the risks, the rewards would be extraordinary.

———

Two days after the wedding, Captain Bull Raskin received a package from Warwick. When he opened it, he found two Rangers badges and a short note from Deputy Sheriff Joe Armstrong.

I have brought retribution for your fellow Rangers.

The captain nodded and smiled as he set the badges on his desk.

———

Joe's other badge, the one that was bent in half from Buck Hogan's shot, was pinned to the wall in the sheriff's office and never failed to awe anyone who saw it and didn't know the story.

Bessie had her second child, another girl just three days after Joe and Cassie were married and named her Amelia Jane.

Cassie thought she'd get pregnant right away and was surprised that she hoped she would. She had gone from being terrified about having a baby to wanting one more than she could have imagined. But even as the summer passed, she hadn't missed a monthly.

It surely wasn't for lack of trying, either. For a young couple who had managed to spend their first night together in bed without so much as a real kiss, they made up for their lost opportunities and after the first three months, Cassie ordered new, heavier drapes for the parlor because her husband chased her out into the front rooms too often in an undressed condition. Of course, more often than not, she was the one who had started the race.

When Bessie announced another pregnancy in September, Cassie began to wonder if all of those wishes she'd made about not having a baby were coming back to haunt her somehow. Even Joe was concerned, not about her failure to become pregnant, but because Cassie was worried about it so much.

When Ellie Sheehy became pregnant again in October, Cassie dropped into an extended depression, and Joe noticed that much of the joy had gone from their lovemaking as it now became almost an obsessive desire to give her a baby and not just the pleasure that they had enjoyed in making each other happy.

She spent a lot of time at Bessie's with her children, which was a blessing to her sister, but only seemed to increase her anxiety.

Joe had talked to John a few times about Cassie and neither could come up with an answer that might help her. It wasn't even about helping her to conceive, but to return her to her normal, happy self.

As October turned into November, Joe finally decided that he'd take the coward's way out and lie to her.

They had just returned from the Warren home where the family celebrated Cassie's eighteenth birthday. She had been given presents by everyone except her husband, but it didn't matter to her as she still considered his return on her seventeenth birthday to be the best gift she had ever received.

When they left the Warrens and Joe was carrying her gifts across the street to their own home, he said, "I didn't forget to get you something for your birthday, Cassie."

"I never need a gift from you, Joe. You are my greatest gift."

"That may be, but still, I arranged for your gift while we were at your parents' house."

Despite her denial about never needing a gift from Joe, she imagined that whatever he gave her would be special and smiled at him as they stepped onto their front porch.

She opened the door and Joe had her wait in the parlor while he retrieved her birthday presents.

Two minutes later he returned with empty hands which surprised her as she had expected him to have an armload of gifts.

Cassie looked at him with the old Cassie sparkle in her eyes as she smiled and asked, “Well, husband?”

Joe stepped over to his wife, took her hand and led her past their big bedroom to the next bedroom and swung the door open.

Cassie looked inside and saw a crib, bassinet, and other baby-related furniture. She turned to Joe almost in tears at his cruelty for mocking her inability to conceive.

“How could you do this to me, Joe? This breaks my heart.”

Joe put his arm around her and said, “Cassie, we needed this because, after tonight, you’ll be carrying our baby. I wanted us to be ready and every day that you come into this room, you’ll know how much I love you and we’ll both love our little girl.”

She looked up at him and asked, “You even know it’s going to be a girl?”

“Yes. Come with me into the room and I’ll show you why.”

She was still holding his hand as he walked into the room and turned, so she could see the wall facing the hallway.

On the wall was a frame and under a pane of glass was a faded letter, the page already in four quarters as its seams had been folded and unfolded countless times by the reader.

Cassie smiled as she read:

Dear Joe,

I know that you can read this by now. You are a lot smarter than you think you are, or I wouldn't want you for a boyfriend.

I still have my pigtails and freckles, but it's only been a few months since you saw me last. I had my eleventh birthday on November 7th. I wish I could have sent you some of my mother's pie that she baked for me, but the best I could do was to send you these cookies that I baked myself. I'll bet you are surprised that I can bake cookies.

My father told me that you thought I was crazy. I can understand that. Sometimes I wonder myself. One of these times, I'll explain why I told you what I did.

Have a good Christmas and write me a letter when you can.

Cassie

"That was the first letter I ever wrote to you," she whispered.

"Yes, my love. It saw me through some terrible times and whenever I thought I might not make it, I read it and thought of that freckle-faced, pigtailed little girl who had written it. That's why I know that the girl who sent it to me will give us a pretty little girl who will someday be the salvation of some wayward boy like me."

Cassie turned to her husband, smiled and said, "Make love to me, Joe. Give me my little girl."

Joe didn't take Cassie to the big bedroom but there in the room beside the new crib, basinet and under the letter that meant so much to him, Joe Armstrong made love to his wife, Cassie Armstrong.

Cassie was so pleased that she would be having their baby that she just relaxed and let herself enjoy the moment more than she had even done those first few times. She let Joe make her feel whole and complete as he did everything that he could to make her happy.

They carried on for more than an hour as Cassie forgot everything but Joe. They rested for an hour and soon, they began again. It was her birthday, and she wanted this gift with all its trimmings.

Joe made sure that he pleasured Cassie as often as possible as he worried about his promise. He'd been told by Dan Sheehy that Ellie had been slow to conceive and that he thought getting her to relax helped. Joe wasn't sure, but he was hoping it would work.

It was a frightening two weeks for Joe as that time approached and Cassie was always on time. On November 25th, a buoyant Cassie greeted Joe when he returned home. She didn't say anything, but he knew why she was so joyful. But it was only one day.

She was just as happy the next day, which was a Saturday, and continued her almost effervescent mood on Sunday. Each day that followed, she seemed to grow even happier and Joe was beginning to hope that she was indeed with child.

When the whole week had passed, and Cassie still hadn't had her monthly, she was ecstatic, and Joe tried to be happy for her, but he needed to be sure.

Cassie didn't have to wait until Christmas to be sure, as she joyously announced to Joe on December 16th that she'd thrown up that morning, which struck him as an odd thing to make her happy until she explained it was morning sickness.

She was happily nauseous right until the holidays, and after missing her second monthly, happily announced her pregnancy to her family at Christmas dinner.

Her morning sickness ended in early January, and she was happy to see it go.

By April, her belly was beginning to show noticeably, and the joys of pregnancy began to fade as her stomach grew. She continued to expand and was glad to have her mother across the street to help her as she approached her seventh month.

Bessie had her third baby, and miracle of miracles, it was a boy this time. They named him Louis John.

Ellie had her next baby, also a boy in July, and that left Cassie as the only wife of a lawman who was still heavy with child.

In early afternoon on the 7th of August, exactly nine months after her eighteenth birthday, Cassie went into labor.

Her birthing room was the same room that Joe had converted into a nursery and where the baby was probably conceived.

Long after sunset, the house was echoing with the sounds of Cassie's cries of pain and effort as she progressed through a long labor. Her mother and Mrs. Williams were with her, switching off to give one of them rest as the evening turned to night.

Joe was in the kitchen with John, drinking his ninth cup of coffee, staring into the almost empty cup wishing he hadn't done this to his wife. Her long-term fears of dying in childbirth were coming back to haunt him.

Suddenly, he heard a loud cry of pain from Cassie followed by her scream of, "Joe!"

Joe dropped the cup, spilling its dregs across the table, raced out of the kitchen, down the hallway, and pushed open the door to the birthing room, not abiding by the strict rule prohibiting men from entry. He had to be with Cassie.

He didn't pay any attention to Mrs. Miller's order to leave the room, or to Cassie's straddled position as he trotted around Mrs. Miller and took a knee at Cassie's head.

Her hair was all matted down from sweat as her entire body was damp and still perspiring as he pulled her hand from where she'd been gripping the mattress, held it tightly and looked into those pained brown eyes.

Cassie was bearing down and grunting as he said, "Cassie, I'm here!"

She had to wait until the contraction slowed before she turned to him and said in a weak voice, "It hurts so badly, Joe."

"I'm so sorry, Cassie," he said as tears began to slide from his eyes.

"No, don't, I…" she replied before another contraction made her grimace and push, her grip almost crushing his big hand.

Joe just watched her face contort in agony and wished he could do something for her, but knew he had no way to alleviate even a tiny part of her pain and what made it worse was knowing he was the cause of her suffering.

When she finished with the last contraction, Mrs. Miller shouted for her to push again, and Cassie's face again twisted into that horrible, painful expression that was tearing Joe's heart apart.

In the brief gap between her quickening contractions, Cassie looked at her agonizing husband and whispered, "I'm happy, Joe."

Joe was weeping as he leaned over, kissed his wife on her forehead, and said, "I love you, Cassie," just before another contraction made her cry out in pain and Minnie finally was able to pull Joe away from Cassie and guide him out of the room, closing the door behind him as he stood in the hallway, knowing that Cassie's last words would be, 'I'm happy, Joe'.

He walked catatonically out to the kitchen and took a seat at the table, not seeing anything.

He thought about Cassie's fear for almost all of her life about having a baby and how that fear had found a home in his heart as he heard her cries of pain. All that talk about risk and reward meant nothing as his only concern was for his wife.

The stressful sounds continued for another forty minutes as Joe just sat staring into nothing. He almost didn't notice when Cassie's voice suddenly went silent and then just seconds later, there was a new voice, a shrill crying voice of a new human being's sudden arrival in the cold world.

When the baby's wailing finally penetrated Joe's nothing world, he blinked and looked at John, but still didn't say anything. *He had a child, but at what cost? Had he lost Cassie?*

The baby stopped crying and all that Joe heard were thumps and rustling from the birthing room that he had set up for their baby.

After another ten minutes of almost unbearable worry, Joe heard footsteps and looked to see Minnie walking out of the hallway entrance, her face split by an enormous smile.

"Joe, you have a daughter and Cassie is fine."

Joe's heart exploded in relief and joy as he popped from the chair, John shook his hand and said something that Joe didn't hear and he quickly followed his mother-in-law down the hallway and turned into the bedroom.

He turned to look at his wife as she lay on the bed under a single, dry sheet, her face still damp, but no longer in pain as she practically glowed in rapturous joy and their baby girl lay in swaddling in her arms.

Joe sat down in the chair that had been placed near her head and his fingertips barely touched her cheek as he asked, "Are you all right, Cassie?"

Cassie was already smiling when he entered and replied, "I've never been happier, Joe. Look at our daughter. Isn't she the most beautiful baby you've ever seen?"

Joe gazed at his daughter for the first time and even though he knew he was biased, agreed with his wife and said, "She had to be, my love, she has you for a mother."

Cassie looked at the tiny face and said, "I never thought my dream could be so simple, but here she is."

Joe leaned over and kissed Cassie on the forehead and passed Minnie and Mrs. Williams before returning to the kitchen to talk to John.

It was almost three o'clock in the morning when Joe finally crawled into bed and as he pulled the blankets up to his chin, he thought about the women he'd met that were mothers; Mrs. Warren, Bessie, Dan's Ellie, the woman who'd died trying to save Michael and now, his Cassie.

At that moment he understood that his mother wouldn't smile if he said, "Mama, I killed those men who hurt you."

He was sure that she was looking down at him with a rapturously joyous face as he whispered, "Mama, you have a granddaughter."

EPILOGUE

Joe and Cassie did her parents one better when little Agnes Lydia was followed by three more daughters, the last, Jolene Charlotte, born on May 17, 1887. Joe loved all of his girls, but there was always a special place in his heart for Aggie.

Bessie, had four more children, finishing with four girls and two boys, while Mary had what amounted to a herd of children consisting of six girls and three boys.

On the night of October 7, 1883, Deputy Dan Sheehy was trying to break up a bar fight at the Lone Texan Saloon and the bartender's scattergun went off accidentally, killing him and one of the other men. His death hit his longtime friend Lou Sanborn especially hard.

His widow initially received financial support from the community, but at a suggestion by Minnie Warren, began taking children into her home during the day to give harried mothers an occasional break. It soon turned into a profitable venture for Ellie and she had to hire two unmarried young ladies to help.

Sheriff Warren didn't replace Dan for almost a year, eventually hiring a young man named Jimmy Lamplighter.

On June 1, 1887, Sheriff John Warren, his left ankle painful and almost unmovable from severe arthritis, stepped down as county sheriff. Lou Sanborn wanted nothing to do with the job, so Joe Armstrong became his replacement.

Joe's first act was to hire John Warren as a consulting deputy sheriff rather than hiring another man. Most of the townsfolk believed it was just a way of providing the long-serving sheriff a steady income, but none objected. Yet to Joe, it was far from that. As he switched badges with his mentor and father, he told him that he still had a lot to learn.

Two years after the birth of Jolene, Cassie asked Joe if she could do something that had been on her mind since the day she'd stormed out of Carlisle's School for Young Women, and Ellie's childcare house made it possible. Joe had not only agreed with her, but later that day, he walked to Philby's Construction and had them draw up plans for a new building on the empty north lot.

On September 1, 1889, Cassie opened the doors to her own school. It wasn't anything like Carlisle's, nor was it like any other school anyone had heard of. When the students entered the doors, the main classroom was dominated by a large, U-shaped table with eighteen chairs. There were inkwells every three feet and large bookshelves along both outer walls. Cassie didn't have a desk, but just a chair at the open end of the 'U'.

Everyone in Warwick referred to it as the U School, and once the initial shock of the school's oddity settled down, it became very popular with the older students and their parents.

Another big difference from Carlisle's was that it wasn't limited to girls. It was, however, limited to students who'd completed their eighth year of traditional schooling. Cassie wanted to help her students achieve their dreams, and in so doing, fulfilled one of her own.

August 11, 1891

Deputy Lamplighter was at the front desk when the door opened, and Aggie Armstrong entered, closed the door and strode across the room in her yellow print dress.

“Good morning, Deputy,” she said as she walked past the desk.

“Good morning, Aggie,” he replied with a suppressed smile as she headed for her father’s office.

Joe heard his oldest daughter’s voice and set aside the report he was writing as she passed through the doorway. She wasn’t smiling as she usually was when she saw him, so that meant she was serious.

Without the smile, Joe couldn’t help but see Cassie as he’d first seen her as he looked at Aggie when she plopped down in the chair. She may not have had the freckles, but the eyes and that look of confidence and determination coupled with her mother’s features couldn’t stop the memories.

“And what do I owe the pleasure of your visit, Aggie?” he asked with a smile.

“Papa, I was just talking to Jo, and she said that because Michael is adopted, he could be her boyfriend. Is that right?”

“Yes, it is, but she grew up with him as if he were her first cousin, just as you have.”

“I know. That’s what I said, but Michael is thirteen now and Jo is twelve and she wants him to be her boyfriend.”

Joe leaned back and asked, “And you want him for your boyfriend?”

Aggie's eyebrows furrowed as she answered, "I don't know yet, but it doesn't seem fair. I'm just a silly little girl and Jo's already growing up."

"You know the story of how your mother and I met, Aggie. It was right here in this jail when she was your age."

"I know. It was just before you went to that horrible reform school."

"And I told your mother that she was a silly, crazy little girl."

Aggie finally smiled and said, "Mama showed me the letter you wrote when you said she wasn't crazy."

"What you probably don't know is that she thought I would want to marry your Aunt Bessie instead of her."

Aggie hadn't heard that part of the story and looked at her father with wide eyes as she asked, "She did?"

"Yes, ma'am. Your Aunt Bessie was closer to my age and, like you just said, more grown up."

Aggie was grinning as she said, "But you married mama."

"I did because when I was away in the reformatory and read her letters, I realized what a special person she was. I wasn't swayed by how pretty or grown-up your Aunt Bessie was, and that made a big difference. I was in love with your mother even though I hadn't seen her in more than four years. When I finally did see her again, I loved her even more."

"But Michael is here and lives right near Jo, too."

"It's not important. You just be yourself, Aggie. Don't ever be anything less."

"That's what mama told me, too."

"Your grandfather believed I was the only boy who could ever marry your mother and he was right. If Michael is meant to be your boyfriend, nothing can change that."

Aggie smiled at her father, dropped from the chair and walked to his side of the desk, hugged him and gave him a kiss before twirling in her yellow print dress, her pigtails whipping around her head and skipping out of his office.

Joe's smile stayed on his lips even as the front door closed, he drifted back to the day that seemed so long ago when another little girl in a yellow dress had entered the jail and changed everything when she had said she was going to be his girlfriend.

She had become so much more. She had become his life.

BOOK LIST

1	Rock Creek	12/26/2016
2	North of Denton	01/02/2017
3	Fort Selden	01/07/2017
4	Scotts Bluff	01/14/2017
5	South of Denver	01/22/2017
6	Miles City	01/28/2017
7	Hopewell	02/04/2017
8	Nueva Luz	02/12/2017
9	The Witch of Dakota	02/19/2017
10	Baker City	03/13/2017
11	The Gun Smith	03/21/2017
12	Gus	03/24/2017
13	Wilmore	04/06/2017
14	Mister Thor	04/20/2017
15	Nora	04/26/2017
16	Max	05/09/2017
17	Hunting Pearl	05/14/2017
18	Bessie	05/25/2017
19	The Last Four	05/29/2017
20	Zack	06/12/2017
21	Finding Bucky	06/21/2017
22	The Debt	06/30/2017
23	The Scalawags	07/11/2017
24	The Stampede	08/23/2019
25	The Wake of the Bertrand	07/31/2017
26	Cole	08/09/2017
27	Luke	09/05/2017
28	The Eclipse	09/21/2017
29	A.J. Smith	10/03/2017
30	Slow John	11/05/2017
31	The Second Star	11/15/2017
32	Tate	12/03/2017
33	Virgil's Herd	12/14/2017
34	Marsh's Valley	01/01/2018
35	Alex Paine	01/18/2018

36	Ben Gray	02/05/2018
37	War Adams	03/05/2018
38	Mac's Cabin	03/21/2018
39	Will Scott	04/13/2018
40	Sheriff Joe	04/22/2018
41	Chance	05/17/2018
42	Doc Holt	06/17/2018
43	Ted Shepard	07/16/2018
44	Haven	07/30/2018
45	Sam's County	08/19/2018
46	Matt Dunne	09/07/2018
47	Conn Jackson	10/06/2018
48	Gabe Owens	10/27/2018
49	Abandoned	11/18/2018
50	Retribution	12/21/2018
51	Inevitable	02/04/2019
52	Scandal in Topeka	03/18/2019
53	Return to Hardeman County	04/10/2019
54	Deception	06/02.2019
55	The Silver Widows	06/27/2019
56	Hitch	08/22/2018
57	Dylan's Journey	10/10/2019
58	Bryn's War	11/05/2019
59	Huw's Legacy	11/30/2019
60	Lynn's Search	12/24/2019
61	Bethan's Choice	02/12/2020
62	Rhody Jones	03/11/2020
63	Alwen's Dream	06/14/2020
64	The Nothing Man	06/30/2020
65	Cy Page	07/19/2020
66	Tabby Hayes	09/04/2020
67	Dylan's Memories	09/20/2020
68	Letter for Gene	09/09/2020
69	Grip Taylor	10/10/2020
70	Garrett's Duty	11/09/2020
71	East of the Cascades	12/02/2020
72	The Iron Wolfe	12/23/2020

Made in the USA
Monee, IL
01 July 2023

38144382R00310